PRIVATE*

THIS SKETCHBOOK BELONGS TO

NORA INKWELL

* I WILL CONSTRUCT A VERY BIG AND VERY BITEY MONSTROSITY TO EAT ANY NOSEY MOOCHERS!

POPPY T. PERRY

uclanpublishing

Dead Real is a uclanpublishing book

First published in Great Britain in 2025 by
uclanpublishing
University of Central Lancashire
Preston, PR1 2HE, UK

Text and illustrations copyright © Poppy T. Perry, 2025

978-1-91674743-2

1 3 5 7 9 10 8 6 4 2

The right of Poppy T. Perry to be identified as the author and
illustrator of this work has been asserted in accordance
with the Copyright, Designs and Patents Act 1988.

All rights reserved. No part of this publication may be reproduced,
stored in a retrieval system, or transmitted in any form or by any means,
electronic, mechanical, photocopying, recording or otherwise; or be used to
train any AI technologies without the prior permission of the publishers.
UCLan Publishing expressly reserves this work from the text and
data mining exception subject to EU law.

Text design by Becky Chilcott.

A CIP catalogue record for this book is available from the British Library.

Printed and bound in Great Britain by Clays Ltd, Elcograf S.p.A.

*For everyone who's finding their
place on the rainbow x*

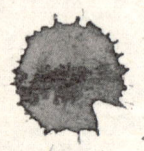

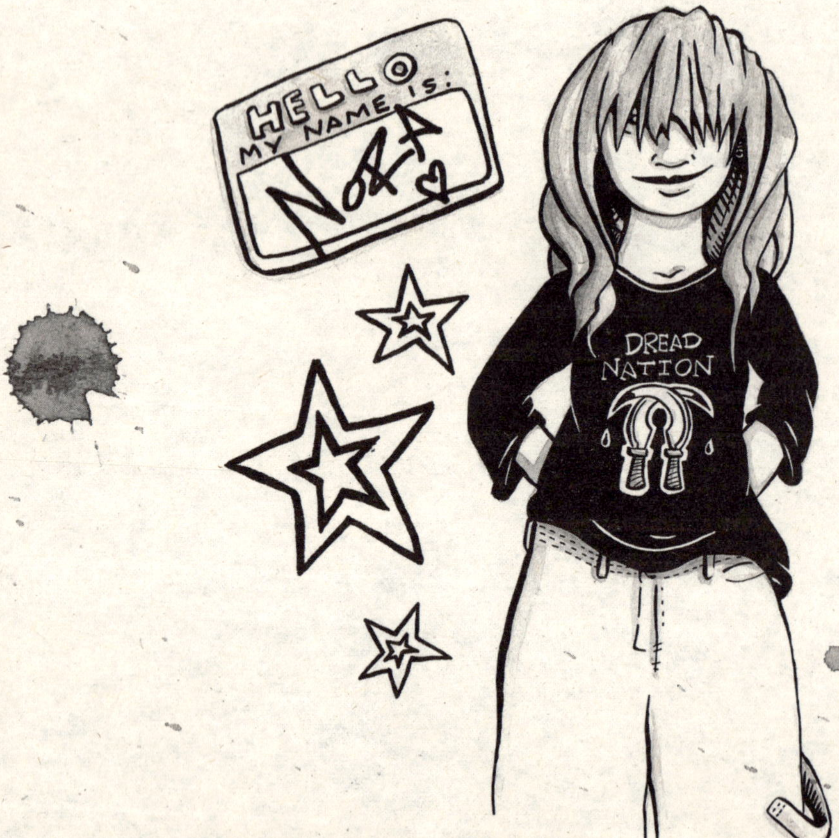
HELLO
MY NAME IS:
NORA
DREAD
NATION

PART ONE

Chapter 1

I'M SURE THERE USED TO BE A FULLY FUNCTIONING brain in my skull, brimming with semi-intellectual thoughts and everything. Now it feels more like a lump of weird squishy meat nestled in there, weighing down my head and straining at my spine.

In opposition to my full skull is my empty belly. The raw gnawing at my core, along with my mouth tasting like I've been licking armpits, drives me to push my stiff limbs onwards. Towards the exit.

I groan and drool with the others as we swarm out of the room that held us captive for so long.

Shoulders knock.

We stumble.

A hollow metal banging accompanies each collision with the lockers that line the corridor.

More groaning. More stumbling.

Our collective mass of bodies hit the heavy doors that bar the way to the outside world. We pile up until the hinges give and they burst open like a vein.

We're free.

The warm afternoon rushes in to snuff out the cold conditioned air. The change in temperature makes me stagger backwards, but the crowd behind keeps my forward momentum.

Our walking bodies flood the quad.

I lift a heavy hand to bat at the sun burning my retinas and a moan escapes my dry lips.

Turning from the glare, I see them. Huge letters sprayed across the blank brick wall.

An enormous "N".

"N" for "Nora".

That's me.

The words sucker punch me in the gut right before something lands on my back and throws me forwards. As I hit the floor, there's a pressure on my eyes and I go blind.

'Guess who!'

'Ruby! What the hell are you doing? Get off me.' My words come out rasping.

In response, Ruby sits on me.

I shake my head to get my best friend's hands off my eyes, but she's strong, and each time I glimpse daylight, they shift and darkness is restored.

'Wow, every single one of you leaving the art studios looks like something off Night of the Living Dead,' she says with a laugh.

I try again to peel Ruby's fingers away, but she's holding tight.

'What do you expect us to be like after five hours of solid arting? My brain's so overused it feels like it's turned to liquid and is trying to seep out my ears.' I give up and lie flat, resting my head on my hands. 'OK. What are you doing?'

'Nothing, just thought I'd come and find you.'

'And sit on me?'

'Why not? Lovely day to sit on someone.' She bounces a little.

'Oof! Can you *please* get off me?'

She gets up, her hands still covering my eyes, which is completely no help as I struggle to my feet.

'Ruby! I've just finished the last of three five-hour exam days for my Art A level. Back-to-back! I'm so not in the mood for this.'

'OK.'

She moves me round in a circle and lets go. Colours pop and swirl as my eyes attempt to focus on our surroundings. The college quad appears hazy at first, then I can see individual leaves on the trees, the wood grain on the picnic benches and the brickwork making up the mishmash of buildings surrounding them.

A smiling Ruby steps into my line of sight, eyes alight, twisting her pink fringe, and any irritation that prickled my nerves seconds ago disappears.

I could gaze adoringly at Ruby for ever. But surely everyone feels like that about their best friend, right?

Especially if they look like Ruby with her pure hazel eyes, smile that lights up every inch of her face, and a sickeningly awesome punk aesthetic.

I was totally punching above my weight in the friend zone the day they put me and Ruby together on a Film Studies project. But from the moment we started talking, our friendship was cemented in a shared passion for cheesy horror, popcorn, feminism, and vegetarian jelly sweets. By the end of the first month sitting next to each other, we'd planned our entire career together.

My exam-addled brain remembers what I saw on the wall before Ruby pounced me. I try to twist round to see, but Ruby's quick.

'So, how did your exam piece turn out?' she asks, pushing her face in close to mine.

All I can see is her.

After a skipped heartbeat at her closeness, I realise what she's doing.

'I've already seen the graffiti,' I tell her.

'Oh,' she says, stepping aside.

The emotional fist to the gut happens again as I see the words for the second time, sprayed up the side of the science block in massive acid green letters.

The shock of seeing it again blasts away any lingering exam fug, but even with my brain functioning better, all I can muster is a defeated sigh.

'Baxter's a dick,' says Ruby.

'He IS a dick. And now I'm going home to hide from the world for ever.'

'He's a dick with balls, though.'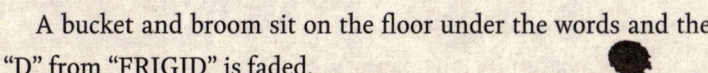
I frown at her.

We move to get a better view.

A bucket and broom sit on the floor under the words and the "D" from "FRIGID" is faded.

'I mean, he must have broken into college last night to do it,' she says and links arms with me. 'That takes massive balls.'

'Oh great, thanks, Rubes. Now we're discussing the fact Baxter's a dick with massive balls? That's kind of what started the whole problem.'

'I had no idea you had a *hole* problem too,' Ruby gasps. 'I would have been more sensitive.'

She giggles as I drag her away from where the caretaker has returned and is scrubbing at the letters. The smell of whatever chemical he's using burns the back of my throat.

My insides churn. This is so bad.

'Did you see it on the way into the exam?' Ruby asks.

'No, thankfully. If I'd spotted it on the way in . . .' The penny drops. 'This was sabotage! He knew I had my Art exam this week. We talked about it Monday night before—' I cut off the sentence; she knows what happened.

The word "FRIGID" is now slowly vanishing with serious caretaker-elbow-grease. It's already clear that it will inevitably leave an echo for generations of students to wonder who Nora Inkwell is and whether she really is frigid.

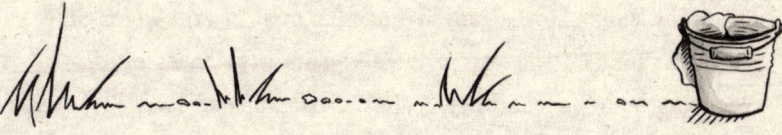

The answer to the most important of these questions is: I think so.

'I'm nearly eighteen and still got my V-plates. That totally makes me frigid, right?' I ask.

There's a painfully long pause.

'No!' Ruby shakes her head a bit too hard. 'No, of course not.'

'You hesitated!'

'I so did not. Anyway, I've still got my V-plates and there's no way I'm frigid – my internet history proves that.'

'You have not got your V-plates,' I say. 'What about that bloke you told me about last year?'

'That doesn't count. I was checking my lesbian status.' She hunches her shoulders and an emotional storm cloud shadows her features.

'Surely you need to sleep with someone the same sex as you to check if you're a lesbian. That's the whole point, isn't it?'

Ruby scrunches her face up.

'Well, that was the original plan, but it turns out it's much easier to bag a straight guy than a lesbian lady. So, I figured, what the hell? And opted for a process of elimination.' She folds her arms. 'When I came out, I thought it'd be easy to find a girl to do all that fun stuff with. Apparently not. Monday night at the gig with Josie proves that.'

I think of Josie, the beautiful drummer from one of the support bands that played that night. The way she'd tangled her fingers with Ruby's and tugged her playfully away from me in the crowd.

Ruby shouted for me not to wait, then mouthed the word "*SEX*" with an impish grin before vanishing into the mass of dancing bodies around her. I blinked back tears. That's when I threw myself at sexy Baxter from Body Combat, who we spotted on our way into the venue. As suggested by the graffiti, that plan didn't go so well.

Later that night, I received a text from Ruby saying Josie had a jealous ex who caught them kissing and chased Rubes all the way to the train station. I pushed the feeling of relief to the same place I'd hidden the jealousy earlier.

So many emotions crammed inside a heart-shaped box, locked away somewhere inside myself, and for the first time I'm worried there might be a limit to its capacity.

JOSIE

Ruby twists her hair again. 'Now I know I'm definitely lesbian, I'm ready to seal the deal. Make it official. I'm hot, right? It should be easy.'

'You're bloody gorgeous,' I say, looping arms with her. 'Anyway, there's no rush. We have our entire lives to lose our virginity.'

'You're joking, right? Nor, I told you this before. Under no circumstances can we go to university as virgins! We'll be literally eaten alive. You don't want that, do you?' She's gripping both my shoulders and shaking me.

'No?' I say.

'No! So, we have eight weeks to lose our virginity.'

I'm already regretting not pointing out that we probably won't be *literally* eaten alive.

'Eight weeks?' I swallow hard. 'As in, two months?'

'As in, one summer holiday. I'm not including the weeks we have left of our exams. I'm not a monster.'

'Haven't we got more like ten weeks' holiday before university starts?'

'Excellent, that gives us two weeks' contingency time, in case things get desperate.' She releases my shoulders and takes my hand, leading me away from the graffiti and towards the exit. 'Nora, my friend, we will succeed. Before we start university, we will have had happy, sexy, fun times, you with a guy, me with a girl, and we will arrive at the next stage of our lives triumphant.'

There's so much about that statement that has me squirming, not least that I don't think I can face reliving the events of Monday night ever again, let alone that soon.

Chapter 2

AWAY **FROM THE GRAFFITI AND CLOSE TO THE** college exit, I hear beats bouncing before I see a cheerful, yellow-striped gazebo at the source. Silver star balloons dance and bob in clusters tied at each corner, sending reflected sunbeams glinting and winking across the surrounding surfaces.

Pop Punk. The happy beats help lift some of the weight pressing down on me. I don't know what the balloons and music are for, and I don't care. I have three things I need right now:

Telly.

Onesie.

Popcorn.

I'm giving myself the rest of the day off before I start revising again tomorrow. I haven't decided what I'm watching when I get home yet, as long as it's suitably crap, and gory enough to float my boat.

The turnstiles that lead off site are so close, but Ruby has other ideas.

'Free stuff!' she says and drags me to join a crowd of students under the gazebo. She points to a sign. 'Free tote bags if we sign up.' Her eyes twinkle.

'Sign up for what?'

She shrugs. 'Some petition?'

I turn to leave, but Ruby still has my arm and she's not letting me go. I'm so not in the mood for this.

'Please,' she begs. 'You don't want to miss out on the pure and unadulterated joy that is a free tote bag, do you?'

'Yes, I really do.'

'Then sign up and give it to me.'

I sigh, knowing we're not getting away from here tote-bag free.

Two women talk to students as clipboards are passed around and a man paces up and down beside them, speaking loudly to himself. I watch, wondering if he's all right, until he turns to reveal an earpiece.

'The sales figures projected are astronomical, we'll need a spaceship to keep track of them.' He pauses and nods. 'Why not? We'll be able to afford to build one.' The hideously fake guffaw that follows triggers my cringe mechanism.

'Just fill in the details and sign on the back,' says one of the women, stepping in front of me and handing over a board with a fresh form on it.

I glance at it before leaning over to talk to Ruby.

'That's a lot of small print,' I point out.

'You're right,' she says, suddenly serious. 'We should absolutely take the time to read through every word on every page to make sure we aren't signing our souls away to the devil.'

'Really?' This isn't like her.

'No way! Free tote bag! Look, it's got a little shark with a heart on its tummy. It's super cute! Just fill it in. People aren't allowed to put anything dodgy in terms and conditions, anyway.'

Too tired to form any kind of argument, with a hand still cramping from hours of meticulously painting details onto elaborate latex prosthetics in my Art exam, I fill in the short form.

'Nora, look!' Ruby elbows me in the ribs and points at the guy who appears to be having an enthusiastic conversation with himself about how important he is. 'It's that rich guy who studied here.'

'Hmmm?' I finish filling in my details, inwardly cursing Ruby for all the random promo crap that'll soon be bombarding my inbox, just so she can enjoy a free tote bag. The shark *is* cute though.

'The, like, super-trillionaire?' I ask, frowning at the man and realising I do recognise him from prize-giving. And our college drops his grinning face onto every piece of marketing they put out. He's their success story. 'Mum showed me him in one of her health magazines a while ago. Doesn't he make diet pills?' The last words curl my features into an involuntary scowl.

'Yeah, him. I think he's married to some director lady.'

'Good for him. Now, can we get the tote bags and go? It's been kind of a long day.' I wave the clipboard about to indicate I've finished filling it in.

The woman returns to collect it.

'Thank you, Miss . . .?' she says.

'Inkwell.' I keep my tone flat and uninviting, hoping she'll just hand over the freebies so we can get away from here.

The rich guy abruptly turns to face me.

'Sorry, I have to go. Something just came up,' he says.

I look around, unsure who he's talking to until he taps and pockets a shiny phone.

'Inkwell?' he asks, striding over. 'Nora Inkwell?'

I blink.

How does this guy know my name?

Apart from Ruby and my tutors, no one here really knows I exist. As a medium-build white girl with average-length brown hair, a regular amount of spots, and no distinguishing features to speak of, I'd say that I'm all but completely forgettable.

'That Nora Inkwell?' Rich Guy points over to where the graffiti is unsuccessfully being scrubbed off.

Oh. I clench my teeth and glare at the ground. Baxter's such a dick.

Taking my lack of response as a yes, he asks, 'Do you know who did that?' His eyes colour with concern and it looks like he genuinely cares. 'You could press charges—'

'No!' I blurt. 'I'm good, thank you.' I hope my voice sounds bolder than I feel, hiding my alarm at the thought of having to talk to anyone other than Ruby about Baxter, and what events led to him breaking into the college campus to deface the hugest and blankest of walls with my name.

People stare as whispers fly around the crowd that I'm Nora Inkwell. *That Nora Inkwell*. I'm glad when Ruby throws an arm over my shoulder. At least, I am until she talks.

'She is totally not frigid,' she says. 'There's this idiot guy who was a rubbish kisser—'

'Thank you, Ruby.' I jab her in the ribs.

'Ouch! OK!'

'And you are . . .' He turns to Ruby and takes her clipboard. 'Miss Ruby Rutherford,' he reads. 'Ruby, Nora, a pleasure to meet you both.' A smile, which I bet has sealed a thousand deals, shines down at us from the top of a blue open-collared shirt.

Rich Guy offers a suntanned hand to us from a rolled-up sleeve. It isn't the kind of tan you get in England and it isn't like Ruby's skin tone that came from countless generations of ancestors living in the heat of the Indian sun. This guy's tan looks like it cost mega money and enough air miles to melt a glacier.

After running a hand down my vintage Evil Dead T-shirt to get rid of any clamminess from the hot day, I shake his. It's soft and dry.

'Elroy Pherson, inventor, entrepreneur, alumni and all-round good guy.'

He flashes a grin my way. We've all seen the photos of when Elroy was a student at our college, looking completely adorable, with puppy fat and glasses. He's grown into a chiselled adult, and it's easy to see that the grin, filled with perfectly straight white teeth, is part of the secret to his success.

'I went to school with an Inkwell,' he continues, my hand now sandwiched in his.

'Yeah?' I say, trying not to look too much like I have better places to be. Even though I do. The sofa awaits.

'Do you have a Henry in the family?' Pherson asks, still gripping my hand.

Well, this is awkward. He's all grin and quiff and holding my hand prisoner. Trying to pull it free I take in the local celebrity. I'd expected his head to be bigger.

'Nope.' My hand pops free. 'No Henrys—' My brain catches up with my mouth. 'Wait, yes, sorry. Dad's

13

a Henry, but no one calls him that.' I flex my recently released digits. 'Everyone calls him Harry.'

Elroy's eyes narrow. 'Really?' He looks me up and down, a smile tugging at one corner of his mouth. Why do I feel like Little Red Riding Hood on her first encounter with the Big Bad Wolf?

'Yep.' I so don't want to be here.

'Perfect.' Elroy lets the first syllable roll like a contented cat, while hugging our forms close to his body. He says it again. 'Perfect.'

Not creepy at all.

When he turns to add our papers to a pile, I take the opportunity to bolt through the turnstiles leading out of college, and power walk to freedom and my sofa. Ruby can have the totes.

Chapter 3

IT'S BEEN ABOUT SIX WEEKS SINCE I FINISHED MY Art exam and as results day sneaks closer, I spend more and more time working on my latest latex creation, trying to distract myself from that dreaded day.

'Nora, Ruby's here!' Mum calls, seconds before the doorbell rings.

She's early!

I look down at my *Sharknado* T-shirt and jeans; the top is awesome, the ketchup mark on it is not. I pull it off and rummage in the bottom drawer for a clean one. *Dawn of the Living Dead*, *Hellraiser*, choices choices. After pulling one on, I glance in the mirror and try to be happy with what I see.

'Nora! Come and help Ruby with her stuff.'

'Coming!' I holler.

My hair's a mess.

While running to the bedroom door, tugging my fingers through my hair, I knock over a pot of red ink I'd been using. It bleeds across the tatty sketchbook I carry everywhere, and a well-thumbed Northern Art School prospectus that arrived in the post weeks ago, on the same day as I sat my last A level exam. I'd hoped it arriving on that day was a good

15

omen, but if it was, what would drowning it in something that looks exactly like blood foretell?

'Shit. Shit. Shit.'

'Hey, Nora, you're keeping your guest waiting,' calls a different voice, one that makes my lips stretch into a smile and my chest go tingly.

'I'm having an inky dilemma! Can my guest come up, grab a load of loo roll, and help?'

'I think she could manage that.' Seconds later there's a thumping on the stairs. Then the sound of toilet paper being spun off its roll, before Ruby appears in my doorway with an armful of tissue. 'This enough?'

'Hope so.'

She drops it onto the spillage. The red seeps bright into the tissue as I pat it down. Ruby helps, her hands a soft oak brown beside my splotchy pink. Soon they're both stained red.

'Looks like we've been doing a spot of murder,' Ruby says in a faux Cornish accent. She looks up and sees the werewolf I've been working on all holiday, a latex mask I'd thankfully put back on its polystyrene head, safely away from the spillage.

'There's my gorgeous girl,' she says, tossing it a wink. 'She's looking hot, Nor. And the hair's epic!'

'Thanks, it's taken me ages.' There's no fighting the blush: Ruby's the only person who has ever really *got* my obsession with monster movies and my dream of working as a special effects artist. Loads of people say it's all gone digital. Losers.

After helping me out with a few moving parts for my creations, Ruby caught the SFX bug herself.

She's an artist as well as an aspiring engineer and she took Graphics at college, so her meticulously detailed technical designs are a thing of beauty. She's even drawing up her own Hayne's Manual for her shiny red Raleigh Chopper.

'Maybe we should have gone with the shark idea? They're way less hairy.' Ruby's lips pull into a smirk.

My eyes trail to the folder crammed full of rejected shark mask plans we spent ages researching. We dropped the idea for the werewolf when Ruby decided it wasn't worth the risk of misrepresenting sharks, after reading something about Spielberg and Jaws.

'You're not allowed to even joke about that after the hours I've put into her coiffure. Anyway, I was adding a hint of rouge around her eyes and lips as a finishing touch, but this . . .' I indicate the scene of inky gore, '. . . is less subtle than planned.'

'I've got a little present for her—' Ruby says.

Before she's even finished, I'm squeaking and pogoing on the spot.

The university said it was OK for us to work together on our summer project before we start. I'm on the mask and Ruby's making the eyes, but she's been struggling with them being *fiddly as fuck*.

'Oh my god! You got them to work?'

'Of course.'

'Let's give them a go.' I throw the mound of scarlet-stained tissues into the bin and lead the way to the bathroom to wash our hands.

'Have you been robbed?' Ruby asks when we get back. 'Where's all your stuff?'

'Away. Mum made me tidy my room for your stay.'

'You have carpet in your bedroom. I had no idea!'

'Ha ha,' I deadpan. 'It's not normally that bad.' But it is.

'Girls,' Mum's voice calls from downstairs. 'Can you get Ruby's cases upstairs and out of the way, please? I'm going to work. I'll see you this evening.'

'OK, bye!' I call to Mum. Then frown at Ruby. 'Cases? As in plural? How many are there?'

Ruby shifts and averts her eyes as she answers. 'Three.'

'Three! You're only here for a week, right?'

'You have no idea how much work goes into making all this look effortless.' She musses the flick of pink at the front of her short black hair before raising her hands and spinning on the spot.

We wrestle the cases upstairs, and prop Ruby's beloved roller hockey stick next to my *Exorcist* poster.

She cracks the largest of her cases and pulls out a tool pouch and a takeaway tub. Two eyeballs peer up at me from within.

'This is going to be so good,' I say, my chest fluttering in anticipation.

'Yeah, it is.' Ruby pulls the lid off, revealing the eyeballs in all their beauty.

Morning disappears into afternoon in the blink of an eye. Well, in the blinks, winks, rolls and twitching of a pair of mechanical werewolf eyes.

It takes a long time to attach the mechanised lids to the latex ones I'd made. Then the glue we use gums up the system and we have to clean it all out, or the eyeball gets stuck mid-roll.

It takes us a while to work out why the left eye keeps rolling back and jamming when the right is working fine, which can only be done after we've stopped laughing at how weird it looks.

Then there's the quiet times, between mugs of coffee, where we each work on our own part of the project. I'm cosmetic, Ruby's technical. In these times she rests her head on my shoulder and I lean my head on hers; side-by-side we work on our craft and I am in heaven.

We've both been offered provisional places to study Visual Effects & Model Making at the Northern Art School. When we finish in education, we've already decided we'll build a woman-strong SFX team to stop the industry being such a sausage fest.

Ruby'll be a special effects engineer and I'll be a special effects artist. Together we'll design and build mechanics and rigs, do model making, pyrotechnics, puppetry and anything that's needed to become the best. And then we'll get to do this together, all day, every day, for ever.

Once everything is finally working, I try the mask on. The wires block the hidden sight holes I've built in.

'I can't see a thing,' I say and turn to where I think Ruby is. Something so big and unmoving, that I can only guess must be the wall, hits me hard in the face. An explosion of Ruby's laughter comes to me, muffled through the latex and hair that softened the blow. By the time I wrestle the mask off, Ruby's bent double, one finger raised and pointing.

'You walked into the wall and her eyeball fell out,' she manages to say before erupting into another fit of uncontrollable giggles.

19

I see the one wolfy eye dangling by a wire, and then I'm laughing too.

A hysterical minute later, ribs aching, we collapse into a heap on the bed. Ruby's head is on my stomach and my hand's draped over her. In that moment of mindless bliss, a shadow moves over me and it threatens to steal all this away.

I jerk my arm back and sit up. A familiar panicked fluttering starts in my chest and expands.

Ruby sits up on one elbow to look at me, her hair mussed, and one perfect eyebrow raised. All the feelings radiating out from my core threaten to drown me.

'You OK?' she asks.

'Yeah! We should get the eyeball fixed.' I jump up and dart back to the desk, leaving Ruby alone on my bed. 'Then we can go find something to eat,' I say, suddenly itching to get out of this room.

Chapter 4

WITH BOTH OF OUR WEREWOLF'S EYES successfully back in their sockets, fully functioning and looking completely awesome, we triumphantly go in search of food.

I didn't realise how late it'd gotten – Dad's already back from work. As we walk through the living room, we find the man with whom I share my chromosomes wearing a pair of glasses made out of a Rice Pops box.

Over his ears are the chunky, noise-cancelling headphones he wears when he wants to watch Mae Rears, the big-boobed survival expert, without upsetting Mum. He's sat in a crouch, balancing over the low coffee table strewn with cuttings, notebooks and drawings.

I'm already cringing, even before he lifts two flaps in his cardboard glasses to reveal his eyes.

Why can't I have normal parents?

Or ones who can at least pretend to be normal when we have visitors?

'Oh, hey, Nor!' he says, lowering his headphones. 'And Miss Rutherford!' Dad beams at Ruby. 'You're staying with us for a while, aren't you?'

'Yeah.' Ruby's smiling widely. 'Loving the specs, Mr I.'

'Thank you very much.' He smiles back and I wonder whether

he genuinely has no idea how completely ridiculous he looks.

Dad flicks a switch on the headphones and the telly's sound comes out of speakers hidden behind the sofa.

'*So, in the blazing hot sunshine, with just a piece of cardboard, you too can combat UV damage to the retinas.*' The annoyingly fake and tinkling voice of Mae Rears is now in surround sound. '*This also works against snow blindness and excessive squinting.*'

Excessive squinting? Really?!

Dad pauses her with the remote control. 'What are you pair up to?' He stands up to his full height and stretches.

'Grabbing some food, then we're planning to watch a movie.' I glance at the telly.

'Well, I'm just about done in here, so please don't let me stop your grand—'

The low purr of Mum's Mini pulling up in front of the house interrupts his sentence.

'—plans,' Dad finishes.

There's nothing miniature about Mum's new car. It's a beast. Through the front window, we see her step out and smooth down the pinstripes of her outfit.

By the time she's in the front door, she already has her phone pressed to the side of her head. 'We can buy them out cheap before the company sinks. Their warehouse must be full of tea tree, chai, and goodness knows what else.' She puts a finger over the mic on her phone. 'Hello, darling,' she whispers, tilting her head and kissing the air in my direction. She nods at where Ruby's watching her with a bemused quirk to one eyebrow. 'Ruby.'

Mum's eyes move from Ruby to the paused Mae Rears on the telly, frozen in her tiny chino hot pants and short-sleeved white shirt with the buttons straining at the task of containing her impractically huge boobs.

Finally, after taking in the room and the mess on the table, Mum looks at Dad. I wish his cereal box sunglasses weren't wonky.

'Harry,' Mum says with a disapproving glare.

'Kim.' Dad smiles, but it falls when Mum turns her back on him and continues talking into her phone. Her voice fades as she heads upstairs, Dad watches her go with puppy-dog eyes.

'Do you need help tidying up?' I ask.

'No, no. It's my mess.'

He moves forwards and starts scooping pieces of hacked-up cardboard into piles. The man looks so lost, watching him feels like an invasion of privacy, so I take Ruby into the kitchen, already regretting telling her she could stay with us.

'Do you want a bowl of these?' I hold a bag of cereal, whose box has recently been repurposed, up to Ruby.

'That would be amazing.'

Our Rice Pops are hardly in the bowl before Mum bounds into the kitchen, head to toe in matching branded sportswear. A vision in magenta Lycra.

Again: why can't I have normal parents?

She fills her favourite water bottle, which has "*GYM AND TONIC*" stamped up the side in lime green, sparkly letters. 'I'll see you at the gym in an hour. I'm going to Body Attack before Combat.'

My cereal snaps, crackles, and pops as cold milk washes over it.

'Are you going to eat that?' she asks.

The first spoonful is halfway to my mouth.

'I was thinking about it.'

'You'll get a stitch at the gym.'

I sigh. 'I wasn't going to come tonight, with it being Ruby's first day here and all that.'

'Fine. But didn't we agree you were going to eat 1% milk because of your skin and your—' She looks me over. 'Well, you need to take care of your figure, if you're ever going to catch a nice boy. Am I right, Ruby?'

Thankfully, Ruby has a mouthful of cereal, so all she can manage is a vigorous shake of the head. Which Mum completely ignores.

'Boys aren't fish, Mum. Anyway, these days there's a lot of emphasis on the fact that people don't need someone else to complete them. I am a strong, independent young woman.'

'Whatever you say, darling.' She dismisses the idea with a small laugh. Before I can say anything else, she air-kisses either side of my disapproving face and jogs out of the room.

The second the front door clicks shut, I stomp over to the row of pots by the kettle, pick up the one labelled SUGAR, dig out a heaped spoonful and savour the time spent sprinkling it over my cereal.

Dad walks in, jams the slips of cardboard into the recycling and sees me at the sugar pot.

'Your mother's gone out then?'

'Yep, just.'

'Oh.' His shoulders roll forwards. He takes off the cardboard glasses and twiddles the leg. 'Are you going to the gym? I could show Ruby how to build a bivouac in the garden while you're out.'

I shake my head and a rice pop stuck to my face dislodges and drops back into my bowl. 'I was going to stay here to hang out with Rubes tonight.'

'Right.' He nods. 'I might go down and do some work in the cellar then.'

'We can bivouac another day, Mr I,' Ruby says.

'Perhaps.' He shrugs and, with a weak smile, heads downstairs.

Sitting at the kitchen island, eating our early evening breakfast, I listen to the familiar sounds of crashing and banging under my feet.

A framed photo of two young people in their graduation gowns hangs on the kitchen wall. The man has scooped the lady up and her mortarboard is frozen mid-tumble to the ground. The couple laugh and gaze at each other as if nothing else in the world exists.

Thinking of the broken man trying to bury himself in the cellar and the human power-suit who's run away to lose herself in the gym, I spoon in mouthfuls of cereal and wonder what happened to those two people who graduated from university so young and in love.

After cereal we settle down, ready for a night of brain-rottingly gruesome horror movies, accompanied by enough popcorn and chocolate to take us way over our RDA of salt, sugar and fat.

Perfect.

We just need to choose a movie.

'*Jaws*?' I ask, as we scroll through reams of movies on the telly.

'Nah, since I learned about those trophy-hunting wankers blasting the great white population after it was released, I just can't. It's too sad.' Ruby rests her head on my shoulder. 'Keep scrolling.'

'Nope.'

'Nah.'

'Definitely not.'

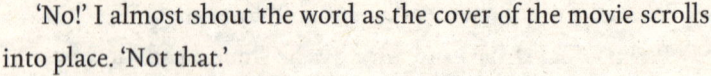

I scroll until Ruby sits up.

'Yes!' She points. '*Little Monsters*!'

'No!' I almost shout the word as the cover of the movie scrolls into place. 'Not that.'

Ruby frowns. 'What? You loved it when we first watched it. We both did. It's got Lupita Nyong'o being epic, killing the shit out of zombies with a shovel. She's gorgeous *and* kick-ass.'

Everything Ruby just said is completely true, but watching Ms Nyong'o in her yellow summer dress killing the shit out of zombies stirs up all the wrong emotions.

'What about one of the Evil Deads?' I counter. 'Bruce Campbell's chin might be exactly what we need.'

'*Resident Evil*?' Ruby purrs. 'Milla Jovovich being awesome in very tight, or very little, clothing, depending on which one we choose.'

'*The Shining*?'

'Nora, if I didn't know for certain that you are a hard-core feminista, I could mistake you – and your unwillingness to watch movies with badass female protagonists – for being a massive sexist. You won't even let us rewatch the *Alien* series. It's a complete classic. And Sigourney, oh my god, don't even get me started about Sigourney in *Alien 3*.' She clutches her heart dramatically.

My insides shut down as I force my lips up into a smile.

'I like them, I just—' My mind scrabbles for something to say. 'I want to watch badass men fight monsters as much as you want to watch badass women fight monsters.' I reassure myself that this is at least partly true, while trying to ignore a sudden urge to cry.

My false smile quirks into something wonky and telling. Thankfully, Ruby doesn't notice because she's grabbed the remote out of my hand and has taken over scrolling duties.

I pull my knees in close and hug them tight.

'Right, we're watching *Dracula*. It's a classic and I'm bored of looking.'

I say nothing as she selects the movie and curls up on the sofa with a lazily contented sigh. I swear Ruby is part cat.

This leaves me gripping my knees to my body, hoping if I squeeze hard enough, I can hold everything inside.

I should talk to Ruby about *it*...

The movie plays, but I'm not taking anything in. As usual, the thought of talking to Ruby about *it* has unzipped a beanbag of emotions and the billions of tiny polystyrene balls are caught up in the storm inside me.

'You OK sitting like that? You look kind of awkward and uncomfortable.'

Yep, that's pretty much how I've felt my whole life.

'I'm good,' I tell her.

'If you say so.'

Later, the front door slams.

'I'm home,' Mum calls.

'Hey,' I reply. The movie rolls in front of my eyes without anything going in, and no matter how tightly I squeeze, I'm failing at holding my insides in.

I need to talk to someone. The telly lights the angles of Ruby's face and the squirming in my chest tightens to something almost painful. I can't talk to her. I think of my dad, with his cereal-box glasses, and know he's not the person for this. That only leaves Mum.

The decision is only half formed in my mind when I'm on my feet.

'Loo trip?' Ruby asks, going to pause the movie.

'Nah, need to chat to Mum. Don't worry about stopping it, I've seen it a million times.'

'All right.' She settles back.

In the kitchen Mum has her little notebook out on the table as she wraps a tape measure around various parts of herself and meticulously records her numbers.

'Measurements never lie,' she says when she sees me.

'I know.' I sigh, already wondering if this is such a good idea, but the need to talk about the thing I've been ignoring for too long has built up inside my chest, suddenly manifesting as something enormous and super important.

It does this sometimes, expanding to fill every crevice of my being so I can't think of anything else. It's happening more regularly, and mostly when Ruby's about.

Most people would just google something like this, but there was this time, in Year 7, I googled a lump on my toe and the results convinced me it was definitely something terrible that would

28

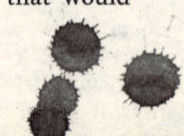

lead to me losing my toe ... and probably dying.

After days of waiting in terror for my toe to fall off, I showed our PE teacher when she found me crying in the changing rooms. Turns out it was a verruca.

So, this sensitive topic is going nowhere near an internet search engine and the prospect of trying to ignore it for the full week of Ruby's visit makes words I've held in for so long explode out my mouth in a hurried whisper.

'Do you think it's OK to like girls as well as boys and—?'

Mum's measuring tape snaps taut with an audible crack that interrupts me before I could mention people who are gender-fluid or non-binary. For a brief and shocking moment, Mum looks like her eyeballs might pop out of her skull, but the measuring tape loosens and her eyeballs retract as she regains composure.

'Oh, Nora, don't be silly,' she says, dismissing my question with an airy wave of the hand and a small laugh. 'That's just a phase people grow out of.'

This gets me worrying. I don't feel like I'm being silly, and it doesn't feel like a phase.

I've had these feelings for a long time. I mean, in that department, I've been a mess from the time I had my first ever crushes, which were, simultaneously, Maid Marian and Robin Hood from the Disney cartoon. The fact they're both foxes only created more confusion.

'Right.' I lick my lips and attempt to go in for another try, but Mum puts away her measuring equipment and moves swiftly towards the door.

'I'm running late,' she says, air-kissing me before pretty much sprinting out the kitchen.

'Good talk,' I mumble and shuffle back in to watch the rest of the movie.

Chapter 5

I COMPLETELY AND ONE HUNDRED PER CENT WILL not be talking to anyone ever again about anything I may or may not feel when watching Lupita Nyong'o or Milla Jovovich fighting zombies. And the less said about Sigourney in *Alien 3*, the better. I manage to tune my brain into *Dracula* just in time to see Winona Ryder, as the beautiful Mina Murray, smooch a decaying Gary Oldman.

It's safer to stick to talking about other crushes. Brooding Brandon Lee in *The Crow* and sweaty Tom Hardy in *Venom* . . . along with a guilty little something for Bruce Campbell in the *Evil Dead* trilogy.

'People in horror movies are stupid,' Ruby says with a stretch and a yawn. 'At the first sign of things getting fishy, just do a runner. Get as far away as you can as fast as you can and look out for yourself. It's the hanging about for other people that inevitably leads to a brutal death.'

We twist so we're sitting on either side of the sofa with our toes touching.

'People don't know they're in a horror movie,' I argue. 'And if everyone listened to you, they'd be on their own. Sometimes you need more than one person to get out of a well-imagined horror bind.'

'No way, I reckon all the problems of getting yourself caught by a monster, maniac or murderer are overcome by the ease of only having to watch out for yourself.'

'OK, so, if we ever find ourselves in a horror scenario, I'm just going to do a runner and not suffer any guilt about leaving you behind?'

'Leave me behind?! My arse!' She laughs. 'I'd be long gone.'

'Maybe I'd hook up with some yummy vampire and leave you to run.'

Ruby's nose wrinkles in that cute way it does. 'Ew. Probably some soft-core twinkly vampire that looks like he's stepped out of a perfume advert. Nor, I thought you had taste.'

'No!' I throw a piece of popcorn and it bounces off her head onto the floor. 'Not one like that. I'd need one with veins running out of their eyes and blue lips. Gothic Edwardian style. Dark and brooding, like.'

'And smelling of dead arse?'

'Of course, that's how I like my vampires.'

'I could get myself a nice little band of succubi. Who knows, we might lure you over to the dark side.' Ruby draws her fingers through the air as though pulling me towards her with invisible tendrils. Her head tilts and, though there's a playful smirk on her face, her eyes are thoughtful.

At that moment, two scenarios play out simultaneously in my mind.

In one I lean forwards to kiss her and she wraps her arms around me, tugging me into a smoking hot, extensive snogging session.

In the other, I lean forwards to kiss her and she shoves me onto the floor, yelling something about me being a wannabe lesbian before storming out of my life for ever.

My chest tangles as awkwardness creeps into the space between us, so I grab a fist full of popcorn and throw it at her.

'Nom, nom, nom.' She chomps at the air, trying to catch them in her mouth. 'I don't want to be a vampire, anyway. Popcorn's much easier to eat than people. And tastier.'

'Less complicated too.'

Ruby's phone vibrates on the coffee table next to us. She throws her hand across to grab it and I'm thankful for the distraction.

'Who is it?'

Ruby looks up at me, her smile eerie in the white glow of her screen. 'There's been some cancellations for tomorrow's gig!'

I stare at her blankly.

'The Interrupters gig.'

'Oh yeah?'

'I put my name on the waiting list for two tickets. And they've just become available!' She squeaks in excitement.

'Who are you going with?' I ask, wondering if she's still in touch with Josie from the gig all those weeks ago.

'You, of course,' Ruby says.

'Yesss!' I pump both fists in the air as joy flicks the switch on a sunshine lamp inside me, obliterating any lingering shadows from my failed talk with Mum.

Ruby shouts, 'We're going to see The Interrupters!!!' And puts the song *Title Holder* on her phone before dancing around the living room, singing along. I laugh as she makes sure the dance is the wrong side of weird.

Ruby introduced me to The Interrupters when we first met and I soon found out that Amy Interrupter, the singer, is as beautiful and awesome as her voice and lyrics. There are other singers from bands who are the same, like Laura Jane Grace from Against Me! and Millie from Millie Manders and the Shutup.

I listen to them all *a lot*.

There's something about the emotions stirred up by their voices, like I can unbox part of myself without getting caught. Aural perving, if you will.

Ruby pulls my hand so I'm up, singing and dancing with her.

'*Fight like a title holder. Stand like a champion. Live like a warrior. And never let 'em break you down. Woo hoo hoooo!*'

We're bum-wiggling, singing *woo hoo hoooo*s and giggling.

When the song finishes, Ruby grabs me in a hug.

'Interrupters tomorrow!' I shout. After a couple of excited bounces, the mood shifts and I'm super aware of Ruby pressing against me.

The hug lingers.

'Oh my god, Nor,' Ruby says, stepping away as though nothing happened. Which, I suppose, it didn't.

She just hugged me.

She always hugs me.

Ruby is one of life's huggers.

'The girls at the gig are going to be so my type. Maybe this is it! Maybe tomorrow's my day for sexy-fun-times.'

I freeze up. Joy about the gig and warmth remaining from the hug vanishes.

'No, scrap that,' she says. 'I'm going to make sure it is. I'm going to throw myself at the first female who shows even the slightest whiff of interest!'

My legs become an abstract concept, and I move back to the sofa before collapsing.

What if it was me?

The question pops into my head fully formed, followed by several other tumbling what-ifs.

What if I showed interest?

What if we—

'I'll do the squelchy with someone, anyone, then bail. It'll take the pressure off my first time if I decide in advance that I'm never going to see her again.'

My thoughts stumble.

'The squelchy?' I scrunch my face at the word. 'Ew, Rubes, you're so grim.'

She smirks at me and I can't help but frown.

'I'm not trying to squash anyone's sexual liberation,' I say. 'As long as everyone involved is having a good time. More sex the merrier and all that. But what about romance?'

'I want to be a proper lesbian and it's called sex-uality, not romance-uality.'

I hate that what she's saying makes so much sense. But I especially hate the idea of her going out and having sex with just some person.

Because you want her to be with you, a small needling voice points out.

'Are you OK?' Ruby asks. 'You look like you've just farted and followed through.'

I don't know why I'm so shocked, I've been silencing that voice for so long. Surely I didn't think I could keep it quiet for ever.

Well, OK, I did think I could keep it quiet for ever. That was the genius plan I'd built the foundation of my happiness on and, even after Mum's certainty that it's nothing to worry about, those foundations are crumbling.

'I'm going to bed,' I say, needing space to work things out.

In the small hours of the following morning, I lie in bed and make a promise to myself.

At some point before the gig, I'll mention to Rubes about the possibility of me being attracted to more than just the opposite sex.

If she wrinkles her nose? I'll shut up and remain silent until we die happy old BFFs surrounded by my abundance of cats and Ruby's abundance of sexual partners.

If she gives me a mischievous grin? Well, then, exciting things might happen.

I fall asleep wearing a hopeful smile.

Chapter 6

THE NEXT MORNING, THE SMELL OF YUMMY cooking wakes me up, but why is anxiety clawing around my stomach like a possessed doll?

Then it hits me.

Today's the day I'm going to *talk* to Ruby.

'Today's the day I'm going to have sex!' Ruby announces.

Oh. And that.

'Morning to you too,' I say to the ruffled Rubes on the inflatable lilo at the end of my bed.

'Girls, pancakes are nearly ready,' Mum shouts up the stairs.

'Pancakes!' Ruby jumps up and grabs her clothes for the day.

'Pancakes?' I scrunch up my face and try to remember the last time Mum cooked anything that wasn't a superfood recipe from one of her health magazines.

In the kitchen, we find Mum playing the role of the perfect housewife-with-modern-day-demands surprisingly well.

Her blonde-highlighted hair bounces as she tosses pancakes with one hand, stirs batter with the other and has her phone wedged between ear and shoulder.

There's no sign of a low-fat cookbook, but the pancakes are cooked in one calorie spray oil and using 1% milk. I should have known.

Dad's in the kitchen too, wearing the eco-warrior T-shirt that

Mum hates, and his dusty brown hair is brushed back. He looks awkward at being in the same room as Mum for longer than it takes for one of them to make an excuse and leave. It's been a while.

On seeing us, Mum finishes her call and herds Ruby to the table where a pile of pancakes awaits.

'I thought we could all have breakfast together this morning, to celebrate you staying with us.' She still has her telephone voice on. 'I trust you're settling in well?'

'Great, thanks,' Ruby says, and checks the time on her phone. 'Mum, Dad and Freddy should be landing in New Dehli in about an hour.' She sniffs. '*So* not jealous . . .'

Mum and Dad move about the kitchen like magnetic robots set to the same pole, repelling each other everywhere they go. I really wouldn't mind if *they* won a prize holiday and were flying halfway around the world, leaving me at Ruby's house.

Judging by Ruby's face, she'd much rather be on a flight to India, but her dad only won two tickets. Her baby brother gets to fly for free because he's only one.

I nudge her with my shoulder. 'We'll have fun.'

'Yeah,' she smiles distractedly.

'Oh! I forgot to tell you, Baxter asked after you last night at Body Combat, Nora,' Mum says. 'He's a nice boy.'

The shadows of fumbled boob grabs and enormous letters reading "NORA INKWELL IS FRIGID" pass behind my eyes.

I don't respond.

'Shall I put on some music?' Mum asks, and before anyone answers, she clicks the radio on. Loud classical music devours the uncomfortable silence. She adjusts the volume to ambient and we all sit down to eat.

Soon Dad's explaining to Ruby the lifesaving potential of knot tying, and Mum's feigned interest is almost convincing. It's good to see Dad so animated, and Ruby's asking all the right questions, seeming genuinely caught up in the conversation. She's brilliant.

A sharp and fuzzy sound pierces the room, invading my head and jabbing at my brain.

'What is that?!' I push my palms over my ears.

Dad's face lights up. 'It's static! We used to hear it all the time. I didn't know that radio had a FM setting.'

'It doesn't, it's just DAB. The electrics have been playing up since we had the new security system put in the other week,' Mum says, walking to the side where the little radio sits shouting its offensive noise. She twiddles the knobs, but the noise grows louder. The pitch changes and words cut in.

'. . .kshhhhhhhhhh
EMERGENCY WARNING
kshhhhhhh
STAY INDOORS
kshhh . . .'

The radio goes dead.

'What was that?' Dad's voice is tinged with boyish excitement. 'Emergency warning?'

'Stay indoors?' I stand up and move to the kitchen window to peer at the cloudless morning. There's only a bright blue sky and an unperilous Saturday waiting on the other side of the glass.

I imagine a meteor shower like one I read about in this old sci-fi horror book, *The Day of the Triffids*. In the book, anyone who sees the meteor shower goes blind and society breaks down. It's brilliantly terrifying.

Ruby moves in beside me. 'Can you see anything?'

'Nothing weird,' I say.

Mum opens the back door and sniffs the air.

'Do you think it's something that would affect flights?' Ruby's eyes are on the sky.

'I'm sure your family'll be fine. It's most likely something localised, like a gas leak,' Mum says, shutting the door.

'Nothing's working,' I say, trying to pull up a news feed on my phone and being blocked by an alert page.

GOVERNMENT WARNING:

STAY INDOORS.

A pulsing starts in my ears.

'Is that the biohazard symbol?' I turn my phone to show the room, and Ruby's face nearly hits the floor as Dad nods.

Fingers moving fast, I tap at my phone, failing to manoeuvre around the alert. The screen floods with the same phrase over and over.

STAY INDOORS.

STAY INDOORS.

STAY INDOORS.

STAY INDOORS.

STAY INDOORS.

STAY INDOORS.

STAY INDOORS.

STAY INDOORS.

I'm suddenly feeling very claustrophobic.

'It's lockdown all over again,' Dad says, his fingers drumming fast on the tabletop, shoulders tense. 'But without the slow build up.'

'And fear of running out of loo roll,' I add. It wasn't long after Mum and I got really ill with COVID that Dad dropped his high-flying job in the pharma world. His survivalist obsession started around then too. And he hasn't let us drop below 24 loo rolls in the house since 2020. 'They can't force us to stay in again, though. Can they?'

'Nobody's forcing us to do anything. But the government appears to be strongly recommending we stay in the house,' says Mum, her lip curling. 'Though, I don't trust this new government an inch.'

'Well, at least it's not the last one,' Dad counters, 'look at how they managed COVID!' He gets to his feet and cracks his knuckles. My parents glare at each other from opposite sides of the kitchen table, and a vast political abyss, until Mum sinks into her seat, picks up her knife and fork, and pointedly begins eating reduced-fat pancakes again.

This throws the room into tension as it leaves Dad, Ruby and I standing, ready for some kind of action, but no idea what.

'It's probably nothing,' I say, choosing words with the same caution as a bomb-disposal expert selecting wires to cut. 'If it is anything disastrous, I'm sure we'll hear more.'

I cast an eye at Ruby, who nods and pulls her gaze away from the window. She twists her nose ring in the same way I've seen her do in exams. I'm glad I didn't share my fear of a meteor shower.

'You're right.' Dad sits back down. Ruby and I do the same. 'And if the end of the world is on the way, it's better to fight it on a full stomach.' I can almost hear his brain running through our food supplies, contemplating slow-burning carbs, energy retention, candle eating, and all the survival stuff he's lived and breathed for the last few years.

'Mrs Johnson!' Dad shouts and drops his fork.

'She'll be fine,' Mum says, patting her mouth with a folded triangle of kitchen roll. 'I took her dinner over last night and everything was fine.'

Holy crap. How haven't we thought of Mrs Johnson until now?

'If she's seen the warning, she'll be scared,' I say. Imagining our little old neighbour all alone in her house has me back on my feet.

Mum shakes her head. 'The woman's lived through World War Two. She'll be fine.'

Dad stares at my mum for the longest time, disappointment in every angle of his features.

'I'm going to check on her,' I say. 'It'll take two minutes to run there and back. I can bring her here until we know what's happening.'

'No one's leaving this house.' Mum's voice is firm and authoritative. 'Mrs Johnson is fine. She won't leave the house without someone there to take her out, she'll be safe until her morning carer comes.'

I step towards the door. 'We can't leave her.'

'Sit down!' Mum slams her hand on the table. 'You're not going anywhere.'

'Who made you the leader?' Dad stands up and glares at her.

'Oh, that's mature, Harry. And I suppose you assume natural leadership as *a man*, do you? If you can even call yourself that,' Mum hurls the words at him.

Instead of buckling under the weight of them, Dad bristles and stands taller.

'I take my job of protecting our little family very seriously.'

'Protecting this family?' Mum snapped back. 'You didn't protect Nora's future when you gave up your job as a Senior Company Supervisor of Pharmaceutica to work for a goddamned environmental charity.' She stands up, knuckles resting against the table. 'Oh no, Harry, I protect this family. Financially. And in this world, that's the only way that matters. You're so old-fashioned, outdated and, and . . .' Mum let out a bitter laugh. 'A joke. You, Harry, are a joke.'

I look at Ruby, eyes wide. This cannot be happening.

'Mr and Mrs Inkwell, I don't think—'

Mum's stern gaze finds Ruby first, then me.

'You pair should leave the room,' she says. 'But don't leave the house.'

We're hardly out of the kitchen when Dad growls in a low voice, 'I'm done with you emasculating me, Kimberly. I've let you carry my balls around in your handbag long enough. Now I'm taking them back.'

'Shiiiiiiit,' says Ruby when we're clear of the fallout.

I dig my face into my hands. 'This is bad.'

'We should've brought pancakes out with us,' says Ruby. 'Do you think they'd mind if we sneak in and grab some?'

'This is serious.' I bat at her arm, but she's laughing too hard to care.

'Lady,' she grins, 'your parents can DISH. IT. OUT.'

'... *handed them to me on a silver platter...*' Mum's sharp voice cuts through to where we're standing in the living room. I wince, almost certain the topic of conversation is still Dad's balls. Gross.

Ruby moves to the window.

'Erm, Nor. You know your neighbour who wouldn't leave the house on her own?'

'Yeah.'

'Is she tiny with a dodgy wig?'

'Yeah. How did you kn— Oh!' I turn and see Mrs Johnson tottering across her front garden.

'She does NOT look well. Does she normally walk like that?'

Mrs Johnson is shuffling oddly, her toes pointing inwards and head twisted at an awkward angle.

'No. There's something wrong with her. I've got to get her.'

'You rebel.'

'Hold the door so it doesn't lock me out. I'll run, grab her and bring her in,' I say, already pulling on my trainers.

'Screw the government warning?'

'Hell yeah! And my mum. I'm only moving across two gardens to get my elderly neighbour. I'm sure I'll survive.'

Chapter 7

OUTSIDE THE DOOR, I PAUSE IN THE SUN'S WARMTH to process everything that's going on: Mrs Johnson looks like hell, my parents are probably going to murder each other, we've been officially warned to stay indoors and a guilty part of me is worrying that tonight's Interrupters gig will be cancelled too.

A short agitated snarl, like an animal bothered by flies, echoes around the houses and brings my focus back onto my neighbour.

Apart from Mrs Johnson, all is quiet in our West Midland suburbia. There's not another person about. On a normal non-government-warning Saturday, there would be kids playing, people heading into town and dog walkers ignoring their pets pooping on the pavement.

'Mrs Johnson, are you all right?' I ask. 'You're sounding pretty raspy.'

She snaps her head round, and cloudy eyes fix on mine. Her wig, which is precariously attached at the best of times, flaps with the motion.

She snarls.

'Whoa, that lady's sick,' Ruby calls from the door.

'Thanks for stating the obvious,' I say. My neighbour's lips and around her eyes are bruised blue and purple. Veins spider-web across her face like a road map, moving between islands of pustulating sores that cluster at the corners of her mouth, eyes and nose. She's tottering on the balls of her bare feet, heels pointing outwards. I clench my fists and fight the urge to run away.

A clattering noise jerks my eyes to where a wheelie bin lies toppled in the road. I only look away for a second, but Mrs Johnson is right beside me, smelling of death and talcum powder. Before I can say anything, she grabs my arm and bites down hard.

I scream.

She bit me. Is biting me. *What the—?*

Our front door slams, then Ruby's there, hesitating at my side.

'I don't know where to grab. I don't want to hurt her,' she says.

'She's hurting me!'

Mrs Johnson's arms fly in every direction, hitting and clawing at anything she can reach.

Ruby catches her by the wrists and a tug-of-war begins. I cry out again as Ruby's pulling makes Mrs Johnson chomp harder, growling like a dog fighting to keep its favourite chew toy.

I reach across and push on Mrs Johnson's chin. The soft skin moves under my fingers. I think of overripe peaches and shudder. Her jaw pops open, and she topples backwards onto the grass.

Old lady spit glistens on my arm and, amazingly, my skin is unbroken.

After hoovering up the surrounding air with a huge gasp, I let it all out with a sigh of relief. It takes a second to remember that zombies aren't real and this can't be a zombie attack, no matter how much it looks like one.

Mrs Johnson struggles to a crouch position, opens her mouth wide and lunges for another bite. Two rows of purple gums fly forwards. A small manic laugh escapes me. She didn't put her teeth in this morning, that's why I'm not bleeding!

'Run!' Ruby pulls me away and we hurry, full sprint, towards the front door.

It's shut. And yet we're both still running.

Ruby hits it first and hammers on the wood. I slam beside her and join in. Fists pounding, voices screaming. A glance tells me Mrs Johnson is close, her arms outstretched, fingers clawing the air as she closes the gap between us.

She snarls and gnashes her toothless gums with a wet popping noise.

We pound harder, scream louder.

Are Mum and Dad arguing so much that they can't hear us? Or have they killed each other and now we're about to get gummed to death?

THANKFULLY IN A GLASS SOMEWHERE

With a roll of nausea, I realise I'm going to have to fight my 90-year-old neighbour.

One hand against the door, I brace myself for a side-kick. It needs to be hard enough to get her the hell away, but not so hard that I put my foot through her rib cage. That would be beyond gross. And morally very bad. Not to mention traumatic and – well, I just need to not kick too hard.

Muscles tense, I can do this. It's self-defence, it doesn't make me a bad person.

Thankfully, before I release the kick, the wood disappears from under my hand and I overbalance, falling through the open door. Ruby jumps over me as I scramble backwards into the house. She pulls Mum out of the way and I boot the door with both feet. It crashes shut in Mrs Johnson's face.

'What are you doing?' Mum runs forwards and turns the latch.

'No!' The shout comes from both Ruby and me before we pounce on Mum.

'You might have killed her,' she says, still trying to get to the door.

We stop and listen. It's so quiet outside. No snarling, no growling or gum popping.

Oh god. I've killed Mrs Johnson.

Guilt sets in so deep and so fast that I laugh with giddy relief when a slow rhythmic scratching starts up on the other side of the door.

'Is she OK?' says Mum.

I open the letterbox and a pair of wrinkled cloudy eyes stare in. A squeal finds its way out of my mouth and I fall backwards.

'I wouldn't describe her as O or K. More like completely F'ed,' says Ruby.

'She's clearly not well. We need to get her in.' Mum goes for the door again.

'Look at this.' I lift my arm to show her the fiery crescent marks left by Mrs Johnson's vicious chomping. They're turning all kinds of red, blue and purple. 'She bit me. Really hard.'

Dad runs in to find Ruby and me wrestling with Mum to stop her opening the door.

'What's going on?' Dad looks at us all, his face tense with confusion. 'What's that noise?'

'Mrs Johnson trying to strip the paint off our front door. Very slowly. With her fingernails,' I say and lift the letterbox. His eyes grow in his head. 'So, quick recap for anyone not keeping up.' I let go of Mum, but I'm still ready to launch myself at her if she goes for the latch. 'There are government warnings to stay indoors, and Mrs Johnson, who's acting and smelling a bit too much like a zombie for my liking, has attacked me.'

The word "*zombie*" weighs heavily in the room as I smooth over the tenderest part of my arm, making doubly sure the skin isn't broken.

'I'll call an ambulance for your neighbour,' Ruby fishes her phone out of her pocket and groans. 'All my apps are blocked with the alert. It won't even let me make an emergency call,' Ruby says.

I check my phone.

'Same.'

I pick up the landline phone behind me. It's dead.

'Zombies,' Dad breathes. 'Poor Mrs Johnson.'

'Well, I blame the hippies she's got a garden share with.' Mum tuts and shakes her head.

'What?!' I stare at her.

'I read an article,' she says, 'about people like that putting their periods onto the garden to help their vegetables grow.'

As if today couldn't get any weirder.

'Well, isn't it obvious?' Mum says. 'That must be where this has all stemmed from. People eating food grown from menstrual blood!'

'No, it's not obvious. That's completely stupid. Anyway, I read that article too and it said it's good for you.' How have I found myself arguing for people to have the right to pour their periods onto their veg patch?

'Perhaps they'll rethink it now.' Mum folds her arms.

'OK, let's forget about period eating.' I fold my arms too.

'I'm going to struggle with that,' Dad says, pure horror written across his face. 'I might see if there's anything useful on the box.'

He flicks it on and I wait until Mum moves away from the door before I follow.

Ruby stands beside me, our shoulders touching.

'I don't think the gig's going to be on tonight,' she says with a pout.

I shake my head, waiting to feel relief that doesn't come.

On the telly, every channel shows the same message.

ALERT!

STAY INDOORS.

'That's helpful.' The screen flickers as though in response to Dad's words.

A newsperson I don't recognise appears. He looks pale and sweaty, not overdone and orange like most newsreaders. He's speaking fast.

'*. . . plague swarming across England. It is travelling faster than could ever have been predicted. Remain calm, keep indoors. Do not attempt to go out to save loved ones. It is every man for himself.*'

'Or woman for herself, or non-binary people for themselves,' corrects Ruby. 'Sexist.'

'*Laboratories are looking into a cure, but the numbers of infected are skyrocketing. What started as a mild curiosity yesterday has turned into a pandemic overnight. Dear god!*' The newsreader drops his papers and leans into the camera. '*Barricade the doors!*'

'Is it restricted to Britain? What about Mum, Dad and Freddy?' Ruby asks the telly, like it can answer her.

The reporter repeats himself with more desperation in his

voice, then picks up a new piece of paper and begins blabbing on about food rationing and avoiding contact with "*the infected*". '*Any loved ones taken ill need to be locked away – for your safety and theirs.*'

Mrs Johnson's still scratching away, and there's a brief pause before it starts again with renewed effort.

A tremor runs up my fingers. I'm not scared, it's just a bit of shock.

OK, maybe I am scared.

And I should be.

I'm the horror geek. I know how these things play out.

Chapter 8

'**SO,' I SAY, ATTEMPTING TO SOUND CALMER THAN** I feel. 'The pandemic that's on the news, we're thinking that's what turned Mrs Johnson into a zombie. Right?'

'The news isn't saying "zombie". Nobody is saying "zombie".' Mum's wide eyes flick between the telly and the front door.

'I'm totally saying "zombie",' I argue, my brain clawing to grab at anything that makes sense.

Dad's crouched in front of the telly, pen and paper in hand. It's the same as I've seen him do, watching hours and hours of Mae Rears, scribbling notes as if his life depended on it. I can almost see the sparks flying up and down his muscles as he bounces on the balls of his feet, looking more alive than I've seen in ages.

There's only really one thing to do at a time like this.

'I'm going to put the kettle on,' I say.

'I'll give you a hand.' Ruby follows me as Mum crumples onto the sofa.

The methodical motion of making tea settles some of the chaos flying around inside my head.

'Definitely no gig tonight then,' Ruby moans beside me. 'No Interrupters.'

'No Amy Interrupter,' I say, before I can stop myself.

Ruby doesn't notice, she's following her own line of thought. 'No hot alternativ-o girls in the crowd.'

No urgency to see if Ruby thinks people who are floating somewhere between straight *and* lesbian are untrustworthy spawns of Satan, or—

'No squelchy times for me tonight,' Ruby adds with a heavy sigh.

'Ruby! Can you stop saying that? It's freaking me out!'

'All right, all right, but I'd got myself psyched up.'

I know how she feels. But then again there's nothing stopping me from going through with my plan to ask her. Just because there isn't the threat of her throwing herself at some other girl to force me to do it, doesn't mean I can't.

Hope blossoms inside me. Hope that I won't always be hiding part of myself from the world and, more importantly, from Ruby.

By the time four brews steam away on the side, I've decided that I'm still going to ask her today. Now, in fact.

I deliver two cups to my parents in the living room and carry ours to the kitchen table, where Ruby's dipping a cold pancake in sugar and lemon juice.

I copy her, rolling mine up tight, sending it in for a fortifying dunk in the tin of golden syrup and folding it into my mouth.

After chewing and swallowing, I ready myself, trying to find the right words. My vision goes hazy around the edges and sweat glands all over my body kick into overdrive as I lick my lips and prepare to speak.

'Whatever this thing is,' Ruby cuts in first, 'I hope my family are away from it all.' Ruby takes another bite of pancake and gazes at the sky through the window.

The damp patches on the pits of my T-shirt slow their rapid spread – this is not a good time to ask.

'If we can't get the phones working, maybe we could go to

the airport?' I suggest, wanting to clear the worry that's got her twisting her nose ring again. 'They might have some information.'

The radio starts up again, making us jump.

'STAY HOME. STAY ALERT. STAY SAFE.'

That was weird – I'm sure it was switched off.

'But we could make our way to the airport, no problem.'

No sooner have I said the words than the radio replays its previous warning.

'Rubes,' I whisper. 'I think the radio's listening to us!'

'Everything listens to us nowadays,' Ruby says with a shrug. 'It's probably through our phones or something.'

I move my plate out of the way and lean forwards until my face is resting on the table and sigh.

What a mess.

Maybe it's best Ruby interrupted me. The last time I talked to anyone about the inconsistency in my crushes, it didn't go well.

Once, in Year 9, I spent a sleepless night searching my insides for an answer to the question: *Is it just me who feels like this?*

When morning came and I had nothing to show for my night's work, except extreme bed head, I decided in my sleep-deprived state that it would be a good idea to talk to my three best friends about it at first break.

Pixie had told us she liked girls the year before and we'd had a coming-out party. The memory gave me courage. I was only part way between Pixie and my other friends, and I wasn't coming out as anything. I just needed some gentle reassurance.

'Hey, guys,' I said, approaching our usual bench behind the art room. We've been friends since Year 7 and surviving secondary school together as *the outcasts* made us close. The three of them greeted me and I knew that the fear gripping my chest was stupid. They wouldn't judge me.

'So,' I said, sounding as offhand as I could. 'Morning quiz: What do we know about girls who don't just fancy guys?'

An awkward silence followed that lasted several heartbeats longer than was comfortable.

Nazia smiled encouragingly at me. She was my closest friend here, but unfortunately also the quietest.

'Pixie's our resident lesbian,' said Molly, diverting our attention to Pix, who chewed thoughtfully on her lip. 'Grace us with your queer wisdom.'

'Are you asking for yourself, or a friend?' Pixie asked.

This was a loaded question, what with them being my only friends and all.

'For myself.'

'Hmmm,' Pixie pondered. 'Have you heard of the word "bisexual"? It means both sexualities, like, being straight and gay at the same time.'

'Is that a thing?' It didn't sound real.

'Yeah, it's totally a thing. It's the B word in LGBTQIA+.'

'The B Word,' I echoed.

'Oh babes, congratulations,' Molly shouted and ran at me for a hug. 'You're bisexual!'

Pixie joined in the hug. Nazia reached a hand round and gave mine a supportive squeeze. A bombardment of mixed emotions had my throat tightening and my eyes welling up.

'I'll be back in a second.' I disentangled myself from them and ran to the loos.

Several deep breaths and runny-nose-blows later, I smiled at myself in the mirror.

There.

That wasn't so bad.

Hello, I'm Nora Inkwell and I'm a bisexual.

I winced.

Still, it was better than my alternative.

Hello, I'm Nora Inkwell and I'm a complete freak of nature.

Bisexual?

Bisexual.

BISEXUALLLLLLLL!

The more I thought it, the more it began to fit.

I walked back to my friends with a carefree bounce in my step that had been absent for some time.

On the way to our bench, I heard them chatting.

'She's absolutely trying to tag on to your lesbian popularity, Pix,' said Molly. My steps slowed.

'I know, that's totally what I was thinking, but didn't want to say anything.'

'She's like a total wannabe lesbian.' Molly's laugh that followed hit me hard.

Pixie added, 'A friend online told me gays shouldn't get into relationships with bisexuals because they can't be trusted.'

What?

'If being gay gets a bit too much for them, they can get a partner of the opposite sex and hide. They're sneaky like that. And apparently they're right slags too.'

I didn't fully understand what a slag was, but from what I knew about it, it sounded bad. I also didn't fully understand what a bisexual was, but now that sounded bad too.

'This is all totally just another one of Nora's attention-seeking things. Do you remember when she told us her toe was going to drop off?'

Nazia looked between Molly and a nodding Pixie, drinking in every word, and tears blurred my vision. The sob that snuck out alerted them to the fact I was standing right there.

'Nora, my bi babes!' Molly's smile was flawless and shining. That smile hurt more than her harsh words.

That was when I promised myself I would ignore crushes on anyone that's not a guy, so I never had to talk about it ever again.

'Please don't call me that. I'm straight. I *was* actually asking for a friend.' I pushed the tears off my cheek. 'Sorry.'

'I knew it!' said Molly, rolling her eyes at the others. 'People shouldn't want to be with both girls and guys. When you think about it, it's just being greedy, really, isn't it?'

'Yeah, I guess it is,' I said, shame soaking through me. I'd even liked some people who weren't guys or girls too. Did that make me extra greedy? The thought made me shrink inside.

In the weeks that followed, my friendship with the group

drifted. I hated myself as much as I hated them and being near them made me miserable. Even Nazia, who'd kept quiet.

I left the group and buried myself in scary books and movies. Molly thought they were stupid and I'd pretended I didn't like them for the years we hung out.

I huff out a sigh at the memory of it all and the lonely years that followed.

At the kitchen table, Ruby lies her head beside me and my stomach flutters as the smell of her strawberry shampoo fills me up. I don't want to lose her too and if I tell her, I might.

At least we're together in whatever's going on right now.

Together, but not alone ...

I lift my head off the table, things are very quiet on the parent front.

'I'm going to check on the rentals,' I say, heading to the living room.

They're standing side by side, staring out the window.

'Mum, Dad, you OK?'

'Jan and Phil are walking the dog,' Mum says in a hollow voice.

Outside, Maisy-dog is barking and running round her owners as they shuffle, arm in arm, down the street.

'They're ill too,' she continues.

That's an understatement. Jan has a huge part of her cheek torn away and deep purple bruises circle her eyes. Phil looks much the same, apart from the hand holding the lead is mostly ripped flesh and exposed bone.

It's weird how normal they look, except for the way Jan's jaw is hanging at an odd angle and wobbling with each step.

'They look like actual zombies,' I say, my voice dry.

Dad raises an eyebrow.

'Well, the way I see it . . .' He walks over to the sofa, pulls it out and flips it onto the backrest.

I know I shouldn't really be surprised, but I kind of am, to see a massive axe strapped to the sofa's exposed hessian bottom. Dad uses two hands to rip the axe off, looking like he could do some serious damage with that thing.

Mum looks like she might argue about him hiding weapons in the house, but Dad speaks first.

'. . . something somewhere has gone horribly wrong and now it's survival of the fittest.' He gives the axe a couple of trial swings.

'Could they be acting?' Ruby says, side-stepping away from my axe-wielding father and towards the window, where more of our neighbours shuffle into view. Some are jolting and jerking unnaturally while others snap randomly at the air.

'I don't think they'd be that good,' I say. 'I'd imagine an old-fashioned George A. Romero, *Night of the Living Dead*-style zombie act from our neighbours, rather than the modern *World War Z* thing we have here.'

'What?' Mum looks at me as though I'm speaking a different language.

I sigh. 'It doesn't look like they're acting,' I say. 'And as spritely as Mrs Johnson is, I doubt she could keep going for as long as she has without at least four cups of tea and a packet of bourbons.'

'I'll put the kettle on again,' Ruby says, leaving us to stare disbelievingly at the scene out the front of our house.

When I finally follow, I find Ruby finishing the washing up. She turns to see me staring at her.

'What? Just because there may or may not be zombies in the neighbourhood, doesn't mean

I can't be polite about staying with your family.' She carries on clearing the table.

She looks so beautifully out of place in our normal, boring house. I take in her heavily black-dusted eyes, with a hint of red and twinkles of pink. Her red beaded necklace and fitted Against Me! band tee over a long-sleeved red string top, hooked over her thumbs. The blacker than black shredded jeans running down to stripy red and black socks. She's like a gem from a different world in our middle-to-upper range IKEA fitted kitchen.

I'm going to blame zombie-induced fear for the fact I am completely failing to build my usual walls around the feelings I have for Ruby.

I totally fancy her.

I've fancied Ruby Rutherford from the first time I saw her stomping across college, sparkly boots twinkling in the sunlight, to our Film Studies class.

It took all the willpower I had to avoid her for an entire year; she kept trying to talk to me on the way into and out of class. But when we were put together for a project at the beginning of Year 13, we started chatting and haven't stopped yet.

Being around Ruby makes me so happy and, for some reason, she seems to enjoy being around me too.

Looking at her now, on the morning of what appears to be a zombie outbreak, I'm smiling dopily to myself. If anyone saw, they would see the truth written across my face and I'd be exposed for the fraud I am. Untrustworthy and sneaky. A wannabe lesbian.

My smile blinks out of existence.

I turn my back on her and make more tea.

Chapter 9

A SCREAM FROM THE STREET OUTSIDE MAKES US all rush into the front room.

Through the big window, we see Mr Hansdale from the grocery shop running down the street. He spots our neighbours Jan and Phil looking creepily gruesome and stalls as they turn on him. The scratching on the front door finally stops and seconds later, Mrs Johnson totters her way across our lawn towards him too.

We bundle to the door and pull it open. Dad has his axe gripped tight in both hands.

'Over here!' he calls.

Mr Hansdale hears and starts running in our direction. The noise brings out more peaky-looking, gnashing neighbours, but their shuffling is no match for the grocer's adrenalin-fuelled, full-pelt sprint.

He's going to make it...

He runs past the corner of the house opposite and three more shambling neighbours lurch out of nowhere and pile on top of him.

...or not.

Dad moves to help, but Mrs Johnson is on her way back towards us. Her black pupils sit like cloudy pools among the red veins running through her eyes.

Dad raises the axe and hesitates as Mr Hansdale lets out

another scream; this one chills my blood. Hansdale's feet kick. A blue-veined fist reaches high with a handful of something bloody and pink dangling from clenched fingers.

'Oh my god, are those his—?' I feel sick.

The shock and horror of seeing our greengrocer disembowelled is quickly replaced by fear, with more sick people shuffling our way.

'We can't help him,' Dad calls, running back with Mrs Johnson close behind.

'Shut the door!' Mum shouts, pulling Ruby and me out of the way. Dad jumps into the house and she slams the door behind him. We all hear the thump of a little old lady running into the other side.

'They ate him. They're eating him. They—' Mum's eyes are wild and her voice pinches high at the end.

'Kim, calm down.'

'Calm down? Our neighbours ate our greengrocer!!!'

'Well, I suppose that's what will come to you if you overcharge for sprouts every Christmas,' Dad says, with a dry chuckle that doesn't match the harrowed look on his face.

A hair-raising screech from the front room, like a fork being dragged slowly across a plate, makes us all wince. I crawl to the window and peer out.

'They've lost interest in Mr Hansdale,' I say, trying to keep the panic out of my voice.

'You mean they've taken an interest in us,' Dad corrects me. We both stare at the bruised, bitten and pustulated faces now pressed against the front window. Some are attempting to bite through the glass, giving a nastily clear view of inside their mouths. Part of me is tempted to run and grab my sketchbook and pens; it's kind of amazing and kind of horrible at the same time.

Where their gums should be pink and healthy, they're blue, black and grey.

'Oh, ew! Someone's been neglecting their flossing duties.' Ruby puts her face closer and examines them. 'These are all your neighbours?'

'Yep.' My one-word answer is punctuated by another tooth catching on the glass, letting out a second screech that sends goosepimples shivering down my spine.

'OK,' Mum's voice is loud and decisive. 'We need to pull this together, get all our ducks in a row.' Oh no, she's switched into motivational-speech mode. 'First rule of success: to be a winner you must dress like a winner.' She looks down at herself in her floaty shirt and mum-jeans. 'Oh god, I need to change.'

She turns and runs upstairs with purpose.

'This might be the making of that woman.' Dad looks impressed. 'She's right, though, you two could probably do with changing too. We need tight-fitting clothes, nothing baggy that anyone might grab hold of in a chase.' He hooks a finger in Ruby's net top to demonstrate its unsuitability. 'Tie your hair up for the same reason, Nor.'

I don't want to. Of course I don't want to. I need my hair to hide behind! But one glimpse of the survival expert bubbling away beneath the surface of my dad's specific instructions, and I know I should listen.

'And put a spare pair of pants in your pocket.'

'Where does it say that in the survival books?' I ask.

'Nowhere, it just makes good sense. We don't know if we'll need to leave the house yet, but in case we do, we should be prepared.'

'With spare pants?'

He nods seriously.

'Right.' I run upstairs and hear Ruby behind me.

'What are you going to wear?' she asks.

'It could be the zombie apocalypse. It's our duty as horror nerds to dress in something completely badass.'

'You always look badass,' Ruby says before grabbing some clothes from her suitcases. 'Fortunately, so do I,' she adds, sticking her tongue out before vanishing into the bathroom. I'm left grinning stupidly to myself before I shake it off and focus on the terrifying concept of wearing anything fitted.

I own some less baggy jeans, no problem there, the problem comes with having to wear them without an oversized T-shirt to cover my bum.

The T-shirt choice is painfully difficult, despite only owning one fitted top. It's a white baseball T-shirt with black sleeves and "*Slash the Patriarchy*" with the feminist fist holding a bloodied knife printed across the chest. It is one hundred per cent awesome but I've never worn it before, because I ordered it online and when it arrived Mum said it was too small for me.

Now I'm desperately trying to think of it as *fitted*, instead of *too small*, as I pull on my black high tops and tie my hair up.

I catch sight of myself in the mirror. No hair or excessive quantities of T-shirt to hide in. I'm exposed.

Survival over self-consciousness, I tell my reflection.

On the way out, I spot our werewolf mask on my desk.

'I'll be back soon,' I tell her, though the words don't sound convincing. With her eyes in, she's looking completely brilliant. The stained university prospectus sits beside her and I realise it might be more than just tonight's gig that'll be cancelled.

'Nor! Ruby!' Dad calls.

OK, one thing at a time: worry about wearing a tiny T-shirt during a zombie attack now and worry about losing my higher education – along with all my hopes and dreams for the future – later.

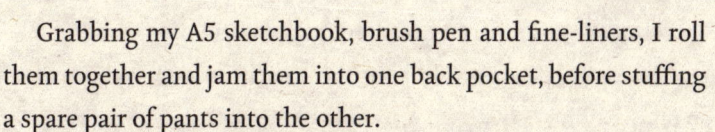

Grabbing my A5 sketchbook, brush pen and fine-liners, I roll them together and jam them into one back pocket, before stuffing a spare pair of pants into the other.

'I'm ready,' I shout back and hammer down the stairs.

'Me too,' says Ruby seconds later, bombing it down after me. 'Whoa, Nora, well done. You officially look badass! Nice top.'

I stop tugging at the T-shirt. Ruby likes it.

'Thanks. You too,' I say, even though she looks more or less the same, except she's swapped her string top for a pink and black striped stretch one and put on her trainers with white skulls printed across the fabric.

She's also grabbed her hockey stick from my room. It's a tall, thin roller-hockey stick, nothing like the stumpy little things we had at school to play field hockey.

'What's that for?'

'What do you think? Self-defence.'

Mum moves down the stairs more cautiously, but her outfit is louder than any of our bounding.

The rest of us stop to take in her matching day-glow pink gym wear.

'Nora,' Mum says, catching sight of me. 'Don't you have jeans without holes in the knees? It looks so scruffy.'

Don't you have an outfit that doesn't make you look like a massive dildo? I don't say. Instead, I answer, 'We're being attacked by zombies! I'm sure they won't mind.'

The activity outside becomes more frenzied.

'I don't think they can get through the double glazing.' Dad's voice drops to a whisper. 'But we should definitely be quieter . . . and maybe keep hidden.'

I shut the curtains. Out of sight, out of mind.

There's only enough time for the muscles across my shoulders to relax before—

SMASH!

We run to the kitchen and see that the glass in the panelled door has given way. The plus-sized recluse from down the road has his head sticking through it, chomping at us.

Chapter 10

THE BACK DOOR IS NOT LOOKING TOO STURDY against several neighbours' shoving and isn't going to hold out for long.

'Follow me,' Dad says, running down to the cellar with the rest of us close behind. When I pull the door shut behind us, I slide a chunky bolt across.

At the bottom of the stairs I find Ruby holding her hockey stick in a mirror image to my dad and his axe. I wish I had a weapon. Mum swings her arms and rubs her hands together, obviously thinking the same thing.

Ruby lets out a low whistle. 'Serious man cave,' she whispers, taking in the toolboxes and workbench.

My nostrils twitch. It's been a while since I've been down here, but I'm sure the place has shrunk. It smells dusty, and parts of the wall look freshly plastered. And come to think of it . . . since when was there a bolt on the inside of the door?

'Zombie outbreak?' Dad looks at us, axe raised almost as high as his quizzical eyebrow.

'Definite zombie outbreak,' I confirm. With a nod, he swings round to a section of smooth pink wall and sinks the axe into it.

'Harry!' Mum shrieks. 'What the hell are you doing? First, you lead us into a dead end and now you're dismantling the place!' She stops and looks at me. 'This is it, Nora, your father's finally gone insane. Ruby, I'm sorry you're having to witness this.'

'Kimberly, will you shut up? I have not gone insane.' He taps a small brass plaque set right below the ceiling with a piece of paper tucked inside. 'Each one represents the survival equipment I've hidden behind it.'

On the one my dad is pointing at, written in his tiny, tidy handwriting, are the words:

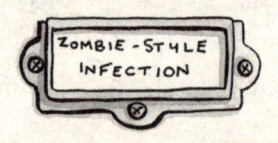

> ZOMBIE-STYLE INFECTION

Around the room there are more plaques with different labels:

GIANT FREEZE

MASS FLOODING

PANDEMIC

HEATWAVE

NUCLEAR WAR

EARTHQUAKE

DROUGHT

I read them under my breath. So, this is what he's spent all his time doing: building a secret survival room. That's not weird at all.

'You prepared for a zombie apocalypse?' Mum asks with a squeak in her voice.

'Zombie-style infection,' Dad corrects. 'It's surprisingly likely, Kim. With some of the stuff I've seen occur in a petri-dish, I felt it needed preparing for. Better safe than sorry.' He turns to me. 'Nora, in that cupboard in the corner, there're two bags. Grab them out.'

I follow his instructions, hauling out two hefty camo-patterned rucksacks.

'Each contains basic survival equipment,' Dad explains, sinking the axe into the wall a couple more times.

While he acts like hacking away at the wall is perfectly normal, the rest of us stare in varying degrees of confusion and worry.

This isn't helped when the wall gives way to a cavity and Dad pulls out a stash of cricket bats from the freshly axed-in cubbyhole. They're followed by a smaller rucksack, speckled pink with fallen plaster. He opens it. *The Zombie Survival Guide by Max Brooks* takes up half the bag; there's also a junior hacksaw, some science-lesson-style goggles, and small mounds of weird shiny fabric.

'The survival guide talks about handguns, but laws about that aren't quite the same over here as they are in America. A good smack from a blunt instrument should do the job.'

He hands me and Mum a cricket bat each. I grip it tight, a weight lifting off my shoulders.

'There's stuff hiding behind each of these panels?' Mum says, the squeak in her voice even more high-pitched this time.

'For different emergencies.' Dad nods. 'Here, this bat might be less cumbersome than that stick.' He moves to swap Ruby's hockey stick, but she pulls it away from him and hugs it close.

'No! Thank you, Mr Inkwell. I'd rather keep this, we've already been through so much together.'

'I don't suppose there is a right or wrong in these situations.' Dad shrugs. 'Now, I went one above *The Zombie Survival Guide* and brought some stainless steel mesh, cut-proof gloves. Custom ordered.'

He pulls out three pairs of gloves made of a daintily knitted chain mail.

'Minor cuts to the hands appear to be a problem that no one addresses in this particular survival situation. Anytime you swing for a hit, your hands are going to be dangerously close to the assailant's teeth, which can break the skin and transfer whatever illness has got them in that state. Unfortunately, I only planned and packed for three of us.' Dad turns to Ruby. 'You have them, I'll go without.'

'You can have mine,' I say.

'No! I was the fool who only packed three of everything. Of course I should have packed spares.' He pushes them into my hands.

They're cold but smooth and fasten with a blue Velcro band at my wrist. Mum and Ruby do the same.

'Now these.' Dad holds up the goofy-looking science goggles by their elastic.

'You are joking?' scoffs Mum. 'And I suppose you don't have enough for yourself, so only we get to wear them and look like idiots?'

'I'm being selfless, Kim. But if you don't want them, I'll wear them. Contaminated blood in the eye could cause infection. *28 Days Later* demonstrates this.' He pulls on the goggles while trying to maintain some level of dignity.

Out of solidarity, I pull mine over my head, and Ruby does the same.

'Good thinking, Mr I,' she says and throws me a wink. She looks adorable.

SLASH
GOOF-BALL

A loud *BANG!* is followed by the sound of many feet shuffling along the carpeted floor above.

'They're in the house,' Mum whispers.

Dad lets out a strangled noise. 'Reinforcing the cellar door was next on my to-do list.'

'We're trapped,' Mum breathes. Then her eyes narrow and she rounds on Dad. 'Have you got any food, water or anything useful in here? Or is it just books, cricket bats and fancy dress?'

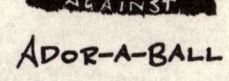

Dad's confidence trips over Mum's words, but he recovers quickly and moves to another section of wall, smiling, and uses one finger to push on the bottom right-hand corner. With a small click, a panel swings inwards to reveal a shallow slope leading up to a hatch above.

'Oh, thank god!' The words fall out of Mum.

'Ooh, escape hatch! Nice work.'

'Thanks, Ruby. Impressive, huh?' Dad adds to Mum.

'Right now, yes,' she says, a little too loudly. 'If, in any other situation, I'd discovered you'd built a secret tunnel in our cellar, I'd have had you taken away.'

A cluster of thumps on the main cellar door makes my heart stutter in my chest.

My eyes stretch wide in panic. 'They know we're in here.'

The banging at the cellar door gets louder and more frantic.

'Whatever we're doing, now would be a good time to do it.' I nod at the escape tunnel.

Dad climbs into the gap and opens a hatch to the outside world.

In the time it takes for me to think *there's no way he'll fit through that tiny space*, he has. He's raised his arms, breathed in deep and squeezed through. He must have done trials because the technique was flawless.

Will I fit?

'All clear up here. Quick, throw up the stuff and then come through,' he whispers.

We get the cricket bats and hockey stick to Mum, who's half tucked into the tunnel and stuffs them through the hatch.

We're working fast, but apparently not fast enough. The pounding gets louder and louder until the cellar door explodes inwards in a shower of splinters.

Zombified neighbours crowd the top of the stairs. They all lurch forwards as one and jam themselves in the doorframe.

'Move, move, move!' I push at Mum.

'What's going on?' Dad's voice travels in from outside.

'Harry, get us out!'

The weight shifts as Mum is lifted out of sight. A juddering, thudding sound makes me turn. Jan is lying bewildered at the bottom of the stairs and I notice her hip clip, full of poop-a-scoop bags, which she always wears when walking Maisy-dog. This small detail stalls my actions and jars my brain.

'Maybe sending the weapons through the hatch first was a bad idea,' Ruby says.

'Yeah, maybe.'

The Zombie Survival Guide lies at my feet near where Jan is clumsily failing to get up. The bottleneck jam in the doorway has been unstoppered and they're coming, ambling down the stairs towards us.

'What are you pair doing in there? GET OUT!' Dad calls.

I snap out of my daze and push Ruby towards the hatch.

'No way, lady, you first,' Ruby says.

Jan grips my leg and opens her mouth wide. Reflexes have me scooping up *The Zombie Survival Guide* and shoving it in her mouth. She clamps down on the book with a puzzled expression before letting go of my leg to hold and gnaw at it. I'm not sure it's exactly what Max Brooks had in mind when he wrote it, but it buys us some time . . . which we then waste arguing.

'What the hell?' I ask Ruby. 'Get out the hatch, it's not an either / or situation, we're both getting out of here.'

'You first then,' she looks at me, eyes hard. Every second we argue is a second wasted, so I launch myself at the tiny exit.

Dad grabs my hands and pulls, my back drags painfully up the metal frame as he lifts. There's one heart-stopping moment when my hips get stuck. I breathe in, twist this way and that, lose a little more skin off my back and I'm out. Dad throws me on the floor. By the time I've turned around, he's got Ruby by the wrists and is lifting her up.

I breathe in relief, moving to take one of her arms.

We nearly have her out when she's abruptly tugged back down into the cellar.

My hands are sweaty and Ruby's grip slips. Desperation runs an icy finger from the base of my skull to the top of my bum as all of Ruby's smiles play through my head. I had no idea I'd been cataloguing them,

RUBY'S SMILES:

'HEY, NORA!' (NORMALLY PRELUDES MISCHIEF)

SNEAKY

CAT-LIKE

THOUGHTFUL

PURSUASIVE

'TRUST ME'

but there they are. Each one brilliant and profound in their own way.

The look on her face just now is pure and gut-wrenching terror.

I readjust my grip and tug hard. She's back out.

'They've got my legs!' Ruby jerks back and forth with every kick of her feet and I focus on keeping hold of her.

We all haul together. Mum's even grabbed me around the middle and is pulling too.

Ruby screams.

We yank.

She screams again.

We tug again, harder this time.

She pops free like Pooh Bear from Rabbit's hole, which now, come to think of it, sounds a little rude. Not the time.

Ruby flies out, and we land in a tumbled heap on the floor.

'Rubes, are you OK?' I run my eyes over her.

She's gripping her foot and my heart is rammed so hard in my throat I think I'm going to puke it up.

'One of them bit me.'

'No!' White splotches fill my eyes as I shakily move in to see.

'Bastards!' Ruby shouts. 'I love these trainers. Why couldn't I have had a gummy old gran, like you, Nor?'

She pulls her hands away from her foot, and I dread the sight of torn canvas and blood. But there are only teeth marks set deep into the white rubber toe of her trainer. No torn canvas. No blood.

I throw my arms around her.

'Don't do that,' I scold. 'I thought they'd got you.' I squeeze her tight, not wanting to ever let go. 'You could have become one of them.'

In the alleyway beside our house, Ruby clutches on to me as tightly as I'm holding her.

'That was fucking scary,' she says, trembling.

Hyper aware that my parents are watching, I reluctantly let go of her.

A blue veiny arm reaches out the hole to the cellar and fingers catch on my shoelaces. I kick out at the hatch and it slams shut with a click.

'Don't worry, Ruby, you wouldn't have turned into a zombie.' Dad's voice is calm. 'What do you think the hacksaw's for? You'd have lost a foot, but I could've hacked the limb off pretty quickly to stop any infection spreading. I've been practising on joints of pork.'

'Of course you have.' I frown, starting to see my dad in a different light. No longer weird, downtrodden or sad, but prepared for more than I ever could imagine might go wrong with the world...

Was he really prepared to saw off Ruby's foot?

← Ruby's Shoe

Chapter 11

RUBY'S NEAR ESCAPE IS STILL REVERBERATING around my mind when Mum turns on Dad.

'How very chivalrous of you to have gone first and left all the girls in the hole.' Each word drips sarcasm.

There are no zombies currently in the alley up the side of the house, but I'm certain it won't take much to change that.

'I *was* being chivalrous, going out first into the unknown.' Dad throws out his hands in agitation. 'Anyway, I thought you were a modern woman. All for gender equality and all that?'

I gather our stuff together, hoping we can get moving before they raise their voices enough to bring more of our chomping, groaning neighbours upon us, and it isn't long before I see we've left behind more than just *The Zombie Survival Guide*.

'Hate to break it to you,' I say, glad to have some bad news to interrupt their argument with. 'Only one rucksack made it out.'

Dad's eyes close, his face scrunches, and his breath grows heavy. 'We're out safe. One pack is better than none, and we have the cricket bats and hacksaw. We'll be OK.' I'm not sure whether he's talking to himself or us.

I glance around at our small band of people. Three of us look apocalypse ready, including shiny metal gloves and plastic safety goggles. But one looks like a lady in her mid-forties wearing florescent pink gym wear. Mum pulls it off better than most, but

I can't help thinking that if we're running away from zombies, she may as well have "EAT ME" stitched across her florescent pink bum.

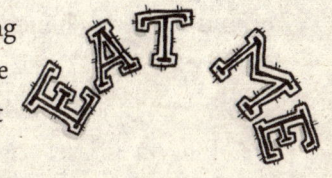

'Right, well, holing up no longer seems to be an option,' Mum says.

'When was the plan ever to hole up?' Dad argues.

'It was an unofficial plan in the absence of other plans.' Mum crosses her arms defensively.

'There was a plan. There's always been a plan. What kind of self-respecting survival expert doesn't have a plan?'

'Survival expert?' Mum raises a sceptical eyebrow. 'Go on then, *Mr Survival Expert*, what's your amazing plan?'

I can't help but feel hopeful.

'We go to Acton Mortimer.'

OK, less hopeful now.

'Where?'

'The middle of absolutely bloody nowhere, that's where,' Mum snaps.

'Acton Mortimer Manor House belongs to a friend I met at a Survivalist Convention. He told me in the strictest confidence that his house is the most defendable place in the UK. A hill on one side, flat fields for miles on the other. It's a little over an hour's drive away from here, in the heart of the countryside. And,' Dad says, like he's been saving the best until last, 'he has a helicopter!'

Dad opens his mouth to explain more, but quickly closes it again and grabs one of the cricket bats from the ground beside him.

He swings it and it connects with a sneaky zombie creeping up behind us, hitting him square across the chest and knocking him over backwards.

My heart jolts. I didn't hear him coming at all! He wasn't breathing, or at least wasn't conveniently grunting and groaning like the others, to let us know he was near.

'We need to get out of here.' Dad hands the cricket bats to me and Mum. I grab the survival pack and pass Ruby her hockey stick.

'I've got my car keys, follow me,' Mum says, running ahead to the end of the alleyway and peering out. She's clearly reluctant to let Dad take the lead on this. If they don't start working together, instead of against each other, this could be a problem.

'The young couple that moved into number twenty-eight last year are near our front door and there's a cluster of people over by Mrs Johnson's house,' Mum stage-whispers as we move up behind her. She takes a deep breath and looks at the car keys clutched in her hand. 'I think I can make it.'

'Kimberly, no!' Dad reaches out, but he's too late. Mum launches from the shadows between the houses at a run. The young couple, who now have sallow skin and bite marks on their faces, lunge at her. She ducks left, then right, the car bleeps, and she's in.

A second later, the engine murmurs into life. She proceeds to do a by-the-book three-point turn. The neighbours that were across the road move in close enough for the fingernails on their grasping hands to scratch at the metal. It's probably only out of fear for her paintwork that Mum puts her foot down and mounts the kerb, narrowly missing Mrs Johnson, who topples over. Mum throws open the passenger door.

'Get in! Now!'

We run and pounce into the car.

After shoving the camouflage pack behind the driver's seat, I turn to see Dad's feet taken out from under him by our elderly neighbour. Then she's on top of him, gums popping. He raises the bat high over his head to strike, and wavers.

I launch myself back out of the car, hitting the ground at a run. With a hand on each shoulder, I grab Mrs Johnson and pull her off. Dad throws his hand forwards, I catch it and tug him up to standing.

Mum drives away, doors open like wings, and we follow on foot.

Dad gives me a knowing grin. We've run side by side, twice a week, for a few years now, so we fall easily into step and it's only then I realise why he's grinning. He's been training me for something like this, and now it's paying off.

Mum indicates and pulls over ahead of us.

Dad jumps in to ride shotgun and I leap into the back.

Doors slam.

'Drive, Kimberly. Drive!'

The car quietly revs under me, the indicator ticks again and we pull away at an alarmingly unhurried pace.

'Mum, you drive like an old man. Put your foot down!'

'But—'

'It's a four-by-four, give it some welly!' says Dad.

She's almost hit 15mph by the end of our road and revs while taking the corner, only to grind to a halt when she sees what's waiting at the school crossing.

Chapter 12

THERE, DANCING IN THE MIDDLE OF THE ROAD, is a one-man disco: a guy who looks a little older than me, dressed in the crossing guard's long fluorescent yellow coat and cap, which glows in the sunlight. The vibrant colour stands out against his dark brown skin and the grey of the street.

I'm amazed that anyone can pull off the look quite like he is. With white earpods hooked into his ears, he's using his giant lollipop stick as a microphone, and hasn't realised yet how close he came to being squished by the world's most restrained apocalypse getaway driver.

Mid-twirl, he opens his eyes. When he sees us, the guy gives an embarrassed smile, flashing a gold tooth, and steps onto the pavement while waving in the universal hand signal for *drive on*.

'What's that kid doing?' Dad asks.

'Waving us by.' Mum drives.

Through the rear window, I see our cluster of zombified neighbours tumbling and staggering around the corner.

'Stop!' I shout. 'You have to pick him up!'

'But we don't know him,' Mum says.

'Mum! He isn't some hitchhiker. He'll be the victim of a mad mauling if we don't get him into the car now.'

'I don't know,' Mum says, but she's slowed down to think.

That's all I need. I throw the door open and jump. It would be amazing to say I land gracefully, scoop the chap up and we keep moving, but sadly that isn't the case.

Instead, I ungracefully miss my footing, go arse-over-tit and take my face out on the pavement. The safety goggles smash into my cheekbone.

The lollipop guy runs over to me and ducks by my side.

'Wow! Are you OK? You just, like, completely jumped out of a moving car.'

'You need to come with us!' I say, my hands, knees and jaw hurting a lot.

'Easy now, you're bleeding. Let's just calm down.' He looks at me, from my wonky goggles to metal gloves, and I'm suddenly aware I need to sound at least a bit sane if I'm going to convince him to get into the car with us.

'Haven't you noticed that not many people are crossing the road today?' I ask, wondering why he's even here on a weekend.

He pulls his cap off and curls the peak in his hands before running a hand back and forth over his short-cut, tightly curled black hair.

'I thought it was quiet, even for a Saturday. I—'

'OK, you need to stop talking now and turn around.'

Our zombie friends are close enough for us to hear their groaning.

'Robbo!' The crossing guy's face

CRACKING KNEES!

lights up when he recognises someone in the crowd and takes a step forwards. He hesitates. 'What's wrong with him? He needs a doctor. Shit. They all need a doctor!'

The mob is so close we can smell the rot.

'Mind if I explain in the car?' I pull off the cracked goggles in an effort to get him to take me seriously.

They're getting too close and I panic. I grab his arm and pull, but he bats me off.

'They're sick.'

'Yep, real sick. Please, get in the car or you will be too.'

He ignores me and walks towards his friend Robbo and the crowd of groanies.

Well, I tried to rescue him.

In the safety of the car, we all watch out the back window as Mrs Johnson makes her way to the front of the crowd. She's the first to seize the guy in his huge high-vis coat and bites down on his hand.

His friend Robbo gets hold of him from the other side.

Crossing Guy is cannon fodder.

There's no hope.

His fluorescent outfit makes him easy to see, even with the others crowding in. He pushes his striped lollipop stick under Robbo's jaw, jamming his mouth shut and throwing him off balance. His friend falls, taking down several of his fellow zombies.

Next, the poor bloke tucks his lollipop under his arm and focuses on getting his hand out of Mrs Johnson's toothless chomp. He pulls as gently as is possible when using your foot on someone's chest for leverage.

It pops free and, without pausing, he dashes to scoop up a black sports bag from the side of the pavement and hurtles towards us. His phone slips out of his pocket and hits the tarmac with a crack. He turns back just in time to see it crushed under his friend's heel.

'Come on!' I swing the car door open and the good-looking guy in neon jumps in. Nice knees too. Zombies or not, you can't help noticing when a cracking pair of knees squish in beside yours.

The stop sign blocks the door from shutting properly, so the crossing guy holds it closed as hands grope the doorframe.

'Oi, nimrod,' Ruby calls. 'Lose the lollipop!'

'I can't, I'll get charged for it.'

'That's the least of your worries!'

'It was my gram's,' he tries to argue, but a veined hand yanks it out the car. As soon as it's gone, the door slams shut.

Ruby shouts, 'We're in. Drive, Mrs I!'

Mum pulls away as fast as I've ever seen her go – which still isn't as speedy as any of us would've liked.

I use the minutes that follow to catch my breath and allow my heartbeat to re-regulate before finally relaxing into our journey to the safety of the countryside.

Beside me, the newest member of our group doesn't show any signs of relief – hugging his sports bag tight, visibly taut tendons run through every part of him not covered in high-vis. From the way he's sat, I think even his bum muscles are clenched as he stares out the window.

I'll give him a minute. We can fill him in on the plan once he's had time to get his head around the current situation.

Outside, the streets are empty.

No cars.

No people.

Just as I begin to enjoy the sensation of putting distance between ourselves and any zombified neighbours, an empty Sainsbury's bag-for-life cartwheels across the road in front of us, caught on a heavy breeze I hadn't noticed before.

Mum pulls over. Mirror, signal, manoeuvre.

'What are you doing?' I ask, looking around for any possible reason why she might have stopped our escape.

'Should we pop to Sainsbury's?' She looks at us like today is any normal day and we might like to pick up a loaf of bread and some milk.

Ruby's eyes light up. 'Popcorn!'

'Though popped corn would be an uneconomical use of space,' says Dad, 'we do need to top up our supplies. We haven't got nearly enough food.' He leans round and looks at the three of us across the backseat. 'Especially now we have an extra mouth to feed.'

My first thought is to panic. Then my second thought is of Woody Harrelson with a banjo in *Zombieland*. All the best zombie movies have an undead ass-kicking supermarket scene.

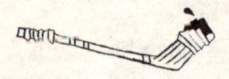

Out the front of the store are a few shufflers, suffering from the same illness as our neighbours.

'Look at them.' Ruby points at an old couple dragging their feet across the road, holding hands. 'It must be so ingrained into them that even in the middle of whatever's going on, they're still holding on to each other. That's love,' says Ruby, and the car falls into awkward silence.

Mum pulls round in front of the supermarket. As if it wasn't enough that the main doors have their roller shutters down, two cars have collided in front of them, acting as an extra barrier, but Mum doesn't seem to notice as she drives into a parking space and removes her seat belt.

'What are you doing?' Dad asks. 'Do you want a pound for the trolley as well?'

She looks at him, puzzled. 'No, I have my key-fob token.'

Dad sighs so heavily it comes out more like a growl.

'Kim, this isn't just some trip to the shops. We're going to have to go in through the side.' He points at the immense glass windows that form part of the wall. Beneath the reflection of the car park, I can make out the café inside. Where it's usually filled with people drinking cups of tea and eating all-day breakfast, today it stands empty.

'But there's no door.' Mum stares blankly at Dad.

'We need to ram it,' Dad says.

'Now we're ram-raiding Sainsbury's? This is getting pretty epic, pretty quickly,' I say to Ruby as my parents argue in the front seat about whether it's an appropriate time to drive Mum's new Mini through a giant sheet of glass.

'The zombies broke into your house, they literally smashed in your back door. We've both been chewed on,' Ruby says with a frown. 'I don't know, lady, I'd say it all got epic a while ago.' She looks out the window at the scattering of clouds above and I know she's worrying about her family.

'But, if this is a zombie outbreak,' I say, 'there'd be a source. There's always a source. Monkeys broken free from science labs, radiation from space, experimental drugs gone wrong . . .' Part way through talking, I become aware Mum and Dad have stopped arguing and are listening to me.

The guy squeezed in beside me comes out of his daze.

'So,' he says. The sound comes out as a squeak. He tries again, 'So, you're saying those people are zombies?'

Dad clears his throat. 'We can't say for certain. Though if they are, there are questions that still need answering. For example: Are they reanimated corpses or people infected with a rage virus?'

'Really, Harry, does it matter?'

'Well, at least it affects how I would feel about myself after hitting someone round the head with a cricket bat.'

'They're trying to eat us!' Mum says, like this is the only fact that matters.

'If this was a movie,' I say, 'I'd be peeved with the makers mixing up their references. These zombies act like one type, then switch to another without warning. Placid and dopey one minute, then faster and more motivated the next. And I don't know if they're breathing. I think Mrs Johnson was—'

'She was.' Dad passes a hand over his face. 'I might have hit her with the bat if she wasn't. But she was. And if they're breathing, that means there may be a cure.'

Ruby sits up quickly. 'There's a plane. Look up there. It's high, but you can see it.'

A dot moves across the blue sky, smudging a faint trail of white behind it.

'Your family are better off being out of the country,' Dad says in a reassuring voice, reading the situation perfectly.

'Right,' Mum says with the loud and definitive air of someone who's made a decision. 'If we're going to do it, there's no point putting it off. Let's ram that window.'

Chapter 13

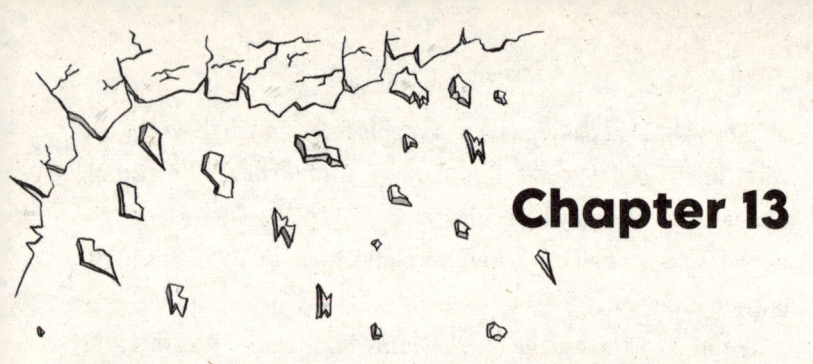

FINALLY DROPPING HER OVERLY CAUTIOUS approach to driving, Mum whips the car out of the parking space and spins it to face the window.

'Seat belts on,' she says.

There's some fidgeting as everyone clicks in before Mum puts her foot down and the car ramps forwards, towards the side of the supermarket.

Rows of sheet glass explode on impact with an ear-splitting crash. It's like we've driven into a waterfall with clear shards raining down on us. The whole thing gives very little resistance ... until we smash into the chairs and tables on the other side.

'Let's see if that draws out the police,' Mum says, unclipping her seat belt. 'Maybe then we can find out exactly what is going on here.'

Dad gazes at Mum in unhidden awe.

'Shall we grab some supplies then?' she asks him.

He's still staring.

'Harry?'

'Supplies? Right.' He swallows. 'Non-perishables. Preferably tins – with ring pulls – and dry goods.'

We all climb out of the car.

Dad whispers low. 'Lollipop kid, you stay here with the car, and keep quiet because noise seems to draw them out.'

'My name's Jayden,' he says. 'And we prefer the title Crossing Guard. Why should I stay here?'

'Because you're in shock and it's the safest place for you.'

'Are you for real?' He doesn't look shocked or confused any more. Just pissed off. 'You're not the boss of me.'

'Exactly, Jayden,' Mum chips in. 'I'm Kim, this is my daughter Nora, her best friend Ruby, and my husband Harry.' She points at each of us as she goes. 'We should stick together in pairs. Jayden, if you would like, you can come with me. Nora can stick with Ruby. And Harry, YOU can stay with the car. Anyone gets into trouble, shout out and we'll all come running.'

'OK,' Dad grumbles. 'Meet back here in five minutes.'

Jayden gently hooks his sports bag over his shoulder, then changes his mind and takes it off. He dithers before lovingly tucking it under the driver's seat, muttering to himself.

Weird.

Inside the supermarket it's dark, with natural light from small windows set high into the wall casting creepy shadows. I walk around the car, Ruby close on my heels.

We see only one sick person, dressed in a Sainsbury's uniform, shuffling about, and breathing so loud we'll hear her coming a mile away.

'That one's a growler,' giggles Ruby before almost walking into a *Back-to-School* display with only two rucksacks left on the hangers.

'This place is creepy as. Let's fill a bag and get out,' I say.

Ruby yoinks the Star Wars bag, leaving me with Spiderman, and we sprint down the aisle.

At the tins, we stock up on dhal, chilli and chunky soups.

And in the toiletries aisle, we pick up toothbrushes and toothpastes. Something shiny catches my eye and I hesitate.

Is this the end of the world?

'We're probably going to die virgins,' I say, wanting to put that piece of information out there. 'The last time a guy went near my pants, I freaked out and left him, possibly concussed, on the floor of an accessible toilet in the O2 Academy.'

'You really need to get over the whole Baxter thing. You said yourself you didn't mean to shove him quite so hard. And then he messed up any chance of you two getting back into that situation again with that shitty spray-paint stunt he pulled. It's not you. That was all him. Anyway, who knows, you might still find the opportunity.'

I sigh heavily, remembering the cold rubbery kisses that came before his tongue invaded and washing-machined my mouth. Then the fumbling, then the freakout.

I cringe. Though it was almost two months ago, the memory's still fresh like a wound that refuses to heal.

'I desperately want hot lesbo sexy times before I get eaten by a zombie. I mean, like, sex is everything! Of course we want to do it, it's the whole reason we've been put on this earth. To procreate.'

'I don't think that works with lesbian sex.'

'Blatant homophobia,' Ruby says. 'How dare you?'

I look at the cellophane-wrapped box that started this conversation. She's right, I don't think I want to die a virgin either.

An image of future me in a *War-Of-The-Worlds*-style dystopian setting, clutching a small wriggling bundle of rags and picking through mounds of rubble for any scraps, flashes at the back of my mind.

What?! That's pathetic.

I readjust my glance into the future to having the baby strapped to my back and me swashbuckling zombies, fighting as part of a resistance.

That's better.

The small square box, with the words "*Extra Safe*" written under the brand name, sits innocently on the shelf. Dystopian futures would be easier without a baby to worry about. Or an STI.

With a glance at Ruby stashing boxes of painkillers in her bag, I move to stealth-grab the pack. My hand fumbles in my knitted metal gloves and the entire manoeuvre isn't as smooth as I'd hoped. I shove it into the back pocket of my jeans as fast as I can.

'Grand plans for Jayden?' asks Ruby at my shoulder. I nearly jump out of my skin.

'No!' I flounder. 'No, I was just—'

She nudges me with her hip.

'Only kidding,' she says, but her voice doesn't sound playful. 'Come on, let's get back to the car. I can hear Growler coming and it sounds like she's found some friends.'

On the way, a shout from the direction of the car gets us running.

Chapter 14

THE BAGS FULL OF TINS JUMP UP AND DOWN on our backs as we run. I readjust the grip on my cricket bat and Ruby raises her hockey stick.

Mum's Mini comes into view and we stutter to a stop.

Beside the car, Dad holds a metal chair out like a lion tamer, jabbing it at two gnashing zombies: a lanky guy in his early twenties and a middle-aged woman I'm sure is the one on all the local Slimmer's Society posters.

She grabs the chair blocking the way to her next meal and bends its legs outwards. Though I seriously want to step in and help Dad, her obvious strength has me taking a shame-filled shuffle backwards.

How many calorie points would she have to count if she ate Dad?

Or just his arm?

What am I thinking?

Ruby runs in to even things up. She uses her stick to flick the woman's hands away from Dad before moving in to fight.

A scream from Mum makes me spin. She's caught in a tug-of-war with a beefy-looking lady who must have spent most of her life lifting weights. Both wrench at opposite ends of Mum's cricket bat. That woman is hench! And she's chomping at Mum's fingers with every tug.

I force myself to move closer, each tentative step accompanied by the crunching of my feet on the shattered safety glass that lies crumbled across the floor.

Heart rate climbing, I grip my own bat, willing myself to follow Ruby's lead of heroically diving into the fray.

Mum lets out another shriek and it snaps me out of my moment of paralysing terror. With my cricket bat flying, I run in and smash it down on the fingers of the hands yanking Mum closer. They release and Mum plummets backwards over a chair.

My bat is wrenched from my hands and tossed away as clammy fingers lock around my arm, jerking me towards a set of champing jaws.

The smell wafting from Hench Lady's festering mouth, along with the close-up of all the manky gunk clinging to teeth jutting out from putrid gums, has me floundering. It takes longer than I'd like to admit to remember that I have another arm. A free arm with a perfectly good hand at the end, capable of making a perfectly good fist, which I could then use to throw a perfectly excellent punch.

I love punching.

Not punching anyone or anything, just punching.

At Body Combat, the high-energy songs with long sequences of throwing jabs and crosses out into the air never fails to motivate me. During a good session I genuinely feel like I could take on the world, and that's what I channel now with the knitted mesh of the gloves stretching across my knuckles as my hand balls into a weapon.

Thanks to all my gym going and running, for a while I've had a sneaking suspicion that I might actually be a bit of a secret badass, waiting for the opportunity to unleash my inner warrior.

Certain this is it, and with no time to hesitate, I throw my fist as hard as I can at Hench Lady's face, scrunching my eyes shut right before the moment of impact, knowing deep in my core that all the Combat classes I've done will give the action some mega heft.

Except it doesn't.

Pain bursts through my hand, wrist and elbow. At the same time, a string of my most graphic expletives erupt from my mouth, and my knees stop working.

Shit the bed!

Why does no one tell you that punching someone hurts like a whole heap of hell? Hench releases my arm, though not because she's flying backwards from the force of my mighty blow. It seems she needs both hands to swat at my piddly fist like it's an irritating fly.

Any belief in my inner warrior blinks out of existence as I crumple to the floor, disappointed in myself in so many ways.

With me out of her eye-line, Hench dithers uncertainly and turns. Struck by the logical idea that she can't bite me if I'm behind her, I launch myself onto her back and wrap my arms around her throat.

Gasps interrupt her groany breathing. This reminds me that she's not a horror movie monster but just someone who's really, really that's-a-hell-of-a-lot-of-gunk-oozing-out-of-your-face sick.

I adjust my grip to reduce any chance of accidentally strangling her and, when it's obvious she can't throw me off or gnaw on any part of me, I cast my eye over the ruined café and the car, looking less than its usual pristine best.

Dad's still beside it, swinging the chair, and it's easy to see that,

RUBY JAYDER NUM DAD

while he's trying to keep his attacker away, he doesn't want to injure him.

Jayden's to my right, fighting with his bare fists.

In attempting to dislodge me, my ride spins to give me a view of Ruby skidding across the floor on her back. She comes to a halt nearby.

'You OK?' I ask, clinging on with everything I have.

'Never better,' she says, the trickle of blood running from her nose suggesting otherwise. 'You?'

'Yeah, not bad,' I reply, scrambling higher on Hench's back to tug my legs out of range of her agitated pawing.

Rubes scoops up her fallen hockey stick and braces herself to take on a new fighter in the ring, a balding man in a Sainsbury's work shirt who's stumbled into the café, dragging a mauled leg behind him. She's awesome.

Mum's found her feet again. She mops her head on the pink sweatband around her wrist before attempting to rescue me from my current predicament.

I'm swept away from her in Hench's continued attempts to extricate me.

Low movement catches my eye. Slimmer's Society is crawling towards Dad. With his attention on the lanky guy who appears to be doing some sort of 80s robot dance while chomping for a bite, Dad doesn't notice her reaching for his leg.

'Mum!' I shout. 'Help Dad.'

She dithers, clearly wanting to stay focused on me, but a holler of surprise from Dad kicks her into action. She moves to grab Slimmer's legs and drags her to a clearing in the mess of tables and chairs. Bodily, Mum flips her over and drops a trainered heel into the woman's solar plexus. Slimmer doubles up, wheezing on her in-breath, groaning on the out. It's an odd combo.

Mum then grabs Lanky Guy by the shoulders, yanks him over backwards and kneels beside him before sinking an elbow hard onto his chest. This causes him to jerk and jolt, legs moving in an awkward mechanical walking motion that makes him spin round on the floor in circles, like some kind of meaty Catherine Wheel, smearing oddly beautiful patterns in blood across the lino.

Even Hench pauses to watch the hypnotic motion. When she rudely continues her efforts to shake me off her back, my screaming arm muscles fail to hold and I'm thrown.

I hit the floor near Jayden, who's in a one-sided boxing match with someone that appears to have misplaced the skin from the lower half of their face – so, even as they receive several powerful fists to the nose, a gory grin remains. I can't help thinking of Skulduggery Pleasant. But more than that, I can't help noticing that Jayden's jabs don't have him yelling in pain and creasing to the floor.

'How do you punch without hurting yourself?' I call.

He stays focused on his bony punchbag as he answers. 'Hit with the knuckle.' I spot a small twist in his fist as he extends, making his knuckles the first point of contact. 'Align your fist, wrist and arm.' He sends out another jab, indicating the line from shoulder to fist with his free hand. 'And hit through your target.' The impact of each knock sends his opposition stumbling. Between strikes, he ducks and weaves around sweeping arms that lunge back at him.

When Hench comes at me again, I clamber to my feet and square up to her, determined to throw at least one half-decent punch and regain some shred of confidence in myself as a fighter.

I squeeze my hands into balls and hold them up to guard my face, just like Body Combat.

Everything Jayden told me plays through my mind as I throw out a jab. This time my shoulder absorbs the impact and any pain is mostly lingering from my first crappy attempt.

Joy overshadows any throbbing as my quarry is forced to take a step back.

I did that!

Empowered, I step forwards and shower my fists on her, but apart from making her stagger, they have little effect and she recovers quickly.

A hand lands on my arm. I shift to attack but recognise the pink sweatband just in time.

'We have to go,' Mum says, pulling me away from the fight I wasn't exactly winning.

We run to the Mini, scooping up our cricket bats en route.

Dad and Ruby arrive at the same time as us. Mum pushes Ruby in first, then stuffs me in after. Dad disappears for a few seconds before returning and tossing Jayden in.

Zombies move towards us.

Mum jumps in the front passenger side and scrambles over to the driver's seat, leaving a space where Dad squeezes in behind her.

The engine starts and Mum puts the car into reverse. We move about a foot, maybe more, before jolting to a stop.

She shifts gear. We move forwards about the same distance and stop abruptly again with a loud, unhappy clunking noise.

'Something's jammed.' Mum hits the steering wheel in frustration.

Hench and the man with the perpetual grin are at the windows, alternating between clawing at the glass and chewing on the wing mirrors. Slimmer's Society scrabbles at the handle, as though some part of her remembers that it opens the door.

'We have to draw them away and remove whatever's under the car,' Mum mumbles, picking at her pink sweatband.

The car's full of the sound of humans recovering from vigorous exercise and us three youths sweating up the backseat are giving off some serious muggy heat.

'Right,' Mum says. 'Right,' she says again, louder this time. She clutches her cricket bat. 'I'm going to get these people away. When they clear, haul out whatever's wedged under the car and get out of here. I'll meet you outside the entrance to the car park in five minutes.'

'Kimberl—' Dad starts to argue, but before he can even finish saying her name, she's pulled on the handle and slammed her foot against the door. She bursts out swinging her bat like a woman possessed, the door closing behind her, and in seconds, she's gone.

I turn to Dad; his eyeballs are bulging and his mouth's hanging open. Right now, I'm not sure which parent I should be more worried about.

Mum's name is caught in Dad's throat as his eyes flash back and forth between me and the now empty driver's seat.

He takes a deep breath before speaking.

'I'm going after her.' He grabs Mum's reliable old sat nav from the glove box and punches in an address. 'When these people move, clear out the underside of the car and get out of here. We'll find you at the entrance in five. I've put the postcode for the manor house in Acton Mortimer in here.' He's speaking fast, looking into my eyes, and I hope his words are sinking into some part of my brain that hasn't got the phrase "*Oh shit!*" stuck on a loop. 'If anything goes wrong, we'll meet you there. It's an hour and fifteen drive, so that's—' he mutters through some internal calculation, '—about twenty hours' walk in an emergency. We'll be back together in three days maximum. But if things are bad, Nor, take the helicopter and get to safety.'

He leans forwards and kisses me on the head.

I want to ask why he's telling me all this when we're going to see him in five minutes. And why he seems to think we'll be able to fly a helicopter.

'Helicopter?' Jayden asks, eyes sparking with interest.

Dad nods. 'With any luck, there'll be one at the manor house.' Eyeing the three of us, he says, 'Look after each other.' Then he's out the door and disappearing into the depths of the supermarket.

Soon after, a loud clanging starts up, like saucepans being hit together over and over and over. Soon the clatter grows, as though another set of pans has joined in.

I imagine Mum and Dad raiding Sainsbury's kitchenware and working as a team to create the distraction. My throat pinches at the thought of it.

Amazingly, the people in tattered, blood-smeared clothes lose interest in us and stumble after the noise.

The second it's clear, Jayden is out the door. A worrying metallic scraping vibrates through the vehicle. He flings a twisted and mangled chair away, then another, before climbing into the driver's seat, starting the engine and flicking the car into first gear. Soon we're out of the supermarket and into the car park.

That's when I rediscover how to use my limbs and lunge for the door handle as Jayden swings us towards the exit. I miss and reach again, fingernails scratching at the faux leather of the door's interior. If I get it open, I can be back across the car park and helping Mum and Dad in no time.

The quiet click of the lock sounds.

I twist around and launch myself at Jayden.

We swerve.

'What are you doing?!' he shouts, one hand on the wheel and the other pushing me away. 'I don't want to die in there, I have stuff to do first.'

Ruby joins in, holding me back too. 'They don't want you there. If you go back, what they're doing'll be for nothing.'

I redouble my efforts, staying focused on my goal of getting my finger to the small lock button on the driver's side door.

'Let me go,' I say, sticking out my tongue and trying to get my forefinger closer to the desired button, but Ruby's locked me in place and I'm going nowhere.

'All right!' I hold my hands up in submission. 'I'm stopping.'

As soon as her grip loosens, I make another dive but Ruby knows me too well – she wraps her arms around my waist and holds me in place.

Damn her strength.

She keeps a tight grip on me as we both wheeze from the scuffle.

'We can't just leave them,' I say.

'We're not, we're going to wait for them. Like they asked,' Ruby says.

Jayden drives smoothly out the exit and pulls up behind a tree. He turns off the engine, shifts in his seat to physically block the button that unlocks the doors ... and we wait.

The illuminated clock on the dashboard measures the longest five minutes of my life. After peeling off my metal gloves and stashing them carefully in the survival bag, I alternate between staring at the clock and staring out the window.

No sign of Mum or Dad.

Ruby is motionless, gazing at the sky while Jayden fidgets, checking his sports bag is still safely under the driver's seat at least three times.

Ten minutes.

'So, I'm guessing trains are probably cancelled.' Jayden's voice slices through the strained quiet.

In answer, Ruby and I glare at him.

'OK!' He holds his hands up. 'I get it. No trains.' He sighs.

Fifteen. At some point I remember the Spiderman bag, left

in the supermarket, but don't have the energy to voice more bad news.

'Where are they?' I moan at the window. No one answers and the silence hurts my heart.

Figures move into view, behind us at first, then in front, but none of them are my parents. By the way they drag their feet and knock into each other, it's obvious they're all sick. At first there's two or three, then more. And they're shambling towards us.

'We have to get away from here,' Jayden says and next thing I know, we're speeding away from Sainsbury's and away from my family.

Chapter 15

I LEAN OVER TO RUBY AND SNOTTILY CRY INTO HER shoulder. The car slams to a stop and we both fly forwards, hitting the seat in front.

'What the hell, man?!' Ruby turns on Jayden.

'Look,' he says, nodding at the rear-view mirror.

I push tears out of my eyes with the sleeve of my top and squint at the tiny mirror where something's flickering in the corner.

Once I realise I can turn around to get a better view, I do, and Ruby joins me.

'There,' she says, pointing at the supermarket behind us. 'Top right-hand corner.'

I follow her finger and see a white roller blind twitching up and down randomly. Something in my brain gives me an internal slap. No, not randomly.

I grab my sketchbook out and start making notes of the twitches.

Jolt jolt. Jolt twitch twitch. Jolt twitch twitch jolt. Twitch jolt.

I note it down, remembering learning morse code with dad from a book, *The Adventurer's Guide to Being Adventurous*, or something like that. We used to go out in the garden at night to have conversations by flashing torchlight.

I write the letters down, any hope I had disappearing as I see they make no sense at all.

MDXA

The want for it not to just be some zombie tangled in the blind's pull chord, keeps me copying out the letters.

MDXAMDXAMDXAMDXA

It's a message repeating.
I write out all variations of the four letters.

MDXA
DXAM
XAMD

'Aha, *Xamd*!' Jayden announces hopefully, pronouncing the X as a Z.

AMDX

I keep writing, hoping something will make sense soon.
'*Amdx*?' Jayden tries, and it sounds like *am dicks*?
This makes Ruby giggle. 'If you say so,' she mutters.
'Hey!' says Jayden, catching on.
And that's all it takes to make the "DX" stand out. My heart glows at the familiarity of it.
Dad always signed his morse code messages like he signs his texts: *Dx*.
'It's Dad!'
I write:

$$D = D\text{AD}.$$
$$X = K\text{ISS}.$$

'They're OK!' I wrap my arms around myself and squeeze.

'But what's the *AM* then?' Jayden asks, plunging the car into thoughtful silence.

'*Acton Mortimer*!' Ruby shouts. 'Where we're headed.'

I reach for the sat nav.

'So, you're meeting them there?' Jayden looks at the screen.

I look from the sat nav to the roller blind still flashing it's little message out.

Acton Mortimer. Dad x

I hesitate on the answer, knowing what we should do, but not wanting to actually do it.

'Your dad is like super survival obsessive and your mum's a badass bitch in pink Lycra. They'll probably get to the fancy house before we do,' Ruby says with a reassuring touch on my arm.

I nod. Take one last look at the message flickering away.

'Let's go,' I say, climbing into the front seat to act as navigator. I wind the window down to hold my hand out in the universal sign for "OK", hoping my parents can see. The blinds fall still and once again, we leave them behind.

We don't get far before Jayden's forced to pick the only routes available through abandoned cars and buses as I stare out the window, numb.

With each turn, the sat nav lady recalculates and tells us, in annoyingly patronising tones, different directions to take. All are impossible to follow.

Where is everyone?

How has everything gone so wrong so fast? My eyes prickle.

The car goes quiet before rolling to a stop.

'Looks like we're out of petrol,' Jayden says with an apologetic smile. 'We might be walking from here.'

I respond with the appropriate look of disbelief for the situation. Mum always has petrol in the car.

'You're joking, right? We can't walk out in the open. There's zombies out there!'

'What can I say? It's dead.' He twists the key and the engine does absolutely nothing.

'Those people out there are probably dead too,' I parry. 'And I don't plan to join them.'

Jayden holds up a finger. 'Well, like your dad said, technically, it might be a rage virus, making them sick rather than zombified.'

'Oh, excellent, we picked up a zombie expert in a stupid hat,' I snap.

'Harsh.' He takes off his fluorescent yellow cap with reflective trim and curls the peak. 'I'm not saying I'm an expert, but I've played enough computer games to appreciate the fact zombies don't breathe,' he answers with a gentle shrug. 'And some of them were breathing.'

Who is this guy? Honestly, I am so not having *his* baby strapped to me in the dystopian future. I—

'So, what does that even mean?' Ruby interrupts my inner ranting.

'I'm not sure. I'm just stating facts here,' he says. 'Zombies, by definition, are dead. The dead don't breathe. Therefore, some of them must still be alive.'

'OK, we get it.' I sigh. 'As we don't really know what's going on, to make life easier, can we just call them *zombies*?' My voice almost breaks on the word.

Jayden chews at his thumbnail. 'Or,' he says, 'we could call them *zoms*? It's quicker and halfway towards being a zombie. Which is what those people seem to be.'

I can't answer, I'm too busy fighting back tears.

Ruby leans over and touches my arm. 'You OK?'

'We left Mum and Dad behind, fighting for us to get away from the zom-whatever-the-hell-they-are!'

'They're OK,' Ruby reassures me. 'We saw the message. Let's focus on getting to the meeting place. And, like Jayden said, with the car out, I think that means walking.'

'You're right,' I agree.

'You sticking with us, Lollipop Kid?' Ruby puts heavy emphasis on the last two words.

'Crossing Guard,' he corrects. 'And, if you're going somewhere with a helicopter, I'm in.'

'OK, then,' Ruby says, glowering at him.

'OK.' Jayden sets his jaw.

'OK?' I say, looking between them. 'Well I guess that's decided, then.'

The sat nav gives another patronising direction we can't follow.

'I just need to do one thing before we go.' The others look on as I rummage in Dad's survival bag and find the paper maps I knew would be there. It takes no time to mark up where we are, our desired destination, and fold it to a size that slides into the waterproof holder with a small compass attached.

I hang it round my neck and feel much better. Paper maps are great. Tried and tested for hundreds of years. You can see where you're going, where you've been, and most importantly, it won't run out of batteries.

Outside, I haul the survival pack onto my back. Rubes grabs the Star Wars food stash and hands me my cricket bat before pulling her hockey stick from the car. Jayden eases his sports bag from under the chair and peers inside before breathing an obvious sigh of relief and zipping it back up. Instead of throwing it over his shoulder, he hugs it to himself.

'What?' he asks when he notices us watching, gently hooking the bag-strap across his body.

'What's in there?' Ruby demands.

'None of your business,' Jayden snaps.

'It is if it's a human head, or anything weird like that,' she snaps back.

He throws up his hands. 'I promise it isn't a human head.'

Ruby raises an eyebrow. 'Or anything weird like that?'

Jayden nods once.

'OK,' Ruby says, apparently satisfied. 'Let's go.'

Ignoring a squirming suspicion that Jayden purposefully avoided actually answering Ruby's question, I turn my attention to the map. It takes a couple of turns to get my bearings.

'Right, so it seems we have two choices,' I say, running my finger up the map. 'We can walk off-road, using footpaths. It's the most direct route, but there might be a few hills, fences to climb, and . . . well, it would be shorter but more unpredictable.'

'What's the other choice?' Ruby sounds doubtful.

'On-road? Might find more people, which could be a good thing or a bad thing, depending on their zom-status.'

'To road or not to road.' Ruby taps her lips and makes a "hmmm" noise.

'Or there's the canal,' Jayden says.

I know he's trying to be helpful and I wonder how to gently let him know it isn't the best plan.

'That's a stupid idea,' Ruby bursts out. 'Towpaths are tiny. If we run into any danger, we'd be completely stuffed. Unless we want to jump into minging canal water, but then we would probably die of rat-wee disease. Or get tangled up and dragged into the murky depths of centuries-old duck crap by an abandoned shopping trolley. Not to mention canals are the longest way to get anywhere ever. We'd have to walk an extra million miles to get where we want to go.'

'Right, thanks, Ruby,' I say, trying to ignore the hurt look on Jayden's face. 'So, that still leaves on-road or off-road?' I say.

Ruby taps her lips again. 'Zoms or ambitious hill walking . . . ?'

'And still the possibility of zoms,' I add.

It's amazing how quickly we've picked up calling them "zoms". The distance it puts between what we're experiencing and what I've seen in horror movies is actually quite comforting.

'Off the roads sounds safer,' Ruby says.

A murmur of agreement through the group sets us on our way.

We're all looking more than a little mussed. Or . . . stylishly apocalypse ruffled.

We walk away from the car and into the unknown. I'm gripping my cricket bat, Ruby has her hockey stick over her shoulder and Jayden has one hand hooked over his bag, the other gripping the strap at his chest.

My inner movie-lover appreciates that if the moment ran in slow-mo, with some Tarantino-esque music playing over the top, they would look mega badass and I would look badass-by-association.

♡ Ruby, Ruby, Ruby

Chapter 16

WE KEEP UP A GOOD PACE UNTIL WE MOVE PAST the last shops on the very outskirts of the town I've called home for my entire life.

The newsagents has been raided and the homes nearby are left wide open. Cars are crashed or abandoned everywhere.

A lorry is jack-knifed across a path and there's another behind it.

'We're supposed to be going up there.' I look at the map. 'Or we can take the next turning and double back.'

After a while my top is sticking to me, my legs are going numb and my mouth is so dry my spit's congealing.

Jayden falls in beside me and asks, 'Why does Ruby keep staring at the sky?'

'Her family were flying to India this morning, but we didn't find out whether they landed.'

'Shiiiiit.'

'Yeah. Where are your parents?'

'Mine?' Jayden says. 'Dead.'

'Oh.' His bluntness leaves me floundering. 'Um. Sorry.'

'It's OK, it happened when I was a kid. My Gram and Gramps raised me. It's just been Gram and me for a few years, but she . . .' His voice dries up and he swipes at his face. Our pace slows even more. When he continues, I see tears build up and catch in his lashes. 'A few weeks ago, she . . .' He runs out of words and shakes his head slowly.

'I'm so sorry.'

'I've not left the house since it happened. Some boss-guy from the council called yesterday, said they can't find a replacement for her crossing duty. She'd done it for nearly twenty years. I figured I could try and do it. I was having a practise this morning, before starting on Monday.'

'Oh . . . I think your gram was my lollipop lady when I was in primary school. On the crossing we found you at this morning?'

'Yeah.'

'Yeah, all the kids at school loved her.'

He smiles and wipes his eyes with the back of his hand.

'Less gossip, more walking, people,' calls Ruby.

'Come on, Nora!'

Now Ruby and Jayden are in the lead as we head towards a bridge over the canal.

They're too far away. If something grabs me, where would I be? Or if something grabs Ruby . . .

That's the thought that has me hitting a sprint. Even with the extra weight of the rucksack dragging on my shoulders, I close the gap between us.

They're over the bridge and striding onwards, both looking fit. I peer at my red splotchy arms. They always go like this when I work out, and so does my face. Urgh!

When I glance down to assess my splotchiness levels, I trip and the ground rushes to greet me. Fortunately, I bump and roll into a bush instead of tumbling all the way into the canal.

While disentangling myself from the twigs, I hear Ruby calling.

'Nor!' There's an edge to her voice I've never heard before. Ruby's possessed of unending levels of cool, calm collectedness, but right now all of that has gone.

The word breaks when she shouts again.

'NOR!'

Her face peers over the wall of the bridge and sees me.

'You absolute cow bag! You nearly gave me a fucking heart attack.' She picks her footing down the hill towards me, swearing, like, really swearing, with each step.

'I'm all right, I just fell.'

She pulls me out of the bush and close up I see her eyes are red-rimmed and glossy.

'Don't do that to me!' she yells. 'I thought something'd dragged you away.'

'Didn't you say you wouldn't go back for anyone?' I say, completely honoured that she cares enough to get this mad.

'Did I say that?'

'Yeah, when we watched *Dracula*.'

She bends her leg around mine and trips me over.

'Fine, I'll leave you here.' She wrinkles her nose, an impish grin showing through. 'Don't want to be carrying any excess baggage.'

She turns to walk off, but I grab her foot and pull. She falls. There's a mad scrabble as we each battle to be the first up.

'No way, I'm leaving you in my tracks.'

'Not if I leave you in *my* tracks first.'

Ruby's hand is pushing down on my face as I'm jabbing my

elbow into her ribs, both of us giggling, when a small cough makes us stop.

We look up to find Jayden standing on the path above.

'Not to interrupt, but you might want to know...' He's speaking to us but looking at the other side of the bridge. 'They're coming.'

'My parents?' My heart jumps.

'Really not.'

My heart falls.

'People?' I ask with little hope.

He shakes his head.

'Zoms?'

He nods.

'How many?'

'Lots.'

'Lots and lots?'

He nods again. 'And lots.'

'Oh.'

'Yep. It's like a swarm of bees.'

'Zom-bees!' jokes Ruby. 'It would be cute for them all to wear black and yellow fuzzy onesies and do a little dance every time they find a pretty flower.'

I love Ruby's brain.

Jayden looks at us like we've lost the plot.

'We have to head to the canal. Now!' he says, moving down the grassy slope towards us.

'I thought we agreed the canal's a death trap?' I call.

He points at the large number of zoms now moving into sight from both sides of the bridge.

'THAT is a death trap.'

'Good point.'

Ruby takes my hand and we run down the hill together. The stability constantly shifts between us, neither knowing who is keeping who up at what point. When we pass through an open gate, we pause to slam it shut behind us.

Despite the obstacle now between us and the zoms, none of us slow our pace.

We side-step onto a path that takes us through inappropriately cheerful dappled sunlight shining between mockingly beautiful plants with their fronds unfurled.

I'm first onto the canal side.

I glance left. Clear.

I glance right. Not clear.

Teeth first, it lunges at me.

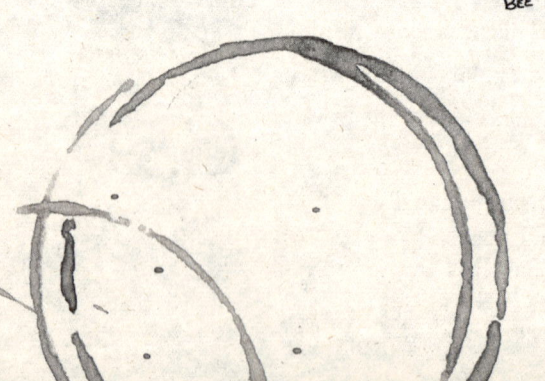

Chapter 17

MY FEET WORK FASTER THAN MY BRAIN AND I weave out of the way of the lunging zom. She fails to stop at the edge of the canal and . . .

Splash!

In the murky waterway, her flailing scares away a pair of mallards.

The waterlogged zom rises with brown sludge streaming down her face and there's even a bit of duck poo stuck in her hair. Nice.

I can't help searching for any sign of cold or disgust registering on her features, but none show. She makes her way to the edge, but it's obvious she lacks the basic motor functions to lift herself back onto the path.

'We need to move before more come,' Ruby says, hockey stick gripped for action. I turn and stare back the way we came.

A hand takes mine. I look round, expecting to see Ruby, and a shock shoots through me when I find that it's Jayden.

'Come on!' he says, gripping tightly and pulling me away.

We bolt down the towpath, following Rubes.

Already exhausted, we soon slow from full pelt to a light jog. Jayden has a small dance in his step, it's there when he walks and disappears when he runs. As we lose speed it returns, making me smile.

The path is clear as far as we can see. For now.

'Man. This. Pack. Is. Heavy.' I pant out each word.

'Yours isn't full of tins,' calls Ruby from the front. 'I feel like I've been beaten across the back with a sack of bricks.' She stops, puts her hands on her knees and sucks in air.

This part of the canal has boats moored along the side. They're each long and low, some with round windows, others square. My favourite are the rustic-looking ones with handpainted names and flowers.

Ruby looks at me with a twinkle in her eye. 'We should hijack a canal boat!' Her eyes snag on Jayden's hand holding mine and her twinkle blinks out.

I drop Jayden's hand. Then the survival pack.

'You seriously want to hijack a canal boat? Possibly the slowest mode of transport in the universe? And don't you have to get off canal boats to open and close locks and stuff?' I ask. 'That would be a prime opportunity to be nibbled on.'

'Well, yeah. But there aren't many locks between here and . . . Where are we getting off?' Ruby tries to grab the map hanging round my neck.

'Exactly.' I pull it out of her reach. 'You don't even know where we're going.'

'To the countryside, right? There's always less locks out that way and I bet there would be less zoms too,' Jayden chips in again.

'How do you know so much about canals?'

'I used to fish down here with my gramps.' An air of wistfulness plays across his face. 'He had mates with canal boats, they used to let me drive them.'

Growling sounds travel up the path behind us.

'Whatever we're doing, we need to do it now,' I say, heaving the pack back up and settling it into the painful grooves forming on each shoulder.

Jayden's checking on his bag contents again and Ruby's already way ahead. She's hopping on and off every canal boat she passes, tugging on the door of each before moving onto the next.

Finally, one swings open.

Her victory is short-lived as the occupier, a broad and beardy man in a black T-shirt with an airbrushed dragon on, stumbles from the body of the boat. His clouded eyes sweep the area and land on Ruby.

I push my feet to carry me forwards faster, to catch up and save her. Jayden moves alongside me until I stop by Ruby and he keeps running. I smack at Beardy Zom's grabbing left hand with my bat and Ruby does the same with her hockey stick to his right.

Jayden appears with a long pole that ends in a vicious-looking hook.

'Move!' he shouts, ducking low to jam the pole between the zom's legs. He jerks the end and the sharp movement knocks the zombified boat owner's feet in two directions at once. He falls and plunges, bloodstained beard and all, into the water.

'And it's a knockout,' Jayden says in a mock sports commentator voice, before dropping the pole and raising his fists above his head in triumph, even adding his own impression of a crowd cheering his name. 'Jay-den, Jay-den, Jay-den. We love yooooou!'

Ruby ignores his one-man celebration and heads into the boat's cabin.

She peers inside and turns back with a smile.

'Looks free now.'

I bend to pick up the weird hook-pole thingy and hand it to Jayden.

'Nicely done,' I say. 'What is this exactly?'

'A boat hook, all canal boats have them.' He puts it back while I examine the beautiful gold and black detail hand-painted on the rich green canal boat. 'It'd be rude not to stop for a brew,' Jayden says, untying the rope that holds the boat to land and pushing it away with his foot.

He jumps and I follow.

'I'll get this thing moving.'

'I'll find the kettle,' I say, and follow Ruby into the belly of the boat.

It is the perfect picture of all that is twee. Everything is miniature and covered in crochet blankets, hand-painted enamel wear, and every inch of wood has been carved into patterns made of dragons and flames.

Ruby is already on a tiny sofa slotted down the side of a mini kitchen area, with the minutest sink I've ever seen. A modest collection of crochet rag dollies sit next to her, a little woolly Daenerys Targaryen, Khal Drogo and three dragons. 'These are cute.' She puts her arm around them. 'The fella keeps the place nice.'

'This feels so wrong,' I say.

'Nora, we can't help those people. They would literally eat us alive.' Her words remind me of a conversation we had months ago, about losing our virginities before going to university. We'd be lucky to get to university now. Our dreams for the future have gone in a puff of zom-infested smoke.

'We need to find safety first.' Ruby's still talking. 'And maybe some other non-zombified humans, like your dad. He's a pharmacist, right?'

'Biochemist,' I correct.

'Right. And together we can generate a cure. So, in a way, we are helping that gentleman by helping ourselves to his tea.' She points to where the man's gnawing on the edge of his own boat.

I fill the kettle and set it onto a single-ringed hob. The floor under our feet shudders, ripples glide across the water's surface as we start moving, and I breathe a sigh of relief.

Once the tea's brewed, we take a cup out for Jayden and find him gazing at something in the distance. I don't like the expression on his face.

'What are you looking at?' I grit my teeth and prepare for the worst.

'There's a camera.' He points up to a black box with a lens mounted on the corner of the bridge. 'It's way too high-tech to be used for surveillance.' He runs his hand across the back of his neck. 'Before I spotted it, I had a creeping feeling, like someone was watching me.'

'That could be there for anything,' Ruby says. 'Like people filming themselves fishing? Or making canal porn? The zom thing happened so quickly it's easy to imagine someone leaving their camera hooked up.'

Ruby ruffles her hair before energetically leaping onto the roof of the canal boat. In landing she pulls a heroic pose, tilting her chin up and pouting at the camera.

'What are you doing?' I ask.

'Well, if we're being filmed, I want them to get my good side.'

'You're right,' I climb up beside her, hook my arm over her shoulder and raise my chin to the camera. We hold the pose for as long as we can before we both burst into laughter tinged with just a hint of hysteria.

Chapter 18

WE COLLAPSE BY THE STEERY STICK AT THE back of the boat, and dappled sun falls through the sweeping trees overhead as we drift along, all of us taking time to recover from the day's events.

'Everything about today's been more like a movie than real life,' I say, watching the water move past the boat.

'At least it's our sort of cheesy horror,' Ruby says, tapping my leg. 'We could be stuck in some smooshy romance.'

Oh to be stuck in a smooshy romance with Ruby Rutherford.

'Yeah,' I say, my palms turning clammy. 'That would be terrible.'

'Well, if I'm the first to die, we'll know this is a movie,' Jayden says, bitterness tugging at his voice.

An awkward silence settles over us as I think on everything I've read about the *Black guy dies first* trope in horror. I want to say something, but everything I think of feels stupid.

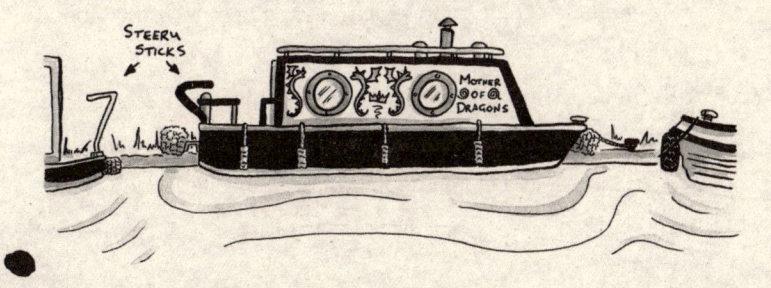

'An old white guy was eaten outside Nora's house,' Ruby says. 'I think, technically, he was the first to die.' I know she's trying to be helpful but it doesn't stop bile rising at the back of my throat at the memory of our greengrocer's demise.

Jayden lets out a humourless laugh. 'Shit, then I guess this must be real.'

There isn't much talking after that.

I get my sketchbook out and draw up some pages, emptying part of my brain onto the paper.

It would have been a beautiful boat trip, if the world wasn't overrun with flesh-eating monsters and I wasn't in a constant state of fretting that Mum and Dad have become zom-munchables.

After some time, Ruby's the first to speak.

'I'm going inside to see if there's any fresh food we can eat. Save our tins for when times get desperate.' She moves towards the cabin.

'Get you,' I say.

'I know.' She points at herself. 'Survival genius!'

Jayden shakes his head. 'How can she think about food?'

'I don't know,' I say. 'Fighting off people with manky faces and parts hanging off has really ruined my appetite. Who knows, perhaps a zombie apocalypse will turn out to be the perfect weight-loss plan.' I pat my stomach jokingly, before immediately regretting drawing attention to it.

'You don't need to lose weight. Why are girls obsessed with losing weight?'

'Wow, gender-stereotyping much? Other people worry about their weight too.'

'Yeah, I guess. Sorry. But you don't look like you need to lose weight.' He doesn't say it like he's trying to compliment me or hit on me. He states it as a fact and I get the feeling that Jayden is one of the good guys.

'I know that, it's everyone else you need to tell.' Or maybe just my mum.

'The dragon-fancier has peanut butter and jam, people!' Ruby shouts. 'And a toaster! Come and give me a hand, Nor.'

'Amazing!' I jump up and all but sprint away from Jayden.

I'm hardly inside the cabin when Ruby speaks.

'I think we need to find more people, like a commune or something.' I move beside her and help prep the food on the cramped work surface.

'That never ends well in the movies. We're best off just the three of us, keeping to the plan.'

'How am I going to get to be with another girl if we don't find more people?'

'What are you talking about?'

'Sex, Nor! I don't want to die without being a proper lesbian.' And I realise she's carrying on the conversation started in Sainsbury's.

'How can your mind be in your pants at a time like this? It doesn't matter any more, does it? Survival matters.' I sound depressingly like my dad.

The smell of toast fills the cabin and despite what I thought minutes ago, I could definitely eat.

Ruby stares at me like I've grown an extra head.

'What?'

'What do you mean, "what"? Nora Inkwell, of course my mind's in my pants! I'm a teenage girl with *all* the hormones flying around inside me. I want to be an official lesbian and it's something I really, REALLY want to do.' Her voice cuts down to a mumble. 'I've kind of thought about it a lot.'

'How do you know, when you achieve your goal, you're not going to be halfway into things when a zom jumps out and shouts, "Gotcha!"'

The toaster pops and we both jump.

'We have to have sex before a zom smears our brains on toast for breakfast,' she says, spreading peanut butter.

Her words set my cheeks burning.

'That might not happen,' I say.

Ruby stuffs a slice of toast into her mouth. 'But it might.'

My insides prickle and the urge to talk to her about us as a potential thing has got me peanut-buttering the toast over-vigorously.

'It's not fair, you have Jayden.'

The knife goes straight through the toast.

'What?!'

Ruby's not looking at me.

'You've got your guy, you're all set. Where does that leave me?'

She's speaking to me like I've done something wrong.

'Do you ever think that maybe I don't want to throw myself at the first person who comes along? Do you never think that I—'

Just tell her.

I like you.

Three words.

That's all.

Unless they go horribly wrong and those three words force Ruby to go off on her own because surviving zoms alone is preferable to the awkwardness of surviving them with someone who has an unrequited crush on her.

Then she would be bitten. And I, of course, would be bitten, if not completely eaten. Companionless, Jayden might become zom meat too. None of us can do this alone. We'd all turn into zoms and it would be all my stupid fault for unleashing those three words.

I look to where Jayden's crotch is perfectly framed in a small round window set into the door. One of his hands reaches down for a good old rummage or a scratch, I can't quite tell which. My head snaps away from the view and Ruby laughs.

I scrunch my face.

'It's not the time to get choosy,' says Ruby.

He's a nice guy, good-looking, with great knees too. I already consider him a friend. How could he not be, after everything we've been through today? But he's just not Ruby.

And to be honest, since the night at the gig with Baxter, the idea of attempting anything that involves anyone else's trouser contents scares me more than a canal path full of zoms.

I'd tried ripping off my virginity like a plaster and look how that ended.

And now Ruby's assumption that I'm just going to throw myself at Jayden pisses me right off.

'He gets a say in it too.' My voice sharpens. 'I can't walk up to the guy and say, "Hey, Jayden, so how about this zombie apocalypse thing? See, I don't want to die with my V plates hanging round my neck and you're the only guy here. Ruby's well gay, so I'm afraid it's not going to work out for you there. I'm your only shot. Let's go somewhere and do it."'

Ruby's face is doing something weird and her eyes are growing wide.

'What?'

I hear a shuffle behind me, followed by Jayden's voice.

'That's very forward of you, but I'm game.'

Shit.

I whip round and see Jayden behind me.

Warmth spreads across my cheeks and my feet go wibbly.

'Easy!' Jayden laughs. 'I was only joking. You should see your faces, it's too funny.'

'Oh god, I'm so sorry, I didn't know you were listening.'

'That's OK,' he says. 'I suppose that answers the question of whether these belong to either of you?'

He holds a small shiny box out to me, sending my hand flying to my back pocket. The condoms are gone, I knew that before I even patted the bum of my jeans, because they're in his hand.

I snatch them back.

'Thanks,' I mumble.

'Anyway,' Jayden carries on, seemingly oblivious to my complete mortification. 'I gotta pee, can one of you take the rudder?'

'The what?' Ruby asks, as I appear to have lost the power of speech.

'The rudder? At the rear? For steering?' Jayden says, waiting for a moment of realisation to land.

'Right,' Ruby says. 'Got it.'

With his sports bag slung over him, Jayden struggles to fit into the tiny bathroom at the front of the boat. What has he got in that bag?

Ruby pulls me to the wooden bench outside, next to the steery stick.

She grabs my hand and looks fiercely into my eyes. I get the impression her brain is screaming at me, willing me to develop some psychic ability so I can know what she's trying to tell me without words.

I'm getting nothing, but the intensity of her dark eyes sets my heart hammering.

It's times like these that I can't help but think about kissing Ruby. Not talking to her about sexuality or labels, just leaning in halfway, her closing the gap and our lips meeting.

My heart batters the inside of my rib cage like it wants to break free and jump into Ruby's arms all on its own, sick of me not acting on its insistence it belongs to her anyway.

I break eye contact to see Jayden stepping out of the boat's cabin.

'It's not long until we should probably find somewhere to stop for the night,' he says.

Ruby raises an unimpressed eyebrow. 'Smooth.'

'What?' Jayden asks with a nervous laugh. 'Oh! I didn't mean like that. I was joking earlier, I'm not trying it on. I'm just saying it's getting late and we'll lose the light soon.'

Ruby and I don't move, but our eyebrows are heading skywards.

Jayden keeps talking. 'There's another lock coming up, so I figured we could park up after that, then we'll have a straight run in the morning.' Jayden shifts awkwardly from foot to foot.

Ruby glares at him. 'OK, sly guy. I guess you're right.'

'I'll get us somewhere safe and tie off,' he says as we swap places with him.

Ruby drags me into the cabin. 'I don't trust him,' she whispers. 'He's trying to get into your pants.'

'You were trying to get *me* into *his* pants earlier,' I hiss.

'I was not! I was only stating your obvious intention to get in there yourself.' She grabs my hand, still gripping the condoms and holds it up.

'I have no such intention!' She's got me so riled she has me talking like someone from a Jane Austen novel. I slam them down on the counter. 'And the poor guy's told you he was joking.'

'He's too much of an eager beaver,' she actually shouts.

'I don't get why you're so upset, you started all of this with your obsession with sex. I just want to live!'

The cheesiness of that last sentence breaks through the tension and sets us both giggling.

Ruby puts an arm around me. 'You're right, I'm being a dope. Though I am starting to wonder whether he really does have a human head in his bag.'

'Yeah, I've been wondering about that too. He's right though, we do need to stop for the night.'

'I know. I'll go help with the lock, then we'll find out what he's hiding in his bag.' Ruby walks out with another piece of peanut-buttered toast in her teeth.

Left on my own, I ignore the food and start wrestling with the sofa, hoping it might be a bed in disguise. Springs squeak in protest until I finally work out which bit I'm supposed to pull on and fly backwards as the cushions *boing* open into a bed. Though it takes up most of the cabin, there isn't nearly enough room for all three of us on this one-and-a-half-person bed.

I upend the contents of the Star Wars bag on the thin mattress and dig out three toothbrushes and a tube of toothpaste.

'Any floss?' Jayden asks with a big toothy grin. He and Ruby stand in the doorway, Ruby looking determined to be grumpy.

'Afraid not. Are we tied up?'

'Yeah, we're next to a thick patch of trees,' Ruby answers, kicking off her shoes and clambering across the bed to settle next to me. 'We don't think a human – or zom – can get through it, it's too dense.'

'Like you?' I ask.

'Oh. Ha ha,' she says, unamused.

The sun vanishes from the sky and it suddenly seems a lot later. Jayden locks the door behind him, carefully places his bag under the bed and climbs up to sit next to us.

'Can I use one of those?' He points to the toothbrushes.

'Yep.' I hold them up for him to choose.

Ruby snatches them out of my hand. 'Only if you tell us what's in the bag,' she says.

In that second, Jayden suddenly looks completely exhausted. He pushes his hands over his face before answering.

'My gram.'

'What?!' Ruby's face shows that she's imagining something truly gruesome as he reaches into the bag. When his hand begins to re-emerge, Ruby leans forwards and I look away.

'She's in there?' Ruby asks, and curiosity turns my head. Jayden's holding a large cardboard tube with an ocean sunset scene on it.

'Well, her ashes are,' he says.

Oh!

'Why didn't you just tell us? We thought there was something weird going on,' I say.

'A guy who carries his gran's ashes about with him *is* pretty weird,' Ruby says to me out the side of her mouth.

Jayden points. 'There! That's why I didn't tell you. Anyway, I don't just carry them around, I took her with me to her crossing point today, to say goodbye.' He runs his thumb over the surface of the tube. 'She loved working there, seeing the kids every day. She said it helped keep her young.' He huffs out a small laugh. 'I had a train ticket to Scarborough to scatter her in the sea.'

'Scarborough's nice,' I say.

'Yeah, apparently my parents treated my gram and gramps to a holiday there for their 50th wedding anniversary. They loved it so much, they decided it was where they wanted to . . .' Jayden sniffs, '. . . you know. When they die.' He pushes at his eyes.

I rub Jayden's arm, while Ruby pats his knee.

'Thanks,' he says with a snuffle. 'We took Gramps' ashes there a few years ago. I just wanted to make sure Gram can join him, but then all this happened, and now I'm scared the tube'll get crushed and she'll end up spilling into my sweaty gym bag.' He finishes with a sad shrug. 'So, now you know.'

He looks so heartbroken as he tucks the tube away.

'We'll help you get her there,' I say, thinking about the helicopter we're hopefully going to find, along with my parents, at the manor house. 'Won't we, Rubes?'

'Yeah! There's not a lot else to do in a world that's gone zom. Why not take a trip to the seaside?'

'Thanks, that would be amazing.' Jayden smiles. 'Can I get a toothbrush now?'

He picks the Spiderman one, Rubes picks Batman and I try not to pout when I'm left with My Little Pony.

We all sit cross-legged on the bed, brushing our teeth and spitting into a pot. Yeah, it's gross, but there's an unspoken agreement to stick together. The full effect of the day can be seen in the sagging of our shoulders and drooping eyelids as we brush.

Once we're finished, I lean over until my body flumps onto the bed and curl up small to make room for the others. Ruby wraps herself defensively around me as I fall into a restless sleep.

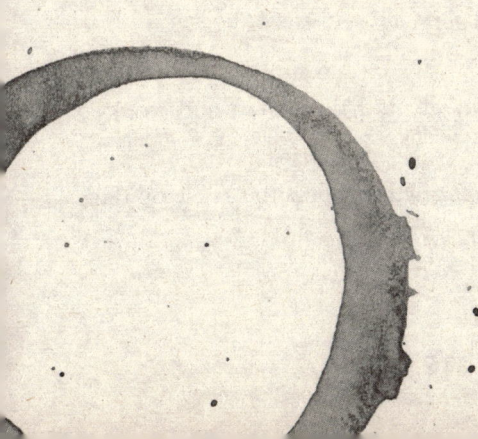

Chapter 19

SOMETHING THAT SOUNDS A LOT LIKE A SNEEZE outside the canal boat breaks my fragile sleep.

My head snaps up. What in the name of Bruce Campbell's chin?

Ruby and Jayden are both still asleep. I hold my breath as the silence that follows pulls tight like a drum.

After a minute, my heart begins the long climb down from the top of my throat. That's when a sharp bang on the roof makes Ruby and Jayden's eyes fly open.

'What the hell?' A disorientated Ruby looks to me for answers I don't have.

I pull back the green flannel curtains to reveal two gurning faces pressed against the glass. The first rays of morning sun illuminate the zoms' grey faces and glint off the puss on their nasty acne clusters.

'Ugh, it's too early to deal with this.' Ruby stretches.

She pulls her hands through her hair, runs a thumb under each eye and then looks her normal gorgeous self.

How does she do that?

'Um,' I say, patting stupidly at my halo of fluff and wonky ponytail.

Ruby leans over and, calm as anything, puts the kettle on the hob and spoons coffee into mugs.

'Jayden, milk, sugar?'

'Um. Yeah, both,' he says, frowning between Ruby and the window to zom-topia. The kettle whistles and Ruby pours out the water.

'I guess there's no way a zom could put a fist through the window, is there? It's double glazed.' Jayden sounds more like he's trying to convince himself than us. 'In theory, we could stay in here all day.'

'That's what I was thinking. That, and there's no way I am taking on zoms without at least one brew. Nora?'

'Yeah, I'll have tea,' I say, standing and stretching. I can at least pretend to be as calm as Ruby. My act is ruined by a hand holding a brick smashing through the window beside me, causing me to stumble backwards and trip over the survival bag.

The sensation of falling is cut short by a thump, accompanied by a sharp pain at the base of my skull and the world switching off.

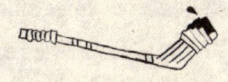

There's a throbbing in my head and a scorching on my arm.

'Get a towel. Soak it in cold water and hold it on her arm. I'll move her into the recovery position.' Is that Jayden's voice?

'Don't tell me what to do!' That's definitely Ruby.

'She's burned and possibly concussed.' Is he speaking really fast or is my brain moving really slow? 'Then we need another to keep rotating them, to cool the burn.'

The tap turns on and I could swear I hear Ruby sniffling. I want to open my eyes and tell her I'm OK, but it's all a bit too much effort right now.

Something cool is placed on my arm. Then one eyelid is yanked open, followed by the other.

'Nora?' Jayden says, his words close to my ear. 'Can you hear me?'

I roll open my eyes.

'Yergh,' I say through thick throat bubbles. It's a horrible noise, but it's enough to get Jayden smiling.

Ruby runs over. 'Oh my god, Nor!' She flaps her hands over the top of me. 'Can I touch her?' she asks Jayden.

'Be gentle,' he says.

Ruby dives on top of me.

'Oof!'

'You dope. I thought you'd brained yourself.' She's actually crying, like not suppressed tears, but full-on wet cheeks and everything. My clumsy fall must have been spectacular.

The sting in my arm gets worse as the wet towel warms and Jayden replaces it with another cold one.

'Where are the zoms?' I ask, my voice slow and eyelids sagging.

'They're still there. Though, for some reason, no longer being so proactive about getting in,' Ruby says, moving away to pull back the curtain.

Yep. They're still there.

'Why does my arm hurt?'

'You fell on the ring of the hob. Burned yourself pretty bad.'

'Oh shit.'

'Yeah. Can you move to the sink? We could do with getting it under the tap for a while,' Jayden says. 'Ruby, is there a freezer or anything cold for Nora's head?'

The move is ungainly, but I get my arm under the trickling tap. The cold water burns and soothes at the same time. Something hard, frosty and damp is pressed against the back of my head and I am thoroughly uncomfortable.

There's another smashing, and another window breaks.

'And now they're being proactive again.' Ruby sighs. 'We need to get the boat moving.'

'Let's do it,' Jayden says. 'You stay here, Nora. Don't fall asleep.'

Leaning over the sink, still quite confused about what happened and holding something to my throbbing head, I listen to the sounds of zoms being splooshed into the canal and the engine starting up.

I think over the last thing Jayden said, something about sleeping. Sleep is such a good idea, I lean my head on the side of the sink and close my eyes.

'No, no, no. Nora!'

And I'm awake again.

'Shit, Nora!' Jayden sounds panicked. 'You shouldn't fall asleep.'

'But I'm so tired.' My voice stretches to illustrate the point. 'Where's Ruby? We can't be in here alone. She'll think we're canoodling.'

'Canoodling?' he laughs. 'She's steering. I'll swap with her soon, she's a bit too bold taking the corners.'

He helps me away from the sink and a defrosting lasagne-for-one that had been my cold compress.

A chill rolls over me, and then again, and Jayden throws the duvet around my shoulders.

'First, I'll take a quick look at that burn.'

No sooner is my arm wrapped in cling film than Jayden is

checking my pulse, feeling my forehead, looking in my eyes again, and questioning me on medical allergies.

'I'm allergic to codeine,' I say.

'OK,' he passes me paracetamol and a glass of water. 'You lie there and rest a bit. Ruby and I can take it in turns steering, while the other makes sure you don't fall asleep.'

'You're like a real doctor,' I say, my words slurring with my seriously woozy vibes.

'Nurse,' he says.

'What?'

'I did one year of nurse training before I had to take a year out to care for my gram.'

Of course he did. 'You'd be the best nurse,' I say, resting my head on his shoulder.

'That's what my gram said.' He looks off into the distance, seeing something I can't. 'But I've decided not to go back.'

'What? Why?' I twist towards him with a squeak of pain.

'I wasn't good enough,' he says, his face a picture of sadness.

'You're helping me,' I tell him and give his arm a hug.

'Well, I guess we're even now – you helped me at the crossing. Thanks for picking me up, by the way. I get that I'm in the way of something between you and Ruby, but I appreciate being here.'

'No! No. You're not in the way of anything. And we like having you here.'

He raises an eyebrow at me, and I amend my previous statement to clear the look of pure disbelief on his face.

'OK. *I* like having you with us. And there's nothing between Ruby and me.' The disbelief doesn't completely leave his features.

Silence.

'I've had two boyfriends,' I blurt, with no idea why I felt the need to share that. When I had boyfriends, it quietened my fears about *the B word* Pixie used. If I was with a boy, then I couldn't be accused of being greedy. Right?

'OK,' Jayden says with a sigh. 'Anyway, your head looks OK. Bit of a bump.'

'Hmm,' I say, wondering if Ruby would think I was a wannabe lesbian.

A sharp judder runs through everything around us and the edge of the canal swings into view through the window with a THUMP!

Ruby runs in.

'Sorry to interrupt your cosy moment, but I've crashed the boat.'

Chapter 20

I CAN SEE BY RUBY'S EXPRESSION THAT SHE'S NOT sorry.

'How the hell did you crash the boat?'

'I ran it into the side of the canal,' she says, like this is obvious. 'These fearless ducks were playing chicken with the boat, I swerved to dodge them and BAM!'

Jayden's on his feet, looking out the window.

'Shit, Ruby. There're zoms out there.' He rubs his hands over his short hair. 'Right, Nora, are you feeling well enough to help?'

The genuine answer is "no way". My head hurts, my arm hurts, I still really want to sleep, and I'm completely shaken to the centre of my horror-loving core by the last time we found ourselves in the middle of a real life zom-fest.

But Jayden and Ruby need me.

All this considered, I give the only answer I can.

'Yep!'

'Amazing. You two keep the zoms off the boat and I'll get us moving again.'

'Will do,' Ruby says, and I'm surprised she doesn't fight against Jayden telling her what to do.

She hands me my cricket bat and trainers. The second I'm ready, she picks up her hockey stick and mounts her foot on the bottom step, looking epic. With the toss of a wink my way, she runs outside. My heart skips and I nearly fall up the three steps leading out of the cabin.

After a smooth recovery, I follow.

There are three zoms, one on the boat grappling with Rubes and two on the path alongside the canal.

I spin to make sure all zoms are accounted for and nearly collapse when I catch sight of what's behind me.

Another zom.

But not just *any* other zom.

THE UBER-ZOM.

There's one in every horror movie, the super manky one that the special effects artists have really gone to work on, the one I always hunted for in monster movies, taking screen grabs to analyse in painstakingly nerdy detail how they'd been created.

And here she is.

Blue veiny boobs nearly tumbling out of her tiny top with each jerking movement, crawling across the boat's roof towards me.

D.I.Y. Uber-Zom — Nora Inkwell Stylee!

Gooey Mouth Drawls:
- Edible Blood?
- Food Colouring?
- Ketchup?!

Injuries & Veins:
- Serious Amounts of Scar Wax?
- Serious Amounts of Make-up?
- Actual Bites & Zombification?!

Limbs At Awkward Angles:
- False Limbs?
- Contortionist?
- Robot?

You'd definitely have to go for animatronics to get those erratic jerking motions.

If this was a movie, and I was the director, I'd totally give the monster-maker bonus points. This zom's her very own brand of evil. The brain-dead look of confusion and hunger mixes with peculiar notes of lust that tug at her agitated features.

I'm really hoping Rubes is doing OK with her zom, because I can't take my eyes off the one crawling closer and looking like she's been dragged up from a deeper layer of hell.

Blood runs from her mouth in oozing strands that prove unhelpful in her progress across the roof, as her hands and knees skid and slide on the smooth painted metal.

I give myself permission to go for her head.

She needs it.

If it was me, I'd want somebody to put me out of my misery.

Wouldn't I?

I can do this.

I raise my bat.

She must be about my age.

I start the swing.

If she's my age, that means she's Rube's age too. The bat halts centimetres from Uber-Zom's head when I realise this person could be someone else's Ruby.

The bat catches her attention and she chomps at it, catching it in her teeth. Any efforts to gently free my weapon are futile and it looks like she might bite a chunk out of the wood.

With a steadying breath, I reach out to push at her head. Stomach acids leak up my throat to fill my mouth as her scalp moves loosely across her skull.

What the hell is wrong with these people?

Panic sharpens my reactions and when she snaps for my hand, I haul it out the way. The clack of her teeth closing millimetres away from my soft fleshy arm numbs my extremities.

It takes me everything to swallow down the nausea and get my limbs working again. My second swing of the bat is lower.

This time I don't stop.

The flat of the wood slaps her arms out from under her and she falls hard, the metal of the roof buckling inwards around her point of impact.

With her down, it's surprisingly easy to nudge Uber-Zom off. There's a satisfying *splash* and I'm awash with relief as she hits the water, though heebies and jeebies are still chasing each other up and down my spine.

I wipe sweaty palms down my grubby T-shirt, watching for her to re-emerge. She doesn't. Is she OK?

Guilt clawing at my chest, I move to assist Rubes.

The first zom she attacked is now in the canal beside us and she's jabbing her hockey stick menacingly at the other two trying to board our vessel.

'How's it going with that engine?' I call to Jayden.

The deck beneath my feet trembles and I fear the worst. I hardly have time to pile blind panic onto my already well-established foundation of terror, when it turns into the smooth vibration I recognise as the boat's engine.

'Haul anchor,' Jayden calls over the now considerable groaning of the latest contestants ready to compete for a bite out of our bee-hinds.

'Haul— what?' I shout. 'Does this thing have an anchor?'

'I was joking. Just shove us away from shore!'

But I know the two zoms on the bank won't let us push off without leaving behind the foot we used to do it . . . and possibly part of the leg too.

'You say that like it's easy,' I call.

'Isn't it?'

'Nope.'

'I've got it.' Ruby moves to the front of the boat, sits down and braces her feet against the boat's brim. Then she hooks the crook of her hockey stick around the backs of the zom ankles and pulls their legs out from under them. They hit the ground with hollow thuds.

'Genius!' I say, jumping down to sit beside Ruby and squelching my trainers hard into the mud lining the canal. She does the same and we push. Chunks of earth fall about our feet and we're moving away from the danger.

I half expect a hand to clamp around my legs or grab my shoes as I pull them back onto the boat. With both feet returned to me bite-free, I breathe a sigh of relief and give them a modest pat of congratulations.

But I celebrated too soon.

Way too soon.

A gargled scream slices the air.

I'm up and traversing towards a wet gurgling noise coming from behind the cabin.

Halfway there, Ruby cries out and it calls me to shuffle back as fast as I can, to where we were both sitting moments ago.

A man the size of a small mountain has Ruby's wrist in one hand and the rim of the boat in the other. He's being dragged alongside us and doing his best to keep his mouth out of the water long enough to chomp on her.

I stamp my heel down on his fingers. The man-mountain roars and lets go of the boat, almost yanking Ruby over the side. I throw my arms around her, holding her tight, feet digging into the corner as I hang on to her with everything I've got.

The zom's hand slips from her arm and we collapse backwards.

Ruby's on top of me, our heartbeats pulsing through every point we're touching. Our eyes meet and my breath catches at the same time hers does.

Our faces are so close.

Our mouths are so close.

The wet gurgling sound pulls me away from thoughts of Ruby's lips.

'Jayden!'

I jolt up and edge my way around the cabin. My eyes take in the scene, but my brain struggles to make sense of the information.

The pure red of so much blood is almost overwhelming.

It's Uber-Zom.

She's back.

Half in, half out of the water, she must have clawed her way up onto the boat. None of the others have been agile enough to pull that off. She sinks her teeth into Jayden's throat, again and again, tearing away at his flesh.

Her arms pin Jayden down, one hand pressed across his face and the other hooked over his chest. As soon as I arrive she starts dragging him backwards.

I dive forwards, seizing his hand. His cool skin is slick and rubbery. I'm trying to hold on to his fingers, but the blood makes them slide from my grasp.

He's going over.

Splash.

Then there's more splashes as the zoms from the shore walk over the edge and into the canal towards Jayden and Uber-Zom.

'Jayden!' I shout, throwing myself forwards.

Ruby pulls me back as the boat gently chugs away from where he's being tugged on like a rag doll. 'He's gone.'

I still struggle, wanting to do something to help.

Man-mountain grabs Jayden from behind, bites down on the back of his head and pulls, bringing most of his scalp and hair away in his teeth. Jayden's screams tear at my ears, and all I can think is how it sounds nothing like him.

I turn to Ruby and push my face into her shoulder.

We'd all been OK a few minutes ago. I wish I could pluck Jayden from the water, and step back that short distance of time to when we were all safe.

The screaming is drowned out to a series of gurgles and splashes until they finally come to an end. I glance back and see only ripples.

We both stand and stare.

Two statues carved of pure helplessness.

The boat cuts gracefully through the water, drawing towards us the pool of red emerging from the point where he vanished.

The monsters under the water come to the surface, eating handfuls of meat and strings of intestines.

'Always the intestines,' Ruby mutters.

I bend over and am so totally sick. Everywhere.

Chapter 21

NONE OF THE ZOMS MAKE A MOVE TO FOLLOW us.

We don't speak for the longest time. I sit on the edge of the boat and bury my head in my hands, not wanting to see any more and not sure if I'm quite done puking.

'We didn't really know him.' Ruby's voice is hard, and it breaks the silence into a million pieces.

'You can be a bitch sometimes,' I snipe back, wanting to collect all the shattered moments of quiet and glue them together again so I don't have to hear any more, or talk any more, about what's happened.

But Ruby keeps talking.

'Listen, Nora, I want to survive this. But I'm not going to be surviving shit if I fall apart every time some guy I've spent a few hours with gets their intestines pulled out in front of me.'

'Twenty-four hours.' My voice is small, and my feet are wet in my trainers. I look at them covered in mud and chunks of regurgitated food. The sharp smell pinches inside my nose and claws the back of my throat. I think I might chuck up again until Ruby pulls my attention away.

'I'm going to see if I can work the boat's brakes. If I can't, we may as well construct a pair of giant happy meal boxes and sit in them until we crash into the next zom-infested hellhole.'

I push away the tears building up in the corners of my eyes. Probably just those weird tears you get after you've been sick. The lump in my throat and ache in my chest is all to do with my stomach contents decorating the floor. And my feet. And is nothing to do with Jayden. Honest.

Ruby's right.

We hardly knew him.

The guy who danced in the street with a giant plastic lollipop and wanted to be a nurse. The guy who fought zoms with his bare fists, loved his gram, and was one of the good guys.

Nope.

We hardly knew him.

More tears come.

Definitely post-puking tears.

Several of the most disturbing images from the last few minutes of my life play over and over in the shadows behind my eyes.

Jayden being bitten.

Jayden being hauled away.

Jayden being eaten.

He didn't need to die.

All the emotions inside threaten to explode out of me, or maybe that's more regurgitated peanut-butter toast.

I don't blame myself. I didn't want to hurt the Uber-Zom in case she was curable, that's all. It was the right thing to do...

OK. Maybe I do blame myself.

I go inside to find Jayden's bag and hug it close. His gram is our responsibility now, we have to keep her safe until we can get her to Scarborough.

Everything feels way too real with Jayden gone. And my parents might be gone.

What if Ruby's next?

My spiralling despair comes to a grinding halt.

I can't let that happen.

Filled with a new-found determination, I pick myself up to set about surviving and, after topping up on painkillers, I up-end the contents of Dad's camo rucksack onto the bed.

Sleeping bag.

Foil bag.

Torch

Penknife.

Kendal Mint Cake.

Candles.

First-aid kit.

Flint and key – as well as a Zippo lighter.

Astronaut food – yep, real life astronaut food, dehydrated, lasts ages, weighs nothing and tastes like crap. I know. Dad made us live on it for a week when he was convinced the government were experimenting with hormones in our food.

Lifestraw – for clean water.

In one pocket I find a bag of vegetarian strawberry shoelaces, a spare A5 sketchbook and a pack of fine-liners – my own personal survival kit.

In another I find a jar of Manuka honey and camomile tea – when combined they make Mum's favourite de-stress drink.

My throat aches and I have to stop. Harry Inkwell is a man with a lot of love to give. There's no denying I've always been a proper daddy's girl. I even tried to keep up with his survival obsession, but I thought he went too far, too fast.

Obviously not.

Obviously, he was prepared just enough for the end of the world.

I tried to keep Mum happy too, by going to Body Combat. That was easier than tracking Dad and his latest theories on how the majority of the population will be imminently wiped out. Now, I'm out in the world, in the middle of a real-life disaster without them and they have, each in their own way, prepared me for it.

A neatly folded piece of paper falls out with the strawberry laces. I unfold it and read:

> My dearest Nora and Kim,
>   Whatever is happening, know that I love you. I've put together this pack to help you survive and, even if I am not physically with you, I am here to help. Each item is labelled with what it is and when you might need it.
>   Harry / Dad x

I re-read it and in a moment of clarity, it's obvious that Dad's survivalist prepping has always been for us. It even started right after we were super sick with COVID.

My heart aches with the realisation that Dad's way of loving us is what drove Mum away. Things got worse when Mum lost herself in work, trying to keep us financially secure after Dad left his high-paying job to become a survivalist eco-warrior. In trying to protect our little family, they both broke it apart.

I'm still examining the tidy, tiny letters that build up Dad's meticulous writing in tight, perfectionist order, when Ruby enters the cabin.

KNITTED MOUSE

'Oooh, Kendal Mint Cake!' The sound of paper being torn snaps me out of my nostalgic fug. A minty waft clears my head and I turn to find Ruby with a face full of survival essential.

'I think that's for when we need an emergency energy boost.'

'What makes you say that?' she asks around her mouthful of pure sugar and peppermint oil.

I point at a small laminated label dangling from the block that reads:

KENDAL MINT CAKE – For emergency energy boost

'Oh.' She re-wraps it and sifts through the survival gear.

'These labels are great! This one says: SANITARY PRODUCTS – For special monthly times.'

'Your dad's cute.' Ruby laughs. 'What are *these*?'

She pulls out something that looks like a collection of small knitted mice, holding them dangling by their tails.

I grin. 'Washable tampons.'

Ruby laughs out loud. 'That's not a thing!'

'Yeah, that's a thing, you're holding them. They're small and reusable. Dad's thought of everything.'

I pull out a bag that hasn't got much in, just some string, or are they shoelaces? On the label, Dad's usually immaculate handwriting has a small wibble in it.

They aren't shoelaces.

'What's that?'

There are only five words on the label:

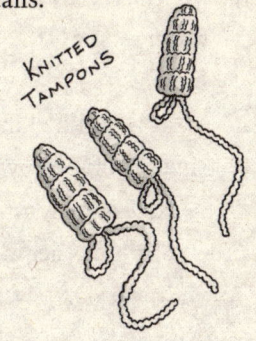

CYANIDE – For the bitter end

Hands trembling at how far ahead my dad has planned, I hold it for Ruby to read. The air falls out of her. 'They can't be real?'

'Dad's worked with ALL the chemicals. They can totally be real.'

Ruby leans in so close I feel her warmth beside me. My heart beats faster and I'm blaming the shock of finding a way to die in our survival pack. That wasn't the plan.

With a little shake, I pull out the strings.

Ruby reaches forwards, untangles one from the other. Each has a small egg-shaped capsule dangling loose at the bottom. They're necklaces. As we pull away, a third drops to the bed.

Jayden.

How much pain had he been in when he died?

'Thanks, Dad,' I say with a grim smile and lift my eyebrows. 'We can now sport the latest fashion accessory in the zom-stomper's line.'

'It would be kind of awesome if it didn't look so much like a suppository.' Ruby unscrews the catch, pulls the ends around her neck, turning for me to fasten it.

She holds her mess of short black hair up, exposing a long neck with soft dark swirls at her hairline. My hands brush them as I

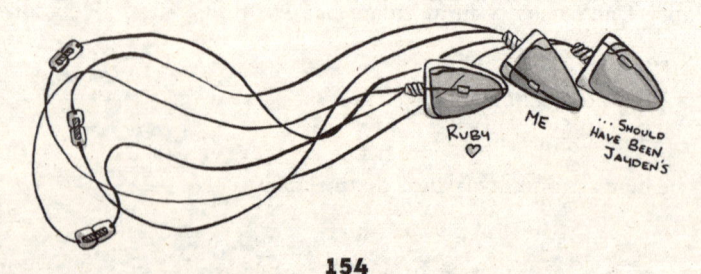

RUBY ♡   ME   ...SHOULD HAVE BEEN JAYDEN'S

take the necklace from her, goose pimples tracing the line of my fingers.

The plastic safety catch is a pain in the bum to re-screw. After some muttered swear words, I get it fastened and Ruby does mine. With the capsule between my fingers, I focus on it, rather than Ruby's breath on the back of my neck and try to imagine a time I might consider taking it.

Jayden's demise flashes through my head and, surprised at how glad I am to have it, I tuck the capsule inside my Slash the Patriarchy baseball T-shirt.

I pick up the small laminated label and turn it over. Across the middle are three small words:

bite and swallow

Good to know.

Chapter 22

WE REPACK THE SURVIVAL BAG, RUBY HELPING me to roll Jayden's gram inside the sleeping bag for safekeeping, and sit, side by side on the bed, picking at jam butties we made for lunch. I don't want to be here; everything about the canal boat reminds me of Jayden and it's too much.

'We should leave,' I say.

'Definitely,' Ruby agrees, eyes flicking to the spot where Jayden slept last night. 'We're stopped at an island, shouldn't take much to get to the side.'

We lash our weapons to our bags for ease of hands-free carrying. Ten minutes later and both burdened with a bad case of the danger parps... we're ready!

Ruby's fingers slide between mine and, despite the fear gripping my stomach, my chest flutters at her touch as we step together from the boat onto the thankfully zom-free towpath.

My heart skips when I recognise a small derelict toll house up the way.

'I've been here before!' I call, running along the path to rummage in the wall of ivy growing thick through wire mesh. 'There's a hole in this fence. Somewhere around here is a shortcut to the railway.'

'How do you know?'

'Loads of Dad's orienteering routes pass this way.'

I move up the canal path, pulling at the fence until I find the point where the heavy gauge, plastic-coated mesh has been snipped.

'Over here!' Thick ivy and brambles have all but closed the gap. 'I'm going in.'

Thorns tear at my skin, they snag and tug at my hair and clothes as I force my way through, dragging the survival pack behind me.

Ouch! A big bramble claws me above my eye. I wipe at it.

Blood.

Can the zoms smell blood on the air, like sharks in water?

Out on the other side of the hedgerow is a big empty field. There's not a creature in sight. No cows, no sheep and most importantly, no zoms.

'Clear,' I call back.

Ruby's rucksack comes first, followed by her head. She's been cut in a similar place to me, above the eyebrow.

'Got you as well, did it?' She points at her own bleeding face as she crawls the rest of the way out of the hedge.

'Yeah.' I'm surprised to find I'm sporting a big smile. We may only be a dense hedge away from the canal, but I already feel lighter.

I try to mentally drop all the memories of Jayden into that section of the journey, to allow us to move forwards without any baggage other than the bulky pack I'm already hauling back onto my shoulders.

'Good job you've been here before.' Ruby grins.

'Dad cut that hole the first time we were here. Our map-reading skills failed us, and we desperately needed to get to the train station in that valley down there, to catch the train to be back in time for Mum to pick us up. Dad always broke the rules when it came to

Mum.' It was so great when my parents made each other happy. 'After that, this became a regular cut through, but we haven't been up here for ages.'

'It's very farmy,' she says, breathing deep.

'Is it the fields that make you say that, or the reek of cow poo?'

'Bit of both.' She looks around. 'Which way we heading?'

'Round this field in a downish sort of direction.'

'Excellent. Let's go.'

As we walk, heavy clouds, with even heavier grey bottoms, move across the sky to sit plump and ominous above us.

It takes longer to get to the railway than planned as we take a more adventurous route than Dad would. OK, we might have taken a wrong turn or two. On the upside, our route has been joyously zom-free since the canal.

We push and pull our way up trees to get over inconveniently placed hedgerows. The hedges separating the fields turn into barbed-wire-topped fences and getting over them becomes more perilous.

The day grows dark around us, thanks to the podgy clouds getting podgier.

One wire fence stands taller than the others. Where the bottom is made of flimsy square mesh, the top has two rows of menacing-looking barbed wire.

'Wow, this farmer really doesn't want anyone to cross their field.' I move to the nearest wooden fence post, which has two lower support struts.

I toss my bag across, jam the toe of my trainer into the corner where wood meets wood, and throw one leg over. Super aware of the danger my bits are in, so close to so many metal spikes, I place my foot very carefully. With the post held tight, I lift my second leg over.

As I land, thankfully unbarbed, on the other side, I let out a shaky breath I'd been holding since starting the climb.

The clouds above choose that moment to release their heavy load. The droplets fall so big, each bounces before forming a small puddle of its own.

Ruby's bag drops beside me. When the rain hits the fabric, it doesn't make a playful *pitter patter*, it's more like a sombre *SPLAT SPLAT SPLAT*.

The wood of the post is spotted all over with raindrops and some is already running down the surface.

Ruby climbs, using the same technique as I did, jamming the toe of her shoe into the angle formed by two wooden struts.

'I've got you,' I say, holding her arm while the rain falls harder and trickles down our faces.

She shifts her weight from one side to the other, straddling the menacing barbs.

'You can let go,' she says. 'I need both hands.'

'Aye aye, Captain.' I let go and salute.

She opens her mouth to laugh and in that second, her foot slips. She falls down hard, the barbed wire between her legs, and her laughter mutates into a scream.

I clamp my hand over her mouth, cutting the piercing note short. She whimpers into my palm.

'I'm so sorry. We don't want anything to know we're here.' I talk quickly, looking into Ruby's wide eyes. She nods and I take my hand away.

Peeling Ruby off the wire is the worst. Every tiny movement brings stifled squeaks of pain. Her face is pinched, and she's biting her lips closed to stop any more involuntary shouts.

This is bad.

Bad. Bad. Bad.

And that's when the rain decides to stop its half-hearted splattering and completely piss it down. In seconds, we're both drenched.

Rubes fell heavy on the wire and she's not coming gently off.

'Shall I pull you off quick? Get it over with and we can get out of the rain to see what the damage is.'

Ruby locks both hands over her mouth and nods.

Only I hear the scream she releases into her hands when I grab the leg left behind and haul, staggering two steps away from the fence before falling under her. All the horrific damage barbed wire could do caught between a girl's legs running through my mind, I move out from under her and help her up.

'Did the wire . . . you know?' I ask, not knowing how to put into words what I was thinking.

She winces, leaning on me heavily as she gingerly sends a hand into her jeans to assess the damage. It comes out covered in blood. The rain washes it from red to pink to non-existent.

She laughs shakily through the pain. 'It caught up the side of my faff and under my left arse cheek.' She laughs again, a little easier this time. 'Shitting hell! Thought I'd lost a flap!'

I imagined worse.

'Amazing! Just a sore bum and possibly tetanus to be going on with.' I try to sound lighthearted, but tetanus is bad. I can't remember the details, something about getting lockjaw and having teeth removed to be fed.

'I had a booster not long ago, after a run-in with some rusty bike parts. So, no tetanus to worry about, just a spot of under carriage and buttock damage.' She tries to walk and lets out another squeak of pain. 'FUCK! It hurts! We might need to go slower, but hey, what's the worst that could happen?'

'I don't know, zoms could jump out of the trees and gnaw on our healthy, nutritious flesh. When they get to our stomachs, they'll reach inside and grab out fistfuls of our intestines to eat, like fat, floppy, human-flavoured spaghetti.'

'Wow. That was weirdly specific.'

I shrug. 'It's always the intestines.'

'A medical professional and some serious painkillers might get me moving quicker,' she says, wincing hard on every step.

We lost the closest thing we have to a medical professional, I think, as the memory of Jayden aches in my chest.

'Unfortunately, I think the best you're going to get is a travel first-aid kit and me. There should be some shelter soon. The quicker I can get you patched up, the less chance we both have of being eaten alive,' I say, trying to sound more upbeat than I feel.

'So, you want to find somewhere to stop and check out my arse, purely for selfish reasons?' Ruby asks.

'Self-preservation,' I confirm.

'Saucy bitch.'

'You love it. The railway lines shouldn't be far. Let's get your battered bum down there.'

Every step is a struggle, throwing one foot in front of the other and hefting Ruby along with me. When we arrive at the train tracks, we shuffle from sleeper to sleeper.

With both hands, I hold a vibrating Ruby tight, digging deep to get us moving faster to find cover, ignoring the rainwater soaking through every inch of me.

'What happens if a train comes?' she asks, loud enough for her words to carry over the rain splattering on the leaves of the trees lining the tracks.

'We get squished and all this has been a failed team-building exercise?' I shout back.

She palms her dripping hair out of her eyes and treats me to some of her finest unimpressed eyebrow angling.

'All right, a bunch of volunteers run this railway, they'll either be zoms or on the run from them. Anyway, the only trains that come down here are steam trains, so we'll hear it miles before it hits us.'

'Even in this?' She points to the canopy *patter-patter-pattering* with rain.

'I'm hoping so.'

'Well, that's reassuring.'

Chapter 23

AS WE TRUDGE SLOWLY ALONG THE TRAIN TRACK in search of somewhere safe to take a look at Ruby's wounded nethers, time passes and my stomach starts to punish me for abandoning my jam-sandwich lunch.

Ruby's movements become more restricted and our progress slows to little more than what an ambitious snail could achieve on a good day. Will we ever reach Acton Mortimer manor house at this pace?

Gloomy thoughts hang over me, even when the rain stops and the mid-afternoon sun finds its way out of the clouds to warm our backs. Finally the tracks split in two, one set continues onwards and the other leads to a dead end where several train carriages sit empty and welcoming.

'This is completely perfect,' I say, knowing it's really not. We could have found a hospital filled with non-zom medical staff. THAT would have been completely perfect – what we have here is a basic rest spot. 'Completely perfect!' I say again.

The passenger carriage looks invitingly comfortable, but I force myself to walk past the upholstered chairs to the luggage carriage, choosing it for the lack of glass. I'm done with zoms breaking windows.

The door opens with a satisfying *pop*, like the lid off a tin of golden syrup. A cough of cold, stale air hits us as I slide it open.

After throwing the packs up, I help Ruby scramble in. Out of the glow of the sunlight, my clothes feel even colder and soggier than a minute ago. They're gritty now too, from the dusty floor of the carriage.

A ladder runs up the inside back wall to a hatch in the ceiling. I climb up for a peer. The square of metal opens to reveal the sun-streaked afternoon sky.

This is a bit more perfect.

The rain has cleaned the roof and, because of a slight curve, all the water's already run off.

A rustling sound behind me stands my hair on end. I've left Ruby alone!

After almost breaking my neck scrambling full-speed back down the ladder, I find Ruby munching a packet of crisps. My relief is accompanied by the *psst* sound of a fizzy drink opening, before Ruby glugs it down.

'This place has a snack trolley,' she says, followed by a hearty burp.

'I can see that.'

Ruby throws me a bag of crisps, the posh, hand-baked sort. I inhale it, along with two others, and wash them down with a glass bottle of cloudy lemonade. It's all old-fashioned and fancy.

'I think it's time for a drop of this,' Ruby says, pulling a bottle of sherry from her rucksack.

'Where did you get that?'

'Nicked it off the boat,' she says with a sly smile. 'Shall I get my arse out now or later?'

'Your bum, your call.'

'Definitely now. It hurts like a bastard.'

'Oh! OK.' That's totally cool. That's what we're here for. 'Um, the roof's nice and bright; we should get you up there. I'll shut this and set the roof up,' I say, sliding the door closed and locking it.

I shudder, not sure whether it's the chill of wet clothes or the fact that the longer we don't see a zom, the jumpier I'm getting. Where is everyone?

'Excellent.' Ruby holds up the bottle of sherry. 'I'll self-medicate.'

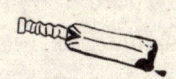

With the sleeping bag laid out on the roof and Jayden's gram safely stashed in the survival bag, I come back down to find a good portion of the sherry already gone.

'How much did you drink?'

'Enough to numb the pain,' Ruby slurs.

It's tough getting her up the ladder; as well as being injured, she's now got her mischievousness that comes out when she drinks. The lady is all limbs, everywhere.

On the roof, I stand on my tiptoes and peer at our surrounding area. 'I can just see the top of what might be the train station in the distance. There'll be a town near there, but we should be far enough away to—' When I glance back at Ruby, my eyeballs nearly plop right out of my face.

She's stripped down to a black bra top, lace criss-crossing over her toned back, which is tense with the effort of peeling off her soggy jeans.

'Son of a bitch!' She winces in pain and downs another mouthful of sherry.

My brain and vocal cords are failing to function at the sudden sight of so much Ruby. Her skin, all over, is even and flawless.

After several moments spent opening and closing my mouth like a bubble-headed fish, I finally find some words at the back of my throat. 'Why are you taking all your clothes off?'

'The metal's warm, our clothes'll be dry in no time.' She's still wrestling with her trousers. 'Give me a hand?'

Helping is hard, what with my looking everywhere but directly at her, as I'm about a million per cent aware that she's only wearing a bra top and black boxer pants.

I lay her jeans out to dry next to her trainers and start on my shoelaces. When I peel off my socks to reveal my toes, I find they've gone all white and crinkly in my wet shoes.

Before standing, I pull my knees in close and allow myself some time to enjoy the warm metal on my bare feet.

She's right.

I know she's right.

We can't stay in wet clothes. I'm just reluctant to get out my spotty shoulders and stubbly legs, especially next to Ruby's spotless shoulders and hairless legs. She must wax.

She lies down and closes her eyes, twisting to one side to keep her weight off the injured bum cheek. I gain the courage to whip off my clothes, at high speed, down to pants and bra, before sitting next to her, knees pulled in tight to my body once more.

'What are we doing now?' I ask. 'Waiting as a zom-smorgasbord?'

'We're putting off the inevitable.'

'Being eaten?'

'No, looking at my arse.' Her eyes are extra shiny and the squeak in her voice makes it obvious she's understating the pain.

'Right, let's find out what's in this first-aid kit then,' I say, jumping to my feet. This is about her sore bum and nothing else, even if I do wish I was wearing more clothes. It's only what some people wear to the beach, the equivalent of a bikini really, I tell myself, as I open a pocket on the side of the survival pack.

The size of the green fabric bag with a little white cross stitched on the front doesn't fill me with confidence. Kits like this are normally made up of a couple of plasters and a pair of blunt scissors.

With mounting anticipation, I unzip, open the bag and . . .

. . . breathe a long sigh of relief.

Of course Dad doctored the contents.

It's packed with sharp scissors, antiseptic wipes and cream, bandages, plasters and pills.

Oh my god, are there pills?!

It's a portable pharmacy in small, neatly-labelled, clear plastic bags.

'Are you allergic to anything?' I ask, thankful for the medical tip I picked up off Jayden.

'Nope.'

'OK, take these.' I hand her two pills from the bag labelled "*Paracetamol*", glad we've got Ruby's stash from the supermarket too. 'Shall we get this done?' I ask, pulling on a sterile glove.

'No.' Ruby throws her hands out. 'I've changed my mind. I'll do it.'

'Have you been secretly training as a contortionist?'

'Maybe I've been doing online circus tutorials.' She tightens her jaw, but the moment passes and her face falls. 'OK, I haven't. But excuse me for wanting to maintain some dignity.' All of her usual moxie has disappeared, and she's looking almost as mortified at showing me her damaged bum as I must at having to clean the wound.

'There's very little dignity in a septic bum,' I say in a matter-of-fact voice and hold out the antiseptic wipe.

'Oh, all right,' she grumps and pulls her pants to one side. The sight takes away any awkwardness.

'Shit, Rubes! It looks like you've had a cheek transplant with a zom! It's all the nasty shades of bruised. And the barbed wire looks like it tried to tear you a new hole.'

'Feels like it too,' she moans.

In focused silence, I clean the crusty blood and gunk from Ruby's injury, flinching away each time she sucks a sharp intake of air through her teeth. The process is slow but once I've applied some antiseptic cream, it's not looking nearly as bad as it did before.

Peach-coloured plaster tape and white bandages sit stark and pale against Ruby's brown skin as I cover the injury to keep it clean.

'There,' I say when I'm finished. 'All patched up and dignity still intact.'

'Thanks.'

We lie side by side in the sunshine for a time, me drawing in my sketchbook and Ruby staring at the sky, both sipping the sherry in heavy silence.

While my silence is heavy with unspoken words, I imagine Ruby's is a bit floaty – she's had most of the sherry.

The day's getting on and the sun has already begun its slow descent. As soon as my T-shirt, jeans and trainers are anything like dry, I pull them back on.

'We should make a move, try to get a bit further before night falls.'

Ruby struggles into her clothes while I wee over the edge of the train. Ruby does the same, but I have to help her. She's unsteady; the sherry really seems to be helping with the pain, less so with the basic co-ordination needed to wee off a train's roof.

We're nearly ready to leave when an ominously rustling bush threatens to ruin our plans.

Ruby climbs down the ladder into the carriage too fast, misses a rung and falls with a hollow thunk. Both the thunk and her swearing echo around the area.

Growling joins the rustling and I throw myself down after her, bolting the hatch behind me.

We've gone from sunshine, warmth and fresh air to cold, dark and dank in a matter of seconds. After a scramble around, I find Ruby huddled in a corner.

'Shhh,' I whisper. 'It might head straight past us.'

The noises outside grow louder. Every hair on my body stands on end as a piercing screech fills the carriage. Teeth on metal?

'Why do they do that? It's completely unnecessary.' Ruby's voice is low but annoyed. She clings on to me tighter than usual and I realise that she's scared.

The fear is catching.

'We'll sit it out.'

Something claws at the door.

'That's going to hold, right?' Ruby whispers.

'I hope so.'

'I don't want to die here, like this. There's still so much I want to do.'

'We won't die here.' I say the words firmly, hoping it will make them true.

'I can't run, I'm a sitting duck.' The sweet smell of sherry infuses Ruby's breath.

'You could be a limping duck, at least. We can get you moving.' But even as I say it, I'm not sure it's true; the last part of our journey here was way too slow to outrun zoms.

We hunch up in the corner as far away from the door as possible. Despite the cold, sweat prickles my armpits and down my spine.

I don't know whether it's the pulse of my heart hitting my ribcage hard enough to vibrate through my entire body, or the chill in my bones that has me shaking.

As the least injured, it's my job to keep Ruby safe. I shift my position so I'm wrapped protectively around her. Ruby's fingers dig into my arms and her knees curl up, resting on my legs. Her warm breath on my neck thaws a little of my chill.

I hold her tight and we stay like that for I don't know how long. Seconds? Minutes? Hours?

There's no more noises outside, but neither of us move.

The pressure of her hand on my arm releases and there's hardly time to miss her fingers on my skin before she presses her palm against my cheek. Her head moves until her breath trickles over my face.

It's too dark to see anything. I picture what the scene would look like if we had any light, our bodies curled together, Ruby's legs turned in towards me.

Her face is up and mine down. Can she feel my heart pounding in my chest?

She trails a finger down my cheek and my stomach melts.

An overactive corner of my brain runs through about a million thoughts a second.

What does this mean?

Should I talk to her about *the B word*?

Is this worth the risk of losing her?

Maybe I could tell her I was a lesbian all along. A knot tightens in my chest – that would be another form of hiding, and a part of me is already wearing thin from playing it straight.

It worked for a while, until Ruby arrived in my life. No matter how hard I ignore the feelings, denying them all the time is exhausting. And I'm so tired.

I've fought wanting this for so long, I don't think I knew how hard I've been fighting. But right now, there's no more fight.

Screw labels, I just want to kiss Ruby Rutherford.

Right now.

My lips tingle at the thought.

And, if I'm reading the signs correctly, she might want to kiss me too.

I turn my head to ask, but she must have been closer than I thought because our lips collide. It's messy and confused and the thrill it sends through me sets every nerve ending in my body into chaos. She pulls away at the same time as her hand moves to my chest and pushes me back.

My mind implodes.

I've misread the moment and murdered our friendship.

My entire everything corrugates inwards, wanting to take the move back, wanting to find words I can say that will delete the seconds before, so we can carry on as we were.

Apologies are forming on my tongue when her hand twists in

the fabric of my top and she pulls me forwards to press her lips on mine a second time. This time it's less clumsy and way more deliberate.

Ruby's fingers trail up my neck and behind my ear. I'm surprised I haven't turned into an actual puddle on the floor; my insides are already liquid and now my skin's going the same way.

She nibbles gently on my bottom lip. I open my mouth to laugh and her breath mingles with mine.

Everything I love about Ruby is there in her kiss. It's intense, but playful. I raise my hand to run my thumb along her jawline. Ruby's gorgeous jawline.

I think of her laugh and smile into our kiss, while my hand plays down Ruby's neck and across her collarbone, wanting to explore more.

She pushes her hips against me and a fire of desire burns low in my belly.

We haven't heard anything from outside in a while and I've almost forgotten that there is an outside. In the time our lips are touching, everything beyond the two of us no longer matters.

Chapter 24

A BANG, LOUD AND SUDDEN, ON THE SIDE OF the carriage makes us jump apart.

'Locked,' says a muffled voice outside.

Excitement shoots through me as I think I recognise it.

'My dad,' I whisper.

'Or some random man?'

'Not a zom, though.'

'Could be a rapist.'

'What the hell, Ruby?'

'I'm just saying.'

A smashing noise makes us both jump a second time. My heart is racing and my head is swimming at the sudden switch from all the feels that came with kissing Ruby and now all the feels that come with finding another non-zom. Hopefully not a rapist.

We stay quiet for a while longer.

'I think they've gone into the next carriage along, let's go look.'

'We can't just pop out and have a gander at who the new neighbours are,' I argue. 'We'll be munched.'

'Not if we go across the roof.'

'Excellent plan, I'll go.'

In the dark, it takes some time to locate and climb the ladder to open the roof hatch.

'I can come.' Ruby stumbles to her feet.

'No, no, really, you stay here. If your battered bum falls off the roof into a crowd of zoms, it's going to be me getting you out again.'

'Talking about my bum now, are you?' she says with a giggle.

I'm up, out the hatch and across the carriage roof in no time. Everything is cast in shades of twilight. With night closing in, it's obvious we're stuck here until morning.

There are rungs across both carriage roofs for me to cling to as I transition from one to the other, wishing I had more limbs to help me get across.

The carriage next to ours is rocking.

Why is it rocking?

It's impossible to see anything from up here. I thought I might be able to peep over, but it appears some more elaborate, hanging-upside-down-type-thing is needed.

The first window is broken and sealed up with a toilet door, so I shuffle further along to peer in.

Hanging over the side of the train, blood rushes to my head and pulses behind my eyeballs as I stare into the darkness of the carriage.

There is something moving in there. I squint but still can't quite make it out. My eyes grow used to the lack of light painfully slowly, my head is throbbing and fingers are sore from holding myself at this rubbish angle.

Who's in there?

Or what?

I make out shadows; someone is in the aisle down the middle of the carriage.

What are they doing?

The person lifts their head out of the shadow cast by the rows of chairs.

Dad!

I nearly fall off the roof in happiness.

He's here!

We can finish the journey together. He can help me move an injured Ruby to safety. And I don't have to be in charge of this car crash of a road trip any more!

I ball up my fist, ready to bang on the window, but something holds me back. Something in the way he's holding himself isn't right.

There's someone lying on the floor beneath him and as my eyes continue to adjust to the dark, I recognise Mum.

What are they doing?

The lack of light makes it impossible to make out exactly what's happening in there. A loud groan escapes from inside their carriage.

My heart inflated when I found them, and now it pops like a spiked balloon.

They're zoms.

My heart cramps and eyes prickle. I move to find Ruby, when more noises come from the carriage – and these are so much worse than the sounds of my parents as zoms.

'Oh, Harry.' That's definitely Mum's voice.

'Oh, Kimberly.'

Oh no.

'Oh, yes.'

Oh no, no, no.

'Oh, yes, yes, YES!' she cries out.

I'm going to be sick.

I crawl as fast as I can to the luggage carriage. Once inside, I bolt the hatch before dropping into a sitting position, knees pulled close in the dark and rock.

'What was it?' Ruby asks.

'I think I'm traumatised.'

'Was it your mum and dad?'

I nod.

'Was that a nod or a shake? I can't see anything in here.'

'Nod,' I squeak.

'Great!'

I don't reply.

'Not great?' She finds her way over to give me a hug. 'You need some of this?' The sherry bottle sloshes close by.

'Yes!' I neck too much too fast, wince and then have more, hoping the alcohol will cleanse the part of my brain that will for ever hold that memory.

'Are they zoms?'

'No.'

'Well . . .' She hesitates. 'What's up?'

'They're . . .' I swallow and try again. 'They're . . .' Another gulp of sherry. The shock of it going down clears the words from my throat. 'They're having sex.'

Ruby bursts into hysterical laughter. 'Lucky them!'

'Let's give them some time before we go find them.' I shudder in the darkness.

I wake with a start. A sliver of light slices through the carriage and across my face.

The weight on my legs is a snoozing Rubes. I gently scoop her off and move to investigate where the light's coming from. What I find is the roof hatch unlocked. *What?* I'm sure I bolted it last night. I examine the bolt, it's fine, just unlocked. Frowning, I open the hatch. Brilliant light beams in as a column from the ceiling.

'Shit!' The sun's up.

Ruby is curled up, cat-like, in the middle of the floor.

'Rubes.' I give her a gentle shake.

'Mmm?'

'It's morning!' Desperation colours my voice.

She blinks awake. 'And that's . . .' she puts a hand to her head and squints at me with a frown, '. . . not good?'

'No. We need to find Mum and Dad.'

'Your mum and dad?'

'Yes.'

'They're here?'

'Yes,' I sigh and hand her a glass bottle of sparkling water from the refreshments trolley, knowing she probably needs it. 'Don't you remember?'

She's quiet for a full minute, and that minute sets my heart hammering. How drunk was she?

'There were zoms, weren't there? Or a zom?' She's rubbing her hand back and forth over her head, messing her hair back into its usual tousled flick. 'Honestly, after pissing off the roof, I'm a bit hazy. I think mixing painkillers and sherry was a bad idea. Did we . . .?'

The pause is almost too much for me to bear; she's trying to read my face for clues. I stare at the ground, my chest threatening to implode with disappointment.

'Nope. Sorry, I've got nothing,' she says.

OK, my chest doesn't actually implode, but something that feels very similar is going on right now. 'You don't remember?'

We kissed.

We kissed, and it lit up my insides like a neon sign that reads "COMPLETELY PERFECT"!

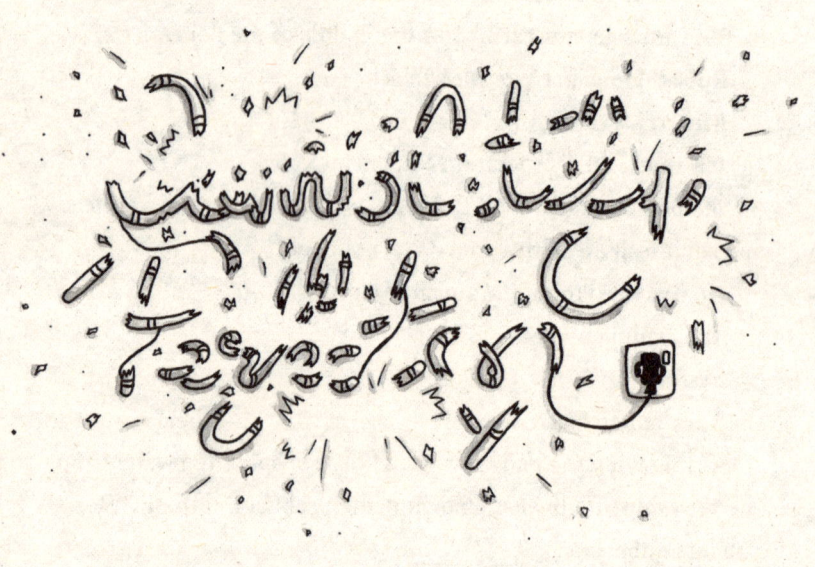

I have so many questions, she couldn't possibly know the answer to all of them, but for such a short and beautiful time, I thought we might have been able to work some of them out together.

Not any more.

The empty bottle of sherry lies next to us. I give it a kick, and it rolls away.

As I pack, I give Ruby speedy highlights of the night before, ignoring my own sherry-induced ache behind my eyeballs, and the ache in my bones that reminds me I've slept on a hard floor. The ache in my heart, I haven't got the energy to examine.

She has to clamp a hand to her face to muffle the sound of her laughter when I tell her about hanging upside down and discovering my parents in an intimate and vocal embrace.

Another shudder runs through me. I'm still not over it.

'Great, thanks for the sympathy, I'm going to be mentally scarred for life. Now, let's find out if there are any zoms outside and whether my parents are still next door.'

The answer to both things is no.

No zoms.

No parents.

We're still on our own.

At least we know Dad and Mum are alive . . . and for some reason, having sex. *Ewwwwwww!*

Without talking, I half drag my friend and her damaged buttock along the remainder of the railway and then up to the road, following the map.

We're over halfway to the manor house, but still have a long walk ahead of us. However we also have shortbread and chocolate, robbed from the train's refreshment trolley, so it's not all doom and gloom.

Hopefully my parents aren't too far in front. God knows what Dad's survivalist hero Mae Rears would say if she saw us fuelled on fast-burning sugars, with alcohol being used as a numbing agent . . . and mixing it with painkillers. Is she somewhere putting her own survival tips to use? Thriving with her own stash of sunglasses made out of cereal boxes?

More importantly, why did Ruby kiss me? And how does she have such soft lips?

We cut onto a dual carriageway, it's odd walking up the middle of one with not a car in sight. Horizontal lines on the tarmac lead past a speed camera. We keep walking until we see a sinister column of black smoke rising into the sky on the horizon.

Chapter 25

A BAD SMELL CATCHES ON THE WIND. TOXICALLY evil, like burning rubber, paint and petrol evil.

Then comes the smoke.

Thick and dark.

'Ain't no smoke without fire,' Ruby mutters, holding her sleeve up to her mouth to breathe through.

'We should be nearly at a massive bridge,' I say as the dual carriageway turns into a single.

Unfortunately, when the bridge comes into view, so does the source of the fire; the hugest crash and burn situation I've ever seen outside of a Hollywood movie, and it's blocking the entire road.

In fact, if anything, it looks a little too perfectly laid out. For a second it dawns on me how unreal these last few days has been.

I rub my aching head and look at the map, pushing away unhinged thoughts of people setting up fake zombie apocalypses to focus on the task at hand.

We need to find a way round this . . .

'There is literally no way round this,' Ruby moans, peering over the edge of the bridge.

. . . or not.

'The river's too wide to swim and we don't know what undercurrents are going on down there.'

I look at the map.

'If we head to the next bridge, it means going all the way through the town,' I say. 'That adds at least half a day to the journey, and that's not including possible zom encounters.'

We both stare at the burning heap made up of a bus on its side, two overturned mobile homes and countless cars. All are burned out or burning up. Flames emerge from cracks all over the place.

As I attempt to plot a path through the carnage, a loud roaring fills my ears, then my head, dislodging any useful thoughts it might have been harbouring. It continues to rumble through the tarmac under our feet.

Hope leaps into my chest.

This is the bit in the zombie movie when a squad team pulls up in a huge armoured vehicle to pick up the survivors. They'll give us a cup of tea and tell us it's all OK, before draping a scratchy blanket over our shoulders and taking us to the safe place filled with other survivors. A place where people with bigger boots than ours are taking care of the whole situation, and there's a bunk laid out with utilitarian, but surprisingly soft, sheets just waiting for us.

They'll tell us that Mum and Dad are safe and we can see them as soon as we've had some sleep.

Proper sleep.

Because I am so, so tired and this roaring noise is really fucking scary if it isn't our amazing and imminent rescue.

Both my hopes and my fears diminish as the sound thins to something less like an armoured truck and more like a bumblebee with a killer PA system.

Ruby and I automatically move back-to-back, weapons raised, a protective kill-circle of two.

WARNING! BIG-HEADED BIKERS AHEAD

A motorbike appears on the road behind, heading right for us.

'Nice bike!' Rubes lowers her stick.

'Don't let your guard down!'

'Lady, I don't think you get zoms on motorbikes,' she says.

The bike skids into an overly showy stop about five metres away, the tyre-burn adding to the already overwhelming stink of rubber, and the accompanying screech hurts my ears.

Thanks.

The biker raises gloved hands and lifts off their black streamline helmet. Purple-streaked hair bounces around the rider's shoulders.

Ruby's stick clatters to the floor behind me. I turn to see her face has become detached at the jaw and her mouth's hanging wide open.

OK, the biker is smoking hot, but that's no excuse to lose control of your weapon. Or your face. Let alone both.

'Rubes!'

Hot Biker examines the crash before raising an eyebrow at each of us.

When neither of us speak, she slams her helmet back on and gives a brief wave before powering away from us and the fire.

← THERE'S ONE!

An involuntary gasp escapes me when the bike spins an impressive one-eighty. With a couple of revs, she bombs it towards the burning wreck. Seconds before smashing into it, the bike manoeuvres to perform a back-wheel bunny hop, mounting the underside of the burning bus. She speeds up it and launches off the other side.

As the bike hangs in the air, a groping hand reaches out of the cabin of an overturned campervan. She pulls a machete from somewhere, leans over and lops off the hand, before landing safely on the other side of the wreckage.

The biker stops, turns to tap an index finger against her visor in a salute before tearing away, leaving a black tyre-burn on the tarmac behind her.

We both watch until the sound of the engine disappears into the crackling of the nearby fire.

'Show off,' I say.

'I'm in love,' says Ruby.

'Of course you are.' I pick up Ruby's hockey stick and hand it back with a little shove that wasn't entirely necessary.

'What's with you? That was Veronique Janvier!'

'Who?'

Ruby sighs and waves her arms about in excitement. 'VJ! She's on like three of my posters at home. She's the number one female competitor in international Streetbike Freestyle and she's only something like two years older than us. She's incredible! I've seen about every single YouTube video of her stunts at least ten times.'

She drags her fingers through her hair and spins on the spot.

'Whoa. I mean, wow!'

She lets out a giddy laugh and shakes her head. 'Amazing. She must be filming over here. I know she does a lot with Marvel and—'

Alarm bells ring in my head and I look at the carefully laid-out crash site. This does feel more like a movie than real life. I wonder whether to voice my thoughts to Ruby, but seeing the love hearts in her eyes as she stares at where the biker vanished into the distance, anger takes over.

'We finally come across someone who might actually help us, but instead we're treated to a stunt show!' I'm almost shouting.

'It was brilliant.'

'No. It wasn't. If anything, the sound will attract every zom in the universe. Really brilliant. Thank you, mysterious biker lady of completely NO HELP!'

'Hey, don't say that about my future wife.'

I know she's joking, but I'm so not in the mood. I pick up my pack and walk towards the fire, hoping nothing's going to explode as I work out how to get over it.

Chapter 26

CLOSER TO THE CRASH SITE, BLACK SMOKE makes my eyes sting and water, which seriously hinders my efforts to pick out which route the bike mapped for us over the burning wreckage.

'Where are you going?' Ruby asks.

'We need to get the hell moving!' I shout. 'We have a helicopter to catch and we're taking too long.'

'Why are you so angry? You should be happy. We aren't the only survivors!' She gives a nervous chuckle. 'Takes the pressure off you, maybe I could repopulate the planet with her!'

Again, I know she's only joking, but screw her. Wrong place and wrong time.

'Populate the planet with whoever you want. I'm getting over this wreckage, finding the wreckage that is my family, then getting away from here to find out what's going on in the rest of the world.'

'Easy now, Nor, what's up?'

'Nothing.'

I secure my bat to my rucksack so my hands are free and touch the first car.

Shit! It's hot!!!

I tug my sleeves over my hands and try again to mount the underside of an old-skool Beetle. Ruby's still staring at the point where the biker disappeared.

'Are you coming, or are you going to stand around with your tongue hanging out all day?'

'All right, I'm coming.'

We pick our way over the mess of cars, staying alert and on the lookout for any movement below. We get to the apex of the mountain of hot twisted metal safely, but then the car I'm standing on moves under my feet.

I slip and grab the frame of a shattered windscreen to stop myself falling. The sloping feeling in my stomach has hardly passed when shards of glass, like jagged teeth, bite into my hand.

I cry out and blood runs warm down my fingers. Pretty much at the same time the first droplets fall between the cars, the fire blazes bigger.

'Shit, run!' Ruby shouts, grabbing my arm and tugging me over the rest of the wreck, jumping from car to car. We hit the tarmac, Ruby calls out in pain, but we're still running.

The explosion deafens me before the wall of heat knocks us off our feet. We land on our stomachs, hands clamped over ringing ears.

I can see Ruby saying something, but I can't make it out. As my hearing gradually comes back, I realise she's swearing over and over.

'Are you OK?' I ask slowly, exaggerating the mouth movements for each word, in case her hearing's gone too.

She holds up grazed palms and I look at the mess that is my own hands.

I bite at a tear in the bottom of my Slash the Patriarchy T-shirt and rip a strip off. Instantly self-conscious about the part of my belly showing, I regret the decision, but the need to stop my hand bleeding quickly is greater than the need to hide my midriff.

With the fabric wrapped around my injured hand, I use my teeth to tie a knot as tight as I can bear and flop back to gaze at the space above me as searing pulses of pain throb through the points of me that made aggressive contact with the floor. Add those to the pain echoing from my bump to the head yesterday, the burn on my arm and now the cut in my hand, and I'm wondering if we're doing so well.

Black clouds billow upwards from the blast point and fatigue has me wanting to lie here for ever.

Ruby plucks at my sleeve. 'We have to go, the noise'll bring more zoms.'

It takes time and teamwork to get us both vertical again. Together, we stagger away from the wreck. We get a good distance before my head clears and it dawns on me how close we came to being blown to pieces.

Things are bad.

And the fact we're moving too slowly is not even the beginning of it.

'We should find a car or something—'

'You've not got your license yet,' Ruby interrupts.

I huff in frustration. 'As long as the zoms don't require me to do a three-point turn or parallel park, we're good.' A little further on I sigh, defeated. 'It doesn't matter anyway. If we find a car, what are the chances of it having keys?'

Ruby shrugs like it doesn't matter. Which makes me wonder...

'If we found one, could you hot-wire it?'

'Who do you think I am?' she asks with open-mouthed shock. 'I'm an aspiring technical engineer, not a car thief.' The entire response is completely theatrical and topped off with a roguish grin. After a brief pause she continues, 'OK... yeah. Probably. It depends on the car, some newer ones need a device to hack in.'

I can't hide the surprise from my face.

'What?! There's literally nothing you can't learn online.'

And that's when I remember I'm mad at her.

'I'm surprised you have time to learn anything online, with all the stunt-bike videos you watch.' The words come out so cold, I'm surprised they don't freeze up and stick to my lips.

She doesn't respond and as soon as we're capable of supporting our own weight we drift apart. Ruby stoically hobbles ahead, using her hockey stick as a crutch. I don't offer to help and she doesn't ask for it. The distance between us grows with the kilometres we leave behind.

Around the time we pass a sign for a caravan park, and I'm considering suggesting a break, leaves of the greenery along the side of the road start moving.

Oh no.

'Run!' I shout.

It doesn't take long for Ruby, with her limp getting worse by the second, to fall behind. Any hint of my jealousy or anger vanishes and I drop back, determined to keep her ahead of me.

Ruby cries out, 'Wheels!'

Turning, I clock the vehicle.

'You're kidding, right?'

'What?'

'It's a bloody tractor!'

'Only a little one, and it has keys!'

'This thing looks like it belongs in a museum,' I say, climbing beside Ruby on the open-top tractor, where we both perch uncomfortably in the metal scoop seat definitely designed for one bum at a time.

'She's got a hint of vintage about her, but she's red!' Ruby says.

Over Ruby's shoulder, I catch sight of zoms flooding out of the foliage and shuffling towards us.

'I'm sold, let's go.' I turn the key and hope fires up to the sound of the engine doing the same.

'You can drive this thing, right?' Ruby looks at me like suddenly this might not be the best idea.

'Looks straightforward enough.' I shift a lever out of neutral and we roll. 'Well, that's a good start.' I put my foot down and we go faster, but we top out at about five miles an hour before the revving gets dangerously dodgy-sounding and a worrying smell accompanies it. I try to move the gear stick, twiddle some random knobs, flick some switches, but nothing helps.

One glance tells me we've lost the distance between us and the zoms – they're almost at our chunky rubber back wheels.

At least we're moving. Even if it is slow.

Hopefully not too slow.

'Nor!' Ruby's voice is several octaves higher than I've ever heard before.

'What?'

'Jayden,' she answers, her voice a ghostly whisper.

'What?' I follow her line of vision and see him.

My stomach contracts.

His movements are jerky and awkward, but not exactly like the other zoms.

They're each a little different, I'm getting that now. I suppose that's the difference between reality and movies. There's no one to choreograph their performance, making sure they're all working to the same model of undead, though face pus appears to be a common trait among most of our own personal zombie takeover crew.

As he gets closer, I can make out the details of Jayden's injuries. From the chunk missing in his neck to the torn and ragged flesh around his hollow stomach cavity.

After two days in zombie meltdown, I'm starting to recognise that when anything really shit happens, the thoughts in my head are never appropriate to the situation.

And right now, all the inappropriate thoughts cram in, one after another.

Like: Being a zombie gives Jayden a gory, horror villain edginess to him. Everyone loves a bad boy (/girl/other) and they don't get much badder than wanting to munch on your brains, using your skull as a decorative bowl.

It's only when I'm wondering if his T-shirt has changed colour, that Ruby speaks.

'Nor, we left him in the canal. How is he here?'

'Things aren't adding up,' I say, willing the tractor to pick up speed.

Chapter 27

THE TRACTOR'S SPEED WITH ITS UNCHANGEABLE gears is still capping at about five miles per hour, but as we hit a hill, we slow to little over three and things are looking grim.

In a zombie movie, this is the bit where the footage would slow, gentle instrumental music with a melody that picks at your heartstrings would start up – something like 'Mad World', not the eighties version, but the one made famous in the cult classic movie *Donnie Darko*.

Ruby and I would both know the fight for survival is over and I'd set the tractor on a course to drive off the edge of a cliff.

The music would play through a final embrace and a pause for us to gaze into each other's eyes, showing there's still so much between us left unsaid, emotions unexplored, that now never will be.

Rubes might even have a flicker of a memory of our beautiful kiss, a flashback spliced in before the zoms swarm the tractor.

Naturally, we'd take some zoms out before we die. Cave in a few skulls, crush a couple under the tractor's wheels. Then, inevitably, there would be the first bite, super zoomed in on, to show teeth tearing skin. Then the next bite. And the next. We'd be buried under a pile of bodies, all clambering to taste our flesh.

When the viewer thinks the shot is done, the tractor will drive over the cliff.

Don't forget the tinkling melodic music, as Ruby and I, tattered and torn, gripping our weapons, launch from the tractor and go down fighting.

The End – thank you very much for taking an interest in our story.

Except it's not a movie. Is it?

The many inconsistencies in the zoms and collection of events that haven't quite added up, flash in my mind. But the zoms are within sniffing distance, and they hum convincingly, like festering meat and sweaty watch straps. They show no sign of tiring – strong weapons in the zombie's armoury are their persistence and strength in numbers. Both are working against us right now.

'This can't really be happening,' I say to Ruby. 'We can't genuinely be stuck in the middle of a zombie apocalypse.'

'It would seem we are.'

'On a tractor.'

'Yep.'

'With loads of them following us.'

'Yep.'

My eyes sting.

'I don't think we're doing it right.' My voice breaks. 'In all the books and movies, survivors sneak around, avoiding the undead. But we have a whole zom fan club in tow.'

Ruby leans across, wraps her arms around me from the side, and rests her head on my shoulder.

'Maybe we aren't doing it the right way, but it's our way.' She pauses before adding, 'And if you don't look back, you can kind of forget they're there.'

She's right. The upside to the tractor's roaring engine is that it drowns out the zom's groans.

Once it's obvious that even the most ambitious of the shambling zoms can't catch us at this speed, instead of relaxing, I become fixated on the petrol gauge and whether we'll have enough to get to Acton Mortimer.

After a long, hard tractor run, in which Ruby instigated several games to pass the time, I check the map, then the petrol gauge again.

'We're going to make it!'

Why did I have to say it? No sooner are the words out of my mouth than the engine makes a weird noise.

'What is that?' I ask, turning to the on-board aspiring engineer.

She frowns. 'I don't know. I've never heard an engine make a sound like that before, it sounds more like—'

Sheep.

Ruby doesn't need to say it, because we turn the corner and a herd of the woolly bastards fill every inch of the road ahead. Standing and staring.

'Run them over,' she says.

'I can't run them over, I'm a vegetarian!'

'So am I! But I can't be a vegetarian if I get eaten, and I'll be too dead to appreciate the irony of the situation.'

I honk the horn.

Sheep shuffle around us, ears twitching in displeasure at being hustled out of the way by an amateur tractor driver.

We jolt to a stop.

Jolt to a start.

Jolt stop.

Jolt start.

Jolt.

Jolt.

'I'm going to puke if you don't stop that.'

'OK, sorry,' I say, pressing hard on the horn. The sheep jump at the noise, clearing a little faster, helping us move through them like a spatula through solidifying Plaster of Paris.

'Well, the good news is that the sheep are slowing up our friends' progress too,' Ruby points out.

I turn, expecting to witness carnage. But the zoms don't care about the woolly obstacles and, in their doddering, clumsy way, they mostly fall over the sheep. A mixture of relief and sadness plays over my heart when I see Jayden is no longer behind us.

A woman in a summer dress is closest to the tractor – she's taken out by a sheep and falls towards us.

A crunching, squelching, popping noise makes Ruby gasp.

'What was that?' I spin to face forwards.

'Nothing,' she says and points over my shoulder. 'Let's admire the view over there for a bit, shall we?'

I immediately look in the opposite direction to where she's pointing and see the tractor wheel covered in bits of exploded sheep going round and round.

'Oh no! I squished one!'

A sheepy limb hangs on to the tyre tread, giving me a sad little wave each time it slowly comes round, until Ruby nudges it off with her hockey stick. I glance behind and see a group of white sheep splattered red.

I'm a murderer.

After that, I can't even bring myself to feel happy when the woolly roadblock thins and we're back to the full five miles per hour up the winding country road.

We put the first bend between the zoms and us. Then another. When there's no sight or sound of them, I ease my grip on the steering wheel. Ruby rests her hockey stick between us and relaxes. She rolls each shoulder and lets her arms hang loose.

'I'm going to need some kind of next-level sports massage after all this. If we find a survivor commune, let's hope they have a physiotherapist.'

And it's then.

In that moment of dropping our guard.

It. Happens.

I open my mouth to reply, but there's a groan before I speak and Ruby cries out.

The middle-aged woman, summer dress billowing in the wind, clings to the tractor, Ruby's hand between her teeth. It takes several high-speed heartbeats to recognise her as the woman who tripped over the sheep earlier. She must have fallen onto the tractor and hung on.

With some effort, Ruby liberates her fingers. I grab my cricket bat and swing it at the zom's head, really fucking hard. She falls away, a spray of deep red spattering the air in her wake before she hits the tarmac with a nasty cracking sound.

The tractor's veering off the road. I haul on the wheel but it's too late. With both feet, I stamp on the brakes to soften the blow as we crash, very slowly, into a tree and come to a standstill.

I grab Ruby's hand. The pad of her pinkie finger's torn open.

'The skin's broken!' I say, and it's obvious that I'm completely freaking out.

'Do you think?' Ruby says, pulling back her bleeding hand and hugging it to her.

There's no sign of more zoms yet. We've got time to sort this.

I unzip the top compartment of the survival pack to get out the thing that's been hidden for our entire journey.

Ruby flinches when I hold it up and the light catches the jagged blade.

'What the hell have you got that out for?'

'You know.'

'Oh, hell no!'

'We need to do this quickly,' I say, 'before the infection gets into your bloodstream.'

'You keep your woodshop skills to yourself, Nor, you're not coming near me with that.'

I lay the hacksaw across my legs and grip her arm.

'Ruby! You'll end up like one of them.'

'We can't stop, there's no time.'

'We have to. Just long enough to get this done.'

'But we need to keep going, or they'll catch us up.' She's speaking fast and sweat is beading on her forehead like she's fresh out of a hockey game.

'I can't lose you!' I shout. The words surprise me as much as they do Ruby. I recover quickly from the confession. 'There's no point running. If you're turning into one, they'll get us no matter how fast we move. It has to happen now.'

'You're serious about this?' Ruby's face is turning waxy.

'Dead serious,' I say, wiping at the clamminess building on my upper lip.

Every second we waste could mean we're too late.

Ruby closes her eyes and hauls in a deep and ragged breath. 'You're right.' She squeezes her eyes shut. 'Do it!'

It takes two attempts to pick up the hacksaw with my jittery fingers.

This is it.

I'm going to cut Ruby's pinkie off.

Chapter 28

THERE'S A SCUFFLE AS I GRAB RUBY'S INJURED hand, hold it out between us, and pour water over. The blood washes clear, momentarily exposing the damage where the zom's teeth tore her skin.

Seeing the wound takes the fight out of Ruby and she swallows down a dose of paracetamol without fluids or question before resting her hand on the lip of the metal seat between us.

With my heart pounding in my throat, I place the saw at the base of her pinkie finger, resting it in the groove of where the bones join, hoping it'll be much quicker, easier and all round less grim if I can avoid having to hack through bone.

Previous thoughts of inconsistencies in the zoms behaviour, and how neatly the car crash was laid out, crowd my mind alongside images of exploded sheep and the unmoving woman that bit Ruby, sprawled across the road behind us.

I can't think straight. I'm holding a saw and Ruby's crying.

'It's OK, Nor,' she sobs.

Time is not our friend. Zom poison is most likely in her blood, moving further through her veins with each second that passes.

Everything we've seen for the past two days screams zombie apocalypse. So, I set my jaw, close my eyes, and push the serrated blade backwards and forwards as fast as I can whilst keeping the downwards pressure firm.

Ruby cries out as the saw's teeth tear a path through her skin, muscle and sinew. Dry retches jerk my shoulders unhelpfully as I perform surgery. I only stop sawing when the teeth scrape along the metal of the seat.

People say that blood flows, but it doesn't, when I open my eyes, it just appears. In vast quantities. One second there's none, and then there's loads of the stuff. Everywhere.

My stomach still heaving, I jam a wad of bandages in place and grip them tight to stem the blood. Ruby screams through her teeth. She presses her lips together to stop the sobs, but they still come.

Tears roll down both of our faces, she's so brave and so broken all at once.

I want to stop everything and hold her tight, but I'm not finished yet and distant groans make my hands shake even more than they already are as I wipe the saw clean on my leg. The Zippo is thankfully easy to find in the side pocket of the survival pack. Once it's lit, I hold the flame to the saw blade until the metal glows red.

'Give me your hand again,' I say to Ruby.

Ruby holds it tight to her, staring at the hacksaw and shaking worse than I am. I know I have to be quick, the white wadding is rapidly turning red.

'Ruby, give me your hand before you bleed to death!'

I hold the Zippo for a few more seconds, then slam the lid shut, every nanosecond counts as I grab Rubes' hand, the bandages fall, and I push the flat of the heated blade on to the absence of finger with a sizzle. The smell of cooked flesh accompanies Ruby's wail at the same time as she lashes out, a sideswipe that catches me sharp around the head.

I recover from the blow, blinking.

Shocked.

Scared.

I'm too late. She's turning into a zom.

But when I look into her eyes, relief floods me to see that she doesn't look like a zom, just really, really pissed off. Then she passes out, slumping into the seat, knocking her disembodied finger off the chair. It rolls onto the floor of the tractor.

Delirious, I almost laugh.

It looks like a prop from a movie. I can imagine it lying on a table in a special-effects studio labelled: *The Finger* for *The Finger Scene*.

What am I thinking?

Nearby groaning brings me back to the larger problem. We have to keep moving. With the toe of my trainer, I nudge the finger off the tractor and then squeeze into the seat beside the unconscious Ruby.

I turn the key. Thankfully, the engine starts first time and I reverse out of the tree we abruptly parked in. One hand holds Ruby clamped to my side and the other steers the tractor. I drive and desperately hope blacking out isn't part of the zom transformation.

'It's OK, we're OK, everything's going to be OK,' I whisper over and over, holding her tight and wanting the words to be true.

We move out onto straight country lanes running between fields.

With Ruby's head on my shoulder, and her breath shallow, we press onwards until I recognise where we are.

'We're so close, Ruby,' I say and she mumbles.

At the turning for the Acton Mortimer manor house, I can't believe our bad luck when I see a stone arch at the entrance to the estate. There's no way the tractor will get through.

I shake Ruby.

'Rubes, you need to wake up now. We have to go by foot.'

She blinks dozily.

'Ruby!!!'

'You cut my finger off,' she says in a stilted voice.

She opens her big beautiful eyes and seeing not a hint of a cloud in them gives me a boost.

I park the tractor across the entrance to the path to slow the following zoms. Once I'm loaded with the two rucksacks and cricket bat, I give Ruby her hockey stick. She drops it twice before being able to get a good hold on it in her uninjured hand.

I haul Ruby's arm over my shoulder and shuffle up the path to the manor house, dragging her beside me.

When we stop to look back at the zoms crowding the parked tractor, Ruby leans over and empties her stomach contents all over the road.

Shit, I hope the paracetamol hasn't all come up with that.

After her chunder session, she actually looks brighter and even takes some of her own weight, using the hockey stick as a crutch. We're moving faster than a zom's stumble and that's enough to make me hopeful.

Mum and Dad will be waiting for us in the house at the top of this hill. Along with a helicopter to fly to safety.

We can do this.

We can—

A group of tweedy zoms shamble down the path. Some are in

riding clothes, all expensive wellies and waxed coats. Posh zoms.

'Shit. Shit. Shit.' How are there so many people? Isn't it supposed to be peaceful in the countryside?

A small building on our right looks like the owner got bored with having a normal garage and built turrets on it for fun, because who doesn't want a miniature castle to park their fancy cars in?

I pull open one of the heavy metal doors.

Something launches out of the darkness inside. Hands grabbing. Teeth clacking. I drop Ruby and grip my bat tight. I crack the zom hard and it hits the floor.

Ruby's staring at the tractor, where zoms are finding their way over or around it.

'Persistent fuckers, aren't they?' I say, and that's when I notice my jeans are wet.

Amazing.

I'm the person who pees themself.

In horror movies, that's a definite sign that I'm next to die.

Chapter 29

WITH A CONSCIOUS EFFORT TO HIDE MY terror from Ruby, I help her stagger into the now empty garage. I whip a chain and open padlock from the outside, haul the heavy door shut behind us, and run it between the D-shaped handles on the inside, snapping the padlock shut right before the scratching starts. Nails and teeth on metal. Again.

Ruby slumps to the dusty floor, breath shallow and shaky, a shadow of the Ruby I'm used to.

'Take these.' I give her some ibuprofen and codeine with the last drop of water we have. 'Show me your hand.'

Eyes a little glazed, she holds it up, and a glimmer of pride runs through me. The dim light is enough to see that, though it looks fiery as hell, it's a tidy job.

In trying to be super gentle, my fingers fumble while slathering the injury in antiseptic cream and bandaging it. In an effort to soften the psychological blow of losing a digit, I pack in a roll of cotton pad where her finger would be.

Which is stupid.

Because she didn't lose it.

I cut it off.

An urge to laugh at the ridiculousness of it all flashes through me, and then, just as quickly, I want to cry.

The pop of the saw going through the joint plays over in my

mind as I bandage, my spit turning to water, and I swallow back the sick that would really ruin the calm bedside manner I'm trying so hard to pull off.

The ambience in here is murky, like sitting at the bottom of a pond; the roof being made of thick corrugated plastic, it lets green-tinted light through the moss and leaves on the outside.

One quick look around tells me there's no other way out.

We're trapped.

'I'm sorry,' I say under my breath and am surprised when Ruby pulls herself up to lean on me.

'Don't be a dick.' The hardness in her voice catches me off-guard.

'What?'

'I'm the one who got bitten and was stupid enough to floss her fanny with barbed wire.' I cringe at the visuals.

The doors rattle viciously against their hinges and the padlock doesn't look like it's enjoying the ride.

'We might die here, in this shitty garage. That's just too crap for words. I mean, if this was the end of a movie, no one would watch it. We'd be the only people capable of dying a boring death in the middle of a zompocalypse.'

This comment teases a glimmer of a smile at the corners of Ruby's mouth. She shivers and says something, but the words are lost to the ever-increasing groaning at the doors.

'What?' I call.

Her lips move again.

'Hang on,' I say, eyeing the space for a solution and finding one.

The contents of the rucksack spew out onto the floor as I upend it and put its empty shell in the corner furthest away from the doors, then I move Ruby over to sit on it and put the torch by her. The sleeping bag unravels to show the cheery ocean sunset on the tube containing Jayden's gram's ashes.

I set them carefully to one side and grab the sleeping bag before sinking down beside Ruby and throwing it over our heads.

Our makeshift tent muffles the sounds of our impending doom and I didn't realise how cold it is in the dank garage until I start to warm up.

With a click of the torch, there is light.

'Better?' I ask.

'Much.'

We pull our knees in and tuck the padded fabric cosily around us.

'What were you saying?' I turn to Rubes.

'I wondered if you had something else in mind, to make our ending movie-worthy?'

Our ending.

This is possibly my last chance to tell Ruby.

I breathe deeply, open my mouth, knowing I want to say something, to say everything, but not really sure where to begin.

'You kissed me in the train's luggage compartment,' I blurt. Well, it's as good a place to start as any I guess. There's a heartbeat that stretches on for ever as I wait for Ruby's response.

When it comes, it's a weak laugh with the ghost of her usual energy tugging at the frayed edges of the melodic sound.

'Is that what the kids are calling it these days?' She laughs again. 'That really happened? I thought I dreamt it.'

She rests her head against the wall and a silence settles between us, but I need to say more. To know more.

'Was it painkillers and sherry that made you—'

Before I finish, Ruby leans over.

'May I?' she asks, trailing the fingers of her unbandaged hand up the back of my neck, sending a shiver of pleasure down my spine.

The sound of my racing heart fills my ears as I nod.

Ruby puts her lips on mine and everything around us disappears. No zoms, no garage. I'm not even sure I still have a body.

She moves away and looks into my eyes.

'Nora Inkwell, I've been aching to kiss you since I first saw you in Film Studies, way before they sat us together and I fell catastrophically into the friend zone.'

My brain effervesces and my words come bubbling out, 'Me too. I'm so sorry. I was scared.'

'Of lil' ol' me?' Ruby huffs out a short laugh.

'Of ruining everything from our amazing friendship to Mum's dream of me *finding a nice boy* . . . Or that you'd think I was trying to copy you with the whole *gay thing*. Or that I was being *greedy* because I don't just like girls. I might be being greedy? Other than confused, I don't really know what I am.' Tears have been building in my eyes and one blink brings them spilling down my cheeks.

'Whoa, Nora. Breathe.' Ruby's words are weak and even in the torchlight, I can see her skin is waxy, but she still manages a smile. 'It's OK to not know what you are.

THE BIG MOMENT...

Sexuality is a beautiful spectrum, it took me so long to work out where I sit on the rainbow.'

Ruby runs a thumb across my cheek to wipe away my tears.

'I like you.' The words escape from me like birds bred in captivity finally released into the wild. They'd been caged in my chest for so long I'd convinced myself they didn't know how to fly. 'And if you like me too, I've wasted all the time we could've been together because I was too stupid to tell you.'

'Nor, we didn't waste it. We were together all the bloody time!' She trails her index finger down the slope of my nose. 'And you're not stupid. I picked up on the vibes between us, but I was scared too. I didn't want to trash our friendship, or our epic plans for the future, by making a move. Being your best friend has been . . . well, the best.'

'You too.' I sniff a little chuckle. She's right. We've been with each other nearly every day since we met, together and always having fun.

This time, I lean in to kiss her. It's a timid movement until she reaches up and pulls me into a mind-blowing end-of-the-world snog. In a movie, this would undoubtably make it into the top-ten steamiest on-screen kisses of all time . . . if we didn't have a sleeping bag on our heads.

All the feels flood into every part of me. Fingers, toes, knees, elbows – and all

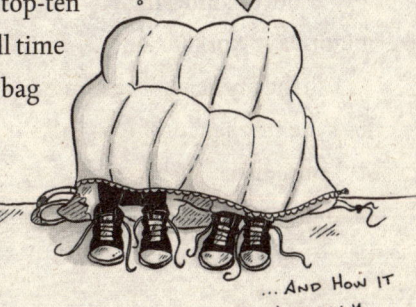

...AND HOW IT ACTUALLY LOOKED.

the bits between – become a shimmering luminescence beneath the surface.

I won't say that I forget we're in a zombie apocalypse, but for the time our lips are touching, I don't care. Ruby moves away and slumps back against the wall.

'Hedging your bets, are you now?' She has mischief written across her drained face. 'Stuck in a garage with one person, last chance to lose those pesky V-plates.' Her voice is frail. It's like she gave the last of her strength into the kiss, and now she looks so weak.

'Can we drop the virginity thing?'

'Probably best, my arse cheek isn't up to much. Or this hand.'

'I don't mind dying a virgin. I don't think it's about the sex, it's finding someone you want to do it with that counts.' I finish and give her a meaningful look.

'I've had my finger chopped off, and the pain is messing with my subtlety receptors. Are you saying I'm that someone for you?'

I nod, and she smiles.

'You're my someone too.' She pauses. 'Which is unfortunate, as it seriously shits on my plans to be a role model for queer female sexual liberation. But to be honest, I think my quest for sex was just my genius way of distracting myself from wanting to be with you. I genuinely thought lots of sex with hot women would take my mind off fancying my straight best friend. Who knows, it might have worked.'

I shake my head. 'I've wanted to tell you for ages. I really nearly told you on the day of the gig with Josie and Baxter.'

I think back to that night.

In the crowd, chest aching, I stared at Ruby as she searched for the drummer who'd not long left the stage.

'Josie's coming to meet me here,' she said, bouncing excitedly.

I was going to lose her. It was my last chance before she had sex with someone. I knew I wouldn't be able to be a good friend and listen to her talk about it, and Ruby would talk about it, in graphic and squelchy detail, because she's Ruby.

I wanted so badly to tell her how she made me feel.

Ruby stopped examining the faces in the crowd and looked at me. 'Nor, you OK?'

'I have to tell you something,' I said, trying to order the words crashing around my head.

Ruby stood still and people moved around us as the next band prepared to go on stage. She took both my hands, looked into my eyes, and I could swear she knew what I wanted to say. Was willing me to say it.

But there's always so much going on behind those big brown eyes, the magical world of Ruby lives in there.

If I told her and it went wrong, I would lose my golden ticket that allowed me access.

The words didn't come.

Instead, I said, 'Be safe,'

She looked disappointed. 'I will.'

And that's when Josie found us. The main band of the night stepped on stage, began playing, and the rest, as they say, is history.

Injured Ruby, looking a little sweaty inside our sleeping-bag tent, bites her lip. Her eyes have gone glassy.

'I totally bottled it,' I say.

'I hoped that was what you wanted to tell me.' She laughs. 'Josie didn't really have an ex who chased me to the train station. The truth is, I couldn't stop thinking about you. It didn't seem right to be with one girl when my mind was on another. And I thought the ex story might make you laugh.'

'When I went with Baxter, he wasn't a terrible kisser,' I confess. 'He just wasn't you. I told myself if you were going to prove you were a lesbian by having sex with a girl, I was going to prove I was straight by having sex with a guy.'

'That's dumb logic,' Ruby says.

'Yeah, I wonder where I got *that* from? Anyway, I gave Baxter all the signals, but when he went for the move, I freaked.'

'That's when you pushed him over?'

I nod. 'The whole time I was trying not to think of you so much, that all I was thinking about was you.'

Ruby runs the back of her uninjured hand over mine. 'We're a pair of dopes.'

'Yeah.' I tangle my fingers with hers.

The noise outside is getting rowdier and one peek tells me the chain on the door is not going to last long.

'It's not looking good,' I admit. 'I don't want to be eaten alive.'

'Me neither. And I'm dying without officially becoming a lesbian. Which is rubbish. I really wanted to have sex at least once before I die.'

'Ruby!'

'What?'

'You just said that's dumb logic.'

'That's with you trying to prove you're straight by being with a guy. I'm not trying to prove anything, I'm trying to make what I already know official.'

'That's equally dumb! You are whatever you are, you don't have to *do* anything to make anything official.'

Ruby frowns for a time. It's so cute how her nose wrinkles when she frowns.

She bites her lip and looks at me. 'But I was really looking forward to having sex. You know, it sounds super fun.'

'It does.' I nod.

After a short silence, our heads rest against each other and it feels a bit like giving up.

'We can't die like this,' I say, throwing the sleeping bag off my head. The torch beam judders an erratic path between the contents of the survival pack, now strewn across the floor.

This needs to be the moment we find out Dad's actually packed a stick of dynamite or a flame-thrower that I've somehow overlooked. The moment I find something to save our lives.

Surely no one wants these two young protagonists to die, especially after we've worked out we want to be together.

Like, *together* together.

The contents lie scattered and there's nothing here to help escape a horde of zoms. I grab the penknife Dad packed, open the tiny blade and run it along the wall's mortar in several places. It's disappointingly well mixed and solid; it would take hours to carve our way out.

We haven't got hours. I don't even think we have minutes.

The roof is too high and there's nothing to climb, even then, the plastic looks too chunky to cut through.

I move round the walls, tapping them. All solid as fuck.

'It's fine,' I say, even though it clearly isn't.

The bricks are huge squared-off stones that might have been reclaimed from an old fortification. The space is more or less empty. A fortress with no weaknesses, except the shonky steel doors buckling under the onslaught from the other side.

A shout makes me turn to see Ruby on her feet, looking washed out and determined as she raises her hockey stick above her head and brings it down hard onto the back wall.

The stick bounces off and she screams in pain. Folding in around her bandaged hand, her scream turns into a broken cry. 'I'm never going to see my family again.' She sinks to the floor and presses her face against the cement.

I swallow my own pain of not seeing my parents one last time. What would they do?

I remember them launching from the car into a crowd of zoms at Sainsbury's. They'd go out guns blazing.

I eye the cricket bat and hockey stick lying lifeless on the floor. I know I haven't got a lot of fight left in me and I'm watching Ruby's energy drain from her like someone's pulled out the plug.

Even though I know it's not the cold that has us shaking, I sit her up and wrap the sleeping bag around both of us.

The doors buckle further from the wall, the noise clanging against my nerves as I catch glimpses of chomping faces and clawing hands pressing in.

We watch the horror show and part of my consciousness detaches. I forget we aren't on my sofa watching some crap zomcom. I almost ask Rubes to pass the popcorn, but there's a sharp pain in my hand and I look down. Ruby's woven her fingers between mine and squeezed tight on the cut from the broken glass earlier. It brings me back to the fact that this is very much our reality.

A link on the chain holding the doors twists open and terror jolts a solution from the dark depths of my brain.

It's not a happy-ending solution.

It's a different kind of solution.

'We could go out peacefully,' I whisper.

'Being torn limb from limb isn't very peaceful,' she says, her shaky lips hardly moving around the words.

'We don't have to.' I raise my hand to touch the small lump resting against my chest beneath my T-shirt. Ruby mirrors the action, her eyes getting bigger and shinier as she grasps what I'm suggesting.

Her mouth rounds to form the shape of a soft 'oh' that is more breath than word.

We pull the laces from around our necks and each hold a cyanide capsule in our hand. Dad really was prepared for everything.

'It is this bad, isn't it?' Ruby says.

The door gives its loudest bang yet. It sounds like something structural has given way, and I worry we're too late.

I nod. 'It won't hold them for ever.'

Tears run down Ruby's face and mine trace their own route over my cheeks.

'It's been fun,' she says with a tight smile, the effort of each word visually exhausting her.

'Yeah.' I tilt my head towards her. She does the same. Our foreheads meet and we stay like that for several of our final heartbeats together.

'Bite and swallow,' I say, remembering the words from Dad's label.

'How long will it take?'

'Hopefully not too long.' Chunks of mortar are now falling away from around the door's hinges. A piece tumbles across the room and I see that there is one more thing I need to do.

I grab my sketchbook and scribble

> PLEASE SCATTER IN THE SEA AT SCARBOROUGH ♡

on a blank page, tear it out and put it with the tube of Jayden's gram's ashes in the far corner of the garage

'I'm sorry we didn't get you to your husband,' I mutter to the lollipop lady I remember so well from my childhood. 'Maybe someone else will . . . one day.'

I dive across the open space to scooch back beside Ruby.

'Right. On three?'

'Hug now, hug later?' she asks. 'We're totally going to hug, right?'

Bang, bang, bang.

More cement falls.

The doors are nearly down.

'Poison first, then hug,' I say. 'Otherwise we might bottle it.'

I hold it closer to my face.

'This is the best thing for us to do . . . right?' Ruby examines the capsule.

I lower it. 'I think so. Why? Don't you?'

'No, I do. I do.' Ruby nods like she's trying to convince herself. 'I just hoped you didn't and then we could have a discussion and put it all off a bit longer. But I think it is.'

And as if to prove the point, the door *ka-klunks*, and a zom is almost through the gap.

The groans are so loud now Ruby has to raise her voice to be heard.

'On three?' she says.

'On three,' I agree.

'One. Two. Three.'

With a shaking hand, I put the capsule in my teeth and bite down.

I swallow the sharp-tasting liquid that flows out and move to put my arms around Ruby, but I'm falling.

She's falling too.

We slump onto the floor. Ruby's arm lands across my chest before the world stretches out into blackness.

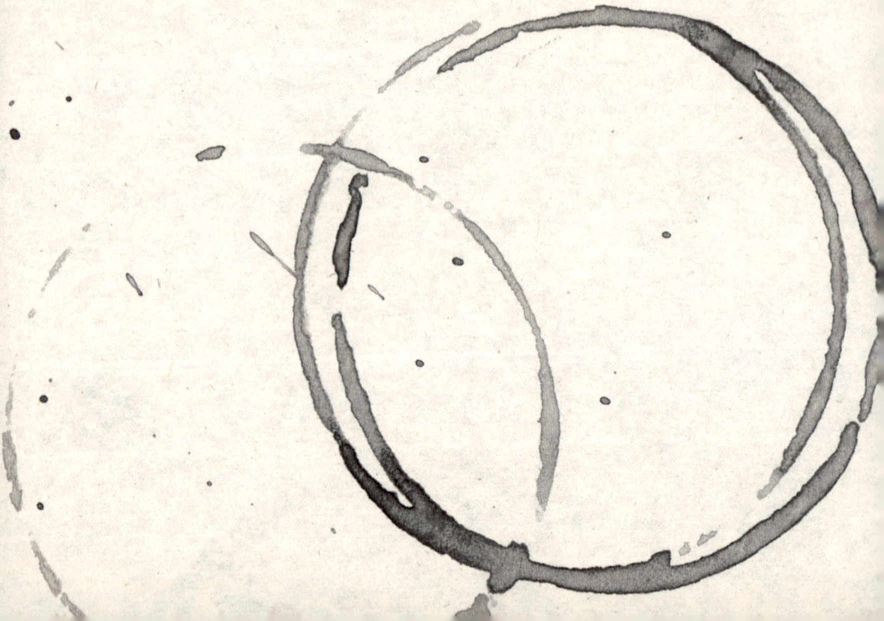

PART TWO

Chapter 30

I BLINK AGAINST THE LIGHT POPPING IN MY EYES.

'Am I dead?' My voice comes out as barely more than a rasp. The nasty taste burning my throat is in my nose tubes too.

Then I remember where I am and make a grab for Ruby's arm. It's still exactly where it fell.

Holding her arm tight for strength, I open my eyes wide against the bright piercing light and see bodies pressing in on me.

The cyanide hasn't worked.

We're going to be eaten alive. Or maybe I've been bitten, and now I'm part of the army of the undead.

I don't feel dead.

Or even undead.

Just groggy as hell, and what is this bastard light in my face?

I lift my head quickly and hit something fluffy. With my first swipe, I catch hold of it and pull it into view.

A boom stick? The sort we use as a microphone in college for making movies.

'Get that out of shot.' An authoritative voice tears at my brain.

I rub my eyes and they clear. 'What the hell is going on?' I say.

No one answers.

The same commanding voice from before speaks again. 'Move the light back.'

I recognise it.

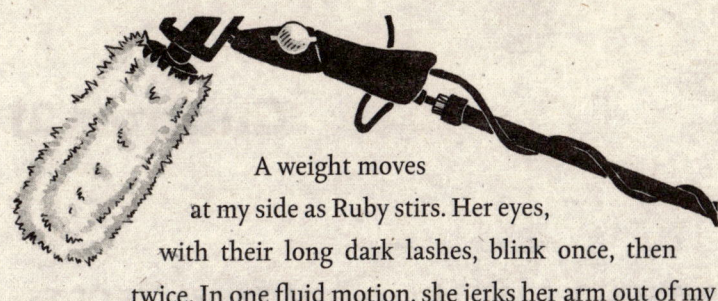

A weight moves at my side as Ruby stirs. Her eyes, with their long dark lashes, blink once, then twice. In one fluid motion, she jerks her arm out of my grip, staggers to her feet and puts up her bunched fists, wincing with the pain in her bandaged hand.

In seconds, she has her surroundings assessed and is ready to fight, while I'm still lying on the floor wondering *Why am I still lying on the floor?*

Inspired, as always, by Ruby, I stand and put my own fists up, but I'm not sure I'd be able to throw much of a punch right now. My muscles are jelly, and so's my brain.

'Here they are. Our two fighters, back from the dead.' It's that voice again.

A man steps forwards through the wall of light, first into silhouette and then into relief.

'You?' Ruby says and her hands drop.

'You!' I say and squeeze my fists tighter.

Chapter 31

THE LIGHT SHIFTS AND I SEE THE FACES OF THE surrounding people.

They aren't growling, pustulated or ruined.

If anything, everyone looks annoyingly well-groomed, with stylish hair and fashionable clothes.

I swear you can hear our brains working as Ruby and I run our eyes over everything, trying to piece together what the hell's going on. There are so many cameras. Some point at us, some at the people around us. Behind them there is someone mending the garage door.

At the same time a frown burns deep into my brow, out the corner of my eye I see a smile blossom on Ruby's lips.

'This is all a set-up?' she says.

The man in front of us – Elroy Pherson, local celebrity, millionaire and recently awarded number-one-dickhead-in-the-universe, as voted for by me – nods. I haven't thought about him since the day I all but sprinted away from him at college; Rubes kept the tote bags. But here he is. Randomly.

'Of sorts.' He beams at us with his super-straight teeth. This time, instead of marvelling at how white they are, I fight a compulsive urge to smash them in. 'You're about the two most famous people on the planet right now. Your adventures over the last couple of days have been filmed and streamed on YouTube.'

Ruby's still grinning.

'There's no zombie apocalypse?' I ask. My muscles have solidified and my fists are so tightly clenched in front of me that my fingernails dig into my palm. 'But we took cyanide . . . WE KILLED OURSELVES!'

'No zombie apocalypse,' he confirms calmly. 'And we swapped out the cyanide for sedatives, so no harm done.'

No harm done?!

I step forwards and smash Elroy Pherson – inventor, entrepreneur, and complete prick who put us through hell – in the face. There's a loud crunch. With any luck, the jab broke the smug nose on his smug face.

'Son of a bitch!' His hands fly up, blood drips down his arm and onto his pristine pastel purple polo shirt.

I shake out a sore hand, but it was worth it.

'After everything I've done for you!' He says it like I owe him something other than a short sharp smack in the face. 'No. Don't stop filming. We'll need all of this.' His voice echoes around the inside of his cupped and bloody hands. 'Someone get me some tissue.'

'Ruby, why are you grinning? You lost a finger because of this complete git.' I turn to the complete git. 'I chopped her finger off because of you, you sick bastard!'

'Well, yes, perhaps things got a little out of hand. But it sent the views through the roof.'

'This can't be allowed.' I look around desperately at all the people in the room watching us. Like putting two teens through actual hell for YouTube views is OK! 'Surely we can sue you or get you arrested or something?' I say, the magnitude of what's happened to us dawning on me. 'This can't be real.'

'This is very much real. Dead Real, in fact.' He gives a self-satisfied little chuckle and if my hand didn't hurt so much still, I'd throw another punch his way. 'I don't want to talk about all the legal ins and outs on camera, but the long and the short of it is you can't sue me because you both agreed to the whole thing. This is my lawyer.'

Someone hands Elroy a fistful of tissues and while he tidies himself up, a young white bird-like lady with loosely tied blonde hair steps forwards, glasses perched daintily on her nose.

'We have all the papers clearly outlining our intentions, that you and Ruby signed the day you both met Mr Pherson at the college. Your parents gave consent through digital signatures. We outlined every detail in the fine print: permission to follow you and film you, and the risks covered range from stubbing your toe to loss of life.' She gives Pherson a toothy smile and a bat of the eyelids.

'Thank you,' he says, returning the lady's lingering smile before turning to us. 'So that's it in a nutshell, though we would never have let it get that far, Nora.'

I remember the tiny print on the form we signed for the free tote bag.

'But Mum and Dad wouldn't agree to anything without reading it through,' I argue.

'Wouldn't they? It's surprising what people click "ACCEPT" to in a hurry to clear their inbox.'

My blood chills. He's right, Mum's always trying to keep on top of her emails and Dad hates computers, so he speed-clicks through his emails.

'But Nora,' Elroy continues, 'you're missing the point: all of this is such a good thing for you.'

'So, the zoms...' I shake my head, hoping everything will start to make sense soon, '...aren't real?'

'Animatronics, actors, special effects, and a pharmaceutical enhancer.' He's positively beaming at us as he reels off the list of ways he tricked us.

'Our families are safe,' Ruby whispers, then she staggers and crumples to the floor just at the same time as I go lightheaded.

I move to help her, but little lights spot across my eyes and my legs struggle to hold my weight. I sink into a squat, hugging my knees and waiting for the dizziness to clear.

So many people rush forwards, all heading to Ruby. Several of them are dressed in green medic's clothes and I really hope they aren't costumes. I'm not entirely sure where reality ends and make-believe begins.

They're all happy to leave me where I am as they strap Ruby to a bed on wheels and give her an oxygen mask and a needle in the back of her hand. A tube leads from there to a bag of clear fluid.

At some point someone must remember I exist, because one person in a medical uniform crouches down to talk to me. She hands me a bottle of water, and as I down it she asks if I'm OK to go up to the house on my own. Apparently there's a doctor waiting to examine me, and now this is all feeling horribly like an entirely different sort of horror movie.

I stand up, swaying.

'I'm fine,' I say and look over at Ruby. Her eyes are closed.

'It's OK,' the medic says. 'We've got her now. She's going up to the house too, we'll get her fixed up.

It's probably the effect of the mild tranquilizers used on you both, and the shock from . . .' The medic struggles to find words and, though she's being friendly to me, she's clearly not happy with this situation. 'Well, you've both been through a lot,' she finishes.

'Ruby's going to the house too?' I ask.

The medic gives a kind smile and a nod.

'We have to stick together and get away from here.' My words come out desperate.

'I can escort Nora up to the house,' Pherson says, like he's doing me a favour. With Ruby strapped to a bed, and my brain straining to untangle my surroundings, I'm completely helpless to resist. 'We'll wait for you to finish sorting Ruby out and then we can all head up together.'

'Right.' The medic turns her attention back to my best friend. My . . . whatever we are.

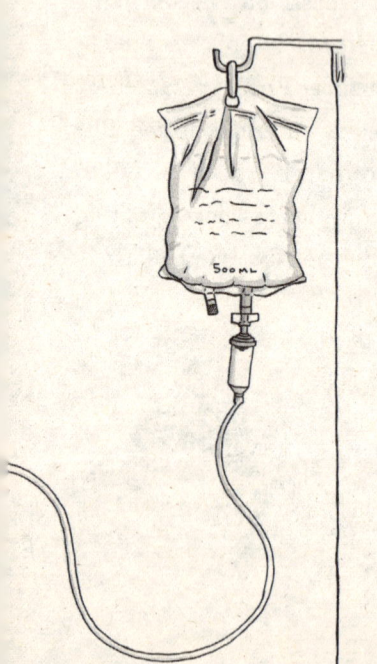

The vague plan forming in my head, of me stealing Ruby and speed-wheeling her down the hill and away from here, is interrupted by Pherson.

'You cannot know how excited I am to finally interact with you, Nora. I imagine you have plenty of questions,' he says, practically bouncing in anticipation.

I don't want to give him the satisfaction of explaining this whole twisted scenario to me. But of course I have questions. Loads of them.

Where to start?

At the beginning, I guess.

'So, all my neighbours were acting?'

He nods approvingly at my choice of question. 'The *zoms* had a little pharmaceutical help, to supplement their performance, but they were all excited to take part.' He nods again. 'We love that you all called them "zoms", by the way, that really gave us an edge on the marketing and makes the merchandise stand out. It goes to show that you can't plan everything . . .'

'So you drugged Mrs Johnson?' I say, throwing my mind all the way back to the beginning.

'That's not quite how it works, Nora, she *was* acting. The pills embellish people's zombie-like behaviour and enhance their strength and stamina.' He chuckles. Yes, actually chuckles. 'Oh, she was more than happy to take part, and key to us ensuring you would respond less violently to our *zombies*. We knew you all care for her and that you wouldn't hurt her.'

'Dad nearly brained her!'

'We were all on standby,' he says confidently. But I was there, I know there was no one else close enough to have stopped him if he brought that cricket bat down on her. What kind of dodgy set-up is this?

My mind is running through the last couple of days.

'So, Mr Hansdale, our greengrocer, isn't dead?' I ask.

'Not at all,' Pherson answers. 'He's alive and well,'

My mouth hovers open as I attempt to process everything.

'And people have been watching us THIS WHOLE TIME?'

He nods. 'There's a thirty-minute delay between footage received and the broadcast. For some light editing. We have a lot of information coming in from different cameras and mics.'

Cameras? Like the canal camera? Then my thoughts land on someone I almost don't want to ask about. Almost.

'Is Jayden . . .' I hesitate, '. . . an actor, or something?'

'Ah, yes! I wondered how long it would take until this came up.' Elroy gingerly thumbs his red-rimmed nostril as he speaks.

'Jayden's a special case. His story is genuine enough. He lived with his gram, but when she died, he locked himself away. He missed all the organisation for Dead Real. So, when you found him doing his road-crossing duties, it was as much a surprise to us as it was to you.' Pherson chuckles again. 'Happy accidents.'

I collect the ocean sunrise tube from the corner of the garage. 'Are his gram's ashes really in here?'

'They are indeed! Jayden was none-too-happy about his speedy removal from the boat. Got a bit of a bump to the noggin and claims we nearly drowned him.' Pherson tuts and shakes his head. 'Not our finest hour, but he was the loose cog in the machine and we needed him out of the picture. Thankfully you took care of the ashes – with them out of harm's way, it was easier to get Jayden on board for his reappearance.'

I remember the loss, the guilt that we hadn't been able to keep him safe, and then the final heartache of seeing him as a zom, following the tractor. It's like someone has slapped me round the face with a cold, hard helping of betrayal.

'He agreed to trick us?'

'He very much did, Nora,' says Pherson, pinching at the bridge of his swelling nose. 'It took a while for him to come round, but in the end, he understood what we're doing here.'

A medic holds up a thumb.

'Ah! It looks like Ruby's about ready to go. Can you walk up to the house OK?' Pherson asks. 'We have a wheelchair if you can't.'

'I'm walking,' I say, trying to hold on to some shred of self-respect. 'I've made it this far, haven't I?'

Every cell of my being screams at me to run, to get away from Elroy and this place, but they've got Ruby and I'm not going anywhere without her.

Chapter 32

WITH THE TUBE OF ASHES IN ONE HAND, I PICK up my cricket bat with the other before following Pherson out of the garage, the space where Ruby and I kissed ... and where we thought we'd die together.

My mind has nothing solid to grasp on to and I can't stop searching every face for pus, bruising or growths.

Outside, the day's still bright. How long were we unconscious for?

Hours?

Minutes?

'You won't be needing this anymore,' Elroy says, all charm as he plucks my cricket bat from my hands and passes it to someone standing nearby.

I hug the tube of ashes close, weirdly comforted by its familiarity.

'Collect all the girls' gear and put it with Harry and Kimberley's contraband. Who knows what it'll fetch at auction.'

'Mum and Dad are here?' My heart skips a couple of victory laps around my chest. With their help, putting some distance between us and this seriously creepy guy, with his fake apocalypse, suddenly feels way more do-able.

'We had to bring them in yesterday. Due to their,' he pauses and appears to be grasping for the right words, 'energetic nature, they're being kept away from the main house,' Elroy explains, before muttering something about them acting like children and then making his way slowly up the hill.

'Where are they?' I scan the small cottages nearby, hoping to see my parents' faces in one of the windows as we walk on, side by side, leaving the garage behind.

Instead of answering, Pherson starts calling out tasks to the people around us.

'Begin the process of flying Ruby's family home. In hindsight, perhaps we shouldn't have sent them as far as India, but we weren't to know how things would pan out. Someone tell Harry and Kim the girls are in, that might calm them down in time for the big reunion tomorrow. We need to keep this tight – no need to get sloppy just because the finishing line's in sight.'

Anger bubbles up at being ignored and my next words arrive harsh and unfiltered. 'If you don't tell me where my parents are, I'll get my cricket bat back and put it through your annoyingly perfect teeth. You got any paperwork that covers that?'

'You're much more hostile than the first time we met.' A flicker of genuine hurt cuts through Elroy's confident smarm. He resets the grin on his face before speaking again. 'Nora, I think you'll feel better once I've explained all the advantages of your current situation.'

'Advantages?! You really don't get what you've put us through, do you? And all for what?'

'To make the world a better place, Nora.' He keeps saying my name. I read somewhere that it's a tool used by business people to make you feel more comfortable around them, but it's just freaking me out. And what the hell is he talking about?

'What the hell are you talking about?'

'All will be revealed tomorrow, Nora,' he says and looks at me with such genuine affection it sends a creeping chill down my spine. 'But I assure you, it has been worth all the hard work.'

'What could possibly be worth all this?' I ask, indicating my tatty and battered self, covered in Ruby's blood along with whole worlds of ick.

He must think I'm talking about my ruined outfit, because he answers, 'Naturally, all costs will be covered. All breakages and losses replaced. Financially, we will reimburse you for everything, down to the last scrap of damaged clothing.'

'And lost finger?' I say, losing my patience.

Pherson tugs at his polo-shirt collar, suddenly looking warm.

'Well, yes, obviously we didn't accommodate for the lost finger. We did everything we could to reduce damage to anyone. As I said, when you found the cyanide pills, we worked fast to make a replacement and exchanged them before either of you took one.'

'How?' My hand moves to my chest, where the capsule had hung. I didn't notice a change.

'In the train carriage, when you slept, we cut through the bolt on the hatch and swapped them out before you woke.'

I remember something being off with the bolt.

Pherson keeps talking, following his own train of thought. 'Your parents kept us on our toes, too. We were working against chainsaws and shotguns. Your dad is a resourceful man! They even raided a doctor's surgery and two pharmacies to set up their own portable research lab and try to find a "cure".' He laughs again.

'They were being filmed too?'

'You were our primary target, you've been my little star from the start.' He smiles like an adoring parent, as if things aren't already weird enough. 'Ruby was a quirky little add-on I decided to throw in when I saw the obvious chemistry between the two of you. And I wasn't wrong, was I?'

My heckles, which I didn't think could raise much further, prove me wrong when he calls Ruby an "add-on".

'But your parents . . .' Elroy continues as we maintain an unhurried pace up this apparently never-ending hill. 'We could never have guessed they would be so entertaining. Harry always was one to think outside the box, even at school.' Elroy laughs to himself. 'The viewers loved them both from the start, so it made good sense, when you separated at the supermarket, to split the filming crew in two and run your parents' footage as well, to bulk out any slower parts of your journey.' He laughs. 'It all kept us really quite busy.

'Your parents even managed to steal blood from one of our extras! But as I said, every second was worth it. You wouldn't believe the views and media attention we got on the night of yours and Ruby's first kiss, and your parents' . . .' He looks at me and winks one crystal-blue eye. 'Well, you know. You were there.'

I suddenly feel sick.

Like, really sick.

I bend and puke over Pherson's expensive-looking shoes and trousers. My stomach is really showing its true colours recently.

He stops, eyes narrow and jaw tight. I'm not sure this is going quite how he planned. I sense anger and frustration boiling beneath the surface of Elroy Pherson's calm exterior, but when he opens his mouth to speak, there's no sign of it. Why is he so determined not to lose his shit at me?

'Right,' he says, shaking my stomach juices off his feet. 'Enough chitchat, let's get you and Ruby seen to by the doctors.'

I'm feeling much better. Not sure whether it's the act of being sick, ruining his fancy shoes or wiping the smug expression off Pherson's face that did it. However, I do manage my first feeble smile since waking up in a zom-free reality.

We are safe.

Mum and Dad are safe.

Ruby's family are safe.

And Elroy is clearly terrifyingly unhinged.

As we walk, camera people swarm around us and every lens I see is focused on me.

Not long ago I would've given anything to see another human, but I find myself wishing it could be just Ruby and me, alone together, fighting zoms again. Things were simpler then.

REBEL GRRRL
(SHE IS THE QUEEN OF MY WORLD)
RUBY IN ASS-KICKER MODE!
K.O.
MY PERFECT APOCALYPSE BUDDY

Chapter 33

IT TAKES A LOT TO TEND THE FAILING FIRE OF energy inside myself, to keep it burning enough to want to find my parents and make some sort of getaway plan. Every exhausted step I take threatens to snuff it out.

We move over the crest of the hill and there it is, sitting amongst a picturesque and well-landscaped setting. The Acton Mortimer manor house. A line of big old oak trees run up to it in one direction, fancy flowerbeds in another, and something that could once have been stables peeks out from behind.

My heart squeezes with disappointment.

We were so close.

The fields on one side are filled with bell tents set up in rows, looking like giant mushrooms. Several more fields are full of cars, with more arriving. Hundreds and hundreds of people press against tall mesh fences marking a boundary around the big old house.

For a heart-stopping moment, I'm certain it must be a zom-horde, because as soon as they see us, they go wild – but they're not groaning or clambering to taste our flesh, they're screaming our names and waving banners.

'I told you, you're famous!' Pherson says with an enormous grin.

I turn to check on Ruby, who's being wheeled behind us. Her

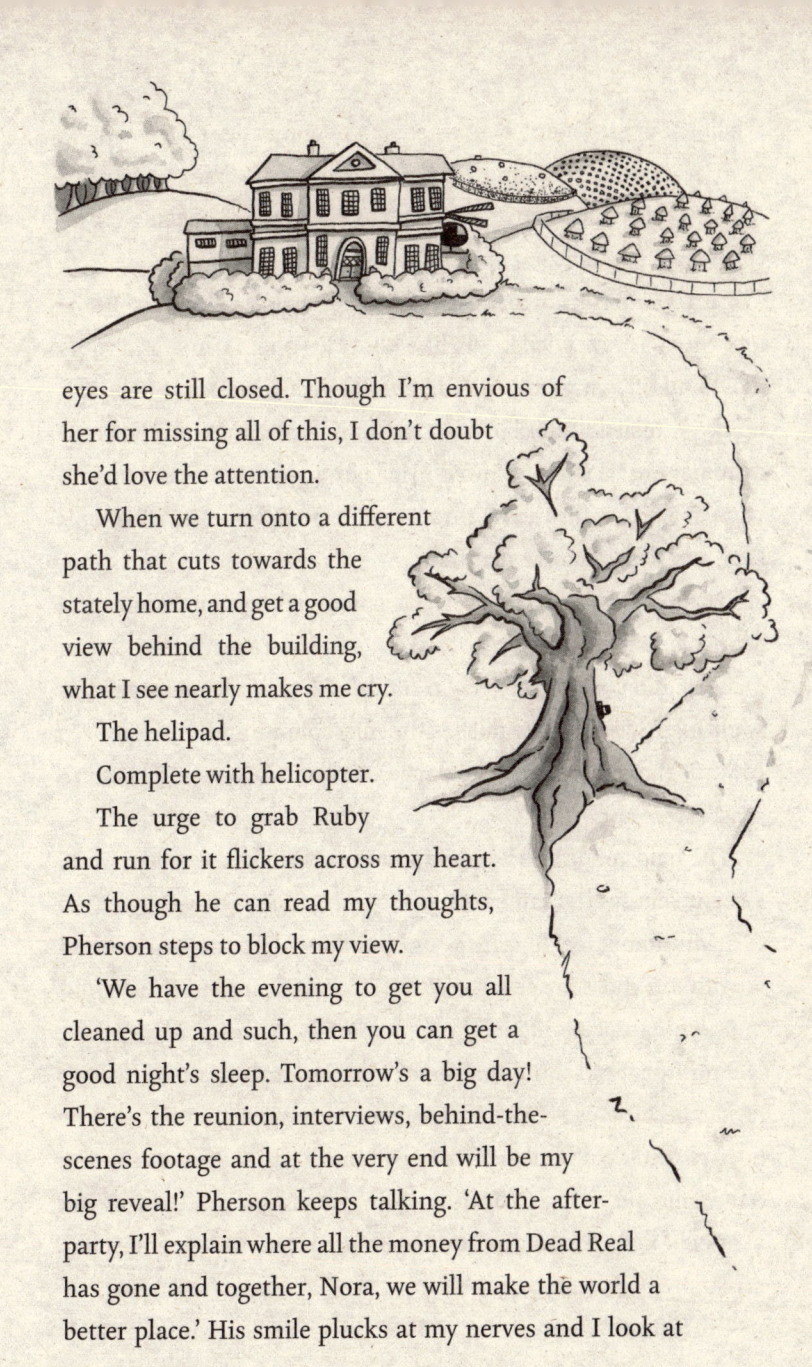

eyes are still closed. Though I'm envious of her for missing all of this, I don't doubt she'd love the attention.

When we turn onto a different path that cuts towards the stately home, and get a good view behind the building, what I see nearly makes me cry.

The helipad.

Complete with helicopter.

The urge to grab Ruby and run for it flickers across my heart. As though he can read my thoughts, Pherson steps to block my view.

'We have the evening to get you all cleaned up and such, then you can get a good night's sleep. Tomorrow's a big day! There's the reunion, interviews, behind-the-scenes footage and at the very end will be my big reveal!' Pherson keeps talking. 'At the after-party, I'll explain where all the money from Dead Real has gone and together, Nora, we will make the world a better place.' His smile plucks at my nerves and I look at the house again, wondering where my parents might be.

'The crew are looking forward to the party, they've worked hard. Zombie apocalypses don't make themselves!' He laughs and the people still buzzing around us force tired smiles.

Further up the narrow path is a gnarled old tree that would be amazing to draw, with knots like knuckles on its trunk and roots like hands clawing into the earth. As we get closer, a woman in a black jacket and blue blouse, clutching a microphone, leaps out from behind it. She's followed by a young guy with a camera. The woman strides forwards, thrusts the microphone in Pherson's face, and fires a question at him.

'Have you any comments on the animal rights groups protesting at your research labs?'

'How did you get into the grounds?' Pherson demands, before shouting, 'Security!' He pushes the microphone away, then moves towards the camera guy, who dances backwards to avoid Pherson's grasp.

The reporter directs her microphone at me like a weapon, while Pherson chases the camera guy.

'How does it feel to learn your big coming-out moment has had 4.3 million views in the last hour?'

'Coming-out moment?' I parrot blankly as the words register. '4.3 million views?' My mouth is suddenly moistureless. 'I didn't *come out*... I mean, I haven't *come out* as anything.'

'Are you saying you and Ruby *aren't* an item?' asks the reporter, her eyebrows pulling together. The camera guy is back at her side now and Pherson is running towards the house, practically screaming for security.

'I-I-I-' I stutter.

'People want to know all about your sexual identity,' the reporter persists.

Staring into the camera, my mind spins back to Year 9, after I stopped speaking to my friends in school. Nazia still waved and said "*Hello*" each time we passed, even though we weren't technically friends anymore. She tried to say more, but I wouldn't let her.

One time she found me in the library, reading an ancient *Point Horror* book and eating lunch under the table.

'I've read up about bisexuality for you, because I know you hate search engines, and I made you this,' she said, tucking a folded piece of paper into my hand.

Real-life horror overtook me. What if someone had heard her?

'And I believed you about your toe dropping off, too,' she added with a kind smile.

'I have a boyfriend!' I shouted, because I did, and everything was good. Mum was getting on at me less about how I looked too. She didn't guilt me for every bowl of popcorn or get on at me about my baggy T-shirts. It was like having a boyfriend meant I was somehow temporarily *good enough*.

I didn't need Nazia ruining all that. I was up and out of the library before she could say another word.

When I looked at what was in my hand, I saw the words "*BISEXUAL: The Facts*" written across the front of the paper with a rectangle below it. She'd coloured it in with pink at the top, blue at the bottom and a stripe of purple across the middle, where the pink and blue overlapped.

I unfolded the paper and glimpsed a list of facts written out in Nazia's bubbly handwriting, part of me excited at the possibility of finding some answers.

Before I had a chance to read anything, I bumped into a couple of girls coming the other way – literally, physically, bumped into them.

The paper fluttered to the floor, the word "BISEXUAL" facing up. I grabbed it, but not fast enough.

'Oh my god, Inkwell's bisexual!' announced one of the louder and less friendly members of the school community.

'What the hell even is that?' laughed one of her groupies.

The reply came quick and was delivered with spite. 'People who are too scared to admit they're gay.'

At that point I used a tried and tested method of self-preservation and ran away, scrunching up Nazia's note as I went and lobbing it in the first bin I passed, trying to ignore the feeling that an opportunity to learn something about myself had gone in the bin with it.

Now the camera is right in my face.

4.3 million views.

With needing to stay close to Ruby, running away from the reporter right now isn't an option. Her last question makes me shrink inside as I remember all the words I've hidden from for so long – *untrustworthy, slag, wanna-be lesbian* – but then also how right it felt each time I kissed Ruby.

How can something that seems so incredibly good *sound* so shamefully bad?

The medics wheeling Ruby in the bed are waiting close behind me. I turn and see them looking uncertain at this unexpected interruption, but making no move to stop it. The lashes of Ruby's closed eyes flutter and so does my heart. She's amazing.

Then I remember that our beautifully private times together

weren't private at all and it shocks my brain out of the stupor I've been stumbling around in. I don't owe this reporter anything – this is all very much my business and none of hers. I decide to channel my inner Ruby.

'Fuck off!' I say confidently, and the act of lashing out loosens a little of the tension knotted inside.

'So, you were pretending?' the reporter asks.

'What?' Wrong-footed, I shake my head, clearly missing something.

'You pretended to be attracted to your friend to comfort her in your last moments together? Was it the guilt of cutting off her finger that made you do it?' The reporter holds her microphone to me, waiting for an answer.

I don't have time to correct her because two bulky women and an equally bulky man, dressed all in black with high-vis waistcoats marked "SECURITY", barge past me and grab the reporter and camera guy.

When I turn to check on Ruby, her eyes are open and they're the saddest I've ever seen them.

'Ruby . . .' I step forwards to tell her that it's not true, but she turns her head away from me as a rumpled-looking Pherson staggers between us.

'Not another word,' he whispers.

'But—' I move to step around him.

'Not one, until we get you both into the safety of the house,' he says, blocking my way. 'It's imperative we maintain sole coverage on this.'

Pherson grips me by the elbow and forcefully leads me towards the big house. At the main entrance, he slows to a stop and his body language changes. As he relaxes, I tense up. I've had enough of being moved around by this man, and right now I need to speak to Ruby.

I've hit Pherson once before and, though the pain in my knuckles is still there, the result was good. It's definitely worth another try. Without too much forethought, I ball up my hands and swing for him again.

He ducks.

'Aha, fool me once ... That time I was ready for you. However, you might want to stop that now, because though you cannot sue me, I most certainly can sue *you*.' His voice becomes low and threatening before bouncing back. 'And it's going to make it very hard for us to be friends.'

Every instinct I have is screaming at me to get away.

'Friends?' I ask, certain I'm missing something.

'Of course, we'll be great friends, once you realise everything I have planned for you, Nora. We still have a long journey together. This ...' he waves his hands at the crowd shouting our names and holding up signs with our faces on, '... is just the beginning.'

Pherson flashes his expensive smile at me and opens the double doors leading into the huge old house, like a crocodile opening its mouth. All of his teeth are on show as he invites us over the threshold.

Chapter 34

RUBY IS WHEELED STRAIGHT THROUGH THE GRAND double-doorway, leaving me no choice but to follow.

Inside, the place is a hive of activity, with people moving around the beautiful old house as they go about their various jobs. Some are setting up tech, moving furniture or looking generally important while holding iPads and talking into headsets.

Everyone and everything smells amazing, like perfume, air freshener and cleaning products.

Except me.

I smell like stale sweat and old wee.

In the middle of the enormous lobby is a massive telly screen, looking completely out of place.

'We've put together a show reel, giving a behind-the-scenes look at the animatronics, effects and makeup. That will be shown as part of the *grand finale*, after the reunion,' Pherson explains.

The telly is set up with two green leather sofas either side. Banners hang from a banister running along the floor above and I stop to stare at the design printed on them.

It's us!

Aware that there's a camera trained on me, and we might still be being watched, I smooth any emotion from my features, trying not to give anyone anything worth watching while I stare at the banner.

FRIENDSHIP, LOVE AND ZOMBIES

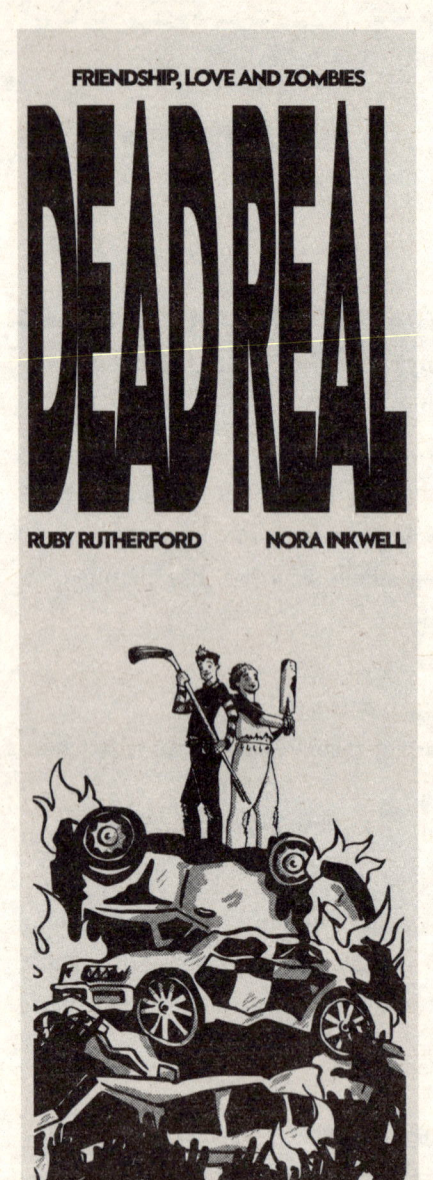

DEAD REAL

RUBY RUTHERFORD   **NORA INKWELL**

Ruby and I are shown standing in our kill circle of two on top of a pile of burning cars.

In the poster I spot the burned-out vintage VW Beetle I climbed up; it gives the shot some serious class. They've pumped the saturation up on the image and we're looking awesome – a bit battered, but mainly awesome – cricket bat and hockey stick ready to swing.

It's hard to figure out what's real and what's fake about the picture. All the hands reaching up from between the cars and grabbing for us definitely weren't there, or the biker would have had her work cut out.

The colour palette is limited to hot pink and acid green behind solid areas of black. It looks like a comic book cover, which is definitely helped by the type printed boldly over our heads spelling out the words: *DEAD REAL*.

'Dead Real?' I read.

'That's the name of the YouTube channel,' Pherson answers my muttered question. 'Came up with it myself.' And it pisses me off that the self-congratulatory grin is back on his face.

Ruby's eyes are closed again. I'd love to nudge her and show her us looking badass on actual banners, but up there she has ten digits and guilt stops me.

Pherson leads me in a different direction to where the medics are wheeling Ruby. Panic shoots through me.

I turn and grab Pherson by his bloodied pastel polo shirt. 'Where are they taking her?'

'She's going to get the medical attention she needs,' he says, his gaze on me softening. 'Ruby's going to be OK.'

I move to follow, but Pherson bars my way.

The only solid thing I trust in the entire world right now is wheeled out of sight.

'Ruby needs me,' I plead.

'Really? Does she need another finger amputating?' he asks dryly.

The comment punctures my already shaky confidence and all the fight flows out of me.

He's right, Ruby doesn't need me.

I need her...

...and she needs a doctor.

'Let's get you up to your room,' Pherson says gently.

I don't trust him, I don't like him and, as soon as I find my parents, we're getting Ruby and doing a runner.

We walk through a room full of small round tables set up with plates and champagne glasses. Every wall we pass is filled with weapons from days gone by: displays of swords, axes and brutal-looking blades that I think actually might be ancient farming equipment.

The sight reminds me that the guy who owns this mansion is one of my dad's survivalist friends, from his online group where they share tips on surviving different apocalypses.

Everything gleams, as if somebody stopped cleaning them seconds before we walked in. I guess there's no need for a discreet cellar like Dad's if you live on your own. In a mansion. Why not hang your weapons on the wall for ease of access?'

With Pherson dismissing people from our group as we move through the house, by the time we walk up a grand set of wooden stairs, a runner of deep red carpet flowing down the centre, there's only Pherson, the main camera operator and two other camera people left, all three with their lenses trained on me.

Above us, a stuffed orangutan hangs from a chandelier. It's kind of horrible and kind of fascinating. Sort of like mine and Ruby's current situation, I guess.

'The old fella who owns the house is a bit of an eccentric old so-and-so,' Pherson explains as we make our way under it. 'He assures me all the taxidermy is Victorian and above board.'

I look at the orangutan, at the sad expression in her eyes, and I'm not sure *above board* is quite how I would describe it.

'We've moved as much of it out as we can safely get to, but with the cost of the chandelier, it being over the staircase, and health and safety, etcetera, we left the ape. No one can work out how he got it up there in the first place. We're keeping all cameras angled downwards anyway, so no one will see it.' Pherson is chattering his way around the house and I get the bizarre impression that he's nervous.

'*I* can see her,' I say.

'No, I mean the public streaming online. We can't be seen to be agreeing with that sort of thing.'

'What about exploding sheep?' I ask.

He doesn't answer, so I try for a simpler question, one that's been bothering me.

'How did you know we were heading here? You've got this place set up as a sort of HQ, but you couldn't have known this would be where we were going before everything started. It was Dad's idea.'

'Ah, yes. It was a little tricky,' says Pherson, positively glowing with joy to explain more. He addresses the cameras and I know the explanation is not solely for my benefit. 'We were set up to lead the project from a studio originally, but as soon as this destination was mentioned, we made a deal with the owner and moved all our gear here.' He beams. 'It adds an element of class to the whole affair, don't you think?'

He doesn't leave room for me to answer.

'So it's from here we tracked all the feasible routes you might take, set up potential roadblocks, etcetera, as we went. We got you down to the canal because it's easier to clear than any other route. You did surprise us with the cut-through at the fence when you left the canal boat. Took us a little while to regroup after that . . .'

The memory of the blissfully zom-free time we had on the walk to the train carriage ignites a flicker of satisfaction that we broke out of his control, even if it was only for a short time.

'Thankfully Harry and Kim took the same abandoned shortcut.

Fortunately neither of you bumped into anyone off-set, and you both headed for the same place.' He shakes his head. 'More happy accidents.'

'So the trains weren't cancelled? We could have been squished!'

'But you weren't. And anyway, it all led to The Big Night in the train carriages. After that, views exploded. Keeping the fans away became a major headache . . .' Unaware of my actively growing hatred towards him, Elroy Pherson jabbers on. 'But the merch has been flying out and money rolling in.'

Pherson stops at a door and rests his hand on the gold knob, a tide of seriousness crashing over his cheerful persona.

'There's a medical team waiting in your room to check you over and sort your burn and that cut on your hand. We're taking this all very seriously. We have a psychologist lined up to work with you over the next year, to make sure there are no . . .' he hesitates, '. . . long-term repercussions. Really, Nora, don't worry, I'm going to take good care of you.'

This feels like an opportunity to appeal to his softer side. I try to make my eyes all big and innocent. 'I just want to see my parents,' I say, pushing out my lip into a wobbly pout.

He glances along the corridor ahead of us, then catches himself and looks back at me. I scrutinise his face. Was that a clue? Are they down there?

He sighs. 'You'll see them tomorrow.' He opens the door. 'This is your room.'

'Dr Glover, Nurse Payne, I'd like to introduce you to your patient, Nora.'

Two women, one in a white coat, the other in a nurse's uniform, sit on chairs beside a large four-poster bed in a room that looks like something an old king or queen might have slept in. My eyes linger at the soft plumpness of the duvet.

Pherson checks his fancy-looking watch.

'It's six o'clock now, there'll be food delivered soon.' He waves away the camera people. 'You're all done for now.'

The second the cameras stop pointing at me, every muscle in my body relaxes just a little.

'Have a rest tonight,' Pherson says, his focus back on me. 'Make-up and breakfast will happen before we start tomorrow's *grand finale*.'

Despite my relief at no longer being filmed, this all still feels so wrong. I step away from the doorway. 'I don't want to be left alone with two strangers. Can't I go in with Ruby? Or my parents?'

A sharp digital ringtone slices the moment in two.

'You'll be fine,' Pherson says hurriedly, reaching into his back pocket. 'There's a bathroom through there and fresh clothes in the wardrobe. Let the doc fix you up and take some time to rest.'

He puts his phone up to his ear. 'Tell me some good news.' He waits. 'Boom! That's the amount we needed.' He takes a deep breath. 'This has to work.'

Elroy turns to me and gives me an encouraging smile before tilting his chin to the room. I walk in and he shuts the door behind me. Part of me is surprised when there's no click. I wait a few seconds before trying the door. It's not locked.

Of course it's not. I'm not a prisoner, just a victim.

Chapter 35

WITH A QUICK GLANCE AROUND THE ROOM, I take in the heavy golden fabrics, fancy gilt everything and all the twiddly bits.

The doctor and the nurse watch me eerily. Saying nothing, just watching. Something Pherson said comes back to me, and I wonder if this is part of the set-up.

'Nurse Pain? Really?'

She has a sweet face and a caring smile.

'I'm afraid so. It's P-a-y-n-e, though, not P-a-i-n. If you don't mind, we'd like to make sure the events of the past few days haven't taken too much of a toll on you and your health.'

'I'd like to wee, brush my teeth and shower first. In that order,' I say.

'Of course,' says the doctor. 'It's great that you want to do those things, shows a lot about your mental state.'

They both continue watching me expectantly. I realise I've been hugging the tube of Jayden's gram's ashes since we left the garage and set them on a dressing table in front of me on my way into the small but welcoming bathroom, and shut the door.

Privacy.

It's softly lit, and clean. Scents of flowers waft around me as I sit on the loo for a wee. I rest my elbows on my knees, bury my face in my grubby hands and heave a weighty sigh.

Even when I've finished weeing, I stay where I am.

Thinking.

About everything and nothing all at once.

My thoughts are like someone is trying to bake an elaborate cake with the contents, constantly adding new ingredients and whisking it all together.

Mmm, cake.

My stomach makes a high-pitched noise that says it's beyond empty.

A toothbrush, toothpaste and wash stuff line a small white cabinet beside the sink. Everything is brand new and calling to me.

I extract my battered sketchbook from my back pocket before peeling off the clothes I've worn for days of battling zoms and untying the fabric from my hand. Shit, it hurts!

Once I've moved all the toiletries I need onto the edge of the bath, I turn on the shower. The water comes out of the huge round head at a perfect temperature and I turn it up to close-on scolding.

The water hitting my skin and working its way in rivulets through my hair to my scalp is amazing. For a time, I stand with my head down and watch the water swirl brownish red around my feet, as days' worth of gore rinses away.

DREAM WASHSTAND

All Animal-Friendly & Refillable ...Of Course!

- Soul Cleanser
- Anti-Trauma Scrub
- Bisexual Confidence Lotion
- Just Plain Deodorant For Post-Apocalypse Stink
- 'In Love With Your Best Friend But You Cut-Off Her Finger' Guilt Relief Shampoo & Conditioner

Ignoring the sting from my injuries, I use a loofah to scrub and scrub and scrub at every part of me, even the grazes, to get the gravel out, wanting this shower to put distance between what has happened to us and whatever will happen next.

All the washing products are the poshest and most yummy, making me smell like strawberries, vanilla, sandalwood, patchouli and some things I can't even pronounce. I brush my teeth with my head under the stream of water, eyes closed and wishing Ruby was here.

Well, not *here* here, but not apart . . . though it would be fun to have her *here* here, like in the shower. Then I remember the look in Ruby's eyes when the journalist twisted my words.

My brain's a mess.

I try to focus on something solid: Mum and Dad are here somewhere. First thing I need to do is find them.

Reluctantly, I finish my shower and get out to use one of the fluffiest towels known to humanity. Warmth glows off my skin and comforts me, until I see my pile of clothes festering in a heap on the tiled floor. My skin crawls at the idea of putting them back on.

Cold air swirls round the bathroom when I open the door a crack, letting the steam escape into the bedroom. I poke my head through.

The nurse and doctor turn towards me.

'Can you not look? I need to find some clothes.'

'Of course,' the doctor says.

With both of them looking in the opposite direction, I run wet-footed to the wardrobe and open it.

'Oh. My. God.' I breathe the words. I'm not sure what I expected, but not this. It's all my own clothes. But not. The T-shirts are the same, same bands but different tours. Same movies but different posters. The jeans are the same brands and cut as mine. It's weird, like they'd got my clothes out of my wardrobe at home and waved a magic wand to make them all new again. With labels and everything.

Creepy as it is, at least it makes the decision easy. I pull on a pair of pants, the baggiest jeans there, and a bra. The T-shirts are smaller than mine. Instead of my usual Large or Extra Large, the labels on these read Medium; annoying mistake for them to make.

I skip over several of my B-movie faves and choose a black-and-white Rocky Horror T-shirt. The clothes are stiff, missing the comforting softness that comes from being washed a million times.

Fully dressed and feeling considerably better for being clean, I shut the wardrobe door that I've been using as a screen between myself and the strangers in the room.

'Are you ready?' one asks.

'I think I might be,' I say, and even manage a semi-sincere smile.

The check-over is almost painless. The light in the room changes over the time they monitor my vitals, ask questions about how I'm feeling, and tend to my cuts, scrapes and the burn from the hob. When out and running for our lives, it all hurt considerably less, but they give me painkillers that take the edge off.

Fortunately, the gash in my hand doesn't have glass in and isn't deep enough to have done any serious damage. Butterfly plasters to hold the wound closed and some antiseptic cream is all it needs.

'Will Ruby be OK?' I ask the nurse, as she winds my hand in a clean white bandage. 'I cut her finger off.'

'This whole thing got out of hand,' Nurse Payne says before making aggravated clucking noises. 'They have a surgeon in to work on her. There was mention of trying to put the finger on ice and sew it back on, until you ran it over with the tractor.'

I cringe. 'I should have known it wasn't real.'

'The debriefing is designed to help you understand where reality stopped and technology stepped in, hopefully giving you some sense of closure.'

'Oh shit! The person I hit around the head, before we went into the garage . . .' My blood turns to ice in my veins.

'. . . was a robot with a head full of meat, I'm happy to say. They saw how you were behaving and stopped allowing real actors close to you,' says the doctor. 'However, the one that bit Ruby was a robot, so it wasn't a perfect plan.'

Her words thaw my innards. I haven't killed or maimed anyone.

I lay back and let them finish their tests.

Once I'm certified healthy and fit as a mildly emotionally scarred fiddle, and they've made sure I've at least picked at a balanced meal, they leave me alone on the bed, dozing. Well, that's what I want them to think.

I give a pretty convincing performance of a teen pooped out from a long few days running from zoms, but the truth is every nerve in my body is on fire with agitation. The ickity feeling under my skin that everything about this situation is not right, keeps me fired up and ready for my next move.

Admittedly, I might have lay in the big snuggly bed for an extra minute or two longer than is absolutely necessary before I spring up and pull on box-fresh high-tops from the wardrobe. They fit perfectly. I'm totally keeping these puppies.

At the door I open it far enough to know there's no one directly outside. A quick peek left and right shows the way's clear. I launch out and run as speedily and soundlessly as I can in the direction Pherson glanced when I mentioned my parents earlier.

The corridor is long and I pass door after door, all left ajar and showing rooms full of filming equipment or camp beds laid out in rows. It's from behind the first shut door I pass that I hear Mum's voice. The sound's muffled, but it's definitely her.

My parents are so close!

Hand trembling with anticipation, I try the door handle. It turns easily and I charge through, desperate to see them again.

I'm so ready for a warm and gloriously human embrace, that I'm thrown by the cold and inhuman wall of technology that greets me on the other side of the door. My eyes and brain take a moment to agree on what I'm seeing.

My parents aren't in the room, they're in one of many tiny windows on a large screen set amongst an impressive editing suite of tech. The monitors look like a security surveillance set-up, showing different people and places all at once, in a grid filling the screen.

Their window is highlighted and I see them in a strange space made up of empty stalls.

Mum reads through a stack of papers, biting her nails. 'He's got a clause in this for everything, even to restrict our movements if our actions put the project at risk.' Since when did she ever bite her nails? 'Surely he must know this doesn't make it OK to lock people up!'

Dad shakes his head. 'All of this suggests Elroy's grasp on reality might not be very strong. Which is why I'm worried about this.' He crouches low to write an equation with his finger in the dirt on the floor. He stares at what he's written, before growling in frustration and rubbing it out with a sweep of his hand.

'You'll work it out,' Mum says, walking over to Dad and stroking his hair. 'We'll get out of here, find the kids, and go home soon. We just might have to play by Pherson's rules for a bit first.'

I watch my dad lean his head into the crook of my mum's arm, and their love in that moment fills me up. They're fixed!

'Elroy Pherson was a good kid when we were at school. I don't get why he would do all this.'

'Let's focus on getting Nora, Ruby and Jayden, then we can work everything else out after,' Mum says.

'I'm on my way,' I say softly and touch the monitor, wanting to be close to them. The window with my parents in pops out and triples in size with "HOUSE.CAM.45:STABLES" across the top.

Touchscreen!

I tap the other small windows, exploring the camera set-up. Several give different views of the main lobby of the house that we walked through earlier.

From a camera labelled "STAR.WARS.BAG.CAM", I see part of Ruby's bag, the camo survival pack, my cricket bat and Ruby's hockey stick, along with a couple of other bags I don't recognise, set on a blue carpeted floor.

There was a camera set into Ruby's Star Wars bag all along?!

It's surprising how sad this revelation makes me feel. All the times we thought we'd been alone . . . someone was watching.

The shock of deception deepens when I tap on footage from a

room I recognise and see it's the bedroom I've just left, the chairs for the doctor and nurse still pulled up beside the bed. The hair on the back of my neck raises: they're still watching us.

Thankful that at least there don't appear to be any bathroom cams, I tap over other windows on the monitor, looking for Ruby, suddenly needing to see her.

Tap. Tap. Tap.

There! Ruby looks so peaceful, asleep in a big fluffity bed, and the muscles clenched tight around my heart relax.

The camera is marked "HOUSE.CAM.21:GROUND.FLOOR.BEDROOM.3".

The sound icon has a small "x" over it. I tap it and Ruby's soft, comforting snores fill the room. I know where my parents are, know where Ruby is. Now I just need to get them.

A toilet flushes in the ensuite to my left, followed immediately by the door opening. A guy with black-rimmed glasses and a beanie hat, steps out.

'Hey, you can't be in here,' he says, making a move towards me.

'Ew, you so didn't wash your hands,' I say, dodging away from him, and in the second he takes to look down at the unwashed hands in question, I bolt out of the room.

NEW!

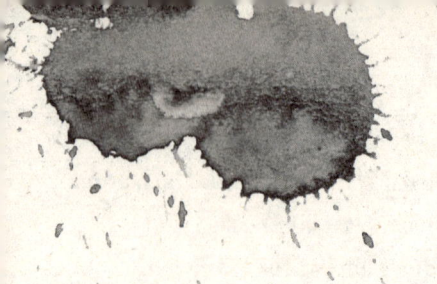

Chapter 36

OUT OF THE ROOM AND ALONG THE CORRIDOR, I clench my teeth and force tired, reluctant legs to kick out some energy. The effort makes me woozy and my head swim, so I grip tight to the banister and take each step as fast as I dare.

At the bottom of the stairs are three doors. I run straight through one, slamming it shut behind me, hoping it might throw off the guy if he's following. I cross the next room, full of ancient riding gear, to an outer door.

Well, that's promising.

Outside, the stables are right in front of me. Where was this luck when I was with Ruby and Jayden?

I take a second to breathe in the cool evening air and a security guard walks close by. I throw myself into the shadows of a woodpile leaning against the back wall of the stables, catching my elbow on landing. To hide my involuntary yelp, I slam my hand to my mouth, crouching low.

As soon as she rounds the corner, I dash out and try each door leading into the stables. With a hard tug on the last one, I'm forced to accept that perhaps my luck has run out.

What was I thinking? Of course Mum and Dad would have tried them already.

I huff in frustration before scooting around the building, back to my trusty log pile. Trying not to think about potentially snapped ankles, I wobble my way up to a barred window that is just a bit too high for me to see in.

'Mum? Dad?' I whisper, clutching the bars and scrabbling my feet up the wall, trying to peer in.

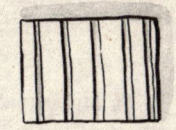

'Nora?' is the whispered reply.

Familiar hands reach up to hold mine where they grip the bars. The small amount of energy I have left drains out and the super new trainers slide down the wall until I'm standing on my tippy toes. I can't see my parents, but I can hear them, and the touch of their hands on mine gets my throat hurting and eyes leaking.

'Oh, Nora,' my mum says, hearing me sniffle. 'We're here, love.'

'It's all right, Nor,' Dad says soothingly. 'Where's Ruby?'

'Ground Floor Room 3,' I answer automatically. 'I thought we could get her and go, but I can't even get you.'

'Your mum and I have a plan to get away tomorrow.' I can tell by Dad's voice that he's trying to sound hopeful.

'This is all so messed up,' I say, using my arm to wipe the tears from my eyes.

'Hmmm,' my dad grumbles. 'Truth is, I think it's more messed up than we thought.'

'Hang on,' I hiss, hearing footsteps approaching behind me. In a couple of seconds, I'm tucked into the shadowy corner again. I hardly breathe as two other high-vised members of the security team walk past.

'I really wasn't expecting a bloody shark!' one says to the other.

'I know, weirdest job ever, right?' the second says.

'You're not kidding.'

The second they pass, I'm back on the woodpile.

'Mum, Dad?'

'Nora!'

'What do you mean "more messed up than we thought"?' I ask, not sure I want to know the answer. 'This is already pretty fucked up.'

'Nora!' Dad gasps, and I know it's only because Mum's there. We swear in front of each other all the time.

'No, Harry, I think she's right. How else would you describe the fact that we're locked in a stables, talking to her through a barred window after fighting pretend zombies?'

Is that really my mum in there? I scrabble at the side of the wall, trying to get high enough to see my parents' faces.

'You're right,' Dad says. 'Anyway, Nor, we managed to get some blood from one of the people attacking us.'

'One of the zombie actors,' Mum clarifies.

'Well, yes.' Dad's voice is rumbling with thought. It's been a while since I've heard him this pensive. 'That's the thing, their blood showed something viral that would explain their behaviour. I've almost found a way to stabilise it, but something's missing.' I can hear his cogs whirring. 'We set out to get a second blood sample.'

'We cornered one of the sick, but when we tried to extract the blood, we couldn't. The needle kept breaking, then the skin tore to reveal it was a sort of robot.' Mum's voice is overflowing with all the emotions appropriate to the completely bizarre situation.

'That was when we were *brought in*,' Dad adds.

I can't help but marvel at the two of them seamlessly overlapping their words, one picking up where the other leaves off, and vice versa, working as a team in every way.

'Naturally we fought,' Mum says. 'We wanted to get you lot back. But the harder we fought, the more security they threw at us, until they tossed us in here and locked the door.'

'Apart from being locked in here, they're treating us very well. I just don't think Elroy wants us ruining his plans.' Dad takes a deep breath. 'But he did mention a drug he's given the actors, and that's where I think this thing's going squirrelly. It looks like something in the drug is acting like a virus. We almost had everything we needed to create a vaccine.'

I shake my head to clear it.

'Dad, the zoms aren't real.' The trauma of everything going on must have gotten to him. So much for them helping me get Ruby away from here. I might need Ruby to help me get them out instead. 'They were acting and we don't need a vaccine. We need to get away from here. Pherson's seriously freaking me out.'

'I know, it's bad, but I've been reading through the paperwork he's kindly provided.' I remember Mum poring over a chunk of papers when I saw her on the screen earlier. 'He thinks he has us wrapped up tight. If we go along with it for now, it might help us get away.'

'Nor, it's getting late,' Dad says, and that's when I notice the light is nearly gone from the day. 'One thing I know for sure is that Elroy doesn't want to hurt us. So, you're safe to get some food and rest. Stay on Elroy's good side until we can work out a way out of here. At the very latest, we'll all be together for Pherson's grand finale.'

'I don't want to go.' I grab at my parents' hands and hold them tight.

'We love you, Nora,' Mum says.

'You're being so strong,' Dad adds. 'Find Ruby and stick together, you two are a great team.'

A mini montage plays in my mind of kissing Ruby, then her looking away after the reporter said I was pretending, and finally, her on the monitor in the editing room, lying asleep in a big snuggly bed.

I know where I need to be.

'I love you,' I whisper to my parents.

'Love you, too,' they both say and it reminds me so much of when I was young, before they drifted apart, that I have to swallow a lump in my throat. I duck down to miss another pass of the security team and sneak back into the house to find Ruby and fix whatever's going on with us.

What's a missing finger, a few stolen kisses and an accusation that one of us was pretending to be attracted to another, between friends?

We're stronger than that.

I hope.

Chapter 37

TRYING TO FIND THE BEDROOMS ON THE GROUND floor is harder than I thought. I pass through a door into a narrow corridor I'm pretty sure even the owner of the manor would have trouble finding. A room ahead has the door open a crack, allowing some lurking light to creep into the darkness.

Ruby could be in there.

Slowly inching forwards to investigate, the boom of Pherson's voice ahead makes me stumble to a halt.

'What?! But it has to be fixed.' Pherson sounds close to tears. The next time he speaks, anger hardens his tone. 'You said you could if I got you the money. It's going live on the market tomorrow! I'll lose everything. After I developed the original compounds, you promised your biochemical formula could fill the gaps! I've gambled everything on this!' By the end, his anger breaks into pleading and he sounds like an executive toddler.

Curious who he's talking to, I sneak forwards, treading carefully not to make a sound.

'Elroy, I honestly don't understand. The science behind the fat-eater pills is sound.' The second voice is thin. 'Its success rate far exceeds the fat-trappers and the fat-burners already on the market—'

'—except it's making people behave like zombies, for Christ's sake,' Pherson finishes. 'People will suffer extreme bloating, constipation or even diarrhoea to control their weight, but they won't pay for this. AND because you insist on growing part of it inside those fish, I've got animal rights activists crawling all over me.'

I peek into the room and catch sight of a small office decorated with all the leather, and unhappy-looking taxidermy birds staring out of glass boxes. The back of Pherson's head blocks part of a screen showing a man wearing a lab coat and a strained expression. When he speaks next, I duck away.

'The incubation period of the bacteria inside the shark's uterus has been integral to the development of the active ingredients—'

'I don't want to hear about the technicalities of the thing. That's what I'm paying you for.' Pherson's voice grows sharper and more threatening and I know I shouldn't be here. I fight the urge to run, forcing myself to tiptoe silently back along the corridor.

'We need to get this thing working. I'm continuing as planned, we go live with it tomorrow,' he continues.

'You can't—' the man begins.

'The wheels are in motion, the promo starts tomorrow. Maybe a little heat will get your grey cells fired up. You guaranteed me that with the extra money you could fix it. Guaranteed. I got you the extra money, now fix it!'

'It doesn't help that you've taken one of our newest specimens to have as a party piece,' the scientist throws in.

'No excuses,' Pherson says, and I use his next little speech as a chance to get out of that corridor. I run, without stopping, until I find myself at the place Ruby and I were separated.

I turn down the only route through the ground floor I haven't tried yet and am rewarded by loud saw-like snoring coming from behind one of four doors.

The ground floor bedrooms!

Through the confusion of what I just heard about Pherson's problems, I remember the room name above the live footage of Ruby sleeping that I'd seen in the editing room, HOUSE. CAM21: GROUND. FLOOR. BEDROOM. 3. I count three doors down and open it, carefully.

It's dark inside.

'Ruby?'

I step over the threshold, take a few steps and trip over a weighty lump on the floor. Arms flailing, I just about manage to keep myself upright, only to take my next step and trip over again. This time I grab hold of something cold and rubbery to keep myself from falling. Heebie-jeebies creep over me as I recognise the shape of fingers beneath my own and it dawns on me that I'm holding a human hand.

Throwing myself back towards the door, I hit a light-switch. Expecting to be grabbed at any moment, I turn and see Jayden sitting in a chair.

'Shit, Jayden!' I hiss, my skeleton almost leaping out of my skin. 'You scared the shit out of—'

He's not moving. I walk closer, to see clouded eyes staring sightlessly ahead and familiar wounds marking his face and neck.

Zom-Jayden.

Next to me is a mound of very familiar items: the camo pack, the Star Wars bag, along with other bags and equipment looking equally as battered as ours, and there, leaning against it all, are my cricket bat and Ruby's hockey stick. The things I tripped over in the dark. I grab the cricket bat and swing it over my shoulder, ready to let it fly, waiting for Jayden to attack. Seconds tick by, allowing my brain to catch up.

There're no zoms.

It's not real.

This is an animatronic.

It takes seeing the remote control to really make it hit home, it's so real.

The sense of heebie-jeebies hasn't fully left me as I lift its hand and move it. It's stuck in a clawing shape with a single movement at the wrist and elbow. The texture's rubbery to touch and close up, though it's pretty good, it's less convincing the more I examine it.

Lifting and releasing the wrist, looking at the make up of the skin and the way it moves, the scale of everything going on crashes down on me and I look around the room, knowing there's a camera in here somewhere, and not just the one built into the Star Wars bag.

The cameras are in every room, though I didn't see any hallways on the surveillance screen.

SURVEILLANCE:
BIG & SINISTER

OR: SMALL & SNEAKY? (*STILL SINISTER)

I drop robot-Jayden's hand and duck out, desperate to be off-camera. In the corridor, I weigh up not wanting to be filmed against wanting to see Ruby. I'm pretty sure they won't throw me out, but I can guarantee they'll be recording, and possibly broadcasting, anything we talk about.

It's something I have to get over, because not seeing Ruby is not an option, and I am already heading to the opposite end of the corridor, hoping the doors are numbered the other way.

I try again.

One. Two. Three.

Can she forgive me for cutting off her finger?

I take a deep breath and open the door.

'Ruby?' I call and step inside.

Heavy curtains are pulled closed and a lamp, with a stained-glass shade, on the bedside table streaks blue and turquoise light around the darkened room.

Once my eyes adjust, I make out the compact figure lying in the middle of an enormous bed. Her left hand is properly bandaged, and she's washed too.

I recognise a clean version of her favourite super-baggy Fat Wreck Chords tee she always sleeps in. I notice they didn't feel the need to downsize her baggy tops. And clean hair – where it would normally be gelled at the front, it's fluffy and droops across her forehead.

She's asleep with no make-up on and I realise she must have been reapplying mascara, eyeliner and hair product throughout our zom escape run. Were they hidden away in her Star Wars bag? She looks softer without it.

'Rubes?' I whisper.

She snuffles mid snore.

In here, with Ruby, I feel safe. Some of the panic that's been building in my chest since they led her away calms. I lie down stiffly beside her, arms at my side and feet together, so close to the edge of the bed that I might fall off.

She rolls over and half wakes up.

'Oh, hey, Nor.' Her voice is thick and gluey. I spot a stack of pills on her bedside table.

'Hey.'

'Apparently I'm a gay icon,' she says, eyelids at half-mast.

'You've always been a gay icon to me.'

'I'm glad you're here.' She puts her arm around me, her bandaged hand carefully placed on my chest, and seconds later, her little snores fill the air again.

Her touch acts like a balm on my aching soul.

'I'm sorry,' I whisper. 'I should have known it wasn't real.'

Chapter 38

A SOFT MORNING HAZE GENTLY WAKES ME OUT of the most peaceful sleep I've had in days. Not wanting to wake Ruby, I ease myself off the soft bed and pull the curtains back to reveal the extensive grounds of the manor house laid out beyond the large sash window.

I slide it open to let some fresh air in. The smell of breakfast butties from food vans set up outside are carried in on the wind, making the empty cavern that is my stomach growl. I wrap my arms around it and promise I'll eat something soon.

The festival of people we saw when we first got here has grown. There are thousands of them now, along with the food vans and small stalls set up under gazebos. Most of the crowd are pressed against the barriers surrounding the perimeter of the grounds. I can just make out that some of them are wearing T-shirts with Ruby, me or Jayden on, and there are even a few with Mum and Dad's faces. Placards announcing statements like "*Nora and Ruby For ever*" or "*Bring Back Jayden*" are waved cheerfully. The hugest banner, held by a group of women with hearts painted on their faces, reads "*We love you, Harry!*"

I laugh out loud. Dad will love that.

Ruby yawns and stretches snoozily.

'So, it was all a dream?' she asks, voice still heavy with medication.

'Not quite. We should find out more later. Your family's coming home soon. I think the competition they won was part of all this, to get them out the way.'

Ruby pulls the duvet over her head and her next question comes out muffled.

'So, were you pretending?' Her words mirror the reporter's.

So, you were pretending?

She looks out of the mountain of crisp white cotton with wet eyes and a wobbling chin. 'You're off the hook now, we don't have to repopulate the planet together any more.'

'Rubes . . .' I walk over, find her unbandaged hand in the folds of duvet and lean forwards. But before I can whisper – for her, and only her, to hear – that everything the reporter said was crap, that I'm so sorry I cut her finger off and that, if she'll still have me, I would happily repopulate the planet with her, the bedroom door swings open.

'Morning, Ruby! Rise and shine,' says a gangly girl walking in backwards, holding a tray loaded with orange juice, milk, cereals and pastries. 'Nora!' she shrieks when she sees me. 'They didn't tell me you were in here too! Dickheads.' Her eyes skip to the top righthand corner of the room and back again. I remember seeing Ruby on the monitor and know from the angle of the shot that the camera's up there somewhere, watching. She looks between the two of us. 'Wait! Did you spend the night?' There's a beat of awkward silence. 'Oh-My-Geeeee! You totally did. I HAVE to catch up on the latest episodes of the show, I've been working all night.'

'Erm . . . who are you?' I ask.

'I'm a HUGE fan.' The words erupt from her like a burst pipe. 'I'm interning at Grave Digger Productions and got to see the process of putting together Dead Real, and I think you and Ruby are, like—' she speaks so fast, waving her hands about as she does, '—so fucking great!'

I frown at her.

'Ruby, you're like super cute and super hardcore and Nora, when you threw your fists around, like, OH MY GOD. I CAN'T EVEN—'

'Thank you?' I don't know if that is the right response, but as soon as it's out, I regret it. She seems to take it as permission to keep talking.

'I'm *Team Norby* all the way! I have some friends who are *Team Jaydora*, but screw those guys, right? But now you're here, I HAVE to ask; Nora, are you lesbian, bi or what? Everyone is DYING TO KNOW. There are bets running. After the news piece yesterday, loads of people are saying you're straight and were just pretending?'

What?! The room is suddenly too hot and too small and my T-shirt's getting soggy under the armpits. A trickle of sweat runs down my back.

'I have no idea who you are,' I say, shakily. 'But I'm pretty sure it's none of anyone's business.'

'I think it's some of my business,' Ruby says.

I whip round to Ruby, my chest aching with all the things I would tell her if we were alone. 'I don't want to talk about this with an audience.'

'Sounds like you're avoiding the question to me,' the intern says, holding her phone out to film. I keep my eyes on the only person that matters.

'Ruby,' I plead, needing her to understand. 'Please don't ask me to talk about this here.'

Ruby's eyes are sad again. 'She's talking about *Team Jaydora*? Like, Jayden and Nora? So, you were *just pretending*.' A tear breaks loose from her lashes.

I take a step forwards.

How does it feel to find your big coming-out moment has had 4.3 million views in the last hour? The reporter's words fill my brain and my ears pump to the rhythm of my heart, pounding like I've got a hoard of zoms on my tail.

'No, Ruby,' I say. The room's spinning, or is it my head? 'There's nothing going on.' I lick my lips and look at the hidden camera. How many people are watching now?

My fumbling for the words to let Ruby know that I'm *Team Norby* – but it should be *Team Rubora*, because she's always first in my thoughts, though they both sound equally stupid – is interrupted by a click from the intern's phone.

Has she just taken a selfie?

'Ruby, I've come to look at your dressings and see how you're getting on.' A nurse steps into the room, then looks from me, to the intern, to Ruby. 'You really shouldn't all be in here. Ruby needs to rest.'

And that's all the encouragement I need. Desperate to get away, I push through the open doorway and run away from Ruby Rutherford, something I never imagined doing.

There are so many similarities in the emotions firing through me now as the day I ran out of the accessible loo, leaving Baxter sprawled on the floor in the O2 Academy. Am I destined to leave a trail of damaged people behind me?

My feet carry me around a couple of corners and up the stairs, past people looking busy and important. I don't stop running until I'm back in my room.

Inside, I find a breakfast tray on the table and I'm filled with relief that I won't have to see that intern again anytime soon.

I flop onto my unrumpled bed and stare at the ceiling.

I know how I feel about Ruby and I really thought Ruby did too.

Apparently, I was wrong.

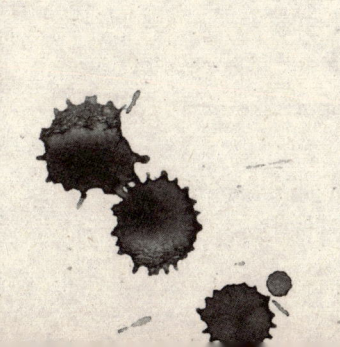

Chapter 39

ALL OF THIS IS PHERSON'S FAULT. IF WE HADN'T met him that day at college, Ruby and I would be pratting about, having a laugh as always. Going to see live music, watching cheesy horror movies and getting excited about university.

Instead, we've been running for our lives, exploding sheep and cutting off fingers.

We need to get away from Pherson.

A knock on my door disturbs a particularly good plot to break my parents out using a hefty vehicle to yank out the bars from one of the windows in the stable block.

'What?!' I shout, finding that everything about this morning has put me in a grim mood and I half want a zom to attack just so I can rip its head off. Or Pherson, and I'll do my best at ripping *his* head off.

But when a head does pop into view, I have no urge to rip it off at all.

'Nora?' It's a young lady with smooth brown skin, bright green eyes, long white locks and a nose ring. She's smiling kindly at me. 'I'm here to do your make-up for the show finale.'

'I'm not doing it.' I want to sound stern and in control of my life, but I'm completely aware that I sound more like a bratty child trying to get their way.

The lady's eyes are sad, and she heaves a gentle sigh.

'You're right. I get it. I'm not sure what we imagined would happen, we each just did our roles as best we could. Each of us focused on our art and didn't even consider the effects it would have on you. I'd be pissed off too.'

'Yeah, I'm pissed off.' I try to stay angry, but the fight drains out of me. She's being so annoyingly understanding. 'It was messed up.'

She looks relieved I'm not shouting now. 'I kind of think even Elroy only half expected this bat-shit plan to work,' she says. 'So he's just excited he pulled it off.'

'This is my life. You can't stick zombies in it and stream it online for people's entertainment. And now complete strangers are acting like they can bet on aspects of it that are none of their business.'

She walks further into the room, wheeling a massive toolbox behind her.

My eyes go wide.

'What's that?' It's red and shiny; Ruby would love it.

'My make-up kit.'

'It's massive!'

'Bet you say that to all the girls.' She laughs. 'Someone said you want to study make-up at uni?'

'As part of a special effects course, learning make-up with latex and prosthetics and stuff. Not normal make-up.'

'They teach you both on the best courses.'

'I've been accepted onto a course at the Northern Art School,' I say, sad that some of the shine has been taken away from it with everything I've been through. Though the Jayden animatronic was awesome – it was brilliant to see how they saved money using a fixed hand and putting the movement into the wrist.

'That's great!' She smiles. 'I worked on the team that designed the zom-bots, as we called them, and helped to transform the actors.'

I cross my arms and put on the same disinterested face I save for Mum's lectures on our body being our temple and how I shouldn't shove crap food into my temple, just because I'm bored or stressed, or both. But I can't keep my treacherous features convincingly stern. I have too many questions.

'How long have you been working in SFX?'

'Since I left uni. I got an internship to work with SFX Animatronix Ltd and made myself so useful they couldn't bear to let me go ... which is a great segue to this.' She pulls a crisp white envelope from the top of the toolbox and offers it to me.

'What is it?' I ask warily.

'They want to offer *you* an internship. A chance to pick up some industry know-how. It's basic tea and coffee, delivery and collection stuff ... but it's a foot in the door.'

A muffled ringing fills my ears as I tear at the paper to reveal some impressive graphics heading an official-looking offer letter – with a thankfully un-suspicious amount of small print.

This is it!

This is how people break into the industry!

I've read about it a million times. My heart flickers with excitement and, just like that, the dream I'd thought had abandoned me is back. This would give me and Rubes a major headstart in the SFX world.

I think of the gangly girl interning for the production company and know we would do a much better job than her.

I'm lost in the warm, familiar daydream of working alongside Ruby to bring all the creations we've talked about to life, when the lady clears her throat politely.

'Are you OK to sit?' She pulls the chair the doctor used over to the dressing table with Jayden's gram's ashes on. I want to say no, but her smile is too kind.

'I'm Clarity,' she says.

'I'm Nora,' I reply automatically.

She laughs. 'I know.'

And everything I'd briefly forgotten comes back in a horrible whoosh. Of course she knows my name.

'Can I ask something?' I venture.

'Anything.' She pauses part way through unpacking her rolling toolbox.

'Pherson streamed us on YouTube, right?'

She nods.

'Did you watch any of it?'

'Everyone watched it.' She points out the window to the field full of people. 'Your fans.'

That doesn't help my churning stomach. 'Did I, you know, come across as a complete idiot-hole?'

She takes her phone out. It has one of those chunky bash-proof covers and is splattered in paint, and I wonder at what point I lost my own phone.

'You were both super cute.' She pulls up a video and presses play. On the screen, Ruby sits next to me on the roof of the train carriage, right before I help with her damaged bum cheek.

'Your friendship has been gorgeous to watch,' Clarity says softly.

My stomach twinges. The angles we're filmed from are odd,

but kind of cool. After a moment, I work out that the cameras must have been set in a tree and it switches to the one mounted in the front of Ruby's rucksack.

We're laughing and my heart aches at the sound of a happy Ruby. My favourite sound.

Watching, I see that Clarity's right. We are cute and I humph a heavily nostalgic sigh for when times were simpler, and we thought a pandemic had turned everyone into pseudo-zombies.

'Are you OK?'

'Things are weird between Rubes and me right now.'

'Yeah, it's been on the socials.'

'What?!'

'Everyone loves you as a couple. And, because your first kiss was shot with night vision, and the second with a thermal heat cam, 'cause you were under a sleeping bag, the country is waiting for your first unfiltered kiss to be captured.'

'That really doesn't help.' I tug my fingers through my hair, frowning.

'I'm just saying, you've got a lot of support.'

'From strangers. Who've been making bets on us.'

There's an awkward beat of silence before Clarity rallies to keep the conversation hopeful.

'Anyway, tonight's event should be epic, and there's nothing like a good party to fix everything.' She scoops up a handful of her locks and throws them over her shoulder. 'Now sit here and your fairy godmother will teach you some useful make-up skills, while we get you ready for the ball.'

'Not too much make-up,' I say, shrinking away.

'I got you, you rock the natural look.' She stands in front of me.

Clarity is a peaceful person and, by some sort of social osmosis, I find myself relaxing. She talks through techniques while attempting to stop me having the face of someone who's been on the run for days without proper food, sleep or facilities.

'Thanks for going easy on our bots,' she says. 'We didn't have to do half the work we were expecting. As time went on, we replaced more actors with them, sure you were going to unleash seven kinds of hell with your cricket bat. But apart from Bob, you were incredibly restrained.'

'I didn't want to hurt anyone,' I say dumbly.

'You're sweet.'

'There was the one I smashed across the head.'

Clarity laughs. 'Yep, that's Bob. We knew he was going to take a beating, you'd been pushed too hard by then.'

I consider how I'd feel if someone smashed in the werewolf mask Ruby and I spent most of the summer building. 'I'm so sorry.'

Clarity shakes her head. 'Honestly, it's fine. Do you want to see how we made the pustules?'

When she's finished, she has zombified half of her own arm, noting down a list of make-up brands, products and techniques for me.

'You really should regard this whole thing as the great opportunity it is. Take on the internship.' She packs her stuff away. 'Most people would give their right arm for it.'

'Or a little finger?' I say, unable to keep my bitterness hidden.

'Yeah, that too.' She smiles sadly.

When Clarity lets me near the mirror, I see that I am transformed. It looks like I'm only wearing a bit of foundation and mascara, but my skin glows and my eyebrows appear naturally shapely ... which they definitely aren't.

'Just one last thing,' she says.

'Hmmm?' I can't take my eyes off my flawless twin in the mirror.

'Don't fight Elroy. He's thrown everything he's got into this and when things don't go his way, he can get pretty scary. His wife – you know the director Maria Garcia-Pherson?'

I shake my head.

'Anyway, she's big in the world of rom coms. She's called in all sorts of favours across the industry to get this together. I heard they're splitting and she's done this to help get rid of him quickly and quietly.'

I can empathise with any woman trying to get Pherson out of her life.

'There were a few times we thought you'd figured it out,' Clarity carries on chatting. 'When you mentioned the radio listening, everyone thought it was over before it even began! Earlier, your mum said about the new security system, that was when they bugged your home, and we were certain one of you would put two and two together. Then we had a glitching robot in the supermarket. But even with things going wrong, Pherson pulled it off! Everything's going to plan so far, except you.'

I don't know whether to feel proud or defensive.

'Which is extra hard for him because you've been his favourite all along. He has a set idea of how he wants this all to play out, and there's a promo side to it that I get the impression you're a big part of. I know you've been through a lot, Nora, but honestly, I'd grab hold of everything Elroy's offering you and think of it as compensation.'

'Thanks,' I say, appreciating the advice, but having no intention of taking it.

I don't want anything Pherson has to offer.

While Clarity finishes packing away her stuff, I drink cold coffee and eat cereal with warm milk to keep myself busy. When I'm done, I take to pacing the floor like a caged animal, trying to build up the courage to see Ruby again.

It's hard to do nothing but wait.

'Chill. You, Ruby and your parents will all be back together again at midday . . .' she checks her phone, '. . . in just shy of an hour.'

Then maybe we can bust out of this place, steal one of the fancy-looking cars outside, and drive off into the horizon.

'I'll be back to take you downstairs when it's time.' Clarity walks towards the door, wheeling her toolbox behind her.

After everything that's happened, suddenly the idea of being alone fills me with dread.

'Wait!' I take a step towards her.

Clarity's sparkling green eyes catch mine.

'Is everything OK?' she asks.

I take a deep breath. 'Could you wait with me, until it's time?'

'Yeah. Of course.' She smiles. 'You draw, right?'

I nod my head, too tense for words.

'You kept your sketches pretty well hidden, but the ones the cameras managed to capture were great. Want to draw now?'

My fizz of anger at the complete disrespect of my privacy is overtaken by a tired resignation, and knowing that right now, drawing would actually make me feel much better.

I nod again.

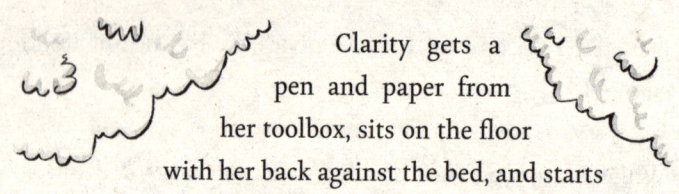

Clarity gets a pen and paper from her toolbox, sits on the floor with her back against the bed, and starts drawing. I fetch my sketchbook, sit beside her and lose myself in my own art until Clarity's phone peeps.

'It's time,' she says. 'You ready?'

I roll my battered visual diary up and tuck it into my back pocket.

'Born ready,' I say, trying to focus on my plan of grabbing the people I love and running, and completely ignoring the fact that whatever Pherson's got planned has my legs going wobbly.

SIMPLER TIMES ♡

Chapter 40

'**YOU'RE GOING TO DO GREAT,**' CLARITY SAYS, giving me a hug before leading me down the corridor towards the main staircase.

The cheer as I round the corner makes me stagger to a halt. A small crowd beside the screen and sofas in the manor's entryway clap and wave. I frown at the size of the crowd. 'Where did all the noise come from?' I ask.

'This is streaming live to the people outside,' Clarity whispers. 'They're hyped to see you.'

I descend the staircase, eyeing the open double doors, letting glorious sunlight pour in. They're obviously not worried about us running. I allow myself a small smile – that's good news for us.

'Nora!' Elroy Pherson is walking towards me, a grin pinching his cheeks, and his arms open wide. Any evidence of the panic and menace I'd heard during his conversation last night is gone.

The small crowd give another cheer, again accompanied by a far louder roar from the fields of people outside. I turn to see Ruby moving down the stairs towards us.

My breath catches. She looks so good, in a Bad Cop Bad Cop band tee, with the sleeves cut off and neckline slashed, above a short chequered kilt and long striped socks. Her hand is neatly bandaged, hair re-spiked and make-up done like it's a gig night.

My first instinct is to run to her, but her expression when she looks over stops me before I even take a step.

When she's closer, I raise my hand in a feeble wave. She flinches away and my organs suddenly feel too big to fit inside my ribcage.

'Isn't this a beautiful thing? Our fighters together again.' Pherson speaks loudly, looking at us and talking at us, but he isn't talking *to* us. He's talking to *them*. The people watching. 'Unfortunately, Harry and Kimberly couldn't join us as we'd previously planned.' He holds his jaw gingerly and moves it as though testing for damage.

'Wait, what?' The words erupt out of me. 'They're supposed to be here.'

'Due to,' he pauses, choosing his next words carefully, 'an *incident* this morning, I'm afraid they cannot be here physically – though they will, of course, be live-streamed in.'

With a sweep of his hand, Pherson directs our attention to the big screen now showing Mum and Dad. Together they look strong, like a solid unit, like I've never seen them before.

Mum has a bandage on her arm and Dad has a plaster on his cleanly shaven cheek. Both are wearing clean clothes. Dad's, like mine, look like he's had a wardrobe match too, but Mum's wearing a pair of jeans with a vest, topped off with one of Dad's shirts, tied at the waist with the sleeves rolled all the way up. They both look great, though, again, I notice nobody got their clothes sizes wrong. Just me and my T-shirts. Huh?

My parents' faces are set in hard lines and though they're on a plush-looking sofa, it's easy to see they're still in the stable block.

'Harry, Kimberly, nice of you to join us,' Elroy says, a strained edge to his voice.

Mum rushes forwards.

'Nora, Ruby! I'm sorry we can't be there with you.' Tears glisten on her eyelashes, blown up large on the screen. Real-life tears. I've never seen Mum cry before, and it's unsettling. 'I'm so glad you're both safe and in one piece,' she says.

'Ruby has a piece missing.' The words are out of my mouth before I can stop them.

Ruby holds up her bandaged hand with a gap where her pinkie should be. 'Only a small piece.'

Mum and Dad's eyebrows react to this information in two entirely unique ways. Mum's shoot up her head in shock, where Dad's lower slowly into a scowl of pure, undiluted fury.

Something's happened to him. He's a changed man, no longer apologetic and broken. He stands and storms around the space they're in, his shoulders broad, his height held full, and he looks menacing.

'There are loopholes in your paperwork, Pherson. I will take you down,' Mum says. Her dangerous business tone mixes with a growl.

'We spoke about this, Kimberly. I don't think you'll want to when you fully understand the commercial potential of your new situation. I've transformed you all into superstars.' He raises his hands at this and the crowds cheer.

Old Mum would have made some kind of indication towards this being a good thing, but the Mum on the screen looks like she's about to go zom on Pherson, to burst through the screen and eat his brains.

'I don't care about that,' Mum says. 'I care about keeping the people I love safe.'

Hang on a minute. Who is this woman?

'We were on top of damage control for the majority. A bot with a glitch bit Ruby's finger.' He waves his hands like he's waving away a minor error. 'You should be glad it ended when it did. Half the team wanted to let the girls get to the helicopter to find out whether they could fly the thing.' Pherson talks through his teeth, apparently determined to maintain his grin, but it's obvious this is not going the way he wanted it to.

Ruby raises her chin and steps forwards. 'We could totally fly it, there's not much you can't learn from online tutorials.'

'We've gone off track, ' Pherson interrupts, turning to the camera and beaming. 'Here we are, joined by *the big four*.'

Someone with an iPad and headset ushers Ruby and me towards one of the two sofas.

'First, we need to say thank you to our sponsors,' Pherson continues, 'who have made all this possible: Brenton and Son's Abattoirs and Lean Meat Solutions.'

'We're vegetarians!' I call out.

Pherson ignores me and announces the next sponsors. 'As well as Champer's Hampers, who are providing all the champagne and vol-au-vents for the evening . . .'

A cheer erupts from the crowd in the room, it's twice as loud as it had been before, and a line of people dressed in smart white shirts, black trousers and waistcoats, carrying trays of mini-foods and champagne flutes, emerge from a door to the right. They walk past the camera and offer their tray contents to us. I shake my head to both, my stomach already regretting the rubbish breakfast I ate earlier, while Ruby scoops up a champagne, downs it in one, and swaps it for another.

In front of where we stand, a monitor shows what's on the large screen behind. Each time Pherson announces a sponsor, a logo flashes up, with my parents looking on disapprovingly from a small window in the top right hand corner.

'And Grave Digger Productions and SFX Animatronix Ltd. Of course.' These get the biggest cheer, as people around us laugh and slap each other on the back. 'And finally, my own company, Global Innovations.'

'Now, back to our four fighters.' Pherson waves a hand towards us. We edge away until the green leather upholstery catches us behind the legs and we both plop onto the sofa. When Ruby realises how close she is to me, she shuffles away, making my throat pinch. I shouldn't have run away this morning, I should have stayed and talked. Now, when we could be working out how to escape, she won't even look at me.

'Let's fill them in on the scale of our little production.' Pherson laughs, seating himself on the opposite sofa. 'We used over 70 extras, 100 cameras and 25 fully remote-controlled animatronic zom-bots.' Pherson reels off the numbers.

I'm numb. This is all so surreal. His words come into and out of focus, much like the faces of the surrounding people.

'... give everyone a little peek ... the preproduction preparations ...'

The screen shows teams of people building zombie robots and making latex body parts. Processes I know well from watching a million *Making Of* videos.

The construction of the Jayden-bot I found earlier is shown and it gives me goosebumps.

We see Mrs Johnson laughing with Clarity as she builds the bite wound onto her neck.

Next, trial runs on animatronic zoms. Then another shot of one being pieced together, and one getting make-up. I recognise the last as the one that got Jayden, the Uber-Zom. And I'm surprised how much it hurts when I see it's Clarity working on her. The camera lingers on her until she stops, puts her arm around Uber-Zom and plants a kiss on its cheek.

I can't watch any more.

I'm on my feet, walking away from the screen. Pherson catches my arm in a painful pinch. 'Sit down,' he says through his teeth.

I shake my head. 'I've got to get out of here.'

Focusing on not vomiting, I yank my arm from his grasp and shove my way through the crowd.

'You've got five minutes,' he snarls behind me, his voice threatening.

I'm swallowing and swallowing, but my mouth's still filling with thin, stringy spit.

I need to find a loo.

Spinning and spinning and spinning, people block me everywhere I turn. I bump into them, moving like a pinball, bouncing between walls of humans until I finally find a door and push it open.

Vision blurring, I stumble across the room behind to the next door and push, then do the same.

I don't find a toilet, but thankfully this last door leads me to the outside and fresh air. A field full of people cheer when I emerge, and they cheer even louder when I bend over and puke in a rosebush.

BEFOULED ROSE

Chapter 41

TO HIDE FROM PRYING EYES, I CRAWL BEHIND the bush I just puked in and curl up small, wishing I had a toothbrush and a glass of water.

There's no way to tell how long I stay like that before someone comes by. The sound of their steps is almost like the beats of a song and I can imagine the dance in their movements. I know exactly who it is.

'Leave me alone. I never want to see you again,' I say.

He sits on the doorstep nearby.

'Harsh. You don't mean that.' Jayden peers around my private sicky bush for one, and a radiant smile lights his eyes when he spots me.

'No, I'm pretty sure I do. You allowed us to believe zoms had taken you away and devoured your insides.'

'Sounds way dramatic when you put it like that. You want some food? I grabbed some when no one was looking.'

He holds out a silver tray of small round puffs of pastry filled with white stuff and topped with tiny black, shiny balls. I frown.

'I think that black stuff's caviar,' I say, moving away from it. 'I'm veggie.'

'Fish eggs, right?' He shrugs. 'More for me.' He picks up two and pushes them both in his mouth, looking extremely chuffed with himself.

'It was "way dramatic",' I say, reminding him of our conversation, 'and traumatic.' I sniff back a bit of sick lodged in my nose tubes. 'You helped them trick us.' Stupid tears sneak out the corners of my eyes and trickle down my face.

'Easy now, I didn't know what was going on. They dragged me off the boat and replaced me with a robot jammed full of meat and stuff!'

He tilts his head down and gives me puppy dog eyes. And I'm ashamed to say, it's working.

'I saw my death scene, it looked crazy realistic. They said I can have the robot-me now it's all cleaned up. I'm going to sell it on eBay or something.'

'OK. That bit wasn't your fault, but then you followed the tractor.'

'That wasn't me, even though they wanted it to be. They were offering good money, so I agreed to a trial. They put make-up on me, gave me one of those weird-ass zombie pills and everything. But it was all wrong. When the effects wore off, I said there's no way, I'm not doing that to you two. So, they used the robot me instead. They wanted my second appearance sooner but, because it was a rush-build, the water gave it some glitches that took a while to fix and then it broke again pretty quickly.'

I lean across to give him a dead arm.

'Ouch! That genuinely hurt.'

'Good.' I climb carefully out of the bush, avoiding chunks of my breakfast hanging from some branches, and we sit side-by-side on the doorstep. 'That's for even thinking about tricking us.'

People at the fences across the way are chanting our names, but it's surprisingly easy to ignore them. The helicopter is harder to ignore, it had been the symbol of our escape and freedom as we ran for our lives.

I turn away to look at the garden in front of us. It's set up for a party: bobbing balloons and waving flags are printed with the same happy shark, with a heart on its tummy, from the tote bags we signed up for at the beginning of this whole warped adventure.

This time they have "*Global Innovation – Fat-Eater Diet Pills*" written underneath.

'They offered me some seriously serious money.' Jayden stands and points at something hidden behind a wall.

I move to see what he's pointing at and my eyes land on a shark tank almost as tall as me.

An actual shark tank.

With an actual shark in it.

'What the hell?' I walk over and press my face to the rounded glass to see the beautiful creature inside swimming round and round what is essentially a party pool with glass sides and some rocks in the middle. I don't know much about sharks, but I'm pretty sure *this* tank is too small for *that* shark, and the flashing, coloured LEDs set into the sides must be pissing it off too.

'The man's got enough money to bring a shark to a party. He must be spending mega money, and did I want to get in on that action?' He walks round to where some metal steps lead up to a small platform. He ducks under some unconvincing red-and-white plastic chain running across the steps to bar the way.

'Well, yes, I did.' Jayden continues. 'But what I said was "*No!*" I said, "*You know you're scaring the shit out of those girls?*" That Elroy guy was all like, "*Well, they've totally signed up for it.*" And I was all like, "*No one would sign up for this shit.*" And he was all like, "*Yeah, *they totally have, and I have the paperwork."* He explained it all to me, sounded legit. So I agreed to them using the bot later.' He scrubs at his hair.

I duck under the plastic chain and we climb the steps.

At the top, I look down into the tank before raising my eyebrows at Jayden. 'Pherson said "*Yeah, they totally have*"?'

'Well, not those exact words, but you get what I mean. Legally, you'd agreed. He also said you would be compensated for everything, and you had a hefty bit of money coming your way. So, I kind of figured that as I'd taken my fair share of the shit, some money should come my way too. Really, like man, I was fucking scared.'

'You were?' The sense of betrayal lessens.

The shark swims round and round and round. It's not a massive shark, but it's got some serious teeth going on.

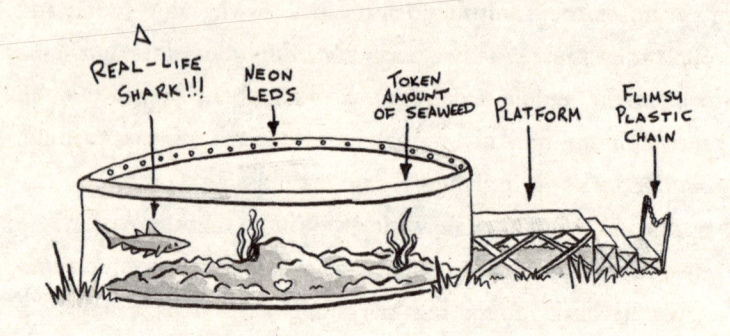

[Illustration: A REAL-LIFE SHARK!!!, NEON LEDS, TOKEN AMOUNT OF SEAWEED, PLATFORM, FLIMSY PLASTIC CHAIN]

My survival instincts tell me that it would be a bad idea to give in to the urge to reach in and stroke it. Instead I hold my hand out as close to the water's surface as I dare.

'Yeah, I hadn't left my house for weeks after my gram died. Then, when I did, BAM! Zombie apocalypse! I mean, if you think about it, really they should pay me as much as you guys. Probably more. Because I didn't sign up for any of it in the first place! That's why they got me out fast. They made me speak to about ten different lawyers after being pulled off the boat, then sign a million pieces of paper. Everything happened so fast.'

He's speaking so quickly and looks really hurt. I hook an arm through his.

'Calm down. I get it. They bound us all up in contracts, paperwork and legalities.'

'I figured the money would tide me over until I make a plan of what to do with my life, now I'm not finishing Nurse Training.'

'You aren't finishing?' I remember him saying something about that on the canal boat, after I brained myself.

'My gram died,' he says, like this is a perfectly reasonable explanation.

'And you were only doing it for her?'

'No, I was doing it because of her. She was a nurse, before she retired and became a crossing guard. She was one of life's carers, she said I was too. And I thought she was right. I loved nursing.'

'Then why not finish?' I imagine Jayden dancing through the wards of a hospital, sharing his smiles out and bringing light to each patient he cares for.

'I told you on the boat, I'm not good enough.' His voice tightens, but he's not crying, he's angry. 'I couldn't keep Gram alive.'

'That's not how these things work.'

His eyes follow the line the shark draws through the water, his face serious. 'I wanted so badly for her to get better. But the illness wouldn't let up.'

'Some illnesses don't. Then it's the nurse's job to make

people comfortable and happy. Something I know from personal experience you're *very* good at.' I lean my head on his shoulder.

'How's the burn?'

'Hurts like a bastard. But it would've been much worse if you hadn't helped.'

'Thanks,' he says, leaning his head on mine.

We stay like that for a time, watching the poor shark swimming nowhere.

'You could use Pherson's money to help you complete your training.'

'Yeah.' He manages a short laugh. 'I'll think about it.'

'You should.'

'I will.' He runs his hand back and forth over his hair. 'Would this be a weird time to ask for my gram's ashes back?'

'Would there ever be a not-weird time for that question?'

Jayden laughs again. 'I guess not. Thanks for taking care of them.'

'It was an honour. They're in my room.'

'Great, I'll grab them later.'

A comfortable silence wraps around us. After a minute I break it with a question that just has to be asked.

'Does Pherson really have a pill that makes people act like zombies? Or is all that part of the hoax?'

'Yeah, it's for real,' Jayden says. 'It's this diet pill.' He waves at the flags catching in the gentle breeze of this warm day. 'It's supposed to work and everything, but it has weird side effects. That's how they got most of the extras to sign up – they're doing clinical trials.'

'Weird.' I repeat his choice of word. It's one way to describe the things I've seen people do over the last few days.

'What's it like, taking the zom-pill?' I ask, curious.

Jayden shakes himself, any hint of his previous smile gone.

'It was like watching myself from the inside, acting like a zom on the outside. My arms and legs moved all awkward, and I heard my heartbeat inside my head. It slowed right down, it was horrible. Then I chomped at things that weren't even there.' He rubs at the top of his head before flicking his hands away in agitation.

'I only took it for the trial and wasn't OK with it. And I wasn't cool with tricking you guys either.'

'It's OK,' I say, even though everything about Dead Real really isn't. Jayden didn't mean any harm, and his role in the whole thing is all a lot less Taming of the Shrew than I'd first feared.

'Is it OK?' He looks at me, face transforming back into his easy smile that radiates warmth, his gold tooth glinting.

I can't help but smile back. 'Yeah.'

'We're good?'

I nod. 'We're good.'

'Good! Now, what the hell is going on with you and Ruby?'

Chapter 42

'**M**E AND RUBY?'

My heart aches. Standing here, next to Jayden, watching a shark in a neon flashing party tank, with a crowd of strangers calling our names, I say the words I've been too scared to even admit to myself.

'I think Ruby hates me.'

'Not possible,' Jayden shoots straight back.

'She thinks I tricked her by pretending to like her. And let's not forget she has a pinkie missing, thanks to my junior hacksaw skills.' The last words are meant to come out as playful, but I ruin the effect by pathetically choking on them.

'She doesn't hate you. I heard that this morning she turned down some internship so that you could have it. That shows she still cares, right?'

There's only one internship? And she's given it to me? My bottom lip wobbles, and tears prickle my eyes again. I thought they'd offered it to both of us.

'She should have it. She's so much better than me and there aren't enough female engineers. It's her dream too. I'll talk to Clarity next time I see her.'

'Talk to Ruby,' Jayden says. 'Sort yourselves out before getting bogged down with anything else.'

'And tell her what? People have been making bets on whether

I'm gay, straight or . . .' I stumble on the last word.

'Bi?'

'Yeah.'

'Who cares? That's for you to know.'

'But Ruby wanted to hear me say it this morning, and I don't think she really gets how many people are watching. And, even if she doesn't, there was someone else in the room.'

'You only need to talk about anything like that when you feel comfortable to. Ruby, for sure, will understand.'

'It didn't seem that way this morning,' I say.

'Well, she's been through a lot. I'm pretty sure she's on extra levels of painkillers. You might need to forgive her if her judgement's a little off. But you two definitely need to talk.'

'Why are people so interested in *labels*? Can't people just *be*?' My hand is still held over the water. The shark's paid no attention to me, but there's a thrill of being closer to it without the glass as a barrier.

Jayden runs his hand over his head. 'I get it, it's pretty shit thinking you have to find a labelled box to squish yourself into. But it's so not like that. Labels don't define people . . . people define labels.'

I look up, face scrunched in confusion.

'They're like rough markers to help people find themselves. And each other,' he says. 'Since I came out as bisexual, I've met so many other people who identify the same and, though we're all different, we're similar in enough ways that it makes me feel less alone.'

'You're bisexual?!' I blurt out, in full admiration of the casual way he dropped the word, considering all the horrible stuff I've heard about it.

'Yeah.'

I'm pretty sure there isn't a greedy or untrustworthy bone in Jayden's body.

'Why are you staring at me like that?' he asks, eyebrows pulled low.

Throughout our friendship, Jayden's demonstrated a couple of times that he's one of the good guys. I think I can trust him.

'Can I tell you something I've never told anyone else?' I ask, lowering my hand to touch the surface of the water.

'For sure.'

Swallowing back fear and shame, I tell Jayden all about the day in Year 9 with Molly, Pixie and Nazia. About being attracted to different genders and *the B word* feeling right until I heard the other words people associate with it.

When I finish, Jayden reaches out an arm and pulls me in tight.

'You've been carrying all that around with you since Year 9?'

I nod.

'That's so shit, I'm sorry. I know how it feels. When I told my friends I wanted to be a nurse, they ripped it out of me. Told me being a nurse was for people not smart enough to be doctors, and that it was a *girls' job*.'

'What?' I say, instantly outraged.

'Yeah, I know. I was pretty pissed off with them. But then my gram helped me see that they'd soaked these stupid ideas up from someone else. At some point in their lives, they'd heard and accepted this bullshit information as a truth, and until someone challenged them, they would go on believing it.'

'Did you challenge it?'

'Well, I spoke to them,' he says. 'Told them they were all being ignorant dickheads. We went our separate ways for a time, people don't change in a day, but time went by and, one by one, they all apologised.'

'And you forgave them?'

'Yeah. They were given a chance to sort that shit out in their heads and they did. That's what matters, I guess. Like I said, they're good guys, they'd just picked up some bad ideas, and it sounds like your friends were the same. All the crap associated with being bisexual is biphobic bullshit. They were probably spouting other people's ignorance.'

'Yeah, maybe.' I look down as the shark swims right under my hand.

'I'm sorry you've had all that going on for so long.' He gives me another squeeze.

I want to say it's OK. But it doesn't feel OK. These ideas have taken up so much space inside me and made me not always like myself.

'So, bisexual seems to fit a bit, but I don't just like guys and girls, if you get what I mean?'

He laughs. 'Yeah, I get it,' he says nodding. 'Gender's this big spectrum,' Jayden says with a smile.

'Sexuality's a spectrum too,' I say, remembering Ruby's words.

'Exactly, which means there's as many different ways to be bi as there are bi people, and we're all living our own experiences. In the past it's been way overlooked and misunderstood, because the people who wrote the history books wanted everyone to be straight. Then they accepted that some people might be gay, but more than two sexualities was just too much for them. And even now, there's still some misinformed people, and there's transphobes too, who think the term "bisexual" is just exclusive to two genders.' He pauses to look at me with an encouraging smile. 'But thankfully most people get that being bisexual just means being hot on more than one gender.'

In that one sentence, something that's always seemed painfully confusing suddenly seems ridiculously simple.

'That's it!' I almost jump up and down on the spot. 'That fits.' After the first thrill of excitement, I feel myself relax within my own skin for the first time in as long as I can remember.

'Nice.' Jayden playfully ruffles my hair.

My throat pinching, I give him a wobbly smile, barely holding back the happy-tears at finally understanding such a huge part of myself.

'Just remember all the important stuff,' he goes on. 'Like *You be you. Ignore the haters. Be hot on who you're hot on,* and *Love who you love!* Oh, and make sure you love yourself too. Which should be easy, because you're awesome.' He nudges me with a grin.

His words echo around my head. *Being bisexual just means being hot on more than one gender.*

'I am bisexual,' I whisper. 'I think I always have been.'

His smile widens. 'But you don't have to choose a label if you don't want to.'

Be hot on who you're hot on and love who you love – make sure you love yourself too.

I've hated and hidden part of myself for so long, because of all the lies I'd picked up from other people. I'm ready to learn to love that part of myself now, the part that led me to kiss Ruby.

Rogue tears break free from my lashes to tickle at my cheeks, and I wonder if this is what Pride feels like.

'I want it,' I say, with a wide grin.

'Nice! And if you ever want to change it, that's OK too.' Jayden holds his hand up to me. 'Bi-five?'

I laugh. 'That's not a thing.'

'It's totally a thing . . . and one of the best things about being bi. Don't leave me hanging!'

I give him a high-five and burst into giddy laughter.

Jayden sweeps me up into a big hug, then I swipe my hand across the water's surface and flick it at him playfully.

'Bleugh!' He leaps away, splashing a handful of tank water at me. I giggle as it rains down, feeling so light inside.

The second time he puts his hand over the brim of the tank, the shark launches out of the water, breaking the surface with its mouth open wide to snap at Jayden's hand.

My reflexes act faster than my brain and I tug him away. The rows of jagged teeth close on nothing as we both fall backwards off the steps and land on the soft lawn.

'Whoa! I don't think it likes me,' he says, examining his hand, as though he can't believe it's still there.

'That's so weird. It wasn't bothered by me at all,' I say.

'My bad, I shouldn't have messed with its water. Got kind of caught up in the moment.' Jayden laughs nervously. It takes him a second to recover, but when he does, he stands up and speaks, 'Right, shark attack aside, I wasn't going to go to Pherson's bullshit finale, but we need to find Ruby and get you two fixed.'

The part of me that always wants to see Ruby fights with the part that is reluctant to face whatever's going on with us.

Reluctance is winning.

I stay sitting on the grass, watching the shark until Jayden holds his hand out.

'Come on, I'll be with you.'

I put my hand in his and feel stronger.

Chapter 43

INSIDE THE HOUSE, WE MAKE OUR WAY BACK towards the entry hall. Distracted by how I could possibly fix things between Ruby and me, I walk into a couple of doorframes. And people.

I *will* fix everything. I have to.

I'll sit beside her and tell her I'm sorry for running off this morning. I'll tell her I really like her, and if she wants to know my sexuality, I'll lean in close so only she can hear and I'll tell her I'm currently identifying as – deep breath – bisexual.

'Here comes Nora, just in time,' Pherson says, the tension in his voice making it clear he isn't happy about my little vanishing act. 'And she's got Jayden with her. The whole gang's in the house!'

Out of shot of the camera, I freeze. The space I left beside Ruby is filled with the stunt biker lady.

What the hell?

She has her hand on her own leg, but the backs of her fingers press deliberately against Ruby's thigh.

Biker Bitch.

Beside her is Mrs Johnson, waving cheerfully. It's so good to see her smiling face vein- and pustule-free, I forget to be angry that she was in on the hoax.

Alongside her are our other neighbours, Phil and Jan. Jan has a black eye, her arm in a cast and doesn't look too pleased with everything going on, then I remember the fall she took down our cellar stairs.

They all accept a delicate-looking pastry offered by one of the waiting staff still doing the rounds.

Beside them, Ruby is scowling between Jayden and me, at the place where our hands are clasped.

Shit!

In the same moment I drop Jayden's hand, Ruby puts her arm up and around the biker's shoulders.

'Nora, Jayden, why don't you come and sit by me, here?' Pherson's charm breaks as soon as I move between him and the camera.

It's the first time he's not kept a reign on his anger and I get what Clarity meant, it's scary. If looks could kill, I'd be out cold. His eyes tell me that even if I came back as a zom, he'd still be the one munching on my skull contents.

Once we're in place, Pherson's spiel starts up again.

'As I was saying, official merch is on sale now – T-shirts, posters and limited-edition screen prints.' Merchandise flashes up on screen: Ruby and I running from a blast, Mum with a petrol-powered chainsaw, zom-Jayden trudging through a crowd of bloodied sheep. All done in the 1970s grindhouse, B-Movie style, along with the words *"Dead Real"*. They're so good, I catch myself wondering if we could get some free tees out of this.

'And as if today couldn't get any better, you're all invited to celebrate with us via live-stream for the afterparty with the crew and the stars of the show. They've all worked hard and earned a night of fun. Courtesy of Champer's Hampers, bubbly and vol-au-vents will flow. Then later it's outside for the DJ set, bar and barbeque.' Another cheer goes up. 'Party starts in a little over an hour, with a huge announcement from Global Innovations to get things started!'

Pherson's face is set to full beam, and he turns it on me.

'Now, Nora, unfortunately you missed Ruby's interview,' he says.

'Yeah, in which she said the grand total of naff-all,' a member of the crowd grumbles loudly.

Tension flickers in Pherson's jaw before he speaks again. 'It's your turn to tell us about your Dead Real experience.' His words take on a talk-show-host edge. 'What exactly was going through your mind when you saw your first zom?'

He waits for the answer, blue and green light dancing demonically in his eyes. I stare, horrified, until I turn around and I see that his eyes are reflecting footage on the giant screen: it's Mrs Johnson stumbling across her lawn, fully zombified.

The sight pulls me back to the beginning of all of this and I'm sickened by the fear and confusion Pherson has inflicted.

Ruby refused to talk.

Jayden wasn't even going to show up.

Mum and Dad aren't really here, and their thunderous expressions tell me there's no way they're doing an interview.

I stand up.

'No!' The word rumbles round my chest on its way out. I'm not playing his game any more. 'I came here for Ruby,' I tell him.

'Yeah, you did!' Jayden calls, dancing beside me.

I move to stand before Rubes and hold my hand out in an echo of Jayden's gesture earlier.

'Let's blow this shitshow,' I say, with a meaningful look I try to cram full of everything I feel for her.

But the time for Ruby to jump up, grab my hand and run away with me comes and goes. She's still sitting with one arm around the biker, glaring from me to Jayden and back again.

I risk a side-glance at Pherson, who looks like a kettle getting close to boiling. He calls over a person with an iPad and quietly growls instructions at her. The glower he gives me as she taps on her device fills me with dread.

'Please? Ruby?' I stretch my hand out closer to her.

'*So, you were pretending?*' The reporter's words from yesterday play loudly through a nearby speaker and she fills the big screen, a news logo spinning in the corner.

'*What?*' A bedraggled version of me on the screen gawps.

The edges of my vision blur and breathing becomes something I have to work at to draw in enough air.

He's playing yesterday's newsreel.

'Ruby!' I gasp, desperate to leave before the next words are spoken, but it's too late.

'*You pretended to be attracted to your friend to comfort her in your last moments together? Was it the guilt of cutting off her finger that made you do it?*'

Ruby is out of her seat and storming away from me, the biker in tow, their fingers woven together.

The footage stops and silence sucks at my ears as my vision pulses with my heartbeat.

Pherson barges me out the way to stand in front of the main camera.

'Phew, I think everyone could use a little time-out,' he says with a forced smile, his talk-show-host mask back in place. 'We'll take a brief break now and reconvene in an hour. That way we can finish up here and move straight to the live-stream party at the planned time!' He pulls at his shirt collar and chuckles. 'It's Nora and Ruby's unpredictability that we love. Am I right?' He doesn't leave any time for the crowd to answer. 'One hour,' he promises. 'Two at the most.'

He holds a horrific smile until the light on the main camera goes off and it swings to point at the floor. The man behind it puts a thumb up to Pherson, who nods and runs a hand across his face.

Music starts up and the crowd around us move cautiously away and towards a table piled high with bubbling champagne flutes.

'Nora!' an unamused Pherson summons me.

I don't go.

He storms over and I step back, until he has me cornered behind the gigantic TV screen.

'That did not go well.' *You don't say.* 'You're the goddamn star of Dead Real and you disappeared for most of the finale! And when you do turn up, you refuse to speak! Do you realise how bad that made me look?'

All his charm is gone, and his words fly with venom. He takes a deep breath to calm himself.

'You're the heart of all this. Tonight, on live broadcast, I'm going to invite you to be the face of Global Innovation's Fat-Eater Diet Pills. And you, Nora, are going to accept.'

'You what?!' I ask, sidestepping, but he follows easily, giving me no option but to stay pinned to the wall.

'My diet pill will change the world.'

'Right. And I would want to be part of that, why?' I'm pressed against the wall with nowhere to go, but there are people close by and cameras everywhere. He can't hurt me any more than he already has, I tell myself.

'You have no idea, do you, Nora? Look at you! You could be a model, if you cut your hair and dressed properly.' He indicates my T-shirt and jeans.

'I don't want to be a model!'

He laughs at this.

'Don't be silly, everyone wants to be a model. Or at least look like one. And now they can, with my pill. No one will ever be picked on or overlooked because of their size, ever again.'

He's getting closer and I can see the white all the way around his irises.

'I like me as I am,' I say, my throat dry as I try to remember how good I felt about myself outside with Jayden.

'Trust me, you don't want to turn down my offer,' Pherson says, his voice practically trembling.

Sensing danger, I stop arguing.

'Good girl, I knew you would see reason,' he says.

'I need to find Ruby.' I duck under his arm and power-walk away, breathing a sigh of relief when he doesn't stop me.

'Back here in one hour,' he calls.

I keep walking.

'There you are! You disappeared,' Jayden says when I find him grabbing more vol-au-vonts from a passing waiter.

'Pherson cornered me.'

'Oh, shit, you OK?' he asks through a mouthful of fancy finger food while dusting pastry flakes off his hands.

'Yeah, but we need to get away from here and we can't leave without Ruby or my parents.'

Jayden nods.

Another waiter moves past, this time with a tray of full champagne glasses. I grab two and hand one to Jayden. He uses his to wash down the fish eggs and I use mine to wash down the fear of what Ruby might be doing and whether everything between us is ruined.

The bubbles hit my brain, giving me courage and motivation.

'Let's go.' I walk deliberately away from the screen and camera, in the direction I'd go if I was looking for a bit of privacy and didn't know the entire house is bugged with mics and cameras.

We find Ruby at the top of a staircase, her hands linked with the motorbike stuntwoman and their lips locked together.

I reel backwards at the physical pain this causes, and Jayden catches me into a hug, turning me away from the sight. The echo of Ruby's lips on mine and now seeing her enthusiastically snogging that flashy leather-clad cow-bag makes me wonder. Maybe she was the one pretending.

'What is that girl doing?' Jayden says. 'She's hot on you, I know she is. She's just . . .' Unable to find any explanation, his words run out.

From the corner of my eye, I see Ruby take the biker by the hand and they disappear along a corridor of bedrooms.

I open my mouth to say something offhand, like "*I don't care*" or "*Pffft, never really liked her anyway*," but instead, I burst into tears.

'Hey, hey, hey. It's all right, I get it.' Jayden hugs me as I ugly-cry all over the front of his T-shirt.

All the joy of claiming *the B word* as my own has disappeared. Any confidence I had to use that word to empower myself has shrunk to the size of a full stop. The full stop in mine and Ruby's friendship.

'I'm going to let her go,' I say, snot streaming down my face. 'I don't know what will make Ruby happy, but I don't think it's me.'

'Come on, what're you saying?' Jayden holds me at arm's length and looks me in the eye. 'You've already said you like each other, that's the hard bit done. You just have to get up there and stop her before she goes too far making a point.'

'Making a point?'

'She's trying to make you jealous.'

It's totally working.

'She deserves someone awesome, like a stunt biker. I'm just me,' I whimper, wiping my eyes on my sleeve.

The banners for Dead Real, where we both look zombie-apocalypse-awesome, hang above us. I try to work out what they've done with editing the image to make me look so great, but on closer inspection they haven't changed anything in my face or my body. But I still look just as kick-ass as Ruby.

'*She* wouldn't take this shit,' Jayden says, pointing to the me on the banner.

'We really both looked like that?' I ask, needing outside confirmation.

'Yeah, you're both epic.'

I smile. It wasn't Ruby being badass, with me tagging along.

We were both badass.

We *are* both epic.

And we're both at our most epic when we're together.

'You're right,' I say.

'Always.' Jayden nods, a sly grin on his face.

It's only my own stupidity keeping us apart. This is totally fixable, if I act now.

'We need to find out which room they've gone into.' I start running towards the staircase. 'Quick!'

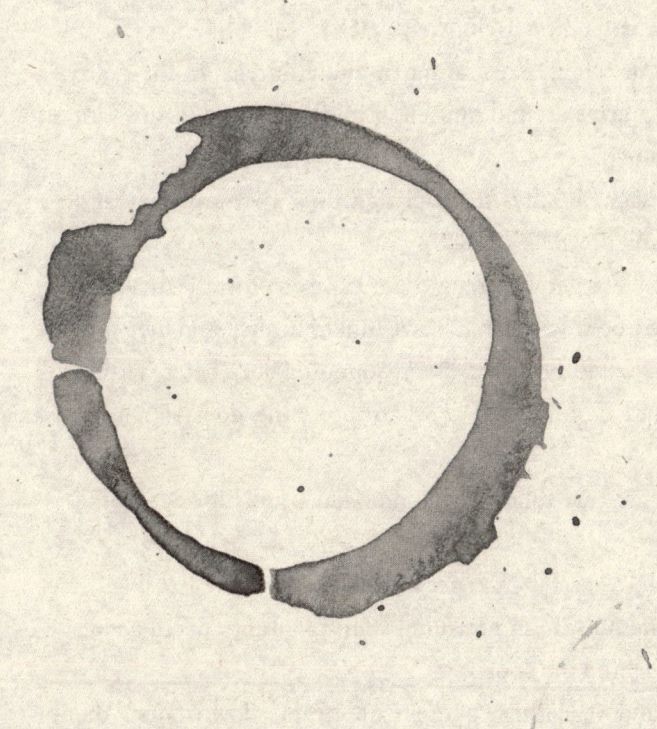

Chapter 44

WE TAKE THE STAIRS TWO AT A TIME. AT THE top we start knocking on and opening doors, hoping to find Ruby before it's too late.

Jayden takes the doors on the left, and I've got the ones on the right. We're making good progress until Jayden collapses to his knees with a thump.

'Shit, Jayden!' I drop back. 'Are you OK?'

He lets out a long guttural moan and crumples to the floor. He wraps his arms around himself, gripping his middle, his face contorted in pain.

'My stomach,' he says through tight lips, his skin waxy and sweat trickling down his head.

'Come on, let's get you somewhere more comfortable than the floor. My bedroom's not far.' I heave him to his feet and help him to my room. Inside, he does a liquid-sounding burp before letting go of me and dashing into the bathroom, the door slamming behind him.

The sounds that follow make me glad I got him out of the corridor.

'Are you OK?' I call. 'Can I get some help?'

'No!' More noises I'm not sure I want to go into detail about, come from behind the door.

Music and cheering pumps up from downstairs; the

celebrations must be starting early. I guess they should have kept back the champagne and caviar until the party started.

I hover, torn between going for help, staying here to make sure Jayden's OK, and looking for Ruby.

She's probably handing over those V-plates right now. The thought scoops out my insides, leaving me hollow and indecisive in the middle of the room.

After a pause in Jayden's sounds of discomfort, there's a flush, the splashing of hands being washed, and the door opens.

He steps out. I tense my face to keep it straight against the smell that leaves the bathroom with him.

'Something's rebelling against my guts.' He staggers to the bed and sits. 'I'll be all right, just need to lie down.'

'Are you sure?' I move to touch his clammy face. 'You look terrible.'

'Always the charmer,' he says. 'Go, find Ruby.'

'I think I should stay with you and—'

'Go!' He rolls onto the bed, holding his stomach.

I muster up all the courage there is to be mustered and put my hand on the doorknob, ready to find Ruby. To walk in on whatever she's doing.

Jayden groans and fear welds my feet to the floor. It's the noise I've come to associate with zoms, being chased, and seeing people eaten alive.

None of that was real, I remind myself. Grave Digger Productions put it all together, with the help of SFX Animatronix Ltd and Elroy Pherson's weird zombie drug.

He curls into a ball, pawing his head. I unstick my feet to shuffle closer to where Jayden's pushing his face into the bed.

I wish Ruby was here.

'My head,' Jayden chokes out, before leaning over the bed and being sick on the floor.

'Holy shit!' Panic comes through with understanding. 'I know what this is. You're having an allergic reaction.' I've never seen it before, but I've heard anaphylactic shock looks something like this. Last thing he ate was the finger food. 'Jayden,' I say, moving forwards as close as I dare. His movements are so awkward and erratic. 'Are you allergic to shellfish? Have you eaten caviar before?'

My brain is stuttering in my head – people die of food allergies.

'No,' he moans.

Is he saying no to the allergy or no to having eaten caviar?

There isn't time to clarify because once the word is out, he's pounding at his skull. I grip his hands but can't stop him. He's going to hurt himself.

'It's like when I took the zombie pill, but worse.' He finishes with a sicky hiccup and starts trembling.

'Shit, shit, shit . . . I'm going to get help,' I call, running from the room to find Ruby.

I continue up the corridor, throwing open every door I pass until I find Ruby and the biker making out, sitting on the end of a bed. Seeing it makes me feel like a zombified hand is reaching into my stomach and pulling out my insides.

Eyes kept firmly on the floor, I shout, 'Ruby? I need your help with Jayden.'

I wait for a response when Ruby bundles me out the door, shutting it behind her.

'Why would I want to help you with Jayden? Looked like you were getting on just fine when I saw you in his arms earlier. Nice and cosy, just like on the boat and when you were holding his hand earlier.'

'He's sick,' I say, talking fast. 'Really sick, we need to do something.'

She raises an eyebrow. 'You only want me to come with you because Jayden's sick?'

'Yes!' I shout. Then realise that wasn't the right answer. 'Wait, no! Well, not exactly. Come on!'

'You pretended to like me, Nor, that was rough,' she says with her usual Ruby bluntness. 'And now you want my help?'

There isn't time to explain about the cameras and the intern watching, about my confusion over my sexuality and not wanting to say anything in front of who-knows-how-many people. Jayden's sick.

I need her to understand that I wasn't pretending. That I've always liked her.

And I need her to understand it really quickly.

The lines of Ruby's face as she waits for my reply are thrown into sharp contrast by the lamp overhead. I think of drawing her to capture her expression and then, I know exactly how I can show her.

The need to get back to Jayden is greater than the privacy of my sketchbook. I pull it out from where it lives in my back pocket.

'I wasn't pretending. It was all real. Everything I said.' I flick through the many pictures of her. 'All real.'

Ruby's eyes grow more with every page she sees, the majority of pictures telling a story of a girl in love with her best friend.

'But I wasn't ready to talk about my . . . identity . . . in front of the cameras, or that intern this morning,' I say, flushing hot pink. 'Can we go now?'

'These are good,' she says. 'I look fabulous as Ru-bee!'

'Not the time, Rubes!' I wave my hands in frustration. 'Jayden!'

'Right, yeah.' She opens the door to the bedroom and calls in, 'Sorry, Veronique, I have to go.'

Veronique shrugs like she really doesn't care either way and Ruby shuts the door.

'That's it?' I ask.

'Apparently.'

And I'm running again, this time with Ruby following. We burst into my dim room and find Jayden looking like he's stuck halfway between human and zom.

'Jayden?' I say quietly, happy to hear he's breathing, even if it is a little heavy, and I see he's not trembling any more.

Ruby looks from Jayden to the puddle of sick on the floor. 'Shit, what's up with him?'

Seeing Ruby calms Jayden down even more.

'You two need to fix things,' he says in a gravelly voice, resting his head on his arm and, closing his eyes, his breath settling somewhere near normal. 'I need sleep.'

'Jayden?'

'Hmmm...'

'How are you feeling?'

'Better,' he mumbles, and it seems he might just need some time to rest and sleep off whatever stomach bug it is.

I flop on the floor near him. 'Phew, I thought he was dying from an allergic reaction to caviar.'

Ruby flops beside me. 'I'd have been ready to jam my fingers down his throat.'

'You think that would've made him feel better?'

'It would've made *me* feel better,' she says with a short laugh.

'You OK to wait with us? Make sure he's OK?'

'Yeah, Nor, of course. And I'm sorry. It wasn't fair to expect you to talk about your sexuality in front of the reporter or that random girl.'

'Thanks,' I say. 'That means a lot.'

She holds up her bandaged hand. 'The painkillers are good, but I would say I'm not the sharpest tool in the box right now. Is there anything I've missed? Like, between you and Jayden?'

'No! But all the rooms have cameras in and we're still being filmed.'

'What?!' Ruby looks around and I point at the corner, where, if you look closely, there's a tiny camera painted to camouflage into the plasterwork.

'And my parents are locked in a stable behind the house, there's a shark in the garden—'

'Really?!' Her face sparks with interest.

'Yep. And Pherson wants me to be the face of his new diet pill.'

'What?!' Ruby's face falls from the shark-related excitement to a scowl.

'Well, I think that's you just about caught up.'

'And we're OK?' she asks.

'As friends? You're with some hot, nonchalant biker now, right?'

Jayden chooses this moment to be sick again. Violently. Ruby and I jump out the way as it flies across the room and splats up the wall.

'We need to get him medical help,' I say, turning on the main light. That's when I see blood in his sick.

Lots of it.

In fact, it's mostly blood.

'Fuck, Nor, I don't think people get that with an allergic reaction,' Ruby says, moving close and placing a hand on Jayden's arm. 'Jayden, I'm going to find a medic. Nor'll stay here with you.' She speaks gently.

Jayden lets go of his head and looks up at us. The twinkle of light that constantly plays in his eyes is gone and the pressure of the vomiting has broken blood vessels in them, streaking red through white.

Desperation tugs on his features, like he wants to escape his own body. Ruby snatches her hand back and edges away. The next moan mutates into a snarl, bearing bloodstained teeth. He raises up onto his haunches, looking like a wildcat ready to pounce.

'OK, we should probably go get help together,' I say, not wanting to be left in the room with him. 'Like, right now!' I'm backing towards the door, pulling Ruby with me.

A hunger burns in Jayden's eyes, and his teeth gnash. I expect him to launch through the air and grab us. Instead, he unsteadily stands and walks off the end of the bed, folding to the floor on impact. He straightens up and moves towards us, hands clawing, in a slow trudge we're both painfully familiar with.

'This is so bad,' I say.

'Part of the hoax?' Ruby looks set to bolt.

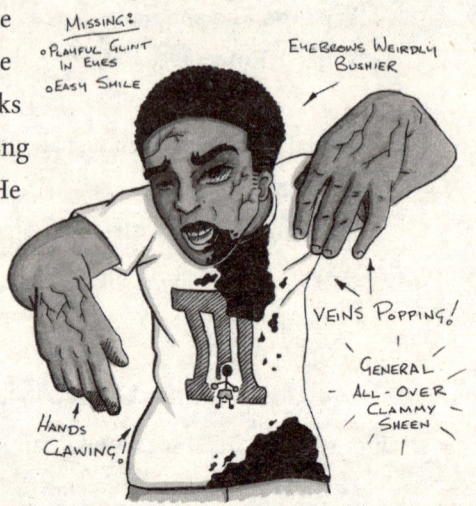

'I don't know . . .' I look closely to see whether the individual joints in his fingers are moving. Unlike the Jayden-robot, they are. 'I don't think so.'

My nose is full of the sharp smell of blood and sick. It smells too real. 'We have to get out of here.'

We scramble to the exit. I pull an elaborate golden key from inside the door before we run out and slam it shut behind us. With a shaking hand I lock it and follow Ruby down the carpeted corridor towards the staircase and the party.

Before we reach the stairs, I slip over. The stink of whatever I slipped in is horrific. I push myself up with blood-slickened hands and recognise it as being the same as Jayden's stomach contents, but this is worse. So much worse. Because it's all over my arms AND it belongs to some random.

'Urgh!' I wipe my hands on my jeans and try to stand up, slipping again and getting more on me.

'I don't think Jayden's the only one suffering,' Ruby says, stating the obvious and hauling me up. 'Food poisoning?'

'I think it's the caviar.'

We get to the top of the stairs and get a full view of the lobby we recently left. What I'd taken to be wildly happy party noises are actually shouts and cries for help, masked by loud music.

It's a bloodbath. A rancid smell of human waste rises off it. I hook the neck of my T-shirt over my nose and look down on the carnage.

People are eating each other.

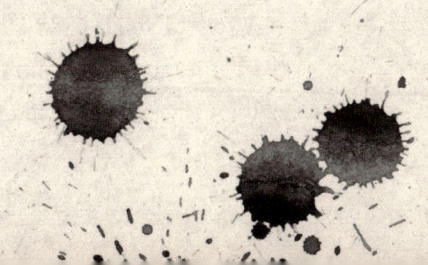

Chapter 45

THIS CAN'T BE HAPPENING,' I SAY, EVEN THOUGH it clearly is. Right here. In front of us.

It's so messed up and beyond real.

How did we fall for the special effects tricks of Dead Real, when this is obviously what a zombie apocalypse would really look like . . . Eugh! And smell like?

A horde of my neighbours bar the front door, including Phil and Jan. Eyes sunken and bruised, they lean in to tear away chunks of flesh from what looks like the remains of some SFX Animatronix Ltd crew members. I guess there might be more than one opening for the internship now.

'It's all the same people,' Ruby says. Her words are pretty vague, but I see exactly what she means. Everyone dining on other humans are the same people who were pretending to be zoms before.

'I don't know what it means, but we have to get out of here.'

We scramble back the way we came, holding hands to support each other as we slither through more puddles of bodily ick.

I direct us to the rear of the house, or, more specifically, to the wall filled with old farming tools artistically hung in geometric patterns that I saw when Elroy walked me to my room yesterday.

A row of small hand sickles hang appealingly within reach. I unhook two from the display as Ruby reaches for a huge scythe that would make the grim reaper envious.

'What's with you and long weapons?'

'Maybe I'm overcompensating.' She sticks her tongue out at me.

A thought crosses my mind, and I look up.

'Pherson, you sick bastard, if this is more of your tricks, I'm not playing any more,' I shout as loud as I dare. 'This is a warning: I'm really freaked out.'

'And we're pissed off,' Ruby adds, copying me and calling out to no one in particular.

'Yeah,' I agree. 'And we're pissed off. We're taking these weapons, and if anyone comes at us, I'm cutting their fucking head off.'

'Wowsers, hardcore. You really think this is part of Pherson's set-up?'

'No,' I say. 'Anyway, if it is another hoax, they'd have replaced these with fake blades or something.'

'True.'

An innocent fern sits in a large pot in the corner of the landing. Ruby swings the scythe's blade round the green fronds and tugs. The leaves tumble to the floor as the blade slices clean through.

'Whoa!' Ruby's eyes go big and round. 'This baby's lethal.'

I eye the blades of my sickles. 'Shall we?' I ask.

'Let's.'

Just like old times, it's the two of us together, running from zoms. I suppose you should be careful what you wish for.

Jayden's gone again too – not in a canal this time, but trapped in a room, alone. The same sadness I felt the first time we lost him hits me and I almost turn back, but I know we can't help him if he eats us.

Right now, we need help. 'We need to get my parents,' I say, finishing the thought aloud.

We run along a corridor lined with open doors leading onto bedrooms of varying sizes and levels of grandness.

Ahead, someone falls out of a doorway. Most of the skin and muscle of her left arm is torn away to the bone, bleeding over her white blouse and shimmering, silver-pleated skirt. Someone was ready to party. At first I think it's fear that has her trembling, but as she looks up, I see I'm wrong.

She's laughing.

Hysterically.

We help the woman to her feet and I recognise her as Pherson's lawyer.

'Is this part of the show?' I ask, gripping her shoulder and talking slowly.

She tugs herself free.

'This . . .' she says, showing the wound pumping blood down her outfit and dripping onto the floor, filling the air with a rich metallic pang, '. . . isn't in the plan. He thinks it is, but it's not. He thinks this is funny! I suppose it must be.' She erupts with another burst of manic laughter before passing out and collapsing to the floor.

The editor with a beanie and black-rimmed glasses shambles out of the same room the lawyer fell from, his eyes red with popped blood vessels. He grabs for Ruby and she swings her scythe. The beanied-zom grips it, pulls it out of her hands and throws it aside.

Shit. Shit. Shit.

He's doing the same frenzied gnashing as Jayden, teeth scarily close to Ruby. She struggles to get free and they trip over the lawyer, falling together backwards into the room.

I run after them and see Elroy Pherson standing in the doorway to the bathroom, buttoning up a fresh shirt and laughing at the scene playing out in front of him.

Without time to waste on fathoming what everyone's finding so funny about all this, I take a quick itinerary of the room. There's nothing obviously helpful; a dressing table, a bed, some filming equipment, wires and unused screens stacked in the corner next to a massive wardrobe that you could probably find Mr Tumnus at the back of.

'Help us,' I call to Pherson before dropping the sickles, not ready to use them. Jayden is still close to the surface of my thoughts, along with the familiar hope that these people are curable.

Ruby pushes hard at the underside of the zom's jaw, clamping it shut. I'm tugging on various parts of the zom and really wishing I had my cricket bat, when Pherson talks.

'How *did* they get you two in on it? Oh, they're good. I suppose you think you're getting your own back, do you?'

'Help us! We can discuss whether it's real later, dickhead,' Ruby shouts, pushing with both hands on the jaw of the zom so hard I'm wondering whether his neck'll snap, which would be too nasty.

With wires tangling around my dancing feet as I shuffle this way and that, looking for a way to help, I have an idea.

As fast as I can, I wind up a length of cable and tie the zom's ankles, ignoring the kicks I get from Ruby's flailing feet.

'Ruby, get the zom to sit up.'

'How?!'

'Crawl backwards?' I suggest. She struggles back, and the zom lifts enough for me to get a couple of loops around his shoulders and pull it tight. One zom hand loses purchase on Ruby and she uses it to her advantage, breaking free.

The dressing table is well positioned for me to tie the zom to, and, thanks to my dad, I'm certain the knots will hold.

One second Ruby is beside me and the next she's being carried bodily across the room by Pherson.

'Hey! What are you doing?' I pull on his arms, but it has no effect on his purposeful stride towards the wardrobe.

He tosses her in and throws the door shut behind her. Next he wraps a cable in a figure of eight around the decorative door handles, trapping Ruby inside.

'What are you doing?' I ask again, louder this time. 'Let her out.'

Pherson rounds on me, grabbing the front of my T-shirt and lifting me until my feet actually leave the floor.

'I've had enough of this. You and the effects team think you can fool me?'

His anger is taken to the edge of something else. Desperation? Humiliation?

'The difference between you and me is that I know what's real and what's not.' We're moving back towards the gnashing zom I just tied up. 'And I've had enough of you all being ungrateful shits.'

He holds me in a way that I can only bat feebly at his forearms. Unable to fight my way out, I try to explain what's going on.

'Jayden ate the caviar and got sick. He's gone zom. Like that guy – he took the zombie drug too, right?'

'How do you know?' Pherson asks, caught off guard for a moment before snapping back. 'Oh, ha ha!' His teeth grit together, making the sound aggressive and forced. 'I've got animal rights hassling me about the fish, and they thought they'd have a dig at that as well, did they?'

'We aren't tricking you,' I say, but he might be on to something;

the fish could be the link. He shakes me and any useful thoughts get jumbled.

I point at the lawyer sprawled across the floor outside the bedroom, desperate to prove my point. 'Look, do you think she's acting?'

'Well, there's one way to find out how real this is, isn't there?' The air in my lungs is knocked out when Pherson slams me to the ground, pant-wettingly close to the teeth of the zom-editor.

As I thrash my arms and legs against his iron hold, my fingers brush over something smooth on the floor. The handle of the sickle.

'Of all the people in the world, I chose you, Nora Inkwell, for Dead Real. I made Ruby a part of it, but you were always my poster girl.'

'Poster girl?' He's lost me, but it could be the teeth gnashing nearby, messing with my ability to process information. I'm also trying to stealthily work the sickle into my hand.

'You looked so pathetic that day I met you at college.'

'We just wanted free tote bags.'

'It's surprising how few questions people ask when signing up for free stuff,' he says with a rough laugh. 'When I saw the graffiti, I wondered if you might be related to Henry Inkwell. Then I met you and I knew you were perfect.' Pherson relaxes his grip, allowing me to move a safe distance from danger, palming the sickle's handle at the same time.

With a second to think, his words settle in.

'Hang on!' I say, disbelievingly. 'You selected me because of my appearance after five hours of an art exam and finding my name slandered in graffiti?'

A chain of events connects in my mind and I see how this is all my fault.

All those weeks ago at the gig, if I'd been brave enough to tell Ruby I liked her, she wouldn't have gone with Josie. Then the entire Baxter thing wouldn't have happened, so there wouldn't have been any graffiti to make Pherson feel sorry for me. Without that, I wouldn't have been chosen for Dead Real and Ruby wouldn't have been dragged into it with me . . .

'It's OK,' says Elroy. 'When I was at school I was picked on too, for being too big and too clever. Your dad stuck up for me. Helping you was a way of saying thank you to him.'

A bead of sweat runs down my head.

'I think what really nailed it for me though was that you were wearing a zombie movie top that day too! That was how I knew it was meant to be. A sign that you were the one. That I could rescue you from your pathetic life . . .'

I really wish he'd stop using the word "pathetic" when talking about me; it's knocking my newfound confidence that I might be a little bit kickass.

'. . . help you slim down, get a stylist to fix your wardrobe and hair. We've already started with a small change to your T-shirt sizes. I think you'll agree it's a vast improvement, with it hugging your figure, instead of drowning you in fabric.'

I wonder at the hypocrisy of wanting to show off my figure in the same mouthful of words that he's telling me to lose weight. But then again, not much of what he's saying makes sense.

'When we're done with you, Nora, you'll be perfect. It'll teach that idiot who sprayed the graffiti. You'll be the person everyone wants to be with.'

I don't want to be the person everyone wants to be with, though. I just want to be the person Ruby wants to be with.

'You don't get to tell me what size T-shirt I should wear or that I need to slim down.'

Blood glistens on the looming zom teeth and I push myself as far away as I can, focusing everything on keeping a grip on the handle of the sickle. The thuds of Ruby trying to break out of the wardrobe drive me on.

'I made you the star of Dead Real, Nora. It's my gift to you. When I met you, you reminded me of myself at your age. I especially recognised the same self-loathing in your eyes.'

This makes me pause in my struggle to get free.

'Think you're confusing self-doubt for self-loathing. And I'm seriously over that now.' As I say it, I know it's true. 'There's some mega projection of emotions going on here.'

Pherson's grip strengthens and he leans in until his cheek nearly rests against mine. 'Oh, it does look real, doesn't it? They've done a good job.'

'It is real!' I plead through clenched teeth.

The wooden handle of the sickle now sits so tight in the palm of my hand it hurts. The meaty zom-breath fills my nostrils and, if I don't act now, those teeth are going to gnaw a hole through my face.

Pherson rearranges his grip on me and I use the opportunity to throw everything I've got into one powerful movement, thrusting backwards and swinging the blade up in front of me as I climb to my feet.

'Stay the hell away from me.' I don't want to hurt anyone, but I'm hoping the blade will be enough to scare him.

Pherson laughs. 'You're not going to do anything with that,' he says with a confidence that shows he knows me.

Either way, I don't lower my blade. 'I'm freeing Ruby from that wardrobe, then getting my parents and getting out of here. You have a serious situation on your hands.'

This is when I see whatever it is inside Pherson flip: any efforts to restrain himself disintegrate and a wild look twists his features.

'You ungrateful little bitch,' he roars. 'Millions of people would give anything for this opportunity!'

'Sadly you chose the wrong one,' I say, moving to get Ruby. 'We're leaving now.'

He gives another dangerous roar and I spin, blade held out defensively before me. Pherson's mid-air, diving for me, his hands held out for my throat. He only stops as the sickle's blade sinks into his stomach.

I let go with a squeak and scramble away from where he's left swaying in a dazed stupor.

'You stabbed me!' He stumbles backwards onto the bed. I thought he would be livid, but when he speaks again, he sounds so upset. 'Why would you do that?'

'You kind of stabbed yourself,' I argue. 'I was scared. You locked Ruby in the wardrobe and were going to strangle me, and . . .' I wave my hands at the outcome of his actions.

'Why are you acting like I'm the bad guy?' he whimpers.

'Pherson, you *are* the bad guy.'

This has a huge effect on him. His chin quivers and his eyes go glossy. 'But I'm trying to make the world a more beautiful place.'

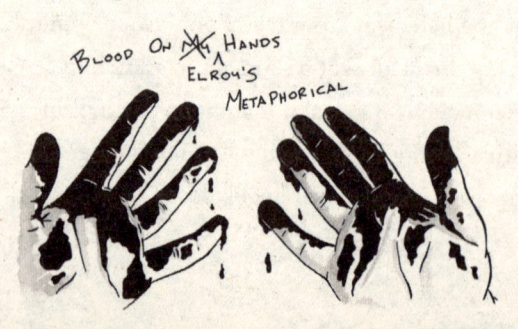

BLOOD ON MY HANDS
ELROY'S
METAPHORICAL

A tear escapes his eye. 'My diet drug works. It'll help people everywhere get the perfect body with next to no effort. Kids won't have to live through the bullying I faced.'

The more he speaks, the more a scowl gnarls my features. Mum's always nagged me about what I eat, so I can look a certain way to *catch a nice boy*. It's based on her idea of what people should look like and should want in life. Ideas that have been pushed on her through media and magazines. Magazines filled with people like Elroy Pherson.

He might have been a victim once, but now he's part of the problem.

I think of Jayden's theory of learned ignorance – it definitely applies here too.

'The idea that there's a *perfect body* is so damaging. People come in all shapes and sizes, and as long as they're healthy and happy, that's OK. Why couldn't you have bought into promoting body confidence instead of selling body perfection?'

The zom's still chomping away on the floor.

'And I wouldn't exactly say your pill works. There are still some major kinks to iron out. But I'm not surprised your scientific messings have gone so wrong – the quest for universal perfection is ugly. Everyone is different, with different needs and desires, and that, Elroy Pherson, is OK too. We are all imperfectly perfect,' I conclude, feeling proud of myself and kind of wishing the guy from the editing suite wasn't zombified, so he could have captured and streamed my one moment of epic lucidity and wisdom.

Pherson lies on the bed gawping like a fish.

'I was trying to help you,' he says, tears leaking down his cheek.

'I didn't need your help.'

The lawyer is moving awkwardly onto her hands and knees. Juddering, and looking rough as hell, she crawls towards Pherson, mouth open wide.

'And now,' I say, 'you need to move.'

'Come on, I know it's a set-up.' He bats her away.

'Pherson, you've been stabbed! You still think this is a joke? Move!'

'No! Now you listen to me—' His self-pity turns into anger as the lawyer lunges forwards and sinks her teeth into the softest part of his stomach. The noise he makes is more rage than pain. Her hands reach in and sharp, silver-painted nails, matching her party skirt, tear away chunks of skin and muscle.

His shouts of pain go through me like teeth on metal. I turn away and retch.

'Nora, save me,' Pherson moans.

'Do you have a cure?' I ask.

'I didn't even know I'd created an illness,' he says, face shredded with misery as reality finally hits him. 'I *am* the bad guy, aren't I?'

A muffled banging has been constant since Rubes was locked away. In the olden days they could really build a wardrobe – she would have been out of my IKEA Flat Pack in two seconds!

I grab the other sickle, wind it into the cable around the handle and pull. The blade slices through easily, freeing Ruby, who launches out to assess the scene of the bedroom before wrapping me in a tight hug.

'We need to help Pherson!' I tell her over the groans of the two zoms and Pherson's sobs.

'Really?' she asks, voice high. 'He'll turn into a zom. And he's a dick.'

'You want to leave him actually *being eaten?*' I step back to glare at her. 'That's dark, Rubes.'

She looks between me and a weeping Pherson before letting out a hefty sigh. 'You're right. You're totally right.'

Unwilling to sink another blade into anyone else tonight, I shake my head as Ruby moves for her scythe.

'We could lock her in the bathroom?' I suggest.

Ruby frowns. 'I guess. Leg and a wing?'

The woman currently licking Pherson's blood from between her fingers is only petite. 'I'll take her arms, you get her legs?'

Ruby nods. 'On three. And watch the teeth.'

She holds up her hand with three fingers. She puts down the first, then the second, and when the third goes down we both dive.

The zom-lawyer is so wriggly and her teeth suddenly seem impossible to avoid.

Ruby yells as the zom's foot thrashes out, catching her under the chin, and she falls back towards the zom on the floor.

The lawyer flips super-fast and lays powerful hands on me, pulling me towards her gory teeth, gnashing in anticipation.

Ruby calls out, but I can't see any way out of this. My panicked flailing is nothing to the zom's solid grip.

'No!' Pherson's shout cuts the air and a second later, he shoves his way between me and the lawyer, pushing me away. She grips hold of him again.

'Save yourselves,' Pherson shouts through gritted teeth, as the woman bites into his chest.

Ruby calls out again, and I don't need to be told twice.

The editor-zom has Ruby's foot clamped in his teeth. She claws at the carpeted floor, trying to crawl away. I move to take her hands and pull, reminded of working with Mum and Dad to get Ruby out of the hatch back home. Was that really just a few days ago?

Ruby's foot slips free and I haul her to her feet.

'Oh, come on!' she says when she sees teeth marks in the toe of her boot. 'These were new!'

'We have to leave.' I take Ruby by the hand and we run to the door, passing the bed at the same time the lawyer tears away more of Pherson's abdomen.

I hesitate.

'Go!' he hollers through the pain, as a portion of his stomach contents spills onto the floor. 'It's always the intestines,' he mumbles before falling unconscious.

Ruby tugs me out of the room and slams the door behind us.

Chapter 46

'**WELL, THAT JUST HAPPENED!**' **RUBY SAYS, EYES** bulging.

'Yeah,' I agree, pretty sure my expression mirrors hers. 'Could we have saved him?' I ask, emotionally flagging after Pherson's demise as we run through the house.

'Nora!' Ruby says, stopping and swinging me close, nose to nose, her eyes locked on mine. My heart thumps like it wants to burst out of my chest and into Ruby's. 'Before he saved us from the zom, which he made by the way, you saved us from him. You're incredible.'

I open my mouth to say something slick and offhand, but all that comes out is, 'Shiiit!' I hug her to me as tight as my trembling arms will allow.

Right now, we're together. We might not be *together* together, but we are physically together and that's better than nothing.

It takes a lot of energy to focus my chaotic brain on what we were doing before we found Pherson.

'We need to get my parents,' I say, voice wavering.

'Which way?'

I point.

Ruby takes my hand and we're moving through the house again.

Skilfully dodging a couple of lunging zoms, we make it to the door Jayden and I sat on the step of earlier.

The crowd outside cheer when they see us and I wonder about

going to them for help, but introducing a massive body of people into a contained zombie outbreak situation could get very messy very fast.

Ruby squeals and I spin, ready to attack her attacker, but she's running to the shark tank. 'She's so beautiful! I love her . . .' She hugs the glass.

'Ruby, we need to work out how to free my parents,' I call.

'Right!' Ruby looks around and her face lights up.

'We could steal the meat van and smash it through a wall?' she says, looking over my shoulder.

I turn, following her eyeline, to see a modern van with a vintage paint job reading "*Brenton and Son's Abattoirs*" on the side, parked near an enormous barbecue.

'I'm not sure about the wall, but there are some doors that might work. Can you get it started?'

'Hell's yeah.' She's already skipping towards it. 'She's got a hint of vintage about her,' Ruby says and, despite everything, I laugh.

She dives into the footwell of the van.

'I've always wanted to do this,' she shouts and, in no time at all, the engine vrooms to life.

'Genius!' I shout.

'Yep!'

We jump in.

'Where do you think the meat people are?' I ask, pulling my seat belt on and wiggling the gear stick.

'Dunno, same place the shark people are?' she says, pointing at the massive marine transport lorry parked down the way.

A memory of the carnage we saw in the entry hall skims across my mind and I decide not to linger on it.

'Let's get my parents.' I shift the van into gear and put my foot down. Ruby prods the radio and we drive straight over meticulously landscaped flowerbeds to the soundtrack of 'Funkytown'.

The stables come into view, and now we're armed with a van, the double doors stand as an inviting weakness in the brick building with barred windows.

I blast on the van's horn, three long toots, and hope that the time between the toots and the point the van impacts the stable doors will be enough for my parents to get out of the way, as I slam my foot down.

The doors explode and I stamp on the brakes, noting this is the second time this week we've driven into a building. This time it's splinters and chunks of wood that rain down.

The debris settles, to the sight of Mum and Dad emerging from beneath a blanket in the farthest corner.

'Nora!' Mum throws the blanket to one side to run over.

Dad follows. 'Blimey, Nor, you didn't give us much warning.'

'There's no time, things are bad,' I say, burying myself in their arms. A tangled knot inside me loosens.

'Are you OK?' Dad asks, grabbing my shoulders and looking into my eyes. He gives me a small shake, as though he can dislodge any trauma settled in my soul and watch it float across my retinas, like a snow globe.

'I'm all right, Dad.'

'You're not. Of course you're not. How could you be?'

'And Ruby,' Mum pulls Ruby into the hug and everything is so perfect, I wish this was the end of our unwanted adventure. Sadly, it feels unsettlingly like the beginning of something bigger, and much badder, than before.

'Where's Jayden?' Mum asks, looking at the van expectantly.

I swallow hard and try not to cry.

'He's not coming,' I say, emotions playing across my vocal cords.

'Oh no.' She purses her lips and her jaw tightens. Mum turns her attention to fussing over Ruby and her missing finger, while I fill them in on everything that's happened, leaving out the minor detail that I was holding the sickle that impaled Pherson.

'I could see something was going on in the original blood sample we took,' Dad says, once I'm finished. 'I've almost found a way to stabilise whatever was going on, but something's missing. A missing piece to the puzzle.'

'That's why we were trying to get another blood sample,' Mum adds.

'Elroy took away our travel lab – we had everything we needed. If I could just get some more blood, there's a chance . . .' he trails off, muttering to himself more than us, '. . . but without knowing more about the drug itself—'

'I overheard Pherson talking to some scientist about it,' I interrupt. 'He was working on fixing the drug. Acting like zoms is the unwanted side effect of his diet pill. They have animal rights activists protesting at their labs because they're developing part of the drug inside shark's uteruses.'

Ruby pulls a face. 'That sicko's been using sharks to make the drug and to promote it? Oh, that's so wrong, like when they put smiling chickens on fried chicken boxes. I guarantee those chickens were not smiling.'

'Yeah, it's proper messed up, but we've already got that perhaps Pherson wasn't one hundred per cent sound of mind. He said earlier he was going to make the announcement about the diet drug tonight, which is probably why he has the shark in the garden.'

'What?' Mum stares at me. 'There's a shark in the garden?!'

'He bought one of the sharks from the lab for the party tonight. I think it's a baby, because it's only about a metre and a half long, but looks like it should be bigger. And it's a bit bitey.'

Ruby's twisting her nose ring, brow furrowed, and I know that expression.

'What is it, Rubes?'

'It couldn't be a sand tiger shark, could it?' she asks.

My eyes grow wide when I catch on to her train of thinking, remembering our shark research at the start of the holiday, before we decided to make our werewolf.

'Shit, that would explain a lot!' I say, heart racing. The tension of the moment is so high, my mum doesn't even call me up on swearing.

'What?' Mum says, her face taut with anticipation. 'What explains a lot?'

'Intrauterine cannibalism,' Ruby and I say at the same time.

'Oh!' Dad's got it.

'What?!' Mum's not.

'Some sharks have a load of baby sharks in the womb,' I explain, 'and the biggest baby shark eats the little ones, until only one or two are born.'

Mum looks green about the gills. 'I'm so glad I've managed to live nearly forty-five years without hearing the phrase "*intrauterine cannibalism*".'

'Anyway, that could be what's causing the side effects with

Pherson's diet drug. It kind of makes sense,' I say and wiggle my fingers mysteriously. 'Science!'

'Pretty serious side effects,' Ruby adds.

'The caviar made Jayden sick,' I remember. 'Fish eggs. Shark womb. Maybe there's a connection?'

'But caviar's from a sturgeon,' Mum says, surprising us all with this unexpected trivia. 'A sturgeon isn't a shark, is it?'

'No, but it might be close enough to trigger something,' Dad says, rubbing his chin before clenching his fists. 'Dammit! I bet the shark's the missing key. If we got some of its blood and some from one of the infected, we would have a shot at making an antidote.' He looks distraught, pacing the stable, which holds a lingering hum of horse poo.

'But surely that's a good thing,' Ruby points out.

Dad heaves a heavy sigh. 'It would be if we had our stuff, but Pherson took it all. It could be anywhere.'

'Oh.' Ruby's shoulders fall as mine lift.

'I know where our stuff is.' I remember the other worn-looking bags piled on top of ours in the room where I'd found robot Jayden. 'And I'm pretty sure your stuff's there too.'

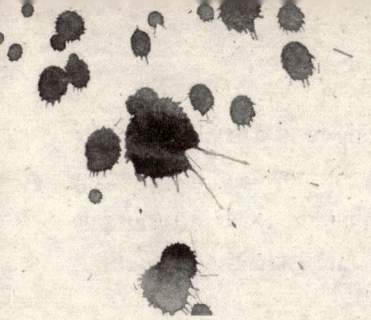

Chapter 47

A ROUGH PLAN IS PIECED TOGETHER AND I drive the meat truck back round to park up by the shark tank. My parents stare like they hadn't really believed there would be a shark in the garden.

We sneak into the house, dodge a couple of zoms to get to the room full of our stuff, and load up on gear. When my parents ask if we'd prefer to get the blood sample from the shark or Jayden, Ruby and I both shout, 'SHARK!' The excitable grin on Ruby's face when my dad agrees makes me think she didn't make the choice for the same reasons I did.

This time, at least, I can hug my parents before we head off in separate directions, each with our own mission to accomplish.

The syringe weighs heavy in my pocket and on my mind as I run alongside Ruby out of the house and into the garden. We agreed on swapping the farming blades for our tried-and-tested sports equipment, so I'm gripping my cricket bat and Ruby's already had to swing her hockey stick a couple of times to get us here.

It's only when we're standing beside the tank, watching the deadly marvel of the evolutionary process cut elegantly through the water, do I realise just how stupid our plan is.

A big blank screen, surrounded by blinking lights, stands beside a stage with a laptop open, ready to play music. This is to the right of a bar, which is across from a massive barbecue, next to a table loaded with sauces, all waiting for a party that's never going to happen. This, combined with the crowds of our adoring fans still cheering every time we come outside, apparently not put off by the after-show running seriously late, is making everything feel extra surreal.

'OK,' I say, walking towards Pherson's party pièce de résistance. 'How do you get blood from a shark?'

'Sounds like the beginning of a joke.' Ruby stands next to me.

'Trust me, I'm not laughing,' I say, watching the shark, certain its teeth are sharper than last time I saw it.

Ruby runs her hands through her hair and twists her nose ring.

I stare at the shark like it's a problem to be solved, until I notice Ruby looking from the nearby tables to the flags, to the barbecue and finally to the DJ rig.

'Aha!' She kicks into action. 'There's nothing you can't find on the internet.' She runs to the DJ's laptop.

Focused, she clicks a few things, messes with others, and the large screen lights up on the YouTube homepage, making the people in the nearby field cheer louder.

Dead Real videos are across the top of the trending list and my lip curls. 'I'm not exactly YouTube's best friend right now.'

'But you will be.' Ruby smiles and types into the search bar:

How do you take blood from a shark?

A load of super unhelpful videos appear, about whether sharks can smell blood and one idiot who swam with sharks while covered in blood. She scrolls past an unbelievable amount of bollocks until she hits on something that looks like it might actually be helpful.

Ruby's cursor hovers and a marine biologist pops up on a one minute twenty-something video and introduces himself. He lets us know that the most important sample he collects from the sharks he rescues is the blood.

The guy tells us he uses a needle and syringe. I hold up the one my dad gave us. 'Check!'

Then he tells us how something called a *peduncle*, by the tail, is the easiest access to a vein that runs along under the spine called the *ventral con*-something.

'Looks easy enough,' Ruby says in uncertain tones. So she has noticed that his shark is littler, less toothy and, most importantly, not in the water.

More clicks and searches later, a "*Sharks Of The World*" poster pops up. One look confirms that our aquatic friend is indeed a Sand Tiger Shark. On the upside, for all its teeth, it definitely has one of the smaller mouths.

I remember drawing shark-fact pages, and I know I did one for Sand Tiger Sharks, but can I remember any of the facts on it?

Ruby types another question into the main search bar.

How bitey are Sand Tiger Sharks?

And clicks on the first link.

Facts About the Sand Tiger Shark:
It is from the same shark order as the Great White.

Really not helpful.

> Its teeth act like dental fishing hooks
> and are perfect for piercing flesh.

Even more not helpful.

> *Violent encounters with humans are very rare.*

Oooh, now that is helpful.

Ruby reads it at the same time and we look at each other with nervous smiles.

'We need to do this,' I say, aware of time ticking away. 'You hold me, I'll lean over, grab her tail and do it.'

'Nor!' Ruby calls out. I turn to see her eyes are big and she's chewing her lip.

'I'll be fine. It's only a baby and attacks on humans are rare,' I say, trying to sound confident and ignoring the fact she already launched at Jayden earlier. Anyway, I'd had my hand over the water for ages before that.

'I'll do it.' Ruby puts her hand on my arm to hold me back. I point at the bandage wrapped around that hand.

'You've lost enough, it's my turn to risk digits,' I say, ducking under the red-and-white plastic chain and climbing the steps to the platform I stood on with Jayden not long ago. 'Please hold me tight, though, I really don't want to go for a swim. In a tank. With a shark.'

I shift myself to sit on the rim and prepare to launch out the way of an attack, but after some initial curiosity, the shark banks away and glides past.

Phew.

Ruby follows me and wraps trembling arms around my waist to hold me as I wait for the shark to make another circuit. When she passes, I lunge for her tail and overbalance, my bum cheek slipping on the smooth brim of the tank.

Everything happens so quickly: Ruby's grip on me tightens and I snatch at her to stabilise myself, only registering the soft touch of the fabric bandage under my fingers too late to stop myself grabbing and squeezing Ruby's injured hand.

She screams and instinctively jerks away.

I fall.

Time slows down as I plunge under the warm water, my feet above my head and the superior predator, who's obviously way above me on the food chain, a blur through my salt-stinging eyes. I can just about make out the jaws opening as she swings round to strike. I open my mouth, my last breath and scream mingling into one, trapped inside a stream of shimmering bubbles racing to the surface.

There's no time to do anything before she bites. I squeeze my eyes shut and wait. My ears are full of muffled sounds of an energetic attack but I feel no pain.

Risking the salt-water sting again, I open my eyes, fully prepared to find blood twisting into the water like red ink, but there's none. Instead, the colours of the irritating neon LEDs dance pink, green and blue through the agitated water. The shark's splashing by the wall of the tank.

Confusion and relief are overtaken by the need to breathe. Once I've located the floor, I push off with both feet, gasping for air as my head breaks the surface. I swim to the middle of the tank, where I can stand on some feature rocks and keep my head above water. It's chest-deep and I remain mysteriously shark-chomp-free. I push at my eyes to clear them and see the shark gnashing at the perimeter of the tank, alternating between hitting the solid glass with her snout and launching herself from the water to snap, exactly like she did at Jayden.

In front of the shark, on the platform outside, Ruby's swinging her hockey stick at a zom leaning on the plastic chain, clawing to get hold of her, with others close by.

Where did they come from?

I follow the trail of them back to see more shambling out through the door to the house.

Oh. Oops.

We should probably have shut that.

The plastic chain breaks with an unspectactular snap and the zoms fall forwards onto Ruby.

'No!' I shout, swimming to the edge of the tank, well away from its agitated occupant, to help. Several zoms beat me there.

The shark moves around, keeping up her menacing thrashing and jaw-chomping. She ignores me, going straight for the zoms. It isn't until Ruby has to fish her hockey stick from where it's been thrown into the water, and the shark takes no notice of her, that I realise.

'Rubes, get in the tank!' I shout.

'What?!' She spins her dripping hockey stick, knocking down the two zoms closest to her, but more are coming.

'The shark doesn't like the zoms,' I shout.

A zom throws themselves at Ruby, their mouth open, ready to take an infectious bite out of her.

'Rubes!' I screech.

The zom narrowly misses and the shark takes a snap at their arm as it passes over the water.

'Trust me,' I try again, desperately hoping this isn't another example of my crap judgement meant to save Ruby from zombification and in fact leading to her losing more body parts.

With more zoms closing in, a flustered Ruby admits defeat and throws herself over the rim of the tank.

I huff out a giddy laugh of relief when the shark pays her no attention, and swim over to lead her to the middle.

'And how is being in here any better than being out there?' Rubes asks, finding her footing on the rocks and pushing wet hair out of her face.

Zom hands reach for us and the shark keeps snapping at them. It doesn't take long for the zoms to learn not to reach over the water, but they still stand in a circle around the tank, groaning eerily as we grip onto each other, protected by our own personal guard shark.

'I really don't think she likes zoms,' I say again.

'No shit.' Ruby breathes the words.

The shark's tail whips me as she moves to let another group of zoms know she means business, and the sudden jolt helps me see this for the opportunity it is.

'While she's distracted, we should take the blood.' The grey brown tail sweeps through the water close by. 'I'll hold her, you get it.'

'What?!' Ruby shakes her head. 'No way, there's a really pissed-off shark attached to the other end.'

I fish the syringe out of my pocket and hold it up to Ruby. 'We might not get another chance.'

Ruby hesitates.

'What?' I ask.

'It's just . . . before we die, I was really hoping we'd get a chance to talk about your sketchbook,' she says. It is so completely not at all what I was expecting her to say that it shocks me out of my determined focus.

'What?!'

'I'm glad you showed it to me, even if it was because I was being an insecure douche bag.'

'They're mostly pictures of you.' My cheeks warm.

'Looking awesome!'

'Ruby!' I say, insides aching at the memory of her kissing the biker. 'I get you want to be with other people. I just didn't want you believing the reporter, and I needed you to help with Jayden.'

'Other people?'

'Your biker.'

'Oh, yeah.' Ruby looks sheepish. 'Veronique is stunning and really friendly and amazing on a bike . . .'

'Ruby! There's no time for this!'

'. . . but, none of that matters because she isn't you,' she finishes hurriedly, and her words make me forget that I'm trying to catch a shark's tail. 'When I thought you'd just been pretending to like me because you cut my finger off, I felt so stupid. Naturally, I hid how much it hurt by trying to have sex with other people again. It's a bad habit of mine.'

'Yeah, it's not the best.'

Both of us speak quickly, in hushed voices, trying not to draw attention to ourselves from our bath-time buddy.

'You're the person I want to be with,' Ruby tells me.

I suddenly want to cry.

'You were being a douche.' I pull her into a hug, then move so I can see her face as I say what I want her to know. 'I wasn't pretending. You weren't my last chance, you're my first choice. But I've been an insecure douche too. I've been so scared of losing you, I almost lost you.'

'I'm not that easy to lose,' she says, leaning forwards.

In water inhabited by an unhappy shark and surrounded by zoms, I crash through the rest of the distance between us.

Our lips smash together in a kiss made up of equal parts passion and fear that this might be our last moment together.

Again.

It's like electricity is dancing across every place we're touching, and I'm surprised there isn't a spark when we move apart.

The sound of the shark crashing into the glass tank pulls my attention back to our task.

My punch-drunk brain flounders.

The tail whips by, nearly catching me again.

'Right! Blood! I'll keep our fishy friend in one place while you extract from the ventra-whatever under its peduncle thingy.'

'Back to business,' Ruby says with a wink and a salute. 'I like it.' Then she grips my arm. 'Please don't get eaten.'

'I'll try.' I give a dry smile.

Worried that if I overthink, I'll bottle it, I waste no time in diving for the shark's tail. I get hold of it and the shark doesn't seem to mind too much, she's too focused on warning the zoms to keep the hell away from her tank...

... that is, until Ruby sticks her with a needle. I hold her thrashing tail for as long as I can before she throws me off and gives me a sharp bump with her nose. The shark then focuses her attention on the zoms she seems to have only just noticed around the rear of the tank.

I pant, heart hammering hard against my ribcage and unable to believe that I haven't got a cartoon-style shark bite missing out of my side.

We need to go again. I'll hold her tighter for longer this time, we'll get the blood and somehow bail without becoming zom-chow.

I turn to Ruby, to see if she's ready for a second attempt, and find her dazed, staring at a vial of blood and muttering, 'We only bloody well did it, Nor!'

I grab the vial and examine it. She's right. It's full.

'We did it!' she says louder and throws herself at me, wrapping me in a suffocating hug. 'You're amazing!'

'We're amazing!' I correct. 'We have the blood.' I look at the crowd of zoms surrounding us. 'Now how do we get out of here without being munched?'

Chapter 48

'**OVER HERE!**'

I look and see Mum and Dad run out the house, both loaded up with bags hanging off their arms and slung across their torsos, a corridor of zoms left floored in their wake.

The crowd of fans let out a loud cheer, calling the attention of the zoms away from us and onto them.

Oh no.

I really hope these zoms can't climb fences.

Dad puts his fingers in his mouth and whistles loudly while Mum claps and shouts, 'Hey! Over here!'

'What are they . . .?' The words slowly die away as the zoms turn from the veritable smorgasborg that is the crowd and start stumbling towards the closer snack, my parents.

Ruby laughs when it's obvious my parents are in complete control, luring them away.

'Go, Mr and Mrs I!'

Like pied pipers of the undead, they run round the corner of the house, whooping and calling, a trail of zoms following behind.

As soon as the last zom moves away from the tank, our shark friend calms right down. She looks at us with tired eyes, swimming in slow circles around us with mesmerisingly admirable elegance, and it's clear she has no grand sharky designs on eating us.

On the next pass, she bumps me gently with her pointed nose.

It's only a minor bump, more of a "*Hello*" than an "*I'm going to eat you*".

Feeling brave, I hold out one hand. The shark does a little snap-gulping thing that makes me jump, but then glides under my hand, close to the surface, so slowly that I'm able to stroke from her nose to her tail. I imagine that if she were a cat, she'd be purring.

'I think she likes you,' Ruby says, giving me a sloshy hip bump before lacing her fingers through mine. 'Come on, we need to go.'

'Yeah,' I agree. The shark passes under my hand again. 'Thank you, Ms Baby Shark,' I whisper, before letting Ruby lead me to climb out.

The second Ruby and I drop, feet squelching in soggy trainers, to the ground outside the tank, I hear shouting.

'Nor! Ruby! Get to the meat van!' Mum calls, zooming past, closely followed by Dad. Not far behind are the zoms they led away.

We run alongside Dad. Mum has the double doors at the back of the van open and the smell of meat, even at this distance, has me hesitating. It doesn't seem like the best place to be with zombies about.

'In!' Mum calls again when we reach her.

I dither. 'Surely, anywhere else would be better?'

'Trust your mum, we have a plan,' Dad shouts to me at the same time as one of his bags falls and its contents scatter across the ground. He stops to scoop them up and we all backtrack to help, throwing ourselves down to grab and shove all the various scientific bits and bobs back into the bag.

A zom gets hold of Dad and he calls out in surprise.

'Not today, bitch,' Mum shouts, launching forwards and performing a perfect roundhouse kick to the zom's face.

Ouch!

Mum helps Dad up, and they pause for a passionate snog that has me averting my eyes, now completely understanding how they've become stars of their own show. Speaking of which, the crowds of people beyond the fence are cheering wildly like this is some stage show put on for their entertainment.

Any time I had to hesitate about locking ourselves in the back of a butcher's van is gone – the zoms are here. We jump in, slam the door shut and are thrust into reeking darkness. Mum flicks a switch and the van's interior illuminates with spotlights.

A slab of wood is set as a chopping block along one side, complete with immense knives hanging on a magnetic strip. At the back, two animal carcasses dangle grimly beside a tower of plastic trays stacked with raw burgers. My nostrils flare, missing the organic smell of the horse-poopy stables.

That's when we learn that these zoms, just like the fake ones, have a thing for dragging nails and teeth along metal. I shudder, as Dad calmly and systematically unpacks all the equipment they must have stolen from their pharmacy raids Pherson mentioned.

'Can we hel—' I begin.

'Shhhhhhhh!' Mum and Dad hiss.

The "*p*" of the word "*help*" pops silently on my lips.

Time passes. Goosebumps prickle over me. Standing in soaking wet clothes in a refrigerated van is not the best idea.

Ruby'll be cold too.

I think about wrapping myself around her, for the warmth and because I'm excited about what the kiss in the tank means for us, but my mum's right there.

Another minute spent dithering and the words "*Fuck it*"

solidify in my mind.

'Mum?' I whisper, wanting them to know my truth before we're separated again by zoms.

'Yes?'

I sidestep and circle my arms around Ruby. The warmth radiating out of my core at being so close to the girl who holds my heart stops my shivering.

'Ruby and I are sort of together,' I tell my parents, hugging her closer, so there can be no doubt in their mind what I mean.

'Not sort of,' Rubys says. 'Pfft! TOTALLY together. Like *together* together,' Ruby adds, wrapping her arms around mine. 'If you want?' she turns to look at me.

'Yeah!' I answer and Ruby moves in to run her nose over mine in a cute but completely parent-friendly show of affection. The whole thing has my insides throwing a party all of their own, complete with flags, lights and a DJ. No sharks though, even my imaginary internal party organiser knows that's not OK.

I face my mum and wait for whatever's coming.

She presses her lips together and blinks away tears. 'Are you happy?'

'Do you mean happy as in gay?' I ask.

'No, I mean happy as in happy.'

The tension tightening the muscles across my back releases. No judgement. No labels.

'I'm happy when I'm with Ruby.'

'That's all we've ever wanted for you,' Mum says through a teary smile. And I know it's true, even if she often went about it the wrong way.

'Blood!' Dad demands, holding out a hand and completely

breaking the moment. When Ruby passes our vial of shark's blood, Dad looks at us both.

'I always thought you two would make a great couple.' He winks. 'But could you please be quiet? I need to concentrate.'

Together and smiling, I squeeze Ruby and she squeezes back. We watch Dad add tiny drops of one blood, then the other, along with some other stuff, under a microscope, shaking his head and muttering. He moves the first concoction to the side, then tries another. After this happens twice, I worry we're going to need more blood.

With the next one, he stays completely still, watching whatever's happening under the microscope. The banging and scraping on the van is getting worse and I wonder how many zoms are out there now.

We wait, though I'm not sure what for.

Time drags on.

And on.

And—

'YES!!!' Dad shouts and the three of us jump out of our skin. 'I have it! The shark WAS the missing element!' He spins towards me and plants a kiss on my head. 'Well done for working it out, Nor!'

I blush. 'It was Jayden really, with the caviar making him sick.'

Mum stands in the corner, tapping her chipped nails on her teeth thoughtfully. 'If it's the key to curing the zombies, could it fix Pherson's diet drug? Seems like there's a lot of money riding on it,' Mum asks, and I see the looming shadow of her former self.

I raise an eyebrow at her. 'Mum!'

'No, no, you're right,' she says, waving her thoughts away. 'It's all best left well alone.'

Dad pulls up one of the two hanging slabs of meat onto the chopping board, chunks off a lump with the cleaver, and injects it with what is hopefully a zom-cure.

An odd sucking sound behind me makes me spin round. Light glows through the growing gap where the rubber seal on a small side door is being peeled away from the outside.

'This isn't good,' I say. Fingers soon claw their way in. The screech of bending metal confirms my words as gnarled, bloody hands slowly twist the door outwards from the bottom corner. We don't have much time.

'How can we help?' I ask, stepping forwards, desperate to get some sort of production line going to speed everything up.

'We need small chompable sections,' he says, lifting the cleaver to demonstrate – the memory of Ruby's finger is all too much. The expression on Rube's face tells me she's thinking the same thing.

'Hang on!' I call out before the cleaver falls. 'Will these do?'

I pull out the burgers waiting to go on the massive barbecue outside.

'Perfect!' Dad gives me a huge smile. Needles are distributed and we speedily inject the beef patties.

We make two full trays of anti-zom burgers.

'Will that be enough?' Ruby asks.

'It'll have to be, unless you both fancy another swim?' Dad's laughter is cut short when a zom shoves their head and one arm in through the small gap peeled open in the bottom of the side door. It gets part way in, then appears to get stuck.

'Seems like the perfect opportunity to trial the product,' Mum says, dropping one of the squishy meaty blobs into the zom's outstretched hand, and we watch as they smash it into their chomping mouth. 'Well, at least they'll eat it.'

I speedily wrap one burger in waxy paper and it feels super gross when I squish it into my back pocket.

'Will it work?' Ruby asks.

'It'll take some time, but I hope so.' Dad's answer doesn't fill me with confidence.

'That's good enough for me,' Mum says. 'Everyone ready?' She's about to open the van door, and everything, from my quaking knees to the nauseous clenching of my stomach, screams that I'm really not ready to face whatever's out there.

Desperate for another idea, my eyes dart about the space and I actually cry out in relief when I find a black square on the ceiling marked out with the words:

EMERGENCY ESCAPE HATCH

Everyone turns to look at me and I raise a hopeful finger, pointing up. 'Can we go out on the roof and throw the burgers down?' I ask, thinking fast. Anything to keep Mum from opening that door.

'It's worth a try,' Dad says, and Ruby's nodding enthusiastically. 'If you two go up, Kim, can you pass the burgers? I'd like to test this one's blood now.' He waves at the zom we gave the first burger to, who appears to be slowing down in their grasping and groaning.

Dad links his hands together to give Ruby a leg up to the hatch, then me, and finally, they move some trays for Mum to stand on and pass up the burgers.

Zoms crowd around the van, clawing to get at us, but the sheer sides keep them away. There's probably about thirty and a couple

Burger tossing in my mind...

more that are dragging themselves out of the house, looking hungrily at our fan club behind the fence. We really should shut that door.

'Them first?' I ask Rubes and she nods, picking up a patty and tossing it from one hand to the other, and back again, a smirk on her face.

'This is going to be so much fun,' she says and, baseball-pitcher-stylee, lobs it at one of the zoms. It splats up the side of their face.

'Ooooh! Not sure why, part of me expected them to try to catch it,' she says. The zom's hand reaches up, scrapes it off their face and pushes it into their mouth. 'Win! Your turn.'

She hands a burger to me and I weigh up the sludgy mass, trying to ignore the slimy ickiness, and decide an over-arm, arching throw is my best bet for distance. I wind it up and let it go.

It splats on the floor in front of my target zom. 'Shit! This is harder than I thought it would be.'

But the zom sniffs at the air before dropping to their knees to snuffle the grass covered in annihilated burger and starts licking the ground.

'Or not,' I amend. 'That's two for two.'

After that we move methodically, making sure we only

get each zom once, which is hard for those clustered around the van, until we work out that if I lie on the roof, Ruby can hold on to me while I drop the burgers into reaching hands.

It seems every zom inside the house has come out to see us. My mum passed up the last few burgers a while ago and the urgency in the zoms is slowing, they're even beginning to look a little confused.

'It's working,' I shout.

'That's good. We're out of burgers,' Ruby says. Seconds later, something clamps painfully around my ankle. Twisting to see what's going on, I find my old nemesis – Hench, from the supermarket – her muscles bulging and hair curled for the party. She's climbed up the front of the van.

Releasing the other hand to get a better hold on me, Hench falls backwards, dragging me with her.

Ruby tries to catch me, but our flailing hands miss each other. I slide down the bonnet and hit the ground so hard it sends a jolt through my wrists and spine.

'NORA! NOR!' Ruby shouts down from the top of the van.

... THE REALITY OF LOBBING BLOBS OF BURGER MEAT.

We've landed near the water tank and the shark's snapping at Hench as she picks herself up to loom over me.

Through my panic, I notice something cold and grim smeared up my back. When I realise what it is, I reach round to scoop up what was once the burger I put aside and smoosh it in Hench's mouth. At the taste of raw meat, she releases me to push more in.

Free, I run to shut the door to the house. If we're out of burgers, we don't want any more zoms stumbling out.

The words "*Zombie Outbreak: CONTAINED*" dance across my mind as the door clicks shut. I turn and bump into Ruby.

'It's really working!' she yells in my face.

'Wow, volume adjust.' I step back and take in the zoms closest. Their jaws are closing, clawed hands unfurling and they're generally looking dazed.

Mum and Dad open the doors to the van and step cautiously out.

'I think we've got the problem contained in the house. Everyone out here's had the cure,' I say.

'I'll check the perimeter, make sure everyone is indeed contained until we can make up more of the antidote,' Dad says, jogging out of sight.

Mum nods. 'There's at least one more person who needs help.' She points to an upstairs window of the house, I follow her finger to see Jayden clawing at the glass like he's seen the cure in action and wants his dose.

Mum walks by, squeezing my hand as she passes. 'I'll see if there's any wounded needing help.'

Nearby, our shark friend has calmed right down as Hench is shaking her head and pawing at her eyes. I gave her the burger I was saving for Jayden.

My knees give out and I sink to the ground, burying my head in my hands.

'Hey,' Ruby says with a tap on my arm that makes me look up. She pulls an indescribably mashed and mangled blob of minced beef from the top of her boot, where she keeps her phone, card and house key when she's not got pockets at a gig. She offers me the sad-looking lump of meat.

'For Jayden,' she says.

'Oh my god!' I jump up. 'You're the best!'

'Not really. It was all my fault Jayden got bitten on the canal. If I hadn't tried to dodge those stupid ducks, all that wouldn't have happened.'

I frown. 'But that wasn't real, and anyway, it was an accident. I didn't take out the Uber-Zom before she got him either. If anything, it shows that we're nice people who don't want to hurt anyone.'

'Or anyduck.'

'Yeah, or that.' A smile dances across my face. We've got one last anti-zom burger for Jayden, and Ruby told my mum we're *together* together.

'What?' she asks, my playful smile catching across to her.

'You like me.'

'Yeah, kinda,' she says, looking up and looping her arms around me. 'But don't get too smug. There's a sketchbook filled with love-hearts and my amazing face that says you like me. You have no solid evidence, Ms Inkwell.'

'Well, Ms Rutherford,' I say, pretending to think. 'Maybe my evidence is that you gave up the chance to hand your V-plates to a Marvel stunt biker to be with ALL this!' I do a little wiggly dance in her circled arms and she laughs.

'I like this new confident Nora.'

'But you liked old insecure Nora too, right?'

She kisses me on the nose and nods. 'I like all the Noras. Now,' she points to the squish of meat in my hand, 'let's deliver that tasty treat to Jayden.'

Really not wanting to go into the house, we drive the van under the window.

'It's a shame Jayden's not the love interest in my story. This would be a very romantic end to a movie, or a book,' I say to Ruby, climbing up to the van's roof, burger in hand.

'I don't know, the kiss in the shark tank was pretty fucking epic,' Ruby calls up.

'Yeah, actually, you're totally right,' I say, and as I'm sliding open the sash window with Jayden behind, I know that friendship is just as important as romance. These past few days have brought me and Ruby together, but it's also given us Jayden, and now I couldn't imagine not being his friend.

I open the window a fraction and slide the burger in. He devours it and I wait outside for the minutes it takes him to calm down, watching, until he sits on the bed, shaking his head woozily. Once the hunger in his eyes is replaced with confusion, I climb in and give him a hug.

'I'm here,' I say and hold him, gently telling him everything that's happened.

'So, you saved me?' he says.

'Well, it was you who kind of saved everyone. Seeing you eat the fish eggs and get sick really helped work things out. Dad mixed the cure, Mum helped inject the burgers, and Ruby had the last burger for you, so we all did something.'

'Yep!' He nods. 'And Jayden saves the day again,' he says in his mock sports commentator voice, putting his hands up in joy. 'Champion!' he cheers, continuing his micro-celebration. 'And the crowd goes wild, Jay-den, Jay-den, Jay-den . . .'

I laugh. 'It was all you.'

'So it's over?' he asks, getting to his feet to look out the window.

'I hope so,' I say, taking his hand. Ruby climbs in to join us.

'I really thought this would all end with me and Nor flying the helicopter away into the sunset, leaving behind zombie-induced mayhem. But this is much nicer,' she says, wrapping her arms around both of us and pulling us in close.

Someone somewhere must have got out a call for help, because that's when we hear sirens approaching.

Chapter 49

'**COME ON, COME ON, WE'RE LATE!**'

And we're running again, but we're always running and always late. Mainly because we're always talking, planning, working or canoodling. But this time it's not our fault, our stupid train pulled into Scarborough nearly half an hour late!

'Oh my god, I can't believe we're finally going to meet the mysterious boyfriend!' Ruby calls from up ahead.

'Ruby! We're here to support Jayden,' I pant.

'Which we won't be able to do if we miss the tide,' she calls back.

I push my feet to run faster.

Me and Jayden have become even better friends in the time since the officials came and sorted out the Acton Mortimer manor house mess; we message nearly every day and speak for hours on the phone. I tell him how Ruby and I are getting on with our SFX course and he shares all the gooiest, icky stuff he's learning about in his nurse training in Birmingham.

He's been up to visit us in Hartlepool twice on the train in the six months we've been away and we caught up a couple of times back home, too. We're definitely reaching bestie-status, no secrets ... besides one.

The man in Jayden's life.

The one who's been making him so happy and sickeningly loved-up, though for some reason, he won't give us any details about.

We run to North Bay beach, and my lungs burn but I push on.

'He said to meet him in front of the first row of rainbow beach huts, near—'

But I don't need to say any more – there he is, sat on the promenade wall, looking out at the morning surfers bobbing on the sea like rubber ducks in a tempestuous bath. He's nodding his head and singing along with tunes drifting from a mini speaker next to him, his arm around a familiar carboard tube, with an ocean sunset scene on it, set beside him. In that moment I see the crossing guard who helped me cross the road to school every day of my primary school life, Jayden's gram, sat beside him, gazing out to sea with her smile-creased eyes.

At the sound of our pounding feet, he turns and greets us with a grin.

'We're here!' We both run forwards and catch him in a big hug. 'We're not too late, are we?'

'Whoa! Easy there! Hello to you too,' he says, laughing and pocketing his speaker. 'No, you're good, we've still got some time.'

I look around and see that, apart from the cardboard tube, Jayden is alone.

'Too embarrassed to introduce us to your fancy man?' I say with an over-exaggerated pout, trying to hide how disappointed I actually am. 'We're not *that* bad.'

'Or maybe *he's* that bad?' Ruby says, hip-bumping Jayden, and I'm surprised to see he's looking genuinely anxious.

'It's none of that. He's here, he went to the shop to buy something to dig with. I'm sorry I haven't introduced you yet, it's just...' Jayden looks up, smiling and waving at someone behind us.

I turn around and see sexy Baxter from Body Combat walking

towards us, carrying a wooden-handled, sunshine yellow trowel. An image of the wall at college with "*NORA INKWELL IS FRIGID*" graffitied across it bricks up my brain.

'... complicated,' Jayden finishes.

'Why's Baxter here?' I ask stupidly. Then I see he's smiling at Jayden. *That* kind of smile. An intimate smile layered with private jokes – and even more private moments – shared.

Oh!

I turn to Jayden. 'Baxter?!'

Jayden's nodding, and I can't work out what expression my face *is* wearing or what it *should be* wearing.

I mean. *What? The? Actual?*

My inner voice screams at me to do something, anything, to make this all seem fine.

Which it is.

Totally fine.

Totally.

'Bi-Five!' I yell in Baxter's face, inwardly cringing that this is the best I could come up with, my hand hovering in the air above us.

Not to leave me hanging, Jayden high-fives me and Baxter shuffles his feet before slowly opening his arms wide to Ruby.

'Big gay hug?' he asks tentatively.

'Always!' Ruby pulls him in for a squeeze, giving me a *Who'd have thought it!* face over his shoulder.

They release and Baxter turns to me. I hope my mouth isn't hanging open.

'I'm so sorry about the graffiti. I was working through some stuff last summer, still kind of am, but Jayden's got me,' Baxter says, looking at Jayden. I'm pretty sure I see actual love-heart emojis flash up in his eyes and I know I can't feel anything bad towards someone so obviously smitten with Jayden.

'Yeah, I got you.' They kiss and it's ridiculously cute.

'It's all right,' I say, and I'm so glad that it really is.

There was a time I blamed Baxter, and his graffiti, for Dead Real happening to us. It was soon after I'd been beating myself up for it being my fault. Then I realised there's only one person responsible for that trauma, and Pherson's dead. So I've been working through all that with my counsellor and it must be working because I wrap Baxter in a huge, sincere hug and I swear I feel a burden lifting from my soul.

'Enough hellos and hugging,' Ruby says. 'The tide's coming in!'

Jayden picks up the cardboard tube and together, the four of us walk across the sand, out towards the water. The early spring sun warms the day and casts the clouds overhead in radiant light. After everything with Dead Real and getting back on to his nursing course, winter closed in before he had a chance to scatter the ashes. Jayden decided to wait until the weather picked up and he was right, it's perfect.

A short way before the tide-line, Jayden stops. He hands me the tube and takes the yellow trowel from Baxter before dropping to his knees and scooping a shallow hole in the sand.

After sliding off the outer section of the tube and pushing the opening in the top, the wind seems to hold its breath as he pours the ashes into the hole and lightly covers it over. The three of us stand close enough for support, but far enough away to allow them privacy in their last moments together.

He drags the sunshine coloured toy trowel through the sand to create a heart shape before standing and walking over to us, his eyes red rimmed, but lips pulled into a smile.

'She'd love this,' he says and we circle him in a group hug.

The tide-line has been washing closer with every passing minute. The four of us stand side-by-side, holding hands and silently watching the heart drawn in the sand until the water rolls over it and Jayden's gram is swept up to dance away in the waves.

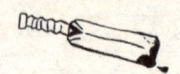

After walking barefoot along the sand, letting the tide chase us slowly back towards the city, Jayden sets the pace as we embark on a day of exploring all the sights Scarborough has to offer until our feet hurt and stomachs grumble that we've missed lunchtime.

'I saw a chippy on the South Bay earlier,' Baxter suggests.

'Yes!' Jayden says. 'That's exactly what we need.'

'And cider?' Ruby asks with a cheeky grin.

Jayden smiles and nods. 'Sounds like a plan.'

'We'll get chips, you two find cider and snacks,' Ruby says, taking Jayden's arm.

He looks between me and Baxter and mouths a silent *Oh!*, before saying, 'Yes! We'll do that.'

And the two of them run towards the seafront buildings giggling.

I look at Baxter and sigh at the unsubtlety of my friends.

'I guess we should find a shop then.'

'I guess so,' he says with a nervous laugh.

It takes a bit of wandering, but we successfully locate a shop that, though limited in snacks, has all the yummy fruity ciders.

Baxter and I make our way to South Bay, our bags clinking triumphantly. We wave at Ruby and Jayden, stuck in an epic queue at the chippy. Serves them right for their devious plan to give me and Baxter time to talk. I'm happy to say we've got this far without hitting any tough subjects.

Wondering if I'll be able to make it through the entire weekend without having to address leaving him concussed on a toilet floor, I say, 'So, you and Jayden?'

I settle on the cool sand and cross my legs. A big dopey smile lollops onto Baxter's face as he does the same.

'Yeah,' he says dreamily. 'He's completely brilliant and gorgeous. Just when I think I couldn't love him more, he does something else that proves me wrong.'

'Yeah?' I beam at him.

'Yeah! Like yesterday he did this full celebration of himself because he aced one of his nursing tests. It was completely adorable.'

I laugh, remembering the times I've had the pleasure of witnessing Jayden do this. 'He's super happy with you too, like, disgustingly happy. I mean, honestly, it's revolting how into you he is.'

Now Baxter's laughing. 'Says you. You and Ruby are like the cutest couple ever. I remember watching . . .' He trails off and I tense.

We've kind of gotten used to it. People still wear the T-shirts and sometimes someone will recognise us from Dead Real, but thankfully, it's mostly caring people sympathising with what Pherson put us through. Though I think about it every day, it's been a while since anyone mentioned it out loud.

I use the Northern Art School bottle-opener keyring they gave me during fresher's week to pop two bottles of fruity cider and hand one to Baxter.

'How's your mum?' he asks, artfully redirecting the conversation. 'She's not been at Body Combat recently.'

'My parents are at sea,' I say and laugh at his confused look. 'They were on a mission to make sure the baby shark could be released into the wild and it sparked something in them. Dad took a career sidestep into marine conservation and Mum sold her cosmetics company to work with him. They're inseparable. Last month they set off on their first ocean run,' I say, beaming.

'Amazing.'

'They are.'

In a surprisingly comfortable silence, we sip our drinks and watch the calming ebb and flow of the waves.

Familiar chattering makes me turn to see Ruby and Jayden walking over.

'My ears have been burning the whole time,' Jayden says, two paper-wrapped bundles in his hands. 'You talking about me?'

'No, *my* ears have been burning, they've been talking about *me*,' Ruby says, plonking herself down and leaning her head on my shoulder.

'Nope,' I say. 'Maybe you both just need some sun cream?'

'It's March!'

Jayden looks nervously between me and Baxter. 'Everything OK?'

We both nod.

'Perfect,' I say.

Jayden grins. 'Excellent! Let's eat!'

The smell of salt and vinegar mingled with fried potatoey-goodness hits me as soon as the paper is unwrapped. I notice Jayden hesitate before eating and I overhear Baxter ask if he's OK.

'Yeah, they cooked them in the same fryer as the fish, that's all. I need to get over this stupid fear of seafood since . . .' His words run out. 'Well, I just need to get over it.' He forks some chips into his mouth. 'Mmm!'

'You're doing great,' Baxter says, rocking sideways to shoulder-nudge his boyfriend.

'Anyone want a bite of my pickled egg?' Ruby asks.

'Ewwwww!'

'Nasty!'

'They're so wrong!'

'Yay! More for me.'

We hang out on the beach for most of the afternoon, watching the sea, drinking cider and talking.

I bring out the snacks Baxter and I picked up.

'What is that?' Ruby points at some bright pink dip.

'The shop was out of salsa and normal hummus, so we got this weird pink hummus.'

'Oooh, looks pretty,' Ruby says.

Jayden uses a tortilla to scoop out a healthy dollop and chomps it down. By about his second chew his features twist in revulsion. 'Eugh! I think it's gone bad!'

Baxter picks it up and sniffs. 'Smells fishy.'

'And tastes horrible!' Jayden swallows thickly, pulling more faces.

I pick up the discarded label and read. 'Taramasalata. Rich and creamy with a hint of lemon juice. Keep refrigerated. Blah blah blah.' I turn it to see the ingredients. 'Oh, yeah, it's got something called *fish roe* in it.'

Alarm bells ring and I'm not sure why. My eyebrows pinch as I try to remember what *roe* is. Jayden washes out the taste with the last of the cider.

'Shall we go back to town to grab some non-fishy snacks and more drink?' I ask.

'Definitely!' Jayden jumps to his feet. We bag up our rubbish and make our way across the beach.

'I have an idea,' Ruby says, flashing her mischievous grin that I love so much. 'We could swing by the chippy and grab a jar of pickled eggs to share. That would sort us right out.'

'You're gross,' I say.

'You love it,' she counters.

'Annoyingly, I really do.' We kiss and it amazes me that every single one is just as exciting as the first. Ruby proceeds to dance alongside us singing a "pickling stuff" song she's making up as she goes along. Baxter joins in, giggling, and I stay back with Jayden.

'It's not like you to miss out on an opportunity to dance,' I say.

'You feeling OK?'

He nods, looking peaky. 'Stomach's acting shady, it feels a bit like—' He cuts off to wipe sweat from his brow.

The word "*roe*" is still clawing its way around my skull and something about this moment transports me back to the manor house.

'Going zom?' I whisper, pulling out my phone and searching: "*What is fish roe?*"

Jayden swallows hard, before shaking his head. When he speaks again his words have their usual upbeat bounciness. 'You haven't told me what your new project is yet.' He links arms with me.

The tension is broken and I pocket my phone before regaling Jayden with our latest concept idea – a horror movie from the point of view of the sharks, making humans the monsters.

'Ruby's already super excited and putting together designs of the mechanics needed to get the movement right on a swimming model shark.' I natter away and leave a space for Jayden to input his usual sounds of interest, but instead, there's a groan.

'Everything all right?' I ask, hairs across my neck prickling.

He swallows again. 'Yeah! For sure, just ate too many chips, that's all.' He laughs it off, but I see the spark of panic in his eyes.

I give his arm a squeeze and throw him a reassuring smile.

'Don't worry, all that's behind us,' I say, 'OK?'

Jayden doesn't answer as he staggers to a stop.

Thinking I might need to call an ambulance, I pull my phone out. It opens on the search results page and my heart stutters in my chest.

***Roe** is a general word for collected eggs of marine animals.*

Oh shit.

Jayden snarls a worryingly familiar snarl.

'Ruby!' I call, backing away from Jayden.

'Yes, my little pickled egg?' Ruby sings, dancing towards us.

'I think we're going to need more anti-zom burgers.'

THE END

Thank you to my parents for instilling a love of books from an early age and to my family for loving me, even with my brain half lost in fictional worlds.

To Beanie and Gogo, there aren't words for the ways you inspire me every day. Thank you both for being so brilliantly and uniquely you.

Luke, you're my biggest champion and, when needed, most honest critic. Your unwavering faith and support over years of chasing my dream has helped it come true! Thanks lovely, your love makes me feel like anything is possible.

Sending love to anyone who's fought, or is still fighting, to get LGBTQIA+ books into young people's hands. I wish teen me had just one of the amazing queer books in the world now.

And finally, to all the readers, librarians and booksellers that make all this worth doing. You're awesome. Thank you x

Desvaux of the Bestseller Experiment, I dread to think how many hours I've listened to you pair natter.

I worked on *Dead Real* over so many years, I can't begin to name all the legends who kindly gave their time to read and critique my words. Thank you all.

While Nora's character is sometimes uncomfortably close to home, naturally, other characters are written outside my lived experience. I want to thank the wonderful people who read *Dead Real* focusing on authenticity of the characters and their stories: Canaan Brown, Karmi Bains, Ian Harris and the members of Dudley Libraries' Rainbow Reading Group 2024: Felix, Grace and Tyra.

Thank you to Iris and Mini Nolan for being brilliant 'limb placement models' and to all my other friends and family I roped into posing for reference pics to draw from.

Thanks to all my Visual Arts college colleagues, especially Heather Chou, for the exciting book chats and promo ideas, Bethan Weston-Smith for all the hugs and mugs of tea when you found me crying in the supply cupboard after a rejection, and Rich Mason, the Vector King!

Unlike Nora, I'm fortunate to have never been secretly in love with a friend. Phew! But throughout my life I've been SO lucky to have THE MOST amazing friends in the universe!!! Through hugs, laughter, nonsense and adventures you've all helped me become the person I am today. I love you all.

A special thank you to the long-suffering Martha O'Brien who's gone above and beyond the call of duty as a cousin by reading pretty much everything I've written and always providing incredible suggestions and encouragement. You're a star!

Acknowledgements

It's taken me some time to get published and I've had so much help along the way...

I count my lucky stars that the first person in the publishing world to take a chance on me is also someone who gets as excited about my story ideas as I do. Thank you for everything Agent Baker.

Huge thanks to Hazel Holmes and everyone at UCLan for seeing potential in Nora and Ruby's story, and patiently answering every one of my many, many questions.

I've been so fortunate to work on this book with a powerhouse of absolute queens:

Tilda Johnson, my amazing editor. Thank you for your bold structural suggestions and being only a panicked email away throughout rewrites.

Nicki Marshall – your meticulous copy editing tightened everything all the way up.

Becky Chilcott, you are an inspiration! Thank you for weaving together *Dead Real's* words and pictures so beautifully.

Over my years as a writer, I've learned so much from so many groups and want to send out monumental thanks to:

The whole of SCBWI, the Central West crew and my scoobie friends. Write Magic and the #sunrisesprint-ers. Lee Wind and the Queer Kidlit Creators who empowered me to 'write more queer'. YALC and the friends I've made attending. Mark Stay and Mark

PLEASE NOTE: No sheep or sharks were harmed in the writing of this book.